DEVIL WITHIN

DEVIL WITHIN

A Nathan Parker Detective Novel

James L'Etoile

LEVEL
BEST BOOKS

First edition

ISBN: 978-1-68512-360-4

Cover art by Level Best Designs

This book was professionally typeset on Reedsy.
Find out more at reedsy.com

"Hell is empty and all the devils are here."

— WILLIAM SHAKESPEARE

Praise for DEVIL WITHIN

"James L'Etoile is such a talented and terrific storyteller! His real-life experience in the criminal justice system gives his compelling, high-stakes thrillers an authenticity that only a savvy insider can provide. You'll be turning the pages as fast as you can!"—Hank Phillippi Ryan. *USA Today* bestselling author of *Her Perfect Life*

"A suspenseful and utterly gripping novel that doesn't shy away from the terror of drug cartels and border violence, James L'Etoile's *Devil Within* is a well-researched, expertly written police procedural with twists that will leave you breathless. This one is not to be missed."—Jennifer Hillier, bestselling author of *Little Secrets* and *Things We Do In The Dark*

"An incredible story that grabs you by the throat and tosses you across the room. L'Etoile is a gem."—J.T. Ellison, *New York Times* bestselling author of *Her Dark Lies*

"*Devil Within* is an exceptional follow-up to L'Etoile's Anthony Award-nominated novel *Dead Drop*. A propulsive thriller with nonstop action, well-rendered characters, and a truckload of twists and turns. Impossible to put down!"—Bruce Robert Coffin, award-winning author of the Detective Byron Mysteries

"Borders are blurred, lines are crossed. Nathan Parker navigates an intensely personal case, uncontrolled emotions threatening his good judgment. Brilliant prose, crisp pacing, and well-developed characters make L'Etoile a must-read for every thriller enthusiast. An unforgettable story."—K.J. Howe, international bestselling author of *Skyjack*

Chapter One

Nia Saldana didn't think today would be the day she died. Why would she? She was careful and avoided situations that drew too much attention. She never wanted to be noticed. When you got noticed, it only led to trouble, or worse.

She cursed herself for snooping around her employer's office as she tidied up. The big man wasn't who he pretended to be. If others knew what she saw...

Nia fought off anxiety driving home after another twelve-hour day cleaning homes on Camelback Mountain, the upscale enclave in Central Phoenix. Commuter traffic on this section of the 101 loop was a field of brake lights, and her hands gripped the wheel, knowing she'd be home after her two girls were asleep. Her sister Sofia never complained when she watched the girls and loved them as if they were her own. Nia regretted every minute away from them, and the envelope of cash on the seat next to her meant she could stop and pick up a little pink box of day-old Mexican pastries for the girls as a sweet surprise.

A job that didn't require hours away from her girls was a dream. She didn't dare look for a better-paying job. There was too much at risk for a single, undocumented mother. One wrong move, like getting caught in her employer's office, and she would join her deported husband in Hermosillo. What would happen to the girls then?

She pushed a worn stuffed animal away from her leg when she caught a sudden blur from the right. A familiar black SUV cut across her path, nearly clipping the front end of her Nissan Sentra. She knew her boss was furious; in a way she'd never seen before. But to chase her on the freeway because of what she'd discovered? Reckless.

A pop caught her attention. Seconds later, the heavy SUV lurched and bumped Nia's sedan into the left lane, pushing her into the gravel median. A second pop sounded moments before the wheel wrenched from Nia's hands, sending the Sentra into a hard spin to the left until it faced back into the oncoming traffic.

Rubber barked on the asphalt as a semi-truck slammed on its brakes, and the trailer jackknifed, a wall of metal rushing toward Nia's windshield. The Sentra crumpled from the impact of the heavy eighteen-wheeler. The thin metal roof folded in, pinning her against the seat. The steering wheel crushed against the driver's seat, and Nia with it. The pressure against her chest made breathing impossible. If her brother-in-law hadn't sold the airbag for a few dollars…. Nia glanced at the blood-spattered stuffed animal and pulled it close to her.

Inside her broken passenger side window, Nia watched as the SUV plowed into the metal rails in the center divider without slowing down. The driver slumped over the wheel after his vehicle came to rest. Why? Why did he?

The grip on the stuffed animal loosened as she grew cold. The faces of her two young girls were the last images she held while she slipped away.

Chapter Two

Detective Sergeant Nathan Parker weaved his way through the snarl of traffic on the freeway. Phoenix dwellers took it in stride because commute hours meant a sludge across the valley with a daily multi-car pile-up, or a disabled vehicle in the tunnel. None of the usual reasons for traffic meltdowns would justify a Major Crimes detective call out.

Parker's Maricopa County Sheriff's Office Ford Explorer was unmarked, but the antenna bristling on the roof and the flashing red and blue lights in the grill gave it away. As he approached, he wasn't certain what warranted a major crimes investigator. Parker spotted the vehicles spun out in the median, the front end of a compact sedan crumpled under a big rig trailer. No one would survive this one.

Fire engines stopped traffic in the two lanes near the accident. A single lane of cars bled through the remaining gap in the freeway, going slow enough to glimpse the gruesome wreckage.

Deputy Marcus Stone called Parker on his cell phone rather than make the call over the department radio frequency. The call was quick on detail, other than Deputy Stone needed Parker at the scene. Parker's mind shuffled through the possibilities as he pulled his Explorer to the far left median. He spotted the wrecked SUV on the center divider, twenty yards from the jackknifed semi-truck. A high-profile victim, or an influential Phoenix power player caught in a deadly drunk driving crash? Maybe. Politics was king, even in the desert. The twisted remains of the Nissan underneath the big rig, however, didn't scream of valley nobility.

Parker spotted Deputy Stone near the rear of the Phoenix Metro Fire Department engine. Stone looked gray.

"Marcus."

Stone didn't take his gaze from the fire crew using an air-powered extraction device, sometimes called the Jaws of Life, to peel back the exposed left front quarter panel of the gutted Nissan Sentra.

"We've got two deceased." Stone jutted his square jaw at the Nissan. "A young woman. In the SUV against the guardrail, our second victim, a middle-aged white male."

"Looks nasty. Any statements from witnesses about how it happened. Why'd you call me out, anyway? Traffic accidents aren't usually our thing."

Stone started toward the SUV. "Come with me." Stone didn't wait for Parker and made a path around the littered wreckage toward the black SUV.

Parker noticed the driver slumped over the wheel after the fire department opened the driver's door and left him in place. From experience, Parker knew fire crews extracted accident victims from the vehicles and tried to administer lifesaving treatment.

The driver's razor-cut gray hair lay matted in crimson. His skull disappeared in a jagged mess of blood and bone behind his ear.

"He's been shot. Dammit, this makes three in a month," Parker said.

"That's why I called you."

Instinctively, Parker glanced at his surroundings. The freeway sat in the bottom of a wash, with city streets twenty feet above on both sides. An unnatural valley, but a natural killing ground for the Sun Valley Sniper.

"Get any ID on this guy?"

Stone held a plastic evidence bag in his hand. Parker hadn't noticed the deputy gripping the plastic envelope since his arrival.

"Roger Jessup. Local attorney, according to the Arizona Bar card in his wallet."

"Can't say I've heard of him before. Gives us an angle to look at—you know, the whole disgruntled client thing."

They both turned at the sound of ripping metal pulled from the Nissan

Sentra. Two firefighters crouched into the passenger compartment, cut the seatbelt, and pulled the driver from the car. They placed her gently on a yellow tarp spread on the gravel shoulder.

"I take it she wasn't a shooting victim?" Parker said.

"No. The collision with the SUV spun her out, and then the big rig finished it. Wrong place, wrong time, poor thing."

"You call in the Medical Examiner?"

Stone shook his head. "Didn't know how you would handle it."

"No problem. While I call the M.E., could you ask the fire crews to set up some tarps to give our victims a bit of respect?"

"On it." Stone strode off to the closest firefighter and started pointing at the scene.

Parker approached the Nissan as the fire department crew draped a tarp over the dead woman. Parker saw she was olive-skinned, young, perhaps in her early thirties, with dark black hair pulled back in a ponytail. She was attractive, but even in death, she carried signs of stress, lines creasing her forehead, and dark bags under her eyes.

Parker dropped to one knee and scanned the passenger compartment. The driver was crushed. If it wasn't bad enough, Parker spotted a well-loved stuffed animal on the seat.

"Oh, man. She's got kids."

He reached for her purse and pulled the inexpensive plastic and cardboard handbag from the floorboard. Parker had seen these knockoff items before, carried by women coming over the border. He fished through the purse for a wallet and ID. Nothing. No driver's license, insurance cards, or credit cards. When he stood, he spotted a blood-stained envelope. When he lifted it from the seat, it held one hundred dollars. No note or message in with the five twenty-dollar bills. The face of the envelope bore a simple inscription: "Nia."

"Nia, what happened?"

Parker thought Deputy Stone might be right. He was about to write it off as another case of a random victim until he found the bullet hole in the Nissan's front tire. The tire exploded outward on the opposite side of the path of entry. Likely sending the compact sedan into an uncontrolled skid, careening off any vehicles in the next lane.

What were the chances of two cars being shot at in evening commuter traffic?

Chapter Three

A plain white van marked the arrival of the Medical Examiner. Parker's phone call drew Doctor Kelly Sherman, the county's Chief Medicolegal Death Investigator. Once he mentioned the link to another Sun Valley Sniper case, Dr. Sherman responded rather than one of her subordinates.

The doctor stepped down from the passenger side, and Parker met her in front of the van. "Thanks for coming, Doc."

"You think this might be another sniper victim?"

"Victims," he said with emphasis on the plural nature of the scene.

"The young woman pulled from the Nissan wasn't hit with a bullet, but her vehicle was. Once we reconstruct the accident, we'll be able to tell if she lost control of the car because of the gunshot."

"And the other one?"

Parker pointed to the disabled black SUV. "He's a little more obvious."

"I'll start with him." She turned to her assistant. "Johnny, let's set up over by the black SUV."

"Got it." A thin young man in a baggy Maricopa County Medical Examiner jumpsuit called out while trotting toward the rear of the van, removing two large black cases.

A Maricopa County Sheriff's Office van pulled alongside, and Tommy Venard hopped out. "Detective, I transferred to the Major Accident Investigation Team to get a break from you dragging me to godforsaken homicide scenes."

Parker shrugged and smiled as he recalled Tommy collecting evidence from squatter's camps, wading through septic tanks, and bagging blood-soaked clothing.

"At least this was in town."

"I'll take the small comfort," Tommy said.

Parker nodded to the crumpled Nissan. "While Doctor Sherman works up our male victim, let's get started over there."

"Shouldn't I wait until the doctor's done with her?"

"I need you to look at the car. Lay out the sequence of events ending with her vehicle ending up tucked under this semi. I'd start with the blowout on the driver's side front."

Parker didn't tell Tommy about the bullet hole in the tire. He wanted to let Tommy unravel the chain of events without influencing the facts the accident investigator might uncover.

"This could take a while to piece together, Detective. I'll keep you posted," Tommy said as he withdrew a bulky 35mm camera.

"Thanks, Tommy."

Parker spotted a barrel-chested man in his fifties sitting on the driver's side running board of the semi-truck. He held his head in his hands and looked pale.

"Excuse me, you the driver?"

The man raised his head, and red-rimmed eyes cut toward Parker.

"I am. I already gave a statement to the other officer."

Parker figured he meant Deputy Stone.

"I'm sure you did. I need a couple of minutes with you to sort out a few things."

"Do I need an attorney? Am I in trouble? I—I couldn't help it. She cut me off."

He wasn't blaming the woman in the Nissan. He was trying to put the events together in his mind to make sense of them.

"Did you see what happened?

He nodded. "The little car lurched and tried to change lanes before the SUV pulled up alongside. The SUV cut a hard left in front of the little car—and me. It hit the car and spun her out. I hit my brakes as soon as I

8

could. She was there, in front of me." He started hyperventilating.

"You need me to get you some water? Can I call someone for you?"

He shook his head.

"I saw her—the woman in her car. I—I tried to steer around her. My tractor missed her, but my rig jackknifed…"

"I get it. I'm sorry."

The driver drew a deep breath. "Damnedest thing was the black SUV."

"How's that?"

"It looked like it was trying to get the other driver's attention. I noticed it cutting in and out of traffic for about a mile until it pulled up next to her."

"Did you see anyone signal or gesture to pullover?"

"No. Nothing." The man stared down at the gravel in the median strip.

"You say you saw her car swerve suddenly? You see what made her do that? Road rage?"

He shook his head. "No, nothing. I saw—and I heard the pop when her tire blew out. Then I heard a second pop. Maybe five seconds apart. Musta been another tire. People don't realize how important good tires are."

Parker agreed, but he knew the "pops" the driver recalled weren't from cheap tires blowing out. They were from two rifle shots, two rounds fired close together. Did the woman get in the way of the intended target? An attorney seemed a more likely target than an anonymous and perhaps undocumented woman.

Parker gestured for a paramedic to come and check on the semi-truck driver.

He stood in front of the semi-truck and replayed the event in his mind as narrated by the truck driver. The car lurched in one direction with the first pop. A second popping sound and the SUV careened into the center divider. The small car first, followed by the black SUV.

It meant the shooter was on the left side of the vehicles and made a shot across the westbound lanes of the freeway to hit these two vehicles. Intentional or random?

Parker scanned to his left and up the embankment. Cars lined the frontage road above the freeway. One space was empty, fifty yards behind him.

Parker fished his cell from his pocket and hit a speed dial number.

"Tully." Peter Tully was a thirty-six-year veteran detective under Parker's supervision.

"You and Barry on your way? Looks like we might have something."

"We started rolling as soon as you called. We were out in Cave Creek on an assault with intent."

Parker gave Tully directions to the frontage road and told him to call when they arrived.

Dr. Sherman was supervising the removal of the man's body from the SUV. The dead man's head bore a blue cover, which Parker always believed looked like a shower cap. The covering kept contaminants off the body, and in this case, helped contain bits and pieces of bone and grey matter.

Parker approached, keeping a few feet from the doctor.

"Can you confirm GSW as the cause of death?" Parker asked.

"Looks that way. His face is distorted from the massive pressure change from a projectile entering his skull—hydrostatic shock. I've noted secondary lacerations from his face impacting the steering wheel and airbag. I can't do much of a wound track at this point until I'm able to reconstruct. It's rather a mess."

"I think I know where the kill shot came from." Parker pointed at the empty parking spot on the elevated frontage road.

"Not much else I can tell you now. I'll need tox and lab results to confirm. I'm thinking the autopsy isn't going to reveal much we don't already know. I'm going to get started with Victim Two." She snapped off a pair of purple nitrile gloves and donned a fresh set.

Parker's cell rang, and the caller ID announced Tully. He pivoted until he faced the embankment, where Tully waved down at him.

"You're standing where our shooter went to work. Tell me what you see."

"You're about a hundred, hundred and a quarter out. Clear line of sight to both east and westbound lanes. Hold on…"

Parker saw Tully bend and wave over his partner to check out an object on the ground. A six-foot-seven Barry Johns stooped and snapped photos using his cell phone.

"What ya got?" Parker asked.

"Could be something. Could be nothing."

"Could you be a little more specific, Tully?"

"You figure our shooter parked here and waited for his shot, right?"

"It's a possibility we need to explore."

"Well, he was waiting for a while then. I got a pile of sunflower seed shells here."

Parker felt the flesh on his neck tingle.

"Please tell me they look fresh...."

"That they do. Freshly chewed up and spit on the sidewalk. You know what that means...

"We've got DNA."

"Barry and I will get to bagging and comb through the scene. We'll canvass the block in either direction and see if anyone saw or heard anything. Mostly light commercial, looks like."

"Thanks, Pete. I'll finish up down here, and we'll regroup later."

Parker ended the call and shoved the phone in his pocket as the gurney with the male victim, Roger Jessup, slid into the Medical Examiner's van.

Doctor Sherman pulled off her exam gloves and jotted notes on a tablet.

Without glancing up from her notes, the doctor noticed Parker approach. "Our female victim—no indication of gunshot wounds or injury other than trauma from the traffic collision."

Parker glanced at the metal shroud that entombed the woman in her final moments. He shook his head. "Did she suffer?"

Dr. Sherman put down her stylus. "She didn't die instantly. I'm afraid she saw everything happen, and the crush injuries probably prevented her from taking a breath. I'll be able to confirm with blood gasses and my post."

"Are you done with the vehicle?"

"Johnny, get everything we need?" Dr. Sherman asked.

"Got it covered. I'll send you copies, Detective."

Parker took a knee at the driver's door. The fire department had peeled it open like a piece of overripe fruit. The steering wheel cut away, and the door itself pulled from the hinges. The shattered windshield glass hung down like a fine crystal curtain, with blotches of blood breaking up the blue-white field.

In this small compartment, a life ended. No matter how many death scenes Parker rolled up on, each one was unique and held the final moments of life. This one was no different. The woman was driving home, a child's stuffed animal next to her. The cleaning supplies fallen from the trunk meant she worked for a cleaning service. Or, based on the envelope of cash addressed to Nia, worked independently.

Parker placed the stuffed animal, the envelope with the hundred dollars tucked inside, and the woman's purse in a brown paper evidence bag. Without an identification, it could prove difficult to reach a next-of-kin.

Parker stole one final glance at the stuffed animal before he rolled up the paper bag. Somewhere a child lost their mother. The fact hit him hard. A hollowness settled in his gut.

Deputy Stone handed Parker a slip of paper.

"The vehicle is registered to Sofia Martinez. Here's the address."

"Thanks." Parker recognized the street name. A neighborhood in The Guad—a community of lower-income housing, predominately Hispanic, with a concentration of undocumented families. Gangs preyed on the innocent new migrants, and crime rates in The Guad were among the city's highest.

"This is about five minutes away. I'll go run by and see if we can confirm an ID and maybe a location on the next of kin."

"Damn."

"What?"

"She almost made it home."

Chapter Four

Parker found the address on Calle Azteca where the car was registered, and the small home didn't stand out from the rest of the street. The squat faded stucco ranch-style residence began life yellow, but lost luster over time to a pale, jaundice hue. Any original landscaping was a faint memory as the desert reclaimed its place. Dirt and sand dominated the front yard. A lone weed struggled against the heat and drought in a battle it would never win.

A few curtains in neighboring homes pulled back as Parker slowed in front of the address. No one came to find out what drew an undercover cop to the place. The residents in these homes were too familiar with government forces, here, and in their home countries.

Parker stole a glance at the vehicle registration on his dash-mounted computer—Sofia Martinez. He grabbed the brown paper bag and strode up to the unit's front door. He rapped with a knuckle.

The door opened immediately, and a woman with deep-set brown eyes appeared through the crack.

"I'm looking for Sofia Martinez."

"Who are you?" the woman responded in slightly accented English.

"I'm sorry. I'm Detective Sergeant Nathan Parker, Maricopa County Sheriff. Do you know Sofia?"

"I'm Sofia. Why do you want to know?"

"Can I come in and speak with you?"

"What's this about? I have a green card. So does my husband."

"I'm not here about anyone's immigration status. There's been an accident...."

The door parted a few inches. A small hand gripped Sofia's leg. A dark-haired girl of no more than five peeked from behind. The sight cut Parker to the bone.

"What kind of accident?"

"We should sit and speak privately. Miss Martinez. A vehicle registered to you was involved in a traffic accident."

The woman's knees buckled slightly, and she caught herself against the door.

"Carmen, take your sister and go play in your room, please."

The girl was more interested in the tall stranger in the doorway.

"Now, Carmen."

"All right," the young girl huffed and stole off to the back of the home.

Sofia opened the door and motioned Parker inside to a small living room. He stood and waited until Sofia took a seat on a sofa. He sat next to her.

"Miss Martinez, who was driving your vehicle today?"

"Oh, my God." She placed a hand over her heart. "What happened? If you're asking, it means..."

"I'm afraid so. I'm sorry. Can you tell me who used your car today?"

"My sister. Nia Saldana. What happened? You haven't said. I need to hear it."

"I'm very sorry, Miss Martinez. Your sister died in an accident on the freeway a little over an hour ago."

The tears started, and Sofia wept in silence for a moment. When she regained her composure, she dabbed her eyes. "She was such a good person. All she wanted was to make a life for her girls."

Parker stole a look toward the back of the home. "Carmen and her sister?"

"Yes. I take care of them while Nia works. God, what do I tell them?"

Rather than pretend to know how to heal a wound as deep as this family's loss, Parker reached for the brown paper bag. "I found a few of her things here. I think you should have them."

She nodded, and he placed the bag between them.

"Did my sister suffer?"

"No, no she didn't." Parker didn't see the need to let Sofia know the prolonged fear and pain her sister felt in the last moments of her life. There'd been enough trauma in this family for one day.

"When can I see her?"

"She's being cared for by the medical examiner now. She's safe and in good hands. As soon as Dr. Sherman finishes her examination, they will call you."

"Do I need to go identify her body, like they do on television? I don't know if I could..."

"It's not like that. You will need to go to the Medical Examiner's Office in the next day or so. You'll make the identification from a photo. If we had dental records, or alternate means, we'd do that. I'm sorry to burden you with this. I know it's difficult. What's the best phone number? I'll give it to the victim's services liaison, and they will pick you up and drive you to the appointment."

Sofia gave Parker her cell number, and he handed her one of his business cards in return. "If you need to talk, don't be afraid to call me."

"Thank you."

Parker stood from the sofa. "You know where Nia worked?"

"Houses up on the hill. I don't know which ones. She'd get referrals."

"I'm sorry. Can I call someone to come and be with you?"

"No, my husband will be home soon."

Parker bid the woman goodbye, and as he left, he glimpsed the young girl stealing a peek at him from inside the home. A coy smile and a chubby-fingered wave. He signaled back and knew the child's world had shattered. Parker didn't envy the task ahead of Sofia.

He caught the shadows behind the curtain across the street flutter. Parker spent enough time in The Guad to know nothing went unnoticed. The question always seemed to be who did the watching? People running in fear of others? Or predators looking for someone vulnerable. Still, there was a collective strength among them. Sofia and the girls would need their support now.

As soon as Parker sat in his vehicle, his cell sounded. He recognized the caller ID as the Avondale Sheriff's substation.

"Parker, here."

"Hi, Nathan. Sorry to call, but we've got a bit of an issue."

Parker knew the voice on the other end of the connection, Deputy Linda Marsh. Linda and Parker met at a foster parents' meeting about six months ago. She'd been having trouble getting a fourteen-year-old boy involved in school. A boy abandoned at the border by his parents, Leon kept to himself and made excuses to avoid going to school, to the point of skipping class. Parker intervened when a Glendale Police officer rounded up Leon and a group of boys spraying graffiti on a brick wall near the freeway.

Parker's experience as a foster parent to Miguel was similar, although Miguel made the trek from El Salvador by himself. Parker met the gangly teen deep in Mexico while running from the Cartel. Both nearly died crossing the border, and they shared a strong bond between them from the journey. Miguel graduated high school and was on to community college. Leon considered Miguel a role model.

"Hey, Linda. What's up?"

"It's Miguel."

Parker's core grew cold.

"What happened? Is he okay?"

"Yes—yes, he's okay. He managed to get himself in a bit of trouble."

Parker's head spun. Miguel never came close to getting involved in anything illegal. The boy knew it could jeopardize his visa as a human trafficking victim.

"What did he do, Linda?"

She sighed and spoke in a soft voice. Parker could imagine her trying to keep others from overhearing the conversation. "It seems Miguel and a group of students from the community college formed a protest in Friendship Park, off of McDowell."

"A protest? He's never mentioned anything coming close to a protest."

"The park protest was the usual pro-immigration rally. Nothing wrong there—until a few of them decided it would be a great idea to block an on-ramp to the 10."

"Miguel did what? I can't believe it."

"It doesn't look like he was one of the knuckleheads who started blocking traffic. One nearly got hit by a guy driving a lifted four-wheel-drive truck. Claimed he didn't see them."

"I'll bet. Where's Miguel now?"

"He's here. I got the responding deputy to let him off with a warning."

"Thanks, Linda. I hate to think you pulled any strings that might get you in trouble...."

"No strings and above board. The deputy didn't really want to spend the next two days writing reports on a protest rally."

"I owe you, Linda."

"You do. I think dinner this Friday would be a good start."

"Why, deputy, did you just ask me out on a date?"

"I got tired of waiting for you to do it, so I guess I did. Now get your ass over here and pick up your delinquent kid."

Parker smiled as he ended the call. He'd thought about asking Linda out but figured she wouldn't be interested. Sure, they had the foster parent gig in common. But she was younger and had her life together. She wouldn't be interested in his mess.

The substation in Avondale was a few blocks south of the 10. Flashing warning signs alerted the westbound drivers of delays ahead. Parker figured it was because of the protestors occupying the freeway on-ramp. He ducked off the freeway and took Van Buren straight to the station.

The receptionist didn't recognize him, so he flashed his ID and asked for Deputy Linda Marsh. The gatekeeper buzzed open the door and gestured down the hall while she took a phone call.

He didn't need to ask where Linda was. She poked her head out in the hallway. Dark brown hair, cut in a short collar-length style, with deep expressive green eyes which glistened when she spotted him.

"Thought I heard you," she said.

Linda stepped into the hall and titled her head to a closed break room door. "He's in there."

Parker thanked her, and she turned to go back to work. Parker noticed her deputy's uniform didn't hide her athletically trim figure. He unconsciously sucked in his gut.

"Don't forget. Friday," Linda said over her shoulder.

Parker opened the break room door and found Miguel at the table, an unopened can of Coke in front of him. The "delinquent," as Linda called him, would turn eighteen in two months. He looked young and vulnerable when he cast his eyes up at Parker to assess how much trouble he was in.

"I'm sorry they called you."

Parker noted Miguel didn't say he was sorry for doing whatever got him hauled into a sheriff's substation.

"Come on. Let's get out of here."

Miguel didn't move. The man-child looked surprised and uncertain. His leg bounced under the table but made a tapping sound on the slick linoleum floor.

"You're not mad?"

"I didn't say that. We can talk about it at home."

"You're letting me come home?"

Parker put his hands on his hips. "Of course, you can. We're family now, Miguel. Just because you did something stupid changes nothing."

"It wasn't stupid. We were protesting the administration's policies on immigration." He puffed up his thin chest.

"The same administration that granted you a visa?"

"That's different—"

"I don't see it that way. Let's continue this at home, before Linda changes her mind and keeps you here."

Miguel stood and slung his backpack over his shoulder. Parker held the door for him. "Linda, huh?" Miguel said in a soft voice.

"Deputy Marsh," Parker said. He could feel the heat under his collar.

"She's nice. I like her."

"So do I," Parker added without thinking. It kind of surprised him. "Let's go. I'm parked out front."

Miguel followed Parker, and they got into his Explorer without another word between them. There would be a time and place for that once they got home.

Chapter Five

The drive to Parker's Litchfield Park home would normally take ten minutes. But the protest was going strong and spilling from Friendship Park onto the roadway. A Glendale police vehicle's flashing lights strobed a warning to oncoming traffic, but they weren't trying to keep stragglers out of the traffic lanes.

"Someone's gonna get hurt," Parker said.

"I didn't think it would get this crazy. It was supposed to be a couple dozen people listening to speakers at the park. It was organized. I don't know what made it blow up like this."

"Who organized this mess?"

"This," Miguel gestured out his window, "I don't know about. The speakers in the park—the Immigrant Coalition sponsored the event."

"The Immigrant Coalition? Please tell me you aren't involved with those people?" Parker said as his knuckles whitened on the steering wheel.

Miguel kept his eyes out the window, avoiding Parker. "I am those people."

"That's not what I mean. You know that. The Coalition gets a little radical in their thinking, and shit like this jumps off."

"It's not like that. The Immigrant Coalition raises awareness. You know what it's like for migrants who cross over."

"Of course I do. We both saw it firsthand down there." Parker and Miguel survived a Cartel drug operation, dropping bodies of undocumented migrants in the desert. Miguel suffered nightmares for weeks following his rescue. Parker's own nightmares began back five years ago, the night his partner was murdered by a cartel coyote.

20

"People need to know what's happening. The families, the conditions, and this government are forcing innocent people into the hands of the cartels. You're the one who told me there are over two-thousand people who died making the crossing, and they never identify most of them."

"I get it, I do. There are ways of helping people caught in the middle without resorting to blocking the freeway and getting people rundown by hardliners looking for a reason to lash out."

Miguel fell silent as they drove.

Parker pulled into their driveway and turned off the ignition. He grabbed Miguel's elbow as the kid stepped from the SUV.

"I don't want to see anything happen to you," Parker said.

"I'm not going to throw myself out in traffic. But I have to do something."

"You could help Billie and me—"

"Collecting medical supplies and food for people stuck near Hermosillo isn't enough. Billie's great and has a good heart, but more needs to be done here to make people's attitudes change."

Billie was Billie Carson, a tough near-survivalist who lived on her own in the desert. She ran from witness protection after the cartel threatened the families caught up in the gang's trafficking network. She'd befriended Miguel during their crossing. As a former coyote, Billie knew the routes across the border, and without her, Miguel would be back in El Salvador at the mercy of MS-13.

Miguel left the SUV, and Parker followed him inside. He admired Miguel for his caring and compassion but didn't want to see him become a target of the racial violence popping up all over the valley. There wasn't a night on the evening news, or a pre-shift briefing that didn't include a mention of hate crimes, militia activity, or deaths of undocumented migrants trying to cross flooded washes.

"Hungry?" Parker asked.

Miguel nodded. "Linda's nice and all, but the chicken sandwich she gave me was—what is it with you white people and refusing to use spices? Back in El Salvador, my mother would make a Pan con Chumpe with turkey, tomato sauce, cucumber, radish, and watercress. Now that's a sandwich.

None of this slab of chicken with a pickle on white bread."

Parker opened the refrigerator and surveyed the scant few items on the shelves: mayonnaise and chicken lunch meat among them. "It looks like takeout tonight. Anything come to mind?"

"Pizza!"

Parker chuckled. Since coming to this country, Miguel had eaten his body weight in pizza. He'd become an American. "Extra cheese, extra pepperoni." Miguel dropped his backpack in the living room and agreed to go pick up the pizza at their favorite local place.

"Be careful," Parker said as Miguel hopped in Parker's Jeep.

Parker changed clothes, locked his service weapon away in a safe in the bedroom closet, and gathered the plates they'd need for dinner.

He grabbed his cell and called Tully, who answered on the first ring.

"How's it going?" Parker asked.

"Finished the canvas and nothing. Barry's in sweet talking with a lady who runs a check cashing store. There's a CTV camera over the front door. It might've caught the parking spot across the street."

"That would be a break."

"Wouldn't it? You contact the next-of-kin for our vics?"

Parker grimaced. He'd forgotten to follow up on the attorney, Roger Jessup. He'd taken a photo of the driver's license to note the address. "Found the sister for the girl—her name was Nia Saldana. I'll hit the Jessup place later. I needed to go extricate Miguel from an Immigrant Coalition protest."

"Yeah, the IC's been getting a bit more in your face lately. Not in a good way."

"Agreed. Compare notes in the morning?"

"Will do," Tully said and disconnected the call.

Parker called the Communications Office and confirmed the Jessup address. No known warrants for Roger, which didn't surprise Parker.

Ten minutes later and Miguel was back with their pizza. The seventeen-year-old wolfed down two slices.

"Listen, Miguel, I know you need to help support people who went through the same things you did. But I'm concerned about the Coalition's methods, and their message might be lost in the antics they pull. Please use your head. You're a smart kid, and I don't want to see you do anything that would come back and bite you on the ass."

He nodded.

"Have you been going to Coalition meetings, or talking to their people? What's with the sudden interest? How did you even get started with them?"

"Jesus, the immigration cops didn't ask this many questions."

Parker left the pizza slice untouched. "I worry. It's what I do."

"No kidding."

"How did you get interested in the Coalition?"

Miguel shoved another mouthful of pizza in rather than answer the question. Parker recognized the delaying tactic and waited him out.

Miguel nodded. "It wasn't her fault. I'd heard about the Coalition on campus. It's not like they're a prison gang or anything."

"Her, who?" The hair on Parker's neck tingled.

"Don't get mad at her."

"It was Billie, wasn't it? I know she gets help from the Immigrant Coalition to fund medical supplies in Hermosillo."

"See, they do good work."

"Did Billie drag you to the meetings?"

"No, like I said, they have a presence on campus, and I went to a rally. The speaker was like me—you know—made the crossing to get away from the violence in his hometown and came here to start new. A chance at a better life. It's all anyone wants. He talked about how the administration in Washington could do more to help people making the journey."

"It's still illegal to enter the country that way. There's a process—"

"You and I both know the official process is broken. Innocent people wait for years for some bureaucrat to look at a piece of paper while lives are destroyed. If the government process doesn't grind them down, then the cartels will. It's a no-win situation for them."

"I know. But blocking traffic on the freeway won't change a thing."

"Yeah, it was stupid. It's going to make people pissed off at the migrant community."

"You realize if they'd booked you for your participation in the mess down on the freeway, it could've jeopardized your visa?"

He nodded. "I didn't do anything but watch them."

"Be careful—" A knock at the door cut Parker off.

Miguel snagged another slice and hefted his backpack, taking advantage of the break in Parker's grilling. "Homework," he said as he hurried down the hall.

Parker glanced through the sidelight of the door and recognized the short person on the front porch.

He unlocked the door and opened it.

"Billie, we were just talking about you."

She wore a sunbaked and frayed Diamondbacks hat pulled low over her eyes. After a quick glance down the block, she darted inside.

Parker hadn't seen Billie this nervous since she discovered the bodies of four men stashed in fifty-five-gallon drums out in the desert.

Parker scanned the street in both directions. "Where's your truck?"

"Next block over. Din't want no one to follow me." She was bouncing on her toes, anxious.

Parker closed the door and motioned Billie inside. "You want some water? I'd offer you some iced tea, but I think you're wired enough already."

"Iced tea would be great."

"You want to tell me what's got you all twisted up?"

"He's back."

"Who's back? What are you talking about?"

"Esteban Castaneda. He's back, and I saw him."

Parker's blood turned to ice at the mention of the man who killed his partner five years ago and vanished.

Chapter Six

"Castaneda's here, in Phoenix?"

Parker felt his knees buckle. Deputy Josh McMillan was stabbed and left to die on the side of the road during a botched human trafficking run. It took four years to identify Castaneda as the coyote who murdered McMillan. Survivor's guilt wormed and festered into Parker's conscious mind because he was less than a mile away and let his partner die.

"Are you sure? It's him?"

Billie gripped the iced tea, and Parker thought she was going to shatter the glass. "I know what I saw. I spotted him comin' out of a machine shop in La Mirage. He got into a car with a couple of gang hitters."

"When was this?"

"About an hour ago. I was comin' back from Tucson and came up Grand—you know where the really good taco place is—West Valley Machine Parts is in the same parkin' lot."

"What did you see, Billie? Slow down and lay it out for me."

She took a deep breath.

"Castaneda was comin' outta the shop. He carried a package under his arm. He waited for this car—the car with the gang bangers—he waited for them to pull up. Then he gets in, and they take off."

"You recognize the guys in the car?"

"Nuh-uh. Not by name. I think I seen 'em before. I got a photo of the car, though." She handed him her cell phone. Through the cracked screen, Parker made out the lowered Chevy Impala with the license plate in clear view. He couldn't spot Castaneda or the occupants in the photo behind the tinted windows. Parker sent the photo to his email.

"Not bad, Billie."

"Why you think he's here—Castaneda?" Billie took her phone back and shoved it in her pocket.

Parker shook his head. "He hasn't surfaced north of the border since he killed McMillan. Have you heard any chatter about Los Muertos running anything up here?"

"Nothing. They've even been quiet down near Hermosillo after Jeannine Cordova lost control of the Sinaloa Cartel."

Parker wanted to believe Castaneda finally surfaced. It meant Parker could make good on his promise to McMillan's wife. He'd find the person responsible and make them pay.

At least once a month, Parker would drop into the gang unit and dig around for any mention of Castaneda or Los Muertos. Until this moment, Castaneda was a ghost. A lone desert scrapper beat the high-tech, high-risk gang to the intel.

"What would someone like him be doin' at a machine shop?"

"That's what I want to find out. You know who runs the business?" he said.

She shook her head. "I don't think it's anyone connected with the Immigration Coalition. I can find out."

"Speaking of the Coalition, what are you doing dragging Miguel into that mess?"

"It weren't like that. He come walkin' in, and it surprised me to see the boy. There ain't nothin' wrong with the Coalition. They been helpin' the people stuck down south."

"If that's all they did, I wouldn't have an issue. You know, I'm hearing they've paid coyotes to ferry migrants over the border. Then they pull a stunt like today, blocking the freeway. I don't want Miguel caught up in that."

Billie nodded and cast her eyes down at her scarred boots.

For a woman who stood up to the Cartel and eked out an existence collecting desert scrap metal, Billie was an enigma. Tough and determined, yet sensitive when it came to finding her place in the world. A world valuing conformity and status. Billie didn't fit in.

Parker regretted taking Miguel's Coalition involvement out on her.

"Billie, I'm sorry. I know it's not your fault. It's mine. If I can't get it across to Miguel these people aren't what they pretend to be. He might get hurt. That's all. I want him to finish school and find a good job. Did you know he wants to go to law school?"

"He'd be a good one. That boy can talk," Billie said.

"Hey, you wanna stay for some dinner? I ordered pizza?"

Billie perked up. "I could eat."

Parker pointed to the pizza box on the kitchen counter. "Help yourself."

Billie dropped a slice on a paper plate and leaned on the counter while she chewed. "Somethin's buggin' me about Castaneda showing up now. He's too careful to risk comin' up here unless he didn't have no choice."

"I'd like nothing more than to tie him to the Sun Valley Sniper cases. Two new victims today. A young mother who got in the way and an attorney."

"Heard about some shooting on the 10. Guess that's what it was."

"Don't know why the attorney was singled out. I need to head out to the Scottsdale address and let the Jessup family know he isn't coming home."

Billie stopped in mid-bite. "Jessup. Roger Jessup?"

"Yeah. How do you know him?"

"Roger helped me out a couple times. Kept the Cave Creek City Council from runnin' me and a few others outta the area when we was campin' on public land. He was a good man. Didn't look down on us on account of we had nothin' and he took our case knowin' we couldn't pay. That's a shame. Really is. Don't know if he's got family. He never mentioned it. Roger'd meet us at his house up there and never saw no one but a housekeeper. I can show you where it is and all."

"I have the address. You don't need to go out of your way."

Billie shrugged. "You be careful with Castaneda runnin' about. I'll keep my ear to the ground and find out if anyone knows why he's popped up."

"Be careful with him, Billie. Keep your distance. You know how dangerous he and Los Muertos are."

"I ain't bout to be no hero."

She tossed her paper plate into the trash and nodded down the hall. "I'll let you know if Miguel takes an interest in Coalition stuff. All the boy's been doin' is listenin'. I think he's lookin' for a link to his past in El Salvador. Wants to feel like he belongs."

"He belongs."

"Easy for you and me to say. He's the one who might not feel like he's welcome here."

Billie slipped out the door, peering down the street before she stepped off the porch.

Parker locked the door behind him. Why would Castaneda appear in Phoenix after all these years? Billie might've spotted someone who looked like the killer. How many men of average height and weight with dark hair did Parker think matched the description? The star tattoo on his left forearm was the telltale mark captured by Deputy McMillan's dash cam in the moments before his murder.

Parker knocked on Miguel's door and poked in. "Hey, buddy. I gotta run up to Scottsdale for a bit. Shouldn't be long. You gonna be all right?"

Miguel hunched over his desk, highlighting sections of text with a thick yellow marker. It gave off a screech as he swept over the words.

"No problem. I've got to do some reading for a mid-term day after tomorrow. Oh, sorry for making you get worried and having to break me out of jail."

"Don't make a habit of it. Be careful. That's all I'm asking. You've come so far, and there's nothing you can't do if you want it. I don't want some fool in the Coalition to ruin it for you."

"I understand. I'll pay attention."

"See you in a bit."

Parker closed the door, strode to his room, retrieved his weapon from the safe, and made sure of the address. Miguel didn't say he would stay away from the Coalition, but only he would pay attention. Parker felt the gray hair sprouting.

Who would he be paying attention to?

Chapter Seven

The drive from Litchfield Park to Jessup's Scottsdale address took less than thirty minutes. He pulled into the cobblestone drive and parked in front of the modern two-story home, which promised a stunning valley view from the back. This was pricy real estate. Jessup must've been a successful attorney.

Before he shut off the engine, Parker noticed the front door ajar. It was one of those ten-foot-tall, massive metal panel doors with a recessed hinge that always made Parker think of a spaceship.

Parker approached the door and rapped on the frame. "Sheriff's Office."

Not a sound in response, so he stepped inside and called out again. "Sheriff's Office. Anyone home?"

Parker squinted against the shadows inside. He spotted a light switch near the door and flicked three of them until the hallway pot lights came on.

Expensively furnished, the home felt more like a museum than a place to put your head. Recessed lights shone down on artwork and sculptures tucked away in niches in the hall. A glimmer of a fully stocked floor-to-ceiling wine refrigerator caught Parker's attention. It must hold over a hundred bottles.

The alarm panel by the front door blinked green letters reading disarmed. A tall table with thin legs lay on its side in the hallway. A blue ceramic vase lay in pieces next to the polished mahogany table.

"Excuse me. Can I help you?"

Parker turned at the voice. A tall, thin woman with long, straight gray hair stood under a Palo Verde tree on the edge of the property. In the evening light, the woman appeared ghostly. She held one thin arm close to her chest while the free hand clutched a cell phone.

"I said, can I help you?"

Parker knew better than to turn his back to an open doorway, leaving him exposed. He moved to the left of the metal door panel. "Sheriff's Office, ma'am."

"Excuse me if I don't take you at your word. You have some identification?"

"I do." Parker pulled his jacket back, exposing the badge on his belt. "Can you confirm if this is the Jessup residence?"

She lowered the cell phone, squinting at Parker.

"Roger isn't home."

As Parker stepped closer, he noticed the woman's wary, light blue eyes. He guessed she was in her seventies and tagged her as the local neighborhood watch. Based on her glare, nothing happened on this block without her knowing.

"Anyone else live here with Mr. Jessup?"

"No. Roger is single."

Parker smiled. The woman kept an eye on the attorney.

"When was the last time you saw him, Miss...?"

"Thomas. Amanda Thomas. I live next door." She tipped her head to the slate-roofed residence to the left of the Jessup home. "Roger should be home any minute. I saw him dash out of here about two—two and a half hours ago. Seemed in quite the rush too."

"You saw him leave? What was he driving?"

Amanda Thomas described the SUV. It matched the vehicle Jessup crashed on the freeway.

"You say he was in a hurry? What makes you think that?"

"Is Roger in trouble? I don't want to say anything to make him cross with me."

"He's not in trouble, ma'am. There was an accident. Now, you said he was in a hurry..."

"Oh, my, yes. I heard a commotion from my yard, and by the time I came around front, Roger was barreling down the street. So unlike him. Usually very courteous. He's lucky the HOA didn't receive a complaint."

Parker figured she probably called the HOA the second Jessup's taillights disappeared. Lucky for the attorney, he wouldn't need to worry about a notice from a meddling association board member.

"What did you hear? The commotion…"

Amanda touched a coral-hued fingernail to her matching lip. "I heard loud voices. His and someone else. I couldn't tell you who. He said, 'Leave it alone.' That's when I came around to see what the fuss was about."

"You didn't see this person, the one he was speaking to?"

She shook her head. "No. I think it was a woman. But I didn't see anyone. Maybe used his cell phone like the kids do, you know, out loud?"

"Like on a speakerphone. Maybe?"

"You didn't see anyone, or another vehicle?"

"No, I didn't."

"Have any idea about who I can contact on Roger's behalf? Did he have any family in the area?"

"Not that I know of."

Parker was careful about using the "next-of-kin" phrase. It carried an emotional wallop, and once spoken, people filtered what they said. Either not wanting to speak ill of the dead, or to conceal an unflattering detail from a conversation, a letter, or encounter with the dead person.

"I need to lock up the place. The door was ajar when I got here. I guess Roger was in a hurry, like you said. You don't have a key to the place, would you?"

"Heavens no. Roger was a very private man. I never saw anyone but the gardeners, the housekeeper, and an occasional visit by the pool man. He wouldn't give any of them a key. You don't give help a key, especially—"

She cut herself off. Parker guessed where this was going. Especially if the help was brown-skinned.

"Thank you, Miss Thomas. You've been very helpful. I'll let you get back to whatever it was you were doing before I interrupted you."

32

Parker needed to secure the home, but he'd need to request a warrant to search, especially in an attorney's home and office. Legal files might require the court to appoint a special master, usually another attorney, who would review the documents and release specific files within a narrow definition spelled out in a warrant. Parker didn't know what might be in there to justify an attorney getting killed.

It was within his authority to make a cursory observation of the home to make sure there was no one inside—the door was open upon his arrival. And the toppled side table was sufficient cause to allow him to enter to make sure there was no one injured in the home.

Parker waited for Miss Thomas to disappear before he entered the premises. There wasn't anyone hiding inside, and no injured parties. He stopped at a home office door and recalled Billie recounting meeting Jessup here. Pretty fancy digs for a lawyer handling property disputes for the homeless. Maybe it was Jessup's good deed of the month.

Something caught Parker's eye in the frame on the wall. Among the photos of Jessup with local and state dignitaries, a gold-lettered proclamation stood out. Not because it testified Jessup was an outstanding citizen, or a compassionate conservative. It caught Parker's attention because the Immigrant Coalition issued it. Roger Jessup was the Executive Director of the Coalition.

Chapter Eight

Parker grabbed a set of keys off the floor near the overturned table. He didn't return the furniture to its upright position, because if the attorney's home became part of a crime scene, he didn't want to contaminate potential evidence. The nosy neighbor mentioned the argument with someone before Roger sped away. He turned out the lights and locked the massive front door, securing the Jessup residence.

The attorney's connection with the immigrants' rights group was troubling. Their executive director was murdered on the same day as the protest. A protest that partially blocked the freeway and slowed traffic to a crawl. The gunman waiting above the freeway used the congestion to make sure he hit his intended target. Parker mulled over the connection between the dead man, the protest, and the Immigrant Coalition.

Miguel was in his room with the door shut when Parker returned. He didn't want to be one of those helicopter parents who doted on and curated every aspect of their child's life. Miguel was almost eighteen and an adult. Miguel rarely talked about plans for his future now that he had one. Parker's formal foster parent status with the State of Arizona would expire at eighteen, but there were provisions for an extension if Miguel stayed in school. He wasn't about to toss the kid out the door. Miguel needed to know he'd always be welcome in his home.

Rather than interrupting Miguel, Parker sent a text, the preferred means of communication for people under thirty, saying he was back and needed to talk with him about the Immigrant Coalition tomorrow.

Miguel replied with a "K." The boy was becoming more of an American every day.

After a fitful night's rest, Parker showered, dressed, and prepared to ask Miguel if he'd ever met Roger Jessup at a Coalition meeting. He found a note on the kitchen counter letting Parker know he needed to go to school early for a meeting with an academic advisor and he'd be home at the usual time. Miguel added, "As long as I don't have a protest to attend, LOL."

Parker grinned at the humor. Hopefully, yesterday's experience sitting in the Sheriff's substation made an impression.

Miguel had made coffee, and the carafe was waiting for him. Parker poured a travel mug full and set out for the cross-valley drive to the Maricopa County Sheriff's Headquarters on West Jefferson.

Peter Tully and Roger Johns were huddled around a video monitor when Parker arrived at the detective bureau.

Tully looked more like a balding college professor than a thirty-six-year veteran detective. His usual elbow-patched sport coat hung on the back of his chair. Morehouse and Spellman Colleges once recruited his partner, Barry Johns, as a professor. Together, Parker thought them the perfect balance.

Johns nodded to the screen as Parker drew near. "We've run this video a hundred times. The shooter never stepped outside the van. He opened the side door and took his shot. There." Johns pointed at the screen. "You see the van shudder under the weight of someone moving around inside before it pulls away."

"Plain vanilla panel van with no rear plate," Parker said.

"Almost. Check this out," Tully said.

He froze the frame on the van as it pulled from the curb.

"Check it out. The rear bumper is out of alignment. It hangs lower on the passenger side, like it hit something. We can get the notice to patrol deputies and ask them to look for a white '90 Ford Econoline van with rear end damage."

"Not a bad start," Parker said.

"MVD says there are over five hundred registered in the valley. Popular with laborers, contractors, and according to I.C.E., coyotes bringing illegals in over the border," Johns said.

Parker flashed back to the last words he heard from his partner, Deputy McMillan, while they watched a remote section of road for undocumented migrants passing through from the border.

"Got one coming my direction. Dark blue panel van riding low. He's not turning around like the others," McMillan said over the radio.

"Nah. A coyote wouldn't be this stupid. Probably a construction worker heading out to Anthem. I'll chase him back out."

Parker heard a click and static over the radio two minutes later.

"Mac? 10-9," Parker said, asking for McMillan to repeat the message.

Another click in response. The hills and washes in this section of the desert caused garbled radio traffic.

"Come again, Mac?"

Parker never heard another word from Mac. The coyote, later identified as Esteban Castaneda, stabbed his partner and left him to bleed out on the side of the road.

"Sergeant, you think of something?" Johns asked.

Parker shook off the painful memory. "No, like you said, there are hundreds of these to chase down. I got some new information on the victim last night, Roger Jessup."

"The attorney in the SUV?" Tully said.

"That's the one. I went to his place last night and couldn't contact next of kin. The self-appointed neighborhood watch said she saw him speed away not long before he ended up shot to death."

"Running to, or running from?" Johns asked.

"Exactly the question to ask. Now put it with another tidbit I discovered—Jessup was the executive director of the Immigrant Coalition."

"Holy crap. He was connected with the pro-migrant movement in Phoenix?"

"Not only connected to it, he ran it," Parker said.

"There's no love lost between them and the anti-immigration hardliners in the Valley. All the militia groups and the 'build the wall' people. The suspect pool just overflowed."

"Pete, hit up Court Implementation and see if they've run across any contact with the Immigrant Coalition."

"Smart. If we go barging into the Coalition, we could violate the Melendres court order. MCSO can't afford to piss off the federal court monitor, at the same time, we're trying to improve relationships with the Latino community," Tully said.

"We need to know where the lines are on this thing before we go upsetting the balance and send someone running to the Sheriff, shutting down this avenue of our investigation. We need to tread lightly."

"Got it."

Parker rubbed the back of his neck. "There's another thing has me concerned about the Coalition connection. The Immigrant Coalition organized a protest and march blocking traffic on the westbound lanes of the 10. The traffic backup made sure Jessup was a slow-moving target for our shooter."

"Whoa," Johns said.

"Might be nothing to it, but the timing of the two events and the Coalition connection are hard to ignore," Parker said.

"What you need me to hit?" Johns said.

"Start putting together a list of disruptive groups, gangs, and anti-immigrant groups who may have a bone to pick with the Coalition. See if the department has a list of complaints."

"I'll check with the gang unit and the HIDTA task force. They have their ear on everything going on in the valley.

Parker knew Johns referred to the High-Intensity Drug Trafficking Area task force, a multi-agency operation designed to disrupt cartel-led drug operations.

"I'm not suggesting the Coalition is running drugs," Parker said.

"Neither am I. The task force uses wiretaps and undercover operations. They've run into an increase in the militia types near the border."

"Got it. Good idea. You two sort out what you can on the Coalition connection—softly—and I'm going to pull the case files on the prior victims.

If the shooter has it out for people connected to the Coalition, it's a new angle we didn't have before."

As his detectives left to gather new intelligence on the pro-immigrant organization, Parker pulled up the case files of the two previous Sun Valley Sniper victims. Unable to find a connection between the first two shootings, it was time to line up all three cases now and see if the Jessup murder added the key to the bigger picture.

The first murder was considered a drive-by shooting until ballistics determined the slug killing Emilio Hernandez came from a .308 rifle round. The large caliber slug caught the storekeeper at the base of his skull and dropped the seventy-year-old man where he stood. The responding officers were quick to write up the initial crime as an attempted robbery. The problem was the cash in the register was untouched, and the fatal shot came through the front window, catching Hernandez as he was sweeping the floor.

Parker opened the case file for Melissa Carson, a twenty-eight-year-old waitress and college student. She was gunned down waiting in line for a concert at the Comerica Theatre. No one in the crowd knew what happened, or where the shot came from. The .308 caliber slug pierced her chest, and the cavitation from the large caliber bullet exploded her heart and sheared off half of her left lung. The slug exited the woman's body and embedded itself into a wall behind her.

In both cases, the victims were in public, and no similarity was found. He worked at a small mom-and-pop store, she as a student and waitress. One male, one female. Hispanic and white. They appeared random.

Adding Jessup to the mix didn't make the picture come into focus. An older white male, an attorney, and civil rights activist. None of these factors connected with the first two victims. Frustrated at the roadblock, Parker flicked the computer mouse away, and he inadvertently opened the crime scene photos from the Hernandez store shooting. The man died sweeping the floor. A broom lay next to him. A small object on the counter made Parker inch toward the screen. It made his stomach turn to ice.

A corner of a poster showed in the crime scene photo. It announced a rally at Friendship Park, sponsored by the Immigrant Coalition.

Chapter Nine

Parker pushed back from the desk. Assuming Hernandez was murdered because he hung a poster in his store was a leap. But, once again, the Immigrant Coalition raised its head in connection with the shooting.

He pulled his cellphone from his pocket and pressed the stored number for Billie—if she remembered to charge the phone and if she was scavenging for scrap metal in a location with cell reception.

The call landed in her voicemail. "Billie, it's Parker. You know about a market near Olive Avenue and Dysart—called Los Aztecas Mercado? Call me when you have a chance. Thanks, Billie."

Parker didn't want to lead her to an Immigrant Coalition connection. If a correlation was there, beyond a poster anyone could've taped up, Billie would find it. Besides, Parker knew he was a stranger in the small Mexican markets, where people experienced the darker side of police officials on both sides of the border.

He pushed back from the desk as his phone rang. "Parker."

"Nathan, good morning."

He recognized the calming voice of the captain's secretary, Monica.

"Morning, Monica. You tell me if it's going to be a good morning."

"That depends…"

"On how quickly I get to the captain's office?"

"See, this is why you are my favorite detective."

"Is he in a good mood? Anyone else in with him?"

"No, and the Undersheriff just left in a huff."

"Great. I'll be there."

Parker hung up the phone and rapped on the captain's door five minutes later.

Monica opened the door from inside the office and slapped a newspaper across Parker's chest as she passed him.

"You see this?" Captain Morris asked.

The captain was a thick-necked bull of a man who was an imposing figure in his youth. From where Parker stood, he was imposing now.

"What is it?"

Captain Morris pointed at a chair and commanded Parker to sit. Parker took a breath and sat, slightly relieved. The last time they summoned him, Parker ended up on administrative time off for a bogus excessive force complaint.

"Today's headline has the county board of supervisors in a panic."

Parker unfolded the newspaper, and the two-inch bold headline explained the concern. "Valley under attack by The Sun Valley Sniper." A quick glance at the article below told readers to avoid open public places, be aware of their surroundings, and alert law enforcement if they observed suspicious behavior.

"The headline's melodramatic, but they seem to give sound advice."

"The Sheriff is being told he can't keep the community safe."

"Good thing he's elected and not appointed by the board."

"If he wants to be re-elected, he needs the public panic put to bed. Which means you need to gain some traction on the case to reassure the public we're on top of this."

"Yesterday's shooting gives us two new victims. One looks like she was in the wrong place wrong time and got in the way of the intended target, a local attorney."

"Random, like the other two?"

"At first glance, yes. Different background, walks of life, and geographically spread apart. But there is a new thread connecting at least two of the victims."

"And that is?"

"The Immigrant Coalition."

"Oh, Christ on a cracker."

"Exactly, we don't need the federal court saying we're profiling when we ask around about ties to the Coalition. I've asked Tully and Johns to walk softly on this. Last night's victim, Roger Jessup, was an attorney, but also served as the executive director for the Immigrant Coalition. Emilio Hernandez was the shopkeeper murdered in his store. And next to his body, a poster for a Coalition event."

"That's all? No role in the organization? No radical public presence drawing right-wing extremists to take him out?"

"Not yet." Parker shook his head. "We've worked the Immigrant Coalition angle for a few hours, so we've only started down the path. Incidentally, Billie Carson came to me claiming she'd spotted Esteban Castaneda."

Morris glanced up from his desk. "The guy we want for killing McMillan? Think she's onto anything?"

Parker shrugged. "I really don't know. I mean, I've learned to trust Billie's instincts, but I'm not sure about this one."

"Have you run this past your girlfriend at the FBI?"

"Lynette Finch isn't my girlfriend. Calling her an ex-girlfriend is even too familiar. Haven't spoken to her in over a year."

"Sounds like you need to put on your big boy pants and call her up. If anyone would know if Castaneda snuck back over the border, she'd know. Make the call, Sergeant. We need to know if that predator is back in our sandbox."

"Understood. I'll reach out. Anything else, Captain?"

"Keep me in the loop on the Immigrant Coalition angle. I have a feeling once it gets out, you're poking around, I'll need to put out some fires. I'll talk to Court Compliance and the Public Information Officer."

"Thanks, Captain."

Parker beat it out of the captain's office and waved to his secretary while she was on the phone. His cell phone sounded as he sat. Billie Carson's name displayed on the caller ID.

"Hey, Billie. Thanks for getting back to me."

"I wasn't sure you wanted nothing to do with me after last night."

"Nothing's changed between us, Billie. You ever been in the market off Dysart? The place where Emilio Hernandez was killed?"

"I know it."

"I figured as much. What can you tell me about the place?"

"It's not what I can tell you. But what I gotta show you. Can you meet me here?"

"What—wait, you're already there?"

"After you left your message, I came on down. Emilio's wife is here, and I think you should see for yourself what Emilio was doin'."

"Will his wife talk to me? I mean, I understand if she doesn't want to see another cop in her market."

"I told her she can trust you."

"Was she there when her husband was killed?"

"I didn't wanna get into it. But they's good people, and Emilio didn't deserve none of it—gettin' himself shot and all. All's he did was help folks who were strugglin' once they came over."

Parker didn't respond. A connection to the undocumented community in Phoenix isn't unusual—then again, the shootings weren't unusual either. The crime scene photo capturing a sliver of the Immigrant Coalition poster registered in Parker's mind. Was Emilio Hernandez targeted for a reason, or was Parker reaching for a connection that didn't exist?

Chapter Ten

Parker pulled to a stop in the broken asphalt parking lot in front of the Los Aztecas Mercado. Billie Carson's battered red Toyota pickup truck was the only vehicle in the lot. Parker entered the store, and a tinkle of a small brass bell on the frame announced his arrival.

The place was familiar from the crime scene photos. Less than ten feet from where Parker stood, Emilio Hernandez took his final breath. In the days since his death, someone scrubbed the worn tile where the shopkeeper fell. They were brighter than the rest of the floor. A slight odor of bleach hung in the air. The front window, shattered by the fatal shot, had been replaced, but it hung as a reminder without the yellow dust patina of the others.

The register off to his left was empty, as was the small butcher counter in the back.

From the rear, Billie ducked from behind a blue curtain.

"Hey, lock the door, would ya?"

Parker turned and twisted the deadbolt on the front door.

"What's going on?"

"Mrs. Hernandez is in the back. She'll talk to you. She didn't want no one comin' in and gettin' the wrong idea."

"Talking to a cop?"

She nodded.

"What aren't you telling me, Billie?"

"Best let her explain it."

Billie nodded to the curtain and parted it for Parker.

Beyond the blue linen veil, Parker expected a market backroom with excess stock arranged on shelves, cleaning supplies, and a loading bay. Instead, the rear of the building was a small apartment. Against the back wall, there were two sets of bunk beds, a small kitchenette to the left, and a threadbare sofa to the side. A metal shelf with a few personal items rested against the cinderblock separating the front of the market from this residential zone.

At a small, yellowed table, an older woman sat with her eyes assessing Parker as he entered. Behind her, a young man in his twenties crossed his arms, and Parker felt the anger seethe from him.

"Señora Hernandez, this is the detective I told you about, Detective Parker."

"Mrs. Hernandez, I'm very sorry for your loss," Parker said.

The young man behind her huffed. "If you were truly sorry, you would've arrested the man who killed my grandfather. Instead, nothing. Because he came from this community—because he didn't look like you—nothing happens, nothing ever happens."

"I understand. I know it must feel like we've forgotten your grandfather. We haven't. It's why I'm here today."

The man began to speak, and the old woman raised her hand, silencing him.

"Forgive Tomaso. He sometimes speaks without thinking."

Tomaso glared at the floor with his grandmother's rebuke.

"He has nothing to apologize for. I'm sure he's had enough experiences with government types."

The woman shrugged.

"Mrs. Hernandez, can you tell me about your husband?"

Her voice softened. "My Emilio was a good man. He didn't deserve what happened here. Emilio was the kind of man who would always help those who didn't have enough. Customers who couldn't pay for food or baby formula, my Emilio would tell them to pay him when they could. Of course, he knew they never would."

"I want to ask you about a photo. There was a poster in the market—wait, let me see if it's still there."

Parker retreated into the market and stood where the shopkeeper's body was captured in the photo. Not only were the bloodstains gone, so was the poster. Not totally unexpected, the rally at Friendship Park had come and gone too. Parker returned to the back room.

"There was a poster out there before. One about a rally in Friendship Park."

Tomaso stiffened. "It was yesterday, so I took it down."

"You know who put it up?"

"Why is it important? It's a poster. We get them all the time from community groups."

"Do you know who put this one up?"

Mrs. Hernandez cleared her throat. "What is the importance of this poster?"

Parker glanced at Billie. "A group which seems to draw a lot of attention sponsored the rally—some of it is not positive."

Tomaso puffed his chest. "The attention the Immigrant Coalition gets is from people like you. Anytime someone from this community makes a step forward, there's someone like you trying to pull us back."

"All I'm trying to determine is if there is a connection between what happened to your grandfather and the Immigrant Coalition."

"Ridiculous," Tomaso said.

"Wait," Mrs. Hernandez said. "A man came to the store a few days before—before it happened. He wanted Emilio to take the poster down. I don't know why he was so angry about it, but he was very loud."

"You were back here when the argument happened?"

"Yes."

"Were you alone?"

Mrs. Hernandez cut a glance at the bunk beds.

"I don't care about who was staying here, or what their status was. I'm trying to find out what happened to your husband. Was there anyone else who heard the argument?"

She nodded.

"Don't talk to him about these things," Tomaso said. "He's trying to trick us."

"Did you or anyone get a look at the man who argued with Mr. Hernandez?" Parker looked through the thin blue fabric into the market.

"He was a white man. I have never seen him here before. Gray hair and wore an expensive suit."

"Would you know him if you saw him again?"

She nodded. "I would remember him."

"You've never seen him before?"

"No, never."

"You said he was upset about the poster. Can you remember what he said?"

"Nothing that made any sense. Bits and pieces. The rally wasn't smart. It shouldn't happen. Then he ripped it down."

Parker stiffened. "He tore it down? Are you sure?"

"He tore it down and crumpled it up in his fist as he left."

Parker rubbed the back of his neck. He saw the poster displayed in the crime scene photo at the time the shopkeeper died.

"You think they killed my grandfather because of the poster?" Tomaso asked.

"I don't know for sure. It's a connection. With the argument over the rally poster, it makes me want to know how it got here and who put it back up after the argument."

"I did."

"What?" Mrs. Hernandez said.

"Please, Grandmother, believe me. I never thought this would hurt Grandfather. It was another angry white man. It meant nothing. Grandfather said I could put the poster up."

"You put up the second one, too?" Parker asked.

"Yes. I was back here with Grandmother, and I heard shouting. After the man left, I saw someone had ripped the poster down. Grandfather told me to leave it alone. But I thought I knew better. No one could tell us what we couldn't put up in our own store. So, I put a new poster for the rally back up."

"Did you get a look at the man?"

"I didn't recognize him," Tomaso said.

Billie cleared her throat and tipped her head away from the group. Parker took it as a signal she wanted to speak to him out of earshot.

"Detective, this don't seem straight-up. I don't see no suit-wearing executive type shootin' Mr. Hernandez. 'Sides, as far as he knew, the poster was down, and that was the end of it. Unless…"

"Unless what?"

"Unless it was Roger Jessup."

"Jessup? Why would he pitch a fit about a rally sponsored by the Coalition? He was the Coalition," Parker said.

"I dunno. But Tomaso in there. I've seen him at the Coalition meetings. Hangs with the radical members. He'd know Jessup."

Parker pulled his phone and made a call. "Let's get back in there."

Billie led the way to the back room. Tomaso was now seated at the table, head in hand, and Mrs. Hernandez was rubbing his back. Sobs came from the boy.

"It's my fault," Tomaso said, his voice quivering.

Parker's phone chimed in his pocket. He opened the text message from Tully.

"Mrs. Hernandez, do you recognize this man?"

He placed the phone on the table in front of her. The old woman bent closer to examine the photograph on the screen. Her eyes widened, and she flinched away from the image.

"That's him. That's the man who argued with my Emilio."

Tomaso leaned in to look, and the young man tried to act uncertain. "I don't think it was this man, grandmother."

"It was. I know it. The eyes. I remember those angry eyes."

"She can't be sure, Detective. She's had a difficult time."

"Don't treat me like I'm la vieja loca."

Parker sat opposite Tomaso and his grandmother.

"Tomaso, why are you covering for Roger Jessup?"

The young man sat upright and looked ready to bolt from the market.

"Sit down. You're not in any trouble here."

"You know this man?" the grandmother asked.

"No."

"Sure you do, Tomaso. I seen you both together at the Immigrant Coalition meetings," Billie said from her spot against the wall.

Parker noticed the kid's left leg begin to twitch, and he couldn't make eye contact with anyone in the room, especially his grandmother. What was he hiding?

"This man—he was from the Coalition?"

"We can talk later, Grandmother."

"We can talk now." She narrowed her eyes, and the boy fell into the chair as if she'd slapped him.

"Tell them the truth."

"I can't. What the Coalition does is too important to risk getting the police involved. You know they'd like to worm their way inside and expose the work we do. What would happen to the people after the government gets their hands on them?"

"Listen, I'm not after any of the undocumented you run through this place. I don't want to know where they are, or how they got here. I want to know why Roger Jessup was here arguing with your grandfather."

Tomaso hung his head, and his shoulders slumped. He fell silent.

In a flurry, Mrs. Hernandez slapped her grandson on the cheek. "You had something to do with this?"

"No!"

"Then tell them what they need to know."

"All right. It was Roger Jessup. He tore down the poster and argued with my grandfather."

"Why would Jessup want to take down a Coalition poster?"

"Mr. Jessup didn't agree with the protest and the planned freeway closure. He said it wasn't the way to build community support for the cause."

"The organizers planned the freeway blockade?"

He nodded. "We wanted everyone to know what it was like not being

49

able to go home. A minor inconvenience for the white privilege you like to throw around."

Parker knew the kid was trying to bait him. "Why would Roger have a problem with that?"

"Ask him."

"I can't. He's dead."

Tomaso wobbled and looked like he was about to faint. "Dead? What happened to him?"

"It's why we're here. Roger Jessup was shot exactly like your grandfather."

"Why—why would someone do that to him? He was a good man in his own way. I mean, he was a little shy about getting in people's faces, and he didn't have any skin in the game—"

"Meaning he wasn't undocumented himself," Parker said.

Tomaso nodded.

"Who organized the rally at Friendship Park?"

"It was the Council. The Immigrant Coalition's Council. They decide for the collective."

"With Jessup gone, who is going to lead the Coalition now?"

He shrugged. "I don't know. I've never been around the Council. Don't know who they are."

Parker doubted Tomaso was honest on that point.

"Who gave you the posters?"

"They were bundled and waiting for me at school. I picked them up and spread them around where I could."

"Why did Jessup come here? Of all the places you put up posters, why here?"

Tomaso glanced up at Parker. "I think he came to see me."

"What gives you that idea?"

"Mr. Jessup is the one who would tell me another family was coming who needed us to give them a temporary place to stay."

"You never told me the Immigrant Coalition was where these people came from," Mrs. Hernandez said.

"I didn't because you said you didn't like their politics. Does it matter?

The people we helped here needed what little we offer. Does it matter who arranged for them to be here?"

"You can ask your grandfather." The old woman pushed back from the table and strode out the back door.

Chapter Eleven

Billie started to follow the old woman, and Parker held her back.

"I think she's gone through enough for one day."

He turned to Tomaso. "You think of any reason someone would want to go after Roger Jessup and your grandfather? Call me." He slipped a business card under the kid's down-turned face.

Outside, Billie leaned on her Toyota. "I know the Coalition finds temporary shelter for migrants makin' the trek north. Jessup would arrange payment to the families to cover expenses and whatnot."

Parker tipped his head to the market. "Explains how they could keep this place up and running. The shelves were bare. Emilio couldn't make enough to pay the electric bill. How many people knew about Roger's role in finding placements for undocumented folks?"

"I don't think it were no secret. He was the Executive Director and was involved in everythin'. Why you ask?"

"I'm thinking out loud here, but planning to hide undocumented people is the thing the immigration hard-liners wouldn't let slide."

"I suppose."

"Ever hear if the Coalition gets hate mail?"

"Seems like they would. I never heard nothin' about it. That wasn't in my purview."

"Who would keep those kinds of records? Complaints, lawsuits, or emails?"

"I don't rightly know. Seems like somethin' Roger would be into—the paperwork and all."

"The Coalition has an office, don't they?"

"Yeah, down on Thunderbird, between Dysart and El Mirage. People drop in for leads on jobs and assistance programs. Help with immigration paper—that kind of thing."

"What say we go pay them a visit?"

The Immigrant Coalition offices took up one storefront in a brown concrete and stucco strip mall. Mixed in with alternative medicine, check cashing, and a pawnshop. Parker thought it a one-stop shop for the hopeless, the desperate, and the broke.

Parker expected a crowded lobby filled with migrants seeking help with asylum claims, immigration visa applications, or help a family member in ICE custody. Instead, the interior held a drab beige insurance office vibe, commercial grade carpet, a desk on either side of the main room, and two offices in the rear.

A woman with jet-black hair and deep-set brown eyes sat at one desk. Her eyes narrowed as Parker entered, but softened when she spotted Billie.

"Billie," the woman called out and jumped up to hug her. "It's so good to see you."

Parker couldn't pin down the woman's age. She looked in her twenties, but the soft lines around her eyes and the sure manner she carried herself marked her as slightly older.

"Isa, this is my friend, Nathan Parker."

Parker received a firm handshake from the woman and noted her demeanor softened after Billie's introduction, which omitted any reference to his association with the Maricopa County Sheriff's Office.

"What can I do for you, Billie? Planning another trip to Hermo—" Isa stopped in mid-sentence and glanced at Parker.

"It's okay. He's been to Hermosillo with me. He knows what's down there."

Parker could never forget the cardboard and scrap lumber encampments where migrants on their way north waited until they saved enough money to buy passage. Coyote or Cartel. They paved the trail north in violence and misery. Men, women, and children risked it for a chance to start over in a country they'd only heard about in stories from those who made and survived the journey. The brutal truth was oppression and scratching out an existence in a foreign land.

"Are you getting ready for another trip down? I don't have medical supplies or water stocked up for another trip yet."

Billie put her palms up. "No, no. I'm not heading back yet. We're here about Roger."

"I got the news about an hour ago. A shame. Do you know why?"

"That's what we want to find out," Parker said. "Roger wasn't the only one killed with ties to the Coalition.

Isa's face hardened. "I'm surprised this hadn't happened before now. There is so much hate speech directed at my community. Not that I expected Roger to be attacked, but we are a target for the extremists."

"You must get hate mail from time to time," Parker said, glancing at the stack of mail on her desk.

"Some of it is vile, way beyond the 'go back where you came from' rhetoric."

"I'm sorry for that. Would you be able to share some of them with Billie and me?"

Isa cocked her head and studied Parker. "You're a cop, aren't you?"

"I am."

"Do you have a warrant, or a court order, to compel us to hand over documents?"

"No. I'd hoped you'd want to help us identify who held a grudge against the Coalition."

She huffed. "That's easy. Get voter registration records for the last election. There was some pretty divisive material coming out of that."

"Isa," Billie said, "We think someone who had it out for Roger is targeting others. There could be more people hurt."

"Without a court order, I don't feel it's appropriate to turn over our files."

Billie turned to Parker. "Did I mention Isa is an attorney?"

"And a good one," Parker said. "You help folks with immigration paperwork, visa applications?"

"Among other duties. I work—worked—with Roger on the Coalition's legal assistance program."

"Mr. Jessup may keep legal documents at his home office. I'll connect you with the special master as soon as one's appointed so you can regain custody of the files."

"Thanks. I appreciate that, but I can't release the files we collect on the threats and complaints."

"You can give it to them," a voice called out from an office door in the rear of the building. A middle-aged man with close-cropped brown hair and an athletic build leaned on the jamb. He wore a crisp button-down shirt, no tie, with the sleeves rolled up. The dark circles under his eyes testified to a long sleepless night. Grief and anxiety spawn from the shadows. The difference between them is sometimes only a heartbeat, or the lack of one. He wasn't a particularly tall man, but his bearing gave him an air of importance.

"Mr. Brunell, I don't believe it would set a good precedent."

"I understand and appreciate your caution, Isa. This is an exception. There is no shortage of right-wing extremists who hate what we do here. If Roger was targeted, I can't let someone else become a victim without doing my part."

The man strode over to Parker and Billie.

"I'm Tim Brunell, vice chair of the Board for the Immigrant Coalition. We've been trying to pull everything together after Roger's death."

Parker shook his hand.

"Looks like you've been burning the midnight oil. How were you notified of his death?"

"Channel 7's newsroom. They wanted a statement from us. Kind of morbid if you ask me."

"The media knew to connect with you?" Parker asked.

He nodded. "Part of my role here with the Coalition is media relations, co-ordinating press releases, answering questions about the struggle migrants face with the broken immigration system, that kind of thing."

"Did Mr. Jessup have any next-of-kin? We're making sure we let family know."

"He didn't have anyone. Widowed and no children. Roger used to say the Coalition was his family."

"Who handled his estate, or did he leave a will?"

Isa stepped in. "I handled Roger's personal legal matters. He has a will. I'll need to reach out to the executor and begin the process."

"Before you begin, please release all the material on the threatening correspondence and incident reports to the detective."

"Are you certain, Mr. Brunell? I haven't gone through them to—"

"Release them. All of them. I don't want another innocent person harmed. If the information in those files will help track down the person or group responsible for Roger's assassination, I want them to have it."

Isa nodded.

"Thank you for your cooperation. I won't expose undocumented people or turn over files to federal authorities. I only want to know who's responsible for shooting Mr. Jessup."

"I appreciate your understanding. I'm risking the trust of the undocumented people who rely on us. Please, don't put them in the middle of your investigation."

"That's not my intent."

"Billie, I don't think we've ever met. It's nice to meet the person Roger told me about. Thank you for everything you do."

"Thanks, Mr. Brunnel. I'm sorry about Roger. Like Isa said, he was a really good man."

"Yes, he was… I'll leave you with Isa to find you what you need."

Brunnel returned to his office and closed the door.

Isa pushed back from her desk. "I'll pull the files for you. I don't like it. But if Mr. Brunnel says you can take them, he's the boss. Wait here."

Isa withdrew a key from her desk and pushed out the front door.

"Smart."

"What's that?"

"The records aren't here. Even if we came back with a search warrant, there wouldn't be any records here on the premises."

Billie smiled.

"You knew that?"

"You notice the storage facility behind this mall? The Coalition uses several storage lockers there. I pick up my medical supplies in one. They must keep their paperwork in another."

While Isa was retrieving the files, Parker noted the red light on the phone flash on next to Brunnel's name.

Isa shouldered open the door and wheeled a dolly with three brown cardboard boxes balanced on the platform.

She noticed Parker's gaze land on the boxes.

"Are the files from the last six months sufficient?"

"You weren't kidding about the hate mail," Parker said.

"There are a lot of closed-minded bigots out there."

"That there are, Isa."

Billie grabbed a box, and Parker hefted the other two while Isa held the door for them.

On the way out, Parker paused and said, "Thanks for helping us try to find who is behind the attack. I won't let these fall into the wrong hands."

She nodded. The glint in her eye was all the warning Parker needed to keep these files safe from harm.

They loaded the boxes into Parker's Explorer. When Parker closed the rear hatch, Billie looked to the Immigrant Coalition offices.

"How come nobody wanted to know about Roger? Like when he could be buried and such. If they was family—like Mr. Brunell said they was—wouldn't family want to know?"

"You heard Isa, she's going to start the wheels turning on his will, and it's not as if we can release Roger's body to anyone before the Medical Examiner is done with her work."

"I get it. If it were me, I'd want to know exactly what happened. When did it happen? How was he killed? Did he suffer? Like that. Brunell never asked for none of it. Kinda cold, you ask me."

"At least he handed over the hate mail to help find who shot Jessup. I appreciate his willingness to cooperate. Isa is right. They didn't need to hand them over. You ever see Brunell before?"

Billie leaned her back against Parker's vehicle. She stretched and rubbed a sore spot on her lower back.

"Roger was the heart of the Coalition. Brunell is the face. He is the one who gets television time, or public appearances where he can shake hands and ask for money."

"Everyone has a role to play, I suppose."

"Yeah, I 'suppose. He ain't no Roger Jessup is what I'm sayin'."

Parker made sure the rear hatch was shut. "I'll run these back to the office and see if they can point us in the direction."

"Want me to come help?" Billie asked. Her face looked hopeful.

"We got this, Billie."

"Oh, Okay. I get it." She kicked an asphalt chunk with the tip of her boot. "You can't have someone like me hangin' 'round with the mucky-mucks."

Parker turned to her. "Billie, it's nothing like that. These documents could be evidence, and I need to document the chain of custody. No one outside of the Sheriff's office should touch them. It's not personal, Billie. After what we've been through together, you know I respect you."

"I thought you mighta had a change of heart, is all."

"Never." Parker opened his door as Billie turned to her Toyota. He realized as tough as Billie came off, she was a sensitive one.

Parker started his SUV, and he froze. Tucked under his windshield wiper a bright brass .308 caliber rifle shell.

Chapter Twelve

After bagging the empty shell casing, Parker's scan of the strip mall lot failed to find anyone lingering. No cameras mounted on the building, as expected. This was a neighborhood where privacy and anonymity meant staying alive another day.

Parker lugged the three boxes into the Major Crimes Unit, dropping them with a thud next to his desk.

Tully appeared in the doorway. "You bring us work? I know it's not from the Immigrant Coalition, because Court Implementation gave us a stay away order."

Parker dropped into his chair and rocked back. "The court unit give you any reason for the keep-away status?"

"Lieutenant Kelly mentioned the federal court monitor wouldn't take kindly to us focusing on an organization representing the same demographic the department's allegedly profiled."

"How's Kelly doing since his transfer from Professional Standards? He was actually fair and aboveboard in his internal affairs investigations, and I think that's what the brass wanted in the new court unit."

"He made it clear he doesn't consider what he's doing as police work. He compared it to divorce mediation between attorneys."

"Kelly would know. He's been through three."

"Ouch." Tully nodded to the boxes. "What ya got for us?"

"Files from the Immigrant Coalition."

"Lieutenant Kelly won't be pleased."

"These were voluntarily given to us by the Coalition's vice chairman, before the lieutenant's edict."

"Doubt Kelly will make that distinction," Tully said. "What did they give you? Can't imagine the Coalition handed over the keys to the kingdom."

"These boxes hold the hate mail sent to the Immigrant Coalition over a six-month period."

"We're at the 'wackos and weirdos' stage of the investigation already?"

"No stone unturned, Detective. Grab a box. Drop one on your partner's desk, too."

Five minutes into reading the hate mail, Parker felt like he needed a shower. Racist rhetoric, anti-immigration hardliners, and scores of complaints blaming uncontrolled immigration for everything from inflation to low-paying jobs for Americans. Parker sorted the letters with threats of violence into a pile to his left. The stack was unnerving in its height.

Tully knocked on Parker's door.

"You can't be done with your box yet," Parker said.

"Boss, you gotta check out the news." Tully strode to Parker's desk, grabbed the television remote.

A wall-mounted screen blossomed to life, to a live broadcast. The breaking news banner on the bottom of the read "Random Killings Incite Widespread Panic."

"Oh, great," Parker said.

The camera focused on a podium in front of Phoenix City Hall, where the mayor stood with the city council and county board members arranged behind him. Parker stood from his desk and opened the blinds. Three blocks away, Parker saw a crowd gathering in the street, swarming past the Phoenix Police Department barriers.

Back on the television screen, Parker caught the Mayor motioning for the crowd to settle down. He was about to speak. The way the gathered mass fell silent told Parker the political rally was planned to drum up support for whatever the mayor had planned.

"We come together today, united from across this great valley, to condemn the wave of random violence threatening our freedom and way of life. Yesterday, the Sun Valley Sniper claimed two more victims. We opened a tip line and offer a ten-thousand-dollar reward for information leading to the arrest and conviction of the individual responsible for these senseless killings."

"Did you know we had a tip line going?" Tully asked.

"Not until now."

The Mayor paused and pinched the bridge of his nose. It was supposed to look like he grieved the loss of the latest victims, but Parker was certain Mayor Thomas didn't know their names. "We, the citizens of this great city, cannot let evil go unchallenged. We must confront it, not allow it to take root in our communities, and fight against this threat."

"I don't like where this is going," Parker said.

"Neither does the Sheriff, check it out," Tully said, pointing at the screen.

The Sheriff didn't shy away from the media. He was an elected official, after all. But he looked like he rather be testifying in federal court than standing there and listen to the mayor's pitch.

The mayor raised his arms, summoning visions of an old-time preacher about to unleash a benediction to his flock. "It is up to us to retake our city, our communities, and make it safe for women, children, and merchants to walk the streets of this great city without fear. If you see something, say something."

The Sheriff couldn't restrain himself and took to the podium. "Thank you, Mayor Thomas. I think the mayor would also like to remind you this suspect is armed and proven dangerous. If you suspect someone, or have any information pertaining to this investigation, please reach out to law enforcement on the tip line. Do not take matters into your own hands. This man is dangerous, and we don't want any innocent people harmed. Please let us do our job."

A few murmurs from the crowd. "You haven't done your job yet!"

The mayor eased back to the microphone. "Yes, yes, the Sheriff is correct. We need to give our law enforcement agencies the opportunity to bring this killer to justice. But make no mistake; we cannot be complacent and allow another random murder in our city. It is up to us."

The mayor turned and strode to the city hall entrance. The television screen cut to a young blonde reporter in the studio.

"The mayor's press conference calls for vigilance, not vigilantism. Four victims are attributed to the Sun Valley Sniper, and law enforcement officials are no closer to solving this case than they were three weeks ago. A break in this case may come from our viewers. Call the tip line number listed on the bottom of your screen if you have any information that may help law enforcement."

The reporter started reading a story about the dropping attendance at Phoenix Coyotes games, and Tully shut off the television.

"What do you make of that?"

Parker leaned back in his chair. "Between the hate mail and the mayor coming close to calling for a citizen's militia to hunt down this killer, it's going to turn really ugly."

Barry Johns entered the office. "You guys hear what the mayor just did?"

"We did," Tully said. "You're first rotation up on the tip line."

"Bullshit, I am."

"Seniority counts around here,"

"Never mind that now," Parker said. "Learn anything from HIDTA?"

"The task force is being run by an old friend of yours, FBI Agent Lynnette Finch."

Parker put his head in his hands. "Of course it is."

"What do they know about the Coalition?"

"The Immigrant Coalition is on their radar. They've been monitoring the group's activity, and they've seen an increase in human trafficking in the last three months. With the human element, they've noticed an uptick in the level of drugs coming across the border with them."

"What happened in three months to spike the numbers?"

"They don't know. They said there is an uptick in women and children being brought over. And where the Immigrant Coalition comes in is the ones they picked up had instruction to connect with the Coalition after they arrived here."

"They get a name to connect with, or a number?" Parker asked.

"I didn't hear the details, but they know to find the Coalition for support."

Parker sighed. "It's not illegal to help them after they arrive here. You know, offer support and some financial assistance."

"I suppose not. The task force was trying to find a link between the Coalition and the drug traffic. I get the feeling they are spinning their wheels and not getting anywhere on that thread."

"I can't see the Immigrant Coalition risking what they built to mule drugs over the border," Tully said.

Parker glanced at the stack of documents on his desk. So many individuals and groups pressuring the Coalition to pull up stakes and move on. Pressure. "Unless the Coalition was receiving pressure to smuggle drugs. The Cartels use NGOs as a cover for their operations."

Parker's desk phone rang, and the caller ID was the captain's number. "I guess the Sheriff made it back from the mayor's press briefing. I'll put it on speaker. Chime in with what you know on the case as the questions come up."

"Parker here. I have Tully and Johns on speaker."

"Good," Captain Morris said. "You need to get down to Tempe Town Lake. There's been another shooting. Multiple victims."

Chapter Thirteen

The park sat on the southern edge of the Salt River and attracted hundreds for events ranging from salsa tasting festivals, concerts, to family movie nights. The radio crackled in Parker's SUV with reports from the scene. With open-air radio traffic, the media would swarm the scene and likely beat them to the location. The responding units cleared the park, set up a perimeter, and started a canvass for witnesses.

The officers didn't mention who had been shot. Parker's mind began running scenarios, picturing the victims and how the Immigrant Coalition factored into these cases. Another shooting victim with a connection to the group would make it impossible for the politicians to ignore. As he drove up Rio Salido Drive, Parker began assessing the locations in the metropolitan public park where a sniper could take their shot. Based on the freeway shooting where the killer used a white van parked on the roadside, there were potential locations on the Tempe Bridge to the north, a parking lot on a high spot in the center of the park, and high-rise buildings to the south.

Parker spotted two Maricopa patrol units parked bumper to bumper, blocking access to the park. One deputy recognized Parker and pulled his vehicle back to let Parker and the second vehicle with Tully and Johns pass.

As Parker swung into the lot, he spotted a pair of bright yellow tarps covering human forms. A few dozen onlookers with their cell phone cameras were taking in the true crime drama unfolding in front of them.

He pulled into an empty slot. He was fortunate to grab one, as the lot was packed, and they held the drivers back from their cars. Parker spotted a deputy at the edge of the lot near a yellow-taped boundary. He held out a clipboard when the detectives approached.

"Hi ya, Detective. Don't see much of you out this side of town," the deputy said.

"You like it out here, Mason?"

"Nice and quiet. Well, mostly," he said, nodding toward the two tarped bodies.

"Two victims?" Parker asked as he bent under the yellow tape.

"One victim, one shooter," Mason said.

Parker stiffened. "The shooter's dead?"

Mason nodded. "Lady who put the shooter down is sitting over there with Deputy Austin." Mason pointed to a patrol vehicle at the far end of the lot. A red-haired woman sat at a picnic table talking with a uniformed deputy.

"Johns, Tully, look at our victims there and see what you make of it. Set some screens up and give the lookie-loos less of a peep show, would you?"

The two detectives grabbed a pair of expandable screens from the trunk and headed toward the bodies.

"You tarp them, Mason?" Parker asked.

He nodded. "We started getting people pushing in for a photo. How'd they like it if one of their family was laid out in the park and some yahoo posted photos on social media?"

"I'll go check in with Austin and the lady over there. Anything I should know."

Mason grinned. "She'll let you know as a sovereign citizen, she has a right to carry a weapon and defend herself."

"Oh, great. Thanks for the warning." Arizona was an open carry state, which meant any qualifying adult could carry a concealed weapon. The sovereign citizen status meant that contact with the woman was bound to be thorny and complicated.

Deputy Austin rolled his eyes as Parker approached. The woman was slight, wore jeans and a green tank top, and was tight-lipped when Parker introduced himself.

"You want to tell me what happened out there, Miss—"

"Parsons, Lucinda Parsons. Am I being detained? I've done nothing wrong. As a free citizen, I have the right to—"

"Let's slow down a little, Miss Parsons. Do you have any identification?"

Deputy Austin handed him a handwritten card proclaiming Lucinda Parsons to be a free sovereign citizen, exempt from the laws of the United States, or any site therein.

"Okay then. Miss Parsons, please tell me what happened out there," Parker said, pointing to the two bodies.

"I was within my rights to defend myself or another person."

"I'm not debating that. What did you see to make you come to your conclusion?"

"I saw a gun."

"It's Arizona. Everyone has a gun," Deputy Austin said.

"Which person had a gun?"

"I saw the man on the left there point a gun and shoot someone. I heard what the mayor said on the radio, and us who live here need to step up and take care of business. I had no choice but to take the man out. Who do I see for my reward money?"

"Let me be clear about what you're saying. You observed a man shoot someone, right?"

"That's what I said."

"Okay, then what made you think the gunman was a threat to you, or anyone else in the park?"

"He'd already shot one man. I wasn't going to be the next one going down."

"You hear any exchange of words before the first gunshot?"

"No, didn't hear nothing until he fired. I was within my rights. Can you give me my gun back and fork over me my reward money?"

As much as it pained Parker, under Arizona law, use of deadly force could be deemed appropriate to defend yourself or others. In a crowded public park, Lucinda Parsons had a point in her favor.

"We're keeping your weapon while we process this scene. You'll be able to claim it at Sheriff's headquarters when we're finished with it. You'll get a call from us and present a valid ID and proof of ownership to retrieve it."

She narrowed her eyes at Parker. "You have no authority to confiscate my personal property."

"Until there is a determination by someone higher than me saying this is a case of appropriate use of deadly force, the weapon stays in evidence. There's a process to retrieve your weapon. Wait here for a second."

Parker stepped closer to the deputy. "You run her for active warrants?"

Deputy Austin developed a sheepish look. "She didn't have ID to run."

"Run her name and description, see if there's a hit. Some of these Sovereign Citizens like to hide behind a new identity because of past criminal convictions."

Austin trotted back to his vehicle.

"You have paper at home to prove the weapon is yours? A bill of sale, or paperwork from a gun store where you bought it?"

"I got it from a private party. I probably have a bill of sale or whatnot I can use."

"Good. Tell me, what made you think the guy you shot was the killer we've been looking for?"

She puffed up a bit at the change in the line of questioning. Her chin up, Miss Parsons said, "I could tell he was no good. He followed the man across the park and shot him. Like the mayor said, this guy targets innocent people, and I put an end to it. You'll put in a good word for me on the reward, right?"

Austin came back and handed Parker a note.

"You've been in a scrape or two before, haven't you?"

"Nothing that matters." She tensed.

"Says here you've got a restraining order against you by your husband—,"

"Ex-husband."

"Excuse me, ex-husband, who says you threatened him with a firearm. The judge ordered you to not possess firearms in public."

"The court has no jurisdiction over a free citizen. I have a right to bear arms. It says so in the constitution.

"The same constitution you claim doesn't apply to you?"

"No court can restrict my freedoms. They got no authority."

"I'm afraid they do. You're in violation of a restraining order, and Deputy Austin here is going to take you into custody."

"I don't recognize your authority!" Parsons said while Austin put her in handcuffs and let her toward his patrol vehicle.

Parker joined Detective Johns standing midway between both victims. Johns held a notebook and hand drew a sketch of the crime scene, noting the distance between the victims and key landmarks.

"Victim 1 over here is a white male in his thirties, has an apparent gunshot wound to the chest. I've secured a Glock 19 found in his right hand. The firearm was not used."

Johns pointed at the second tarped body. "Victim 2 is a white male, also in his thirties. He has an apparent gunshot wound to his upper back. He dropped a Smith and Wesson .38 revolver. I've secured the weapon, one shot fired."

"He shot Number 1?"

"Appears he did, and it's consistent with witness statements. Ballistics should confirm it easy enough."

"Our vigilante shot Number 2 in the back. She claimed she shot him after he put down Victim 1."

"Looks that way."

"This has nothing to do with our sniper. I don't know why these two needed an old west draw down, but the mayor's call for vigilante justice is responsible for at least one of these deaths."

Johns tipped his chin to a picnic table where Detective Tully sat with a young woman, sobbing with her head in her hands.

"She ID'd the victims."

"What's her connection?"

"Boyfriend."

"Which one?"

"Both."

Parker shook his head. "You guys got this one? I'm going to head back and let the captain know our shooter is still at large."

As Parker turned from the lot, a faded blue West Valley Machine Parts panel truck swept past. The address stenciled on the metal was where Billie swore she spotted Castaneda.

Chapter Fourteen

P arker didn't see the driver as the truck as it lumbered by. He pulled behind and tried to catch the driver's reflection in the rearview. Dark hair, olive skin. The driver's elbow rested on the open window.

Dash camera footage from the night Deputy McMillan was murdered showed a star tattoo on his killer's left forearm. Esteban Castaneda's tattoo.

From where Parker sat, he couldn't see the driver's forearm. He edged the Explorer into the left lane and crept up next to the panel truck. As Parker drew closer to the driver's door, the man pulled his arm in the window before Parker could spot the telltale tattoo.

Parker pulled even with the truck at a red light. His hand slipped to his weapon, thumb releasing the retention strap on the holster. He gripped the weapon as his SUV drew alongside the truck. Parker ducked down to catch a better view of the driver. The driver was shorter and a good ten years older than McMillan's killer.

Parker slammed a fist on the steering wheel. He knew it was a long shot, but coupled with Billie swearing she spotted the man, Parker wanted to avenge his partner's murder. Four years and not a single sighting of the man. Parker hoped the Cartel violence down south swallowed the Los Muertos leader. Disappeared. Until Billie planted the seed in Parker's mind with her sighting.

Parker backed off and followed the truck west as it meandered across the valley, making three stops at automotive shops and metal fabrication businesses. Parker was about to give up and swore at himself for his paranoia until the truck pulled into a familiar chipped asphalt parking lot in front of the Immigrant Coalition.

He slid his SUV under a Palo Verde tree down the block. The driver hopped out, trotted into the office, closing the door behind him. Less than a minute later, the driver came out, started his truck, and drove around to the storage yard.

Dammit. Parker couldn't see into the storage facility. Ten minutes later and the truck emerged from the storage yard and headed west, riding lower. The short stopover at the Coalition office added a heavy load, straining the suspension.

The truck drove directly to the West Valley Machine Parts shop, where Billie spotted Castaneda. The driver pulled in front of the shop. There wasn't a loading dock or back alley to unload. The driver didn't notice Parker slip the SUV to the curb across the street, where it blended in with the mid-day customers at a strip club.

The driver jogged to the back of the truck, looked in both directions along the street he'd traveled. He didn't want the wrong people to see what he unloaded at the shop. Parker discounted drugs. He didn't believe the Coalition was moving heroin or fentanyl over the border. He could see them hiding files of the secretive parts of their operation, since he'd made his interest known to them.

When he was satisfied, the driver unlocked the back door. Parker was wrong. There weren't files or business documents. Ten women, five children, and five men stepped from the rear to the truck and hurried inside the machine shop. The window blinds were shut tight, and a closed sign appeared on the front door.

It didn't surprise Parker the machine shop sheltered undocumented migrants. Many small businesses in the predominantly Hispanic community helped wherever they could, like the bunkhouse in the market. What bothered Parker was the connection to Esteban Castaneda. If he and Los Muertos were involved in trafficking people, they weren't doing it for humanitarian purposes.

The closed window blinds allowed Parker to slip to the front door unseen.

He tried the door, but it was locked. Muffled sounds of a metal shop inside hid any evidence of twenty migrants hiding in the building. Parker crept around the back of the strip mall until he found a fire exit marked for the machine shop. Fire access and no parking signs hung on the rear of the cinderblock structure.

The steel fire door didn't budge and likely featured a push bar on the inside. A garment shop three doors down left its door propped open to let fresh air in. The pile of cigarette butts on the asphalt near the rear exit marked where shop workers took their smoke break. Parker figured the additional twenty people crammed in the small shop might speed up the need for a nicotine fix.

Ten minutes later, the steel door popped open, and a thick-built man in a sweat-soaked t-shirt pushed through. He dropped his pack of cigarettes as Parker yanked the door out of his hand.

"Sheriff's Department."

After a stutter step outside, the sweaty man said, "We're closed." He flung the door behind him. Parker shoved his foot in the gap and kept it from closing.

Grinders and bandsaws echoed in the shop.

"Doesn't sound like it," Parker said, stepping between the man and the door.

"Policia!" the man yelled.

No change in the tempo or pitch of the sounds inside meant they couldn't hear him over the machine noise. Parker slipped inside and closed the door on the smoker, locking him out. The thin echo of a palm slamming the door reverberated, and Parker figured there was little time until the man gave up and ran around to the front door.

Parker edged into the workspace. As it should be—a machine shop with lathes, bandsaw, metal stock, and partially completed projects. He spotted six men working on various pieces of machinery. He almost missed it. A metal door was tucked away behind a shelf of machine parts.

Parker put an ear to the door and couldn't hear sounds from within. A thick brass padlock secured the thick metal door. He grabbed a two-foot length of metal stock from a nearby shelf and shoved it between the lock and hasp. The cheap hasp buckled and tore from the door frame, unlocking the door.

Parker opened the door an inch and peered through the crack. A dim, bare light bulb hung from a wire. The illumination reflected in the eyes of twenty people huddled in the bare concrete room. Parker knew a prison cell when he saw one.

He recognized a few of the faces from the panel truck as it unloaded a few minutes ago. The expression of the men and women changed in the minutes after they entered the machine shop. Hopeful and nervous to grim and resigned. They were used to being powerless.

He motioned for them to come.

"Come. Come quickly. We need to get out of here," Parker said.

They sat, unmoving. Few dared to make eye contact with the white man, let alone trust him.

"There's not much time. Come."

"If we go with you, it will make it worse," an older man said. He wore a brown baseball hat and a faded denim jacket. Gray hair shot from under the hat on the sides.

"These aren't good people. We need to hide you somewhere safe."

"What safety can you promise?"

"I can bring you to the right people. People who can help you."

"There is no safe place for us."

"Anywhere is better than here. Come on."

A few bodies stirred from the floor. Parker heard banging on the front door. The smoker made it around to the side of the building. One by one, even the stubborn old man rose from the floor and followed Parker out the back door. He hurried them down the alleyway until they were around the corner from the machine shop.

Parker hid behind a car and motioned everyone down as two men stepped from the machine shop's rear door. One looked angry while he spoke into a phone. The two looked in both directions and stepped back inside the shop.

There was no way Parker could fit twenty people into his SUV and bring them to a shelter.

Maybe he didn't need to...

Chapter Fifteen

Parker knocked on the back door of the Los Aztecas Market.

A deadbolt turned, and a wary Lola Hernandez peered out.

"Mrs. Hernandez. It's me, Detective Parker. I need your help." He tipped his head down the alleyway.

Her eyes grew wide when she spotted twenty people with him. She froze, and Parker could tell she wasn't certain if he was telling her the truth or if this was some sort of elaborate setup.

"Please," he said. A small boy stood behind Parker and sucked a thumb while looking at the woman in the doorway.

She shook her head. "Come. Dentro, rapido."

Mrs. Hernandez pulled the door aside and ushered in the travelers. When the last man entered, she locked the door behind them.

She pulled aside a pair of women with small children and began speaking with them in hushed tones. Parker couldn't make out the Spanish being spoken, but from the eyes cast in his direction, he was a focus of their hurried discussion.

Mrs. Hernandez took the women by the hand and pushed them to the storefront beyond the curtain. They came back with milk for the children and bottles of water.

The travelers began to settle, and Mrs. Hernandez flitted from one group to another, bringing them food and water.

She stood back once everyone was attended to and nodded. A faint satisfied expression came over her. She glanced at Parker and nodded.

"I'm sorry. I didn't know where else to bring them. It wasn't safe where they were."

"Why did you bring them here? What do they mean to you?"

"Look at them. They were about to mix it up with the wrong people. They're not fighters."

"Don't be so sure. They fought to be where they are. They don't need some white savior to rescue them." She took a step back as the front store bell rang. "Did you bring anyone here? Immigration?"

A soft, worried murmur spread in the room at the mention of immigration.

"No."

Parker peered through the thin fabric curtain. "You recognize him?"

Mrs. Hernandez tilted her chin and gave the man a once over. Her shoulders relaxed. "Cálmate, cálmate. I know him. He worked with Roger Jessup."

She pulled the curtain aside, and Parker grabbed her by the elbow as she greeted the new arrival. He whispered, "The Coalition? Don't tell him these people are here. Please don't. They were involved in taking them."

She searched Parker's face and a quick tip of her head before she stepped into the front of the store.

"Hello, Mrs. Hernandez."

"What brings you by the mercado, Juan? It is Juan, is it not?"

"Yes, Mrs. H. Is your grandson around?"

"Tomaso is at school."

"Oh, I must've missed him. We were supposed to meet up and plan for the rally this weekend downtown in front of the federal building."

"The last Immigrant Coalition rally did not end well."

Parker tensed as she mentioned the Coalition.

"I understand if Tomaso didn't want to mention the rally to you. He knows you worry."

She glanced at the spot where her husband died.

"I'll let Tomaso know you came looking for him."

Juan thanked her, and the bell chimed as the boy left the market.

Parker stepped through the curtain and watched Juan climb into an older model Nissan Sentra and back out of the parking lot. The suspicious part of him believed the concern for Tomaso was a ruse to enter the store in search of the lost migrants. Maybe it was as it appeared—a college friend looking for Tomaso. He filed a mental note to make sure Miguel stayed far from any rally at the federal building.

Mrs. Hernandez joined Parker at the front window.

"You don't think he was looking for my grandson, do you?"

"I can't be sure."

"Why do you blame the Coalition for what happened to these people?"

"They were picked up at the Immigrant Coalition offices and locked in a cell in a machine shop."

Her eyes narrowed. "There's more, isn't there?"

He nodded. "I don't know for certain. Billie said she'd seen a man at the machine shop who is a Los Muertos hitman."

The old woman pondered the information for a moment. Parker could see her thinking, looking back to the room where the migrants hid.

"If this is true, you did a great kindness to these people. I've heard whispers about Los Muertos coming back."

"What've you heard about them?"

"Los Muertos killed two coyotes last month, and the migrants traveling north never appeared. We know because one small girl escaped and hid from them while Los Muertos took her family away."

If Parker showed the girl a photo of Esteban Castaneda and she confirmed he was involved, it meant a chance to make good on his promise to McMillan. If Castaneda was on this side of the border...

"Can I speak with her?"

Mrs. Hernandez shook her head. "She is no longer here. She's safe in Colorado, and she needs to stay that way."

He nodded. Parker hooked a thumb at the backroom. "How long will it take to get them out and safe?"

"I need to make a call. They should be on their way in two hours."

He put a hand on her shoulder. "Thank you. Don't involve the Coalition in this until we know what's going on there. Promise me that."

"You're a strange man, Detective Parker. The call I need to make doesn't involve the Coalition. Once the undocumented come to me, I use my own network." There was a sparkle of pride in her voice. She pulled an older model flip phone from the folds in her long dress.

"I'm sure you do."

Parker left through the back entrance and drove the SUV down the alley to the main road. He turned east, and two blocks down, he spotted a silver Nissan Sentra pulled to the side of the street. Parker parked behind the vacant sedan and keyed in the registration on the computer terminal in his SUV. Within seconds of the final keystroke, the system spit back the details for the vehicle. The Nissan was registered to Juan Estrada with an address down in Glendale. No active warrants.

Parker stepped from his SUV and approached the Sentra. The driver's door wasn't closed. On the passenger seat inside, Parker saw a backpack and a cell phone resting in plain view. The closest building was a mud-colored duplex tucked behind a sound wall. The Sentra missed the driveway by fifty feet if he was to visit someone there. Parker locked the Sentra. No reason to give anyone else any temptation.

Parker plodded to the duplex where an ancient woman in a rocking chair sat watching the neighborhood. One eye was milky white, the other light brown, almost yellow. She wore a linen dress with brightly colored designs on the fabric.

"Excuse me," Parker introduced himself and pointed at the abandoned Nissan. "You see the young man who left his car there?"

She rocked in her chair and turned her one good eye to Parker. "Um-hum."

"You see where he went?"

"I did," she said, without a change in the rocking tempo.

"Is he all right?" Parker didn't know anyone Miguel's age who would leave the backpack and phone in an unlocked car.

The old woman stopped rocking. "No, I don't think he is. Two men in a big blue truck forced him to stop there."

"Forced him?"

"Pulled the truck in front of him." She made a motion with her hands, showing how the truck swooped in front of the smaller car.

"What happened to the young man in the car?"

"They took him. Pulled him from the car and dragged him to the back of the truck. They threw him inside like they were tossing out the trash."

"Ever seen the men before?"

She shook her head. "Wouldn't say if I had. Seen their kind before. Coyotes, thugs, gangbangers. I don't want to get involved. I've learned it is best to let them settle their own disputes."

Parker rubbed the back of his neck. "What makes you think the kid was a thug like the others?"

She pointed to the abandoned Nissan. "He knew them. I could tell by the way he acted. The boy talked to them like they were friends. Until he didn't give them whatever they were looking for. Then they yanked him out of the car. And tore off that way." She pointed a gnarled finger eastbound.

Parker thanked the woman and returned to his SUV. He called for a tow to move the car to impound. There was a slight chance the attackers left prints on the door during the struggle to pull Juan from the driver's seat.

Parker scanned the road ahead. Eastbound. Less than three miles to the Immigrant Coalition offices.

Chapter Sixteen

As he put the SUV in drive, Parker's cell phone rang. The number wasn't familiar, and he thought about letting it go to voicemail. The buzz was distracting.

"Parker."

"Detective Parker?" A meek voice in accented English asked.

"Yes."

"It's Sofia Martinez." After a pause, she continued. "Nia Saldana's sister."

"How can I help you, Miss Martinez?"

Parker's mind snapped to the thought of the two young girls left behind by Nia's death.

"You said I should call if I found out where my sister worked. It's probably nothing. I shouldn't have called. I'm sorry, Detective...."

"Sofia? Wait. You called because you thought it was important."

A pause on the line.

"Sofia?"

"My sister worked for several families in and around Scottsdale and Cave Creek."

"Anyone in particular?"

"I don't know them. Nia got all the referrals from one place."

Parker let the silence encourage Sofia to continue.

"The Immigrant Coalition."

Parker's gut twisted at another tie to the migrant aid organization.

"You know who at the Coalition gave her the referrals?"

"No. But I received her belongings from the tow company. You know, stuff in my car."

Parker bit his cheek.

"They probably weren't supposed to release your sister's property to you...."

"I saw the car. My God. I can't imagine what she felt."

Parker clenched his eyes shut. He wished she hadn't seen the metal shell where her sister was crushed to death.

"There was an envelope. At first, I thought it was another one like you gave us—you know, with Nia's cleaning money. It wasn't. The envelope had one of those computer things—jump drives, or something."

"A USB thumb drive?"

"I don't know what you call it."

"Would having a USB drive be unusual for Nia? Schools are using them for homework assignments...."

"Nia doesn't use a computer. No one in the family has one. I can't think of any reason my sister would need one of these things."

"And you say it was in an envelope?"

"Yes, like the one with the money."

"The envelope I gave you had Nia's name on it. Did this one have her name on it also?"

"Let me check." Parker heard paper rustling in the background before she came back on the line. "It says 'RB' in small letters. I didn't see it before. What does it mean?"

"I'm not sure. Maybe whatever's on it will tell us. I'll come by and look."

"Umm—I'm not at home. I'm at work. In Tempe."

Parker got the address and asked Sofia to hold on to it until they met.

As the call ended, the phone sprang to life again, as did the SUV's police radio.

The radio broadcast an excited call from a patrol deputy on scene of a reported shooting. The voice was young and anxious as he transmitted. The caller ID on Parker's phone was Tully.

"You hear?" Tully said before Parker spoke.

"I'm catching it now. This kid's a mess. We have units responding?"

"Johns and I are en route now. The Watch Commander has patrol units responding to the location. Looks like it's at the 303 and Glendale Avenue."

"I'm not far from there. Another freeway shooting?"

"Don't know yet. Not much around there. Open land. North of the prison and south of Luke Air Force Base."

Parker disconnected the call after telling Tully he'd meet up on scene.

The 303 was a north-south expressway cutting from Interstate 10 on the south to let commuters reach the western suburbs. It cut through underdeveloped desert and flat agricultural land. The 303 and Glendale Avenue overpass was a high point overlooking acres of fields and the White Tank Mountains to the west. Parker spotted the flashing red emergency lights as he approached the off-ramp.

The activity was off the freeway, in the field to the east. Parker shot down the offramp and drove to the first patrol unit he spotted. The deputy parked his unit blocking access to the field, and he waved Parker around into the rich loamy soil.

One hundred yards ahead, two additional black and yellow patrol units and an ambulance sat near a blue farm tractor hooked up to a trailer brimming with heads of cabbage. Huddled around the tractor were a dozen farmworkers, and Parker read the fear on their faces as he drew close. One man spoke with a deputy and pointed to a shiny red Ford pickup truck fifty feet behind the tractor.

Parker pulled his SUV into a bare red dirt patch near the ambulance. He approached the assembled group cautiously. It wasn't uncommon for a sudden presence of law enforcement types to spook a group of undocumented workers. He could sense the anxiety of two men at the edge of the gathering. They were taking a step or two away, subtly putting distance between them and the deputy questioning the oldest man among them.

"Hey, guys," Parker said as he joined. The two reluctant participants stiffened and looked like they wanted to bolt.

Parker put his hand out. "We don't care about your immigration status. This is about what happened here."

The two didn't respond but didn't bolt either.

"Hey, Detective. Mr. Valdez here saw the whole thing unfold." The deputy turned to the farm worker. "Mr. Valdez, please tell Detective Parker what you told me."

Mr. Valdez held his baseball hat in front of him and bent his head a little when he was introduced to Parker. The farmworker's sun-weathered skin and short-cropped black hair made it difficult for Parker to guess his age. The deference paid to him by the others marked Valdez as the most senior man in the field.

"I told the deputy we were listening to Marco speak when it happened."

"Marco?" Parker asked.

Valdez pointed to the pickup truck. "Marco is from the union. He was here to tell us about the things joining a farmworker's union could do for us. He was standing in the bed of his truck when—"

Parker looked at the deputy. "Through and through gunshot wound. Knocked the victim off his feet and over the rail of the truck bed. Waiting on the medical examiner before we move him."

"Anyone touch the body," Parker said.

"I did," Valdez said. "After the gunshot, I ran to the side of the truck. I turned Marco over to see if I could help him." He shook his head.

Parker spotted a bit of blood on the man's right hand.

"Did anyone see where the gunshot came from?"

Silence from the men was betrayed by fleeting glances at one another.

Mr. Valdez turned. "If you saw who did this, tell him. We invited Marco here to speak to us. He was killed because he came here. If you know anything, you owe it to Marco to speak now."

One man stepped forward. He was timid and spoke in a soft voice. "It came from the overpass. There." He pointed to the west and the 303 freeway overpass sprouting from the arid desert floor.

"The overpass? Anyone spot a shooter? A vehicle?"

Another man spoke up. "A white van. After the gunshot, I saw the van's side door close, and it sped off."

"I know it's a distance, but did anyone see the shooter? Anything you can describe about them?"

"It is too far. All I saw was the door close, and the van take off."

"Yeah, it's a fair distance. Mr. Valdez, you said the victim, Marco, was invited here to speak?"

"Yes, he was."

"Who else knew he'd be here? I assume the farm owner didn't know?"

Valdez shook his head. "No, Mr. Collins was aware Marco was coming today. He doesn't support us trying to unionize, but he didn't stop us from hearing what Marco had to say. He's a good boss."

"But you wanted to unionize?"

"Marco said there were things we could earn by organizing, you know, like medical insurance and sick time. We wanted to hear him out...

"Did Marco mention any hassles from the owner, or other farmers, before he talked?"

Mr. Valdez shook his head.

One farmworker spoke up. "Mr. Collins isn't like the others. There are some who threaten to fire everyone if they unionize. Mr. Collins said we should listen. He didn't make any promises."

"Who else knew Marco—what was Marco's last name?" Parker asked.

"Cavalrubio," Mr. Valdez said.

"Who else knew Mr. Cavalrubio was going to be here today?"

"It wasn't a secret. We had the word out to our workers. I know Marco was going to farms up the 303 today after he came here."

Parker glanced over his shoulder at an approaching vehicle. Tully and Johns parked next to his SUV. "Where ya want us?"

"The victim is a labor organizer, and a couple of the guys mentioned a white van parked on the overpass."

Johns turned to the overpass. "That's a good two hundred yards. If this is your same shooter, it means he's got some skill."

"I'll make a call to the Department of Transportation. They've got a series of traffic cameras on the new stretch of the 303."

"I thought they deactivated those," Parker said.

"Only the speed cameras. The video is up and running."

"Remind me to watch my driving out here."

While Johns stepped aside to make the call, Parker motioned Tully to the pickup truck.

"Marco Cavalrubio was standing in his truck when he got hit." Parker leaned over the dead man's body. "Looks like Roger Jessup. One shot to the head."

"Not much left of the back of his skull."

Parker scanned behind the truck in the open fields. "Not much of a chance at finding a bullet out here."

"I'll pull some of the lab guys out here with metal detectors, anyway."

Parker stood where the victim fell and looked back at the overpass. "That's one hell of a shot. Not impossible, but to hit the target at this distance means we're looking at a shooter with military, or at least mad range skills."

"Here comes the medical examiner."

"I'll give her some space while she works up the scene." Parker backed away from the body and circled around to the passenger side of the pickup truck.

"Mr. Valdez, is this Mr. Cavalrubio's truck?"

The man nodded in response.

Parker opened the passenger side door and noted a nylon messenger bag on the seat. The top flap was open, and a clipboard lay next to it. A quick glance said it was the union organizer's schedule for the day. The Collins farm was the second entry on his itinerary. There were other stops planned, as Mr. Valdez reported. The schedule was printed out on letterhead from a Farmworkers Union, Local 43. Parker knew there were union groups popping up across the valley. This one, though, wasn't familiar.

He opened the glove compartment and fished through a stack of maps, gas receipts, and fast-food condiment packets until he found the vehicle registration. He could've run it on his SUV's computer, but the paper document was enough for the moment.

Parker felt his breath hitch when he saw the registered owner wasn't Cavalrubio. The printed document claimed the truck was owned by the labor union, but the address was familiar.

The union's address was the Immigrant Coalition offices.

Chapter Seventeen

The medical examiner couldn't provide much new information than Parker, and his detectives found at the scene. The victim suffered a single large caliber gunshot wound to the left edge of the frontal bone. Hydrostatic shock distorted the man's face and blew out half of the parietal bone in the rear of his skull.

Parker watched as Cavalrubio's body was wrapped in a plastic tarp and loaded into a black body bag. Within minutes, the dead man was gone, the farm workers disappeared, and little remained in the cabbage fields testifying to the labor organizer's presence. It was as if he had never existed.

Johns joined Parker at the front of his SUV. "DOT cameras caught us a break. Spotted a white van about a half mile north minutes after the shooting."

"We have a current location?"

"Lost sight of it after the Bell Road intersection."

"Damn. It'll be impossible to find a white van in the fifth largest city in the country."

Johns didn't reply, but a grin spread across his face.

"What aren't you telling me?"

"The DOT camera caught a plate number. The Ford Econoline van is registered to Gary Clement at an address in Buckeye."

Parker perked up. "He could be heading back to his place. Bell Road to the Sun Valley Parkway—it drops into Buckeye. It's a straight shot here on the 10. We can probably be there before he shows up."

"He has a bit of a head start," Johns said.

"He's probably not going to run red lights to draw attention to himself. We might hold the upper hand there."

Parker trotted around to the driver's door and pulled the SUV out of the field with Johns and Tully behind him. He sped back to the 303 and headed south to the interstate 10. Clement's Buckeye address was five miles away, in a sparsely inhabited section south of the freeway.

Johns came over the radio and gave Parker the address on S 199th Avenue. The place was a dilapidated ranch house on a large lot. Adjoining homes on the street were well kept, some with horse corrals and large ornamental desert gardens.

"I'm gonna do a drive-by," Parker replied on his radio.

He cruised by the address. "Place is a mess. The neighbors must love this guy. No visual on the van."

"Garaged?" Johns replied.

"Negative. Garage door looks broken. It's open, and Clement must be a hoarder. Stacked full of crap. No hiding a van in there."

"Musta beat him home," Johns said.

Parker directed Tully and Johns to take a position two blocks to the south, and he'd park on a side street to the north to wait out Clement's arrival.

Five minutes later, Parker's cell rang.

"Tully? You spot him?"

"Not yet. I asked the gang unit to run Clement, and they list him as a White Pride sympathizer. They're a small extremist offshoot of the Aryan Nation. Mostly, they go around posting photos of themselves with weapons and body armor."

"They offer any intel on Clement, specifically?"

"Clement was dishonorably discharged from the Army."

"Any idea why the DD?"

"They didn't know. Don't know what his MOS was."

Parker knew the Military Occupation Specialty code might reveal some of Clement's skill level. It was too much to hope he had a background as a military sniper.

Tully continued, "Clement is a registered sex offender, though. Might relate to his discharge."

"Up to date on his registration?"

"He is. Went into the Surprise substation last month to verify his address and take new photos."

Parker ended the call with Tully and dialed Captain Morris.

Parker gave him an update on the latest shooting, the van sighting, and Clement.

"The Glendale Avenue shooting is making the news already. I caught a breaking news alert, and the reporter made it sound like the sniper targeted the victim as a threat to migrant workers to not pursue unionization."

"Wait until they find out there's an Immigrant Coalition tie."

"No, I don't need this. The Sheriff has a hands-off order on the Coalition. They hold some sway over the Hispanic community's voting in the next election."

"The undocumented can't vote."

"But the Coalition's donors can."

"Money talks," Morris said.

"Three of the shooting victims shared connections to the Coalition. The attorney, Roger Jessup, the storekeeper, and now the labor organizer—all connected to the Immigrant Coalition. Someone could be targeting the group."

"Politically, might be enough to give us some cover to probe what's happening there."

"Tully phoned in a warrant request for Clement's van and residence. There's enough probable cause. Could you light a fire under the District Attorney's ass to speed it up?"

"Yeah, they owe me a favor. I'll call you the minute it's approved."

Parker let Tully and Johns know the plan was to sit on the place until Clement appeared, and the warrant was signed off.

Parker was about to arrange for an unmarked patrol unit to relieve Tully and Johns when Tully called.

"White van coming your way. Passed us from the south and heading up 199th Avenue."

He leaned forward and glanced to the left and caught the flash of white turning into the drive. The van pulled to a stop in what would've been a front yard. Clement used it for parking and a place to dump a used refrigerator and a trailer with lawn and garden tools. Guess the lawn business in the desert wasn't thriving.

A lone white man with stringy brown hair stepped from the van and ambled to the front door. He balanced a heavy fast-food bag in his left hand while he fished the keys from his jeans pocket.

"Eyes on our guy. Entered the residence. Wasn't carrying a rifle. He stopped for tacos—that's why he was late, I guess," Parker said.

"We moving?" Johns replied over the radio.

"Let's hang tight until we get our warrant. If he tries to leave, we'll improvise."

Thirty minutes later, Clement stepped onto his front porch, tipped back a tall beer can before crushing it and tossing it into the yard. He wiped his hands on his shirt and snagged his keys from his pocket.

"He's heading to the van. Once he's left his driveway, we're gonna light him up."

"We got the warrant?"

"Not yet. Follow my lead," Parker said.

Clement started the van, hung a three-point turn in his front yard, and headed down his driveway. Without a pause, he swung north and sped up the road, passing Parker's position.

Parker pulled in behind him, glanced in his rearview, and spotted Tully and Johns. Parker hit his red and blue lights and let the siren bark a quick yelp.

It startled Clement because the van lurched to the left before creeping to a stop at the right shoulder.

Johns met Parker at his door while Tully circled around to the right, monitoring the van's passenger side.

Vehicle stops were unpredictable. A panel van with the rear windows painted over made it difficult to see the driver, except in the few inches of side mirror. Parker locked eyes with Clement.

The face in the mirror turned and vanished from view.

"Tully, watch your side. He's moving."

The Ford van shifted on worn leaf springs as Clement's weight shifted in the back.

A large caliber rifle, like those used in the Sun Valley Sniper killings, would rip through the van's thin metal skin. Parker hadn't seen Clement carry the weapon from the van when he came home, which meant the rifle could be inside with him.

The van shifted, and Clement's face appeared in the side-view mirror, bug-eyed and anxious.

"Sheriff's Office. Driver's license and registration, please," Parker said as he approached the driver's door.

Clement reached to the sun visor and removed the registration from a clip. He shifted his body weight and fished for his wallet.

"You know why I stopped you?"

"How should I know? You guys are always fucking with me."

"Is that right?"

"I don't bother no one. I stay pretty much to myself," Clement said as he passed his license out the window.

"You been drinking, Mr. Clement?"

"I ain't got no probation conditions no more, if that's what you mean."

"What I mean is, drinking and driving is against the law."

"I ain't drunk."

"So, you *have* been drinking..."

Clement leaned forward and spotted Johns in the rear view behind Parker. His lip curled at the big detective.

"I had me a beer or two. I got the right to do what I want in my own home. And what the fuck is he doing back there? I don't trust them people."

"By them people, you mean highly decorated detectives?"

"Prolly got the job on account of some woke quota."

"I need you to step out of the vehicle, Mr. Clement."

"The fuck I will. I done nothing wrong. You and your black dog can kiss my ass."

"You need to get out of the vehicle. I want you to submit to a field sobriety test. I observed you consuming alcohol immediately before getting behind the wheel. You failed to make a complete stop when you turned onto this public road."

"What bullshit is this?"

"I'm not asking again. If you fail to comply, I'll arrest you for suspicion of drunk driving and impound your vehicle."

"I don't need no sobriety test, and I know my rights say I don't gotta take one. They're a setup anyways. I seen it before."

"This is a DUI checkpoint. I have a breathalyzer in my vehicle. You know you can't refuse without losing your license for at least a year. Take the field sobriety test. Prove to me you aren't drunk, and I'll let you go about your business."

"Man, fuck that. This is a setup. I want my attorney."

Tully stepped to the passenger side window and tapped on the glass. "Come on. Man up and step out of the vehicle."

Clement didn't budge from the driver's seat.

"Have it your way. Detective Johns, call a tow truck and get this junker taken to impound."

"Got it," Johns said.

"You know how much in impound fees this is gonna cost you? All because you're too scared to step out of the vehicle."

"I ain't scared of nothing. Especially you."

"Prove it."

Clement shoved the door open and stepped down from the van. He misjudged the first step and slipped, catching a boot on the door frame. Clement landed on his knees.

"Just how much have you had to drink, Mr. Clement?"

Johns joined Parker near the kneeling Clement. Glaring down at the racist, Johns said, "We have our warrant."

"Mr. Clement, we have a lawful warrant to search you, your vehicle, and residence."

"Search? I told you I ain't on probation no more. Besides, it ain't illegal for someone to have beer in their refrigerator."

"You keep any weapons in the van or at home?"

"Weapons?"

"Yeah, like a rifle, you ignorant hick," Johns said.

"Who you calling ignorant? Go back to Africa, you chocolate-colored piece of shit."

"Actually, I'm from Kansas."

"Hook him up, would you?"

"My pleasure," Johns said as he ratcheted the handcuffs down on Clement's thin wrists.

"Ow. Not so tight, dude."

"Now answer the man. You have any weapons in the van? Anything sharp in your pockets, like needles or knives?" Johns patted Clement down.

"Don't touch me. Get your black ass away from me."

Johns used his six-seven leverage to pin Clement's face against the van while he patted him down. He dropped a worn green nylon wallet to the ground at the handcuffed man's feet. Johns found torn bits of photograph paper in Clement's front right pocket.

"What's this? You keeping a hamster in your pants?"

"Fuck you. I don't gotta say nothing to you."

"That's probably best. Say, you look like you got some Italian in you. We could be related. Bet your Aryan Nation boys don't cotton to no mutts in the gene pool," Johns said as he perp-walked Clement to the back seat of his patrol vehicle.

Parker used the keys Clement left in the ignition to unlock the rear door. Swinging them open, he was taken aback by the uncluttered cargo space. Based on the man's home and personal appearance, he expected the van to be a filthy nest of trash and junk. Instead, the van floor was clear, covered by a thin green carpet. An oversized bean bag chair sat against one wall. Two heavy metal boxes were welded to the floor next to the overstuffed chair.

Parker sought the smallest key on the keyring and unlocked the first box. He hoped it revealed the .308 caliber sniper rifle, perhaps disassembled to fit into the smaller container. Instead, he found a single-lens reflex thirty-five-millimeter camera with a foot-long telephoto lens. The high-end Nikon camera and lens were unexpected, but Parker knew some killers would photograph their victims as they prepared for the ultimate attack.

The second box used the same key to unlock. Parker raised the metal lid, and his gut churned. No incriminating rifle.

But what Clement locked away in his metal box were hundreds of photographs. Photographs of children.

Chapter Eighteen

A search of Clement's residence revealed three-thousand photos and hundreds of digital files. A small bedroom was converted into a photo lab with an industrial printer, computer terminal, and camera equipment.

"How much you think this guy spent on this stuff?" Tully asked.

"It's not cheap," Parker said. "We might track down where they were purchased from, but I'm not sure where it will get us."

Johns flipped through a stack of photos. "I know the guy's a registered sex offender, but I expected more—"

"Kiddie porn?" Tully said.

"Exactly. Everything I've come across here and in the van are pictures of young girls, but they're in public, fully clothed, and nothing indecent. I don't know what to make of it."

"We know details about his sex offense conviction?" Parker asked.

"I'll run it down. Could be he has a type, and this is a lead-up to him acting on his impulses," Tully said.

"Maybe. What I'm not finding is a rifle, shell casings, a loader, things you expect to find in a gun nut's lair. We based the warrant on probable cause that Clement was our shooter. We've got nothing."

"I've asked the lab geeks to run gunshot residue on his hands and inside the van," Tully said.

"We know it was his van spotted off the 303 where the shooting went down. But where's the rifle? The bullets? All we have is his photos—even those won't keep him locked up. Nothing to put him definitively at the scene."

"Hold on there," Johns said.

Johns pulled a photo from the printer tray. "He was there."

Parker glanced at a photograph of a young girl in a playground. She seemed intent on a game of four-square with three other girls.

"How does this help us?" Parker asked.

"It's not about the girl," Johns said. "Look in the background. It's not blurred out, it's there."

Parker took the photo and scanned the buildings and terrain in the distance. Brown box-shaped buildings dominated the background, but to the edge of the photo, a red and white sign appeared. It was blurry because the photo focused on the girl and not the Collins Farms sign two hundred yards in front of her.

"He was there. At the farm. Is there a school nearby?"

Johns was pulling up a map on his phone as Parker asked the question. "Glendale Elementary."

"He was watching the school? Then where's our shooter?"

"Can't rule him out for both yet," Johns said.

Tully popped back into the photo lab room. "Guys, you gotta check this out."

Parker and Johns followed Tully into the musty master bedroom. Clement never mastered the concept of a closet; his clothes lay in a heap on the floor in the center of the room.

"Martha Stewart, he's not," Johns said.

"Over here," Tully motioned to the far wall. Aryan Nation posters created a wall of hate from floor to ceiling. "Notice the specifics in this art collection?"

"Other than our red-neck child molester likes to hang with assholes?" Johns asked.

"What do you think about the Aryan Nation?" Tully asked.

"They hate everyone who ain't like them, don't look like them, and don't think like them," Johns said.

"Exactly. Not a deep gene pool. That's what drew me to this particular artisanal racist gallery. What do you see?"

Parker and Johns looked over the violent images, the rally announcements, and supremacy proclamations.

"What am I missing?" Parker said.

Johns shrugged. "Garden variety racists to me."

"I'm disappointed in you both. Detectives? Really?" Tully stepped close to the hate wall and did his best impression of a game show host, revealing the grand prize.

"These posters are anti-immigrant. They focus on the blight caused by the undocumented. Go back home, build the wall, secure the border, lethal electric fences, and taking jobs from God-fearing Americans. All the stereotypes are here."

"Huh. Good catch, Tully."

"This mean there's a Nation chapter devoted specifically at brown-hate?"

"I don't know, but it is a connection between the anti-immigrant movement and Clement. Check this one out here." Tully tapped on a single poster on the wall. A poorly drawn border wall with crude depictions of dead people in the dirt at the foot of the wall with a "Don't tread on me" flag. On the bottom of the poster was a six-month-old announcement for a counter-protest against the Immigrant Coalition.

"Another Coalition connection? Wonder if Clement was there?"

"I'll check with the gang unit and see if they can give us intel on any rally six months ago."

"Good call, Tully. Still doesn't help with keeping Clement locked up. We have him on driving under the influence, but the charge won't keep him in long," Parker said.

"I'll sort through these photos back at the bureau. I don't think it will amount to much, but in case he did more than watch—I don't want to miss a thing," Johns said.

They bagged up every scrap looking like evidence of ties to the Aryan Nation or hate directed at the immigrant community. It filled the rear of one of the SUVs.

They agreed to meet back at the office after Parker made a stop—at the

Immigrant Coalition offices.

Chapter Nineteen

Parker pulled into the parking lot at the strip mall where the Coalition kept its storefront. It seemed most of their business happened offsite.

When he stepped through the front door, Isa, the attorney, and Tim Brunell were huddled near his office door. Their harsh conversation stopped when Parker entered. The last words from Brunell were, "He can't tell me what to do with my organization." They were reviewing a document, which swiftly disappeared when Isa saw Parker step inside.

"Detective, I wasn't aware we had an appointment today," Isa said.

"Unscheduled visit, I'm afraid."

"How can we help you, Detective?" Brunell said.

"A couple of things popped up involving the Coalition. I hoped you could help me make sense of it."

"I'll try," he said.

Parker handed a plastic envelope to Brunell. "Found this in a residence we were searching. What can you tell me about this rally?"

Brunell glanced at the Aryan Nation poster. "You hang with some interesting people. I guess you can call them that. The poster doesn't mean much to me. It references an event months ago. I don't recall it. Isa, you?"

She shook her head.

"I told you we get the haters coming out at our rallies on a regular basis. Wouldn't be a bit surprised if these extremists came out as well. I can tell you I don't remember a particular disruptive or violent act in the last six months." Brunell handed the poster back.

"Any reason they'd specifically call out the Immigrant Coalition in their hate speech?"

"They're a bunch of racists and xenophobic trash?"

"Thought you should know what we ran across. It's a bit concerning."

"Thanks for your concern. We're used to it."

Parker craned his neck and made a show of looking behind the pair.

"Can I help you, Detective?" Isa asked.

"Where's Marco Cavalrubio's office?"

Isa jerked like someone slapped her. She regained composure quickly. "The Coalition doesn't have an employee by that name."

"Mr. Cavalrubio was a labor organizer with the local Farmworkers union. He was shot and killed today."

Brunell cut a glance at Isa. "Marco's dead?"

"You knew him?"

Brunell slumped at a nearby desk.

"Marco wasn't a Coalition employee. But we had him on contract to do work for us. What happened?"

"Shot and killed like Roger Jessup."

Isa shot a hand to her mouth. "Oh, my God. Do you know why?"

"I hoped you both could shed some light on it for me. Why don't we start with the contract between you and Mr. Cavalrubio. What services did he perform?"

Brunell rubbed his temples.

"Marco was an employment specialist. He would help some of our clients find jobs."

"As farmworkers?"

"Primarily, yes. Many of the undocumented coming here need a temporary arrangement until they can save up enough money to move on to their destination with family or friends. Marco would get them set up and make sure the farm operators paid them."

"Did Marco ever tell you if he ran up against any resistance, placing undocumented people in these jobs?"

"From time to time, he did. The government has done nothing to make it easy for undocumented people to find and hold legitimate employment. Businesses demand government forms, proof of citizenship, and birth certificates. Our people have none of those. What makes them worth less than anyone else? They want to work and do a full day's work for a full day's pay—that's all. Where's the crime?"

"You won't get any argument from me. Marco knew where he could place undocumented workers with the owners taking at least a blind eye about it."

"Farmers need laborers to get their crops to market. Marco made sure they paid our people a fair wage."

"The obvious question is, who'd want him out of the way?"

"Anyone who felt slighted by people coming over and doing a job they were too lazy to do—like your Aryan Nation friends."

Isa found her chair, removed a pair of athletic shoes, and put on a pair of heels. "The big labor unions didn't approve of him taking potential dues-paying members from their ranks. Every man or woman he took on was one less they could hook into an apprenticeship, and they couldn't take a portion of their wages for union dues."

"How much did he collect in dues from your people?"

"Nothing. He got them training, experience, and linked them to healthcare options for people without legal status. We'd work on setting them down the legalization path to citizenship," she said.

Parker shifted. "What do you do with the people who don't sign up to work in the fields?"

Brunell squinted. "I'm not sure I follow. You know we find placements for those making the journey."

"Do the placements include temporary lodging in the storage yard behind these offices?"

Brunell and Isa exchange a glance.

"We don't keep anyone living in storage units, Detective," Brunell said.

"Would it surprise you if I said I don't believe you? A group of twenty men and women were loaded into a van and taken from here. I followed them to a machine shop where they were held."

"When was this?" Brunell leaned forward.

"This morning."

"Are they all right?"

"You know who I'm talking about, then?"

Brunell nodded.

"Don't say anything," Isa warned.

"I need to know if they're okay."

"They are."

His shoulders relaxed. "Good, good. This is getting out of control, Isa. It has to stop."

"What has to stop?" Parker asked.

"We arrange movement from south of the border to this community. We offer the resources and opportunities to help the undocumented find a new life here. We do good work. You believe me, right?"

"What's out of control, Mr. Brunell?"

"You don't know what it's like for these people. What happens to them when they're trapped waiting for their opportunity to make the crossing? It's inhumane. We rely on people to help move them."

Parker well knew who moved people over the border. Coyotes. Some were reputable, like Billie Carson had been. Criminal elements, opportunists, or worse, ran the rest.

"You work with coyotes to move people up here. I'm not surprised. You know how many alleged rapes, kidnappings, and assaults are reported by the people we apprehend crossing the border?"

"We're aware. In our attempt to save as many people as possible, we fell in with the wrong people."

"The cartels influence most of the human trafficking over the border, often in exchange for smuggling contraband for them. It's not new. You know all this."

"Which is why we made arrangements with someone else. Someone who turned out to be worse than the cartels—Los Muertos."

Chapter Twenty

The mention of Los Muertos sent a chill through Parker. Billie was right, after all. She had seen Esteban Castaneda here. Parker should've never doubted her.

"How is Los Muertos involved with the Coalition?" Parker asked.

"You shouldn't talk about this, Tim," Isa said.

Ignoring the counsel from the Coalition's attorney, Brunell continued, "They aren't involved with what we do to help migrants once they cross the border. We don't work with them, and I resent the implication."

"You're the one who said you had arrangements with them. What do you mean, exactly?"

"People were getting kidnapped for ransom their families couldn't pay. Women were raped, children were taken from their mothers, and sold into trafficking rings. You know how the Cartels use violence and fear, intimidating people traveling north."

"All too well," Parker said.

"We needed to bring people across safely. A way to avoid the Cartel's influence. A man came to us. He said he knew a way to work around the Cartels."

"Los Muertos?"

Brunell nodded. "Yes, but we didn't know it then. It started slowly. A handful of asylum-seeking families, women with children, and sometimes children alone. They would make the crossing, and we were told where to pick them up. It was as if our prayers had been answered."

"What changed?"

"Eight or nine months ago, two groups of undocumented migrants came across. There were supposed to be eight asylum-seekers. We picked them up at the agreed-upon location and found no migrants, only eight criminals. This was the first time I heard of Los Muertos. They were armed and threatened our drivers before stealing their cars and leaving them in the desert."

"Were you there?"

"No. Roger was. He was pissed and wanted nothing to do with these thugs from then on."

"Your connection to them didn't end, did it?"

"No. We have people in need of safe travel."

Parker pulled his cell phone out and thumbed through several photos until he found the one he wanted. "Have you seen this man?" Parker held the phone to Brunell.

Brunell stared at the image and bit his lip. Isa leaned in, and her eyes widened. "That's him. It's the man who first came to us claiming he'd help work around the Cartels."

"Are you sure it's him?"

"I think so," Brunell said. "It looks like him, but after all these months…."

"It's him," Isa said.

"His name is Esteban Castaneda," Parker said as he pocketed his phone. "He's running Los Muertos. He murdered my partner four years ago. When's the last time you heard from him?"

Brunell brushed Isa aside. "We haven't been in contact for a while. I think two months ago."

"How do you contact him?"

"I don't. He always initiates the call. Different number every time."

The doorbell sounded, and Parker turned to find Miguel entering the office. Miguel froze with one foot in the doorway.

"What are you doing here?" Parker asked.

Miguel raised his chin a bit. "I could ask you the same. How did you know I was coming here?"

"I thought we agreed it wasn't a good idea to stay involved with the

Coalition."

"We didn't agree. I told you I would back off on the protests. Now you're checking up on me?"

"Miguel, we can talk about this later—"

"You two know each other?" Isa asked.

"You could say that," Miguel said.

Brunell used the distraction to break off with Parker and offered to call if he heard from Los Muertos again.

"Miguel, why are you here? Don't you have classes today?" Parker asked.

"I was supposed to meet up with a friend and study, but he never showed. I thought he might be here."

Miguel turned to Isa. "You haven't seen Juan today, have you?"

"No, was I supposed to?" she said.

"I don't know. I know he comes here sometimes. He's usually on time for everything. It's not like Juan to flake."

Parker perked up. "Juan? Juan Estrada? Does he drive a Silver Nissan Sentra?"

Miguel's brow furrowed. "You profiling my friends now, or something? Not cool."

"I think he's in trouble. Some gangbangers snatched him out of his car a few hours ago."

"What? And you're wasting time here bothering the Coalition? You need to send people out looking for him."

"It's not that easy."

"It was easy enough to send riot police out at Friendship Park to break up a peaceful demonstration. I guess one missing brown boy doesn't make a difference." Miguel turned on his heel and stormed from the offices.

Parker started after him. He paused at the door and let Miguel drive off. Nothing he could say would change his beliefs. He'd hoped the months living in his home would convince Miguel he could trust him. The experience of watching his family murdered in El Salvador while the police did nothing left a deep scar on the boy's soul. A few hot meals and a warm bed would not heal those wounds.

"He's right, you know?" Isa said as she joined him at the front window.

"He usually is."

"Our people are over-policed and over-incarcerated. Yet when we need help, they're never around. It makes you wonder what kind of message it sends to the community."

"It's more complex than that."

"Is it? The community's perception is we are on our own out here. We're reluctant to call 911, because we'll be arrested, or worse. Miguel was right, and it comes down to priorities. Riot police clamped down on a demonstration because they blocked a few rich people in their cars. Yet when one of ours goes missing, where is the police response? We're told to wait."

"I'm not saying you're completely wrong. It's a complicated issue, especially when politics and money get involved. The table isn't even. Everyone knows it, but no one wants to admit the system doesn't work for everyone."

"Give the kid a break. Miguel is smart. He'll come around."

"You know him?"

"From the college, and he drops by here occasionally to pick up things for the events and meetings. He was a little quiet and reserved when he first showed up. He found people like him, with shared experiences, and began opening up." Isa glanced over at Parker. "He mentioned a foster parent who gave him an opportunity when everything seemed lost. I guess he meant you."

"That would be me. I guess he's outgrown what I can provide for him."

"Don't sell yourself short. You gave him the foundation to grow and experience this new life. It's up to him to make the most of it. If I had to wager, I'd bet he'll achieve great things."

"I hope so. I want the best for him. Which is why I'm worried about him getting wrapped up with Los Muertos."

"For what it's worth, Miguel hasn't been exposed to the people-moving side of the business, or the horrible decision to bring Los Muertos on board. I can't believe Roger and Tim did it. It's the opposite of who we are."

Parker thanked her and grabbed the door when he spotted a small table near the entrance with an assortment of pamphlets, brochures, and resource guides for the undocumented. A single brightly colored leaflet with Tim Brunell's face plastered across the surface stood out. The face of the Immigrant Coalition, Parker figured. A little tone-deaf, with Brunell playing the great white savior.

Parker snapped the leaflet up, and instead of the altruistic mission statement he expected was a one-sentence declaration: Tim Brunell for State Senate, a man for all people.

Parker waved the leaflet toward Isa. "When did he decide to run for office?"

"He hasn't officially announced. There's a press conference later this week to formally announce his campaign. Tim's been mulling over a senate run for a month or so. He thinks it might be a way to get our cause noticed." She shrugged.

"You don't agree?"

"Like you said, when politics get involved...."

"Thanks, Isa."

Parker left the Coalition offices and couldn't help but mull over the connections to the Immigrant Coalition and the Sun Valley Sniper cases. All the shooting victims were connected to the relief organization. The storekeeper, Mr. Hernandez, Roger Jessup, the group's attorney, and Marco Cavalrubio, the contract labor specialist—all involved in the Coalition's helping undocumented migrants.

He glanced at the dash-mounted clock in the SUV and figured Gary Clement would be worked up from sitting in the interview room for an hour. Parker knew from experience suspects needed to talk. When you cut off their ability to explain themselves, they tend to blurt out damning admissions when he sat down to interview them. The same thing with silence. Suspects loved to fill the uncomfortable silence.

Parker made a mental list of questions for Clement to uncover the location of the rifle used in the murders when his cell rang.

Captain Morris's caller ID filled the screen.

"Captain?"

"You headed back this way?"

"Yeah. I'm about fifteen to twenty out."

"Make it fifteen. You got an FM radio in whatever it is you're driving? Tune in and step on it."

The captain disconnected the call, and Parker tuned the radio to a local FM news station. He recognized the mayor's voice immediately.

"After intense pressure from my office, the Maricopa County Sheriff's Office has apprehended the shooter in the series of killings plaguing the valley."

"Oh, Jesus," Parker muttered.

"Gary Clement is in custody and will be charged with three murders. What we know about this criminal is he is a member of a white supremacy organization built on the hate of anyone who can't trace their ancestry back to the Mayflower.

"We have it on good authority Clement targeted members of an organization devoted to helping those less fortunate than most of us. We will not tolerate hate and violence against any member of the undocumented community. We are all united in our support of the migrant community who bring so much to our neighborhoods."

Parker turned off the radio and pressed the gas pedal harder. A shitstorm was brewing, and he was in the eye.

Chapter Twenty-One

Parker made it to the detective bureau in fourteen minutes. Tully and Johns were tucked behind their computer monitors typing up reports of the Clement arrest.

Tully popped his head up first. "You heard?"

"The captain called. He wants a briefing ASAP. I need you two to stall him while I talk to Clement. I need to pull what I can from the guy before some legal aid attorney swoops in and tells him to zip it."

"Got it. Why don't Pete and I go tell the captain what we have, and if you get Clement to crack, give me a text."

Parker agreed, and he grabbed a small voice recorder and a notepad before entering the interview room.

"About damn time," Clement said. He was worked up and pacing.

"Sit."

"This is bullshit. And you know it."

"I said sit down," Parker said.

He waited for Clement to drop himself into a stiff metal chair before Parker dragged the opposite chair out and sat.

"You got yourself involved in some bad stuff here, Gary."

"All I done is drink a few beers on my property before you, and your boy entrapped me."

"You were drinking and driving on a public road. It was our public safety duty to pull you over."

"Man, I'm as sober as you are."

"You know, I did some digging into your past. Your sex crime past.

109

"I done my time. I told you I ain't on probation no more. It's all in the rearview."

"Is it?"

Clement fidgeted in the chair. "Yeah. It is."

"See, thing is, I found these photos of little girls in your van and at your house. You care to explain how you got them?"

"Ain't nothing illegal. You didn't find nothing illegal."

"You went to sex offender treatment, right, as part of your probation?"

"You know I did."

"Then you know about the behaviors sex offenders exhibit before they re-offend. Behaviors like targeting their next victim. Grooming them comes next. You start grooming one or two, Gary?"

"I ain't done nothing."

Parker plopped a file on the table between them. He made a show of slowly opening the file, exposing dozens of photographs. Parker spread the photos out with the blade of his hand.

"You have a type, don't you? Pretty, aren't they?"

Clement turned his chin away from the assortment of young girls, but his eyes cut to the images.

"Let's talk about this one." Parker selected one photograph and slapped it face up in front of Clement. The once-convicted child molester jumped when Parker's hand smacked the table's surface.

"What can you tell me about this one? I found this one fresh off the printer. She is a pretty little thing, isn't she? So sweet and innocent. What is she, ten, maybe?"

"They're not so innocent. Girls like her—girls like that lead a guy on."

A sweat was breaking on Clement's brow.

Parker tapped on the photo.

"Why do they do that? Girls like her—what's her name? Why do they do it?"

Clement expected a confrontation over the photos and relaxed at Parker's understanding of his obsession.

"That one's Katie. I heard one of her friends call out to her."

"Katie. That fits. You couldn't hear the girl from the 303—it's where this was taken, right? Where did you hear the girls talking?"

"You can drive up to the school and park on the street. They're right there on display. It's like they're asking for it."

"Asking for what?" Parker asked. He kept his voice as neutral as possible when he wanted to kick this vile creature out of his chair.

"You know. They want what a man can give them."

Parker paused and stared across the table for a moment. He swept up the photographs and shuffled them back into the folder. Clement frowned.

"You got her to talk to you, didn't you?"

"Nothing illegal about saying good morning."

"She say hi back?"

"She did. So, I know she's into me."

Parker pushed back from the table.

"We got us a problem here, Gary. And by we I mean you."

"What? I didn't do nothing."

"Hanging out at the school, taking photos like these, and communicating with Katie sound like enough for a criminal trespass conviction. With your sex offense prior, you could look at some serious prison time for your peeping."

"But I never touched anyone."

"I don't think a jury will care, do you?"

Clement fell back in his chair. The sense of dread swept over him, and Parker knew he had him where he wanted him.

"What if I could make this all go away?"

"Why would you?"

"You help me, and I help you. Simple."

"What do I gotta do? I can't go back to prison."

"I hear the Aryan Nation is cleaning house of child molesters in their ranks."

"I ain't a member."

"Close enough, though. They wouldn't give you a pass if they found you on a prison yard, would they?"

Clement blinked, his eyes fighting back tears.

"Listen, I know you can help me. Give me the rifle."

"What rifle?" Clement tried to pass it off.

"Your van was spotted on the overpass on the 303 where you shot Marco Cavalrubio, and we have video of the van at the 10 when Roger Jessup was shot."

"I didn't shoot no one."

A knock on the door interrupted the questioning. Johns poked his head inside. "You got a second?"

Clement couldn't look at Johns and kept his gaze focused on the yellowed vinyl flooring.

Parker stood, leaned on the table, and said, "Think about what you're going to tell me. Give me the rifle, and the child molesting issues disappear."

Parker joined Johns in the hall outside the interview room.

"The lab geeks got our rush on the GSR test," Johns said.

"Good, I need to tie this up. Is Pete in with Captain Morris?"

"The captain wants to hear we've nailed him. This isn't going to get us there."

Johns handed Parker the lab report.

"Clement had no gunshot residue on his hands. Okay. Not a deal breaker. Could've worn gloves. A rifle might not leave as much GSR on his hands as a revolver."

"Yeah. We didn't find any gloves in the van, or in his place. Could've tossed them. Still doesn't give us the rifle."

"The report says the van's side door frame was positive for GSR. A rifle was fired from within the vehicle."

A tall, rail-thin man approached the detectives. The expensive suit and long, slicked-back salt and pepper hair combined with a haughty air pegged him as either an insurance investigator or a defense attorney.

"Excuse me, could you direct me to Gary Clement, my client?"

"And you are?"

The man fished a business card from a stainless-steel card holder and presented it to Parker.

"Ambrose R. Turner, I'm Mr. Clement's attorney."

"I wasn't aware Mr. Clement asked for one."

"Yet here I stand."

"Pardon me for asking, but Mr. Clement doesn't seem the type to afford a lawyer like you," Parker asked.

"I appreciate your concern for my client's financial standing, but it's none of your business. My client, please."

Parker shrugged and opened the interview room door.

"Who's the dandy?" Clement asked.

"He claims to be your attorney," Parker said.

Clement narrowed his eyes at the new arrival. "That right?"

"Indeed, Mr. Clement. Now, Detectives, please let me have a word with my client. Privately."

Parker and Johns stepped from the room and waited in the hallway while the attorney conferred with his client.

"Where did this guy come from?" Johns said.

"Don't know. Take his card and see what you can find out about the guy. Arizona State Bar membership, what clients and cases he takes on. Might find a lead off a website. All these ambulance chasers seem to have one these days."

Johns took the card and strode off a moment before the attorney opened the door.

"We're ready for you, Detective."

Parker took his seat opposite Clement. The sex offender was pale after the discussion with the lawyer.

"Gary was about to tell me where he stashed the rifle."

Turner placed an arm across his client as if he were a petulant child.

"My client knows nothing about a firearm and doesn't own one."

"Thing is, we know there was a rifle in the van when your client was out and about peeping at adolescent girls." Parker slid the lab report page, confirming GSR on the van door.

"This doesn't put my client in possession of any firearm. He knows better than to be in possession of a firearm. Could've been left by someone who borrowed his vehicle. He lends it out to friends now and again."

"Counselor, what we can prove is your client was in his van, parked on the 303, when a shot came from the van, killing Marco Cavalrubio."

"You have no weapon, no witness putting their eyes on my client, and I doubt you can even prove he was in the van at the time the shooting happened."

Parker nodded and pulled a photo from the file.

"Have you met Katie?"

Clement leaned into the attorney and whispered.

Turner took an exasperated breath and nodded.

"My client will confirm he was there, but it doesn't portend to make him culpable for any shooting. We'll be leaving now."

Turner stood, pulling Clement up by the elbow.

"Sorry, I'm booking your client on criminal trespass. He's staying with us for a while."

"That's absurd. All you have is a photo of a girl—"

Parker spilled a dozen photos on the table.

"There's a little more to it. With his sex offense prior and if the District Attorney files this as entering a public service facility, this might bump up to a Class 6 felony. Up to five years, Gary."

"It will never hold up. Blatant overcharging, and I'll fight your notion there was ever an entry into a facility, lack of Miranda notice, and unlawful search."

"I told your client I can make it all go away if he tells me where he stashed the rifle."

Clement tugged on the attorney's arm. The dogged expression told he was ready to deal.

"Well, Gary?"

"Don't address my client. You speak through me."

"While I'd love to play a little game of telephone with you and Gary here, I wonder if it's in the client's best interest to get him locked up facing a felony when it can all go away."

"What can you give me, Detective?" Clement said.

"Hush."

Clement hung his head at the rebuke.

"Gary, remember who'll be getting locked up? You or your attorney?"

"That's enough, Detective. Do not threaten my client."

"No threat. I'm booking him for first-degree criminal trespass. You can argue your case in court. A jury's going to be interested in what your client was doing, loitering on school property, peeping at young girls. Let's go, Gary."

Parker led Clement by the elbow into the hall, where a uniformed deputy waited.

"We'll have you bailed out in no time. Don't listen to anything they try to promise you," Turner said.

The deputy led Clement down the hallway.

"Who would want to post bail for him?" Parker asked.

"Doesn't matter to you. You ensure nothing happens to my client, or I'll hold you personally accountable."

"You're the one who put him there, not me. I offered an out."

Parker turned and left the defense attorney stewing in the hall.

Who would arrange for a high-priced attorney for a scumbag like Clement? If he bonded out, Clement wouldn't feel the pressure to cooperate. And who would benefit if Clement walked?

Chapter Twenty-Two

When Parker made it back to the detective bureau, Tully's face warned him seconds before the captain's voice called out.

"Parker, your office."

It wasn't a question.

Tully's eyes rolled.

The captain paced in Parker's office and didn't stop wearing a path when the detective entered.

"You sent your two errand boys to stall for time?"

"I wouldn't call them errand boys. They're both capable investigators, and I thought they could brief you on what we have to the minute while I tried to wrap something else up."

Morris grinned in response. "Close the door."

Parker caught Tully and Johns peeking in as the door closed, trying to assess how much trouble they were in.

"Captain—"

"They are good detectives—Tully and Johns. You've done a good job with them. But I can't help feeling slighted when my detective sergeant blows me off."

"It wasn't blowing you off, Captain. Time was of the essence, and I needed a crack at Clement before his attorney showed up."

"Lawyered up already?"

"He has. Some high-priced flack. Johns is running some background on him and the firm he represents."

"Get him to cop to anything before the attorney showed up?"

116

"Not on the location of the rifle. Pete and Barry told you we didn't find it in the van or Clement's residence. There's GSR on the van door. A weapon was fired from inside. Without the weapon, we can't definitively connect the van and the murders. No one saw the shooter—only the van. Clement was about to crack about the location of the weapon when the lawyer muzzled him."

"You heard the mayor say we have the shooter in custody?"

Parker closed his eyes and let out a deep breath. "We need time to pull the case together. If I work on Clement, I know I can use the kiddie photos to make him roll over on the weapon. Once we have the rifle in our possession, he's toast."

"Why would he give it up? His lawyer told him there's no case without it."

"Thing is, Clement wants to roll with the Aryan Nation boys more than anything. He had a damned shrine to them at his home. Even cockroaches live by a code. The Nation doesn't tolerate child molesters. They've been known to green light a hit on molesters the minute they step on the prison yard. Clement would rather go down for life on the murders than do a few years branded as a kiddie-diddler in the eyes of his role models."

"That is one screwed-up perspective on life."

"These people live in a different world, Captain. I think we can use it to get him to crack."

"How does this help us with the political issue the mayor dropped in our lap? Do we have enough for a conviction on this guy and claim we've solved the case?"

"What we have is circumstantial. A race-hating bigot at the scene of at least two shootings. GSR on the vehicle, not on him. He has a military service record, so he should know his way around a rifle. No eyewitness identifying Clement, no murder weapon, and no confession. I hate to say it, but if we file now, he'll beat us."

"Damn it. If this guy walks, the political backlash will be incredible. The Mayor and the County Board call us incompetent for not catching the suspect, and now that we arrested one, we might not have a strong enough case against the guy." Morris rubbed the knots on the back of his neck.

"The attacks center on victims with ties to the Immigrant Coalition. Tim Brunell, the acting Executive Director, let us go through the organization's hate mail. Clement doesn't show up there, but there is enough white supremacy rhetoric to feed a borderline personality like him to target the Coalition."

"I've hit the wall on intel from our gang unit. Nothing specific or credible threats to any local humanitarian organizations. Was your girlfriend at the FBI able to kick down intel we can use?"

Parker cast his eyes at the ceiling and sighed. "I haven't gotten around to reaching out."

"Listen, whatever is between you two, figure it out. We have an investigation to pull together. Reach out to her. Make it today. If they hold leverage to tie Clement, or the Aryan Nation to the shootings, we need it."

Parker agreed and promised to call Lynnette. They needed closure on the shootings, but Parker also wanted everything the FBI had on the reawakening of Esteban Castaneda.

"We still have a job?" Tully asked after Morris left the bureau.

"For now. We've got to work up some traction on the investigation, and the mayor's premature announcement is giving the brass a political time bomb. I've been ordered to connect with Lynette Finch over at the FBI. They might give us intel on the hate crime angle of the shootings from their civil rights investigators. The Immigration Coalition seems to be the target here, so look for a nexus between the group's activities, online presence, press releases, and the victims."

"I can dive in there," Johns said. "Besides, I doubt Pete knows what social media is."

"Oh, and you're the influencer now because you post selfies in your bespoke suits on Instagram?" Tully said.

"One time. I did that one time."

"Barry, you dig into the Coalition's social media. Pete, I expect Clement will bail out in the next few hours. See if you can find out who posted the bail bond and who picks him up."

"On it."

"He was about to crack before the attorney showed up. Turner. Barry, you find the dirt on him yet?"

"He is registered with the Arizona Bar. Seems to be a gun for hire for criminal defense. The cases range from drunk driving to murder defense. There were a few police misconduct cases where his clients were claiming excessive force. He had a co-counsel listed on those cases. An old friend of yours—Larry Sutton."

"Huh, Larry Sutton represented Cartel hitmen and filed a bogus use of force complaint that got me suspended last year. His involvement with Turner doesn't give me a warm and fuzzy feeling."

"I remember Sutton. He's a sleezebag." Tully said.

"I think I got Clement nervous about the rifle. He had to stash it after the shooting. We lost track of him after the traffic camera near Bell to the time he pulled up to his place. I've gotta try to retrace his trail when I come back from the FBI office. You guys tail Clement if he bails out. If he heads in my direction, dude might lead us to the murder weapon."

Chapter Twenty-Three

Parker passed the holding cells on his way out to the parking lot. It was a bit of a detour, but he needed to bait the hook.

Clement sat in a bare cement cell, and Parker tried not to acknowledge seeing him there. A uniformed deputy monitored Clement and the six others in holding.

"Hey, Detective. What brings you by?" the deputy said.

"Got a break on the Sun Valley Sniper case. Got a tip. A C.I. Says he knows the location of the rifle used in the shooting. Heading out to meet him now."

From Parker's peripheral vision, he noticed a stiffening of Clement's shoulders.

With the bait set, Parker headed out.

The Phoenix Field Office was forty minutes away from downtown, up North Seventh Street in a five-story caramel-colored brick federal building off Deer Valley Drive. Parker turned the air conditioning on full to counteract the hot, dry wind marking the late afternoon swelter. Parking was easy at the federal building, and the lot attendant directed him to the visitor area.

Assistant Special Agent in Charge Lynnette Finch's offices were on the top floor. Parker smiled at the reception desk because an unfamiliar face glanced up and shot him a welcoming glance. Lynne's usual gatekeeper abandoned her post or retreated wherever gargoyles go when they weren't watching the castle gates.

"Can I help you?" the cheery receptionist said.

"Detective Nathan Parker to see Ms. Finch."

"Do you have an appointment? I see nothing on her schedule." The woman frowned at the monitor. "But I'm sure we can figure something out."

"Thank you. You're new here, aren't you?"

She sat a little straighter. "I'm filling in for Ms. Finch's usual secretary. She's out on medical."

"Oh, nothing serious, I hope." Inwardly, Parker wondered how painful a personality transplant would be.

"She should be back soon. Let me ring Ms. Finch and let her know you're here."

Parker stood back while the temporary secretary dialed Lynne's extension.

"Yes, I have a Detective Parker here to see you."

Her face fell flat, eyes wide, and her mouth gaped open.

"Yes, but he—"

The secretary blinked rapidly in response to whatever Lynne was saying.

Parker cleared his throat. "It's about the Sun Valley Sniper case."

"He says it's about—oh, you heard."

"Yes, ma'am. Yes. I understand. No, I won't. I'll tell him."

"Let me guess. Ms. Finch doesn't have time for me, isn't happy I dropped in unannounced and would like you to shoo me from the premises."

She leaned in and whispered. "What was that about?"

"We have history. Some good, and some, well…."

"She said you nearly got her killed last year?"

"Funny, I remember being the one who pulled a bomb from under her car when her boyfriend tried to off her."

"No way."

"Way."

"That's wild. I'm sorry I couldn't help you."

"Not your problem. What's your name, by the way?"

"Rebecca. Rebecca Long."

"Nice to meet you, Rebecca. Can you direct me to the Civil Rights Division?"

Rebecca gave him the office number and called ahead to let the agent on call know Nathan was dropping in. "Ask for Agent Collins."

"Thanks again, and give Lynne my love."

"I should probably keep that to myself."

The Civil Rights Division's offices featured a waiting room. The fact they needed one told how unbalanced the system was. This was the place of last resort for those whose complaints of hate crime, police misconduct, and interfering with the right to vote fell on deaf ears within local agencies.

Parker was escorted to the agent on call, a thin, balding black man. Judging by the flecks of white on the man's receding hair, he was nearing retirement age.

"Agent Collins?"

"You must be Detective Parker. Rebecca said you'd be paying us a visit. How can we help Maricopa County?"

"We're working a case with hate crime overtones."

"Haters always hating. What are you seeing?"

"You hear about the Immigrant Coalition?"

"Pro-migrant group based here in Phoenix, funded by community donations and grants. They seem to be focused on social service, housing, and resources for the undocumented."

"That's the group. They are involved in getting their clients over the border, contracting with coyotes and such."

"That's not really our thing. ICE might be interested."

"How they show up isn't what I'm here about. I'm working three shooting victims—all tied to the Coalition. One theory is our shooter is targeting the group because of what they do to help migrants."

Collins sat forward. "You're talking about the Sun Valley Sniper."

"Right."

"The victims. What can you tell me about them? Are they migrants?"

"It's not clean. One was an older man, a Mexican American shopkeeper, a labor organizer working with migrant workers—"

"Hispanic?"

"Yes, but the third is a white male. The Executive Director of the

122

Coalition."

"Huh. Any communication or intel on the director being targeted because of his work?"

"No. Looking at his death, apart from the others, it looked random. Random until we found his connection to the Coalition. We picked up a suspect with ties to the Aryan Nation. Had all kinds of anti-immigrant propaganda at his place, including a poster for a counter-demonstration at an Immigrant Coalition rally."

"We've been watching the local Aryan Nation regulars. Haven't picked up chatter specific about them going after immigrant groups. They don't like them, to be sure, but their hate seems focused lately on the Black community in response to the Black Lives Matter movement."

"The counter-demonstration posters I saw...."

"With these guys, I'd be worried when they go radio silent. Posters, demonstrations, and posturing are like waving the flag. The real insidious activity happens in the dark. Synagogue bombings, rat pack muggings are their style. Don't see much of a military following—if you were thinking a shooter might hide in their ranks. It's always possible, but it's not their go-to move. Give me the guy's name, and I can run him on our database."

Parker gave him Clement's name, and Collins tapped the information in on a keyboard.

"Not someone we've seen on our radar. No field contacts, and he hasn't come up linked to a hate crime."

"Thanks for looking. If something pops on him, or the Coalition, would you let me know?"

"Nathan, I heard you were wandering the halls," Lynnette Finch said from behind him.

It was hard to read her expression. She'd gained the skill in the year she'd been tossed into the political side of running a major FBI field office. He remembered the old Lynne, who was open, vulnerable even, but their jobs changed both of them. It was easy to understand. You see the worst humanity has to offer—the suffering and the loss. It takes a toll on a person. You hope there is a little soul left in the aftermath.

Lynne protected herself behind emotional barriers, which Parker couldn't blame her for building. His relationship with her flamed out, and he should've ended things better, but at least he didn't try to kill her like her last boyfriend. That kind of trauma takes a lifetime to unpack if you're lucky.

Parker thanked Agent Collins again and stepped out into the hall with Lynne.

"I like your new assistant, Rebecca. She's friendly, unlike—"

"Rebecca doesn't know you yet," she said, but it came with a smile.

Rebecca's expression while she tried to tell Lynne he needed to see her said she got a crash course on all his many failings.

"How have you been?" Parker asked.

She leaned against the wall. Slight dark circles under her blue eyes. It looked like she was trying to get out and run regularly, which made Parker suck in his gut and repeated a silent vow to exercise again.

"It's been a madhouse. The Attorney General wants a push on voting rights violations, which caught my interest when I heard you were looking for our Civil Rights office. Something I need to know about?"

"Hate crime related—or probably is. Three victims with connections to the Immigrant Coalition."

"Can't say I know who they are. Pro-immigrant, I presume."

"They are. I think their heart's in the right place. I don't agree with the methods they choose. Miguel's become involved in their on-campus activities."

"How is Miguel?"

"The boy is amazing. I can't really call him a boy anymore. He's almost eighteen, already taking college classes, and he has a compassion for others I never believed he'd find after his ordeal."

"Getting taken by the Cartel and left for dead would break most people."

"It would. He found some strength in all of it. The whole 'what doesn't kill you makes you stronger' bit. Part of me wishes he'd be a little reserved and less trusting. His sense of justice and compassion is getting him in trouble."

"He got that from you," Lynne said.

Parker smiled. "Could be some truth there. I've asked Agent Collins to let me know if the Immigrant Coalition pops up in any hate crime intel. I hope that's all right."

"Sure. I'll mention it to the Border Security Task Force and see if our counterparts in Homeland, DEA, and ICE pick up a mention."

"That'd be great, Lynne. I have a favor to ask when you reach out to the task force...."

She narrowed her eyes at Parker. "Your favors have a way of biting me in the ass, Nathan."

"I know. This one is personal. I've gotten word that Esteban Castaneda has been seen in Phoenix. Los Muertos is involved with undocumented migrants, either getting them over the border or moving them once they arrive here. Either way, it will not be a good outcome."

"Castaneda? Here? I haven't seen any intel reports on him since he disappeared after the leadership of the Sinaloa Cartel changed. We would know if he surfaced. He's flagged and on the Most Wanted List for your partner's murder. Where did you hear it from?"

Parker sighed. "Billie Carson said she spotted him."

Lynne crossed her arms. "Billie? Really? She's your intel?"

"I know how it looks. Billie's a loner living in a broken-down trailer in the desert, collecting scrap metal for a living. But she knows the players in the border smuggling game."

"Because she was one."

"And worked with the U.S. Attorney to prosecute high-level members of the Sinaloa Cartel."

"Exactly. She was in that world. If she told you Castaneda was operating up here, I'd believe her."

Parker didn't expect Lynne to put stock in Billie's report because it didn't come from within the Bureau's curated intelligence sources.

"I want to believe he's up here, so I can nail him for McMillan's death. What worries me, if it's true, is why he's here?"

"I'll ask the task force to let me know the minute they alert on him or Los

Muertos."

"Thanks, Lynne. I appreciate it."

"Glad I could help. How are you doing? Seeing anyone?"

"I'm treading water with this Sun Valley Sniper investigation. A person of interest, but we don't have enough to charge him. The local politicos are pushing for a quick solve—you know how it goes. I make sure Miguel gets off to school and try to keep him from doing something emotional that might jeopardize his immigration status. I have little time to do much else."

The fast click of heels on the floor behind Lynne captured their attention. Rebecca tracked down her boss.

"Excuse me, the Assistant U.S. Attorney on the Marks case is in your office."

"Good seeing you, Nathan. I'm glad to see you, and I'm sorry if I've been—distant."

"Good to see you too." Parker left the 'distant' comment alone. She refused to take his calls after they broke off their relationship and made it clear she wanted nothing to do with him. Was she warming up? He'd felt them grow apart, her in her political world and him in his local law enforcement role. Different orbits, different lives.

Parker watched Rebecca lead Lynne away, handing her the file she'd need for the meeting. A slight pang of loss swept through him. They were good together—until they weren't. There wasn't much he could have done to salvage the relationship, and she still looked great. Another reminder to suck in his gut.

His cell phone vibrated in his pocket.

"Parker."

"Detective Parker?" A quivering woman's voice asked.

"Yes."

"This is Maria Hernandez from Los Aztecas Mercado."

"Yes, Mrs. Hernandez. Did our friends get off safely?"

"They did, but I'm calling you about my grandson."

"Tomaso? What happened?"

"He's gone. I think they took him."

"Who took him?"

"Los Muertos."

Chapter Twenty-Four

Parker pulled into the parking lot at the Los Aztecas market twenty minutes after he hung up with Mrs. Hernandez. Clearly worried about her hothead grandson, she had reason to fear if Los Muertos nabbed Tomaso.

The bell on the door tinkled when Parker pushed through. The front of the store was empty.

"Mrs. Hernandez?" He called out.

He parted the thin linen curtain. "Mrs. Hernandez?"

He found her slumped over the makeshift kitchen table. Her face was bruised and swollen.

Parker ran to the table. He pressed his finger to her neck, relieved to find a pulse. Weak, but it was there.

"Hang on, Mrs. Hernandez." Parker pulled out his cell phone and called 911. He gave the dispatcher his name, badge number, and the location of the market. The calm voice on the other end said an ambulance was on the way.

The old woman moaned but didn't regain consciousness. Parker worried a beating this severe would send Mrs. Hernandez into shock. He felt anger welling up at anyone who would attack a vulnerable old woman.

She suspected Los Muertos had taken Tomaso. Parker glanced at the table in front of her, looking for the phone. He couldn't spot it on the kitchen counter, either. He remembered the old woman using an old flip phone to summon help for the twenty undocumented people he dropped on her doorstep.

Sirens sounded from the front of the store, followed by the bustle of paramedics entering.

"Back here," he called.

Two paramedics found Parker and the injured woman in the back room. Parker stepped aside while they started oxygen and took her pulse and blood pressure.

"You know what happened to her?" the younger paramedic asked.

"Found her like this. I was on the phone with her twenty minutes ago, and she was fine."

The two paramedics gently lifted the frail woman onto a gurney with the help of the fire department engine crew responding to the call. Parker followed the gurney outside to the waiting ambulance, where a small crowd gathered to find out what happened in the market.

An older pair of gray-haired women spotted Mrs. Hernandez on the gurney and blessed themselves with synchronized Sign of the Cross motions. The grim expression on those in the crowd bore a blend of worry and respect for the woman.

While the fire personnel loaded her into the ambulance, Parker edged toward the people waiting for one of them to speak first. He knew from experience if he pressed for information, they would disappear. Fears over their unlawful immigration status, distrust of police, and suspicion of anyone outside their community made the bystanders elusive witnesses.

"Is she going to be all right?" A quavering voice whispered behind him.

Parker half turned and found an older woman standing nearby.

"I hope so."

"She's been through so much. I'll pray for her."

"I know she'd appreciate the prayers."

"First her husband and now this. This used to be a safe community. We could look out for one another. Now we have this." There was a venom in her pronouncement.

"Why would anyone hurt an innocent woman? First her husband and now this," Parker asked, being careful not to be too direct.

"Evil is what it is. They've turned away from the church's teachings and are consumed with sin."

"Why Mrs. Hernandez? She's willing to help anyone who needs it." Parker left anyone as vague as possible. From the nod, the old woman agreed.

"It has gotten worse in the last six months. Used to be families and people who wanted to work to send money home to their people. Now, it's mixed with drug smugglers and criminals."

"I've seen it too. Did anyone here see the ones who did this to her?" Parker finally turned to face her.

"They weren't from here."

He nodded. "I've heard there are criminals coming up from Mexico. Some call them Los Muertos."

The old woman blanched at the mention of the gang. She spat on the ground and crossed herself again. "Los Muertos are evil. They are capable of unthinkable violence. The Cartels used to keep those dogs under their thumb. Now they run free and prey upon innocent people. I know of them, but this was not their work."

"Not them? Are you sure?"

"They were like you."

"Me? Police? You're saying police officers hurt Mrs. Hernandez?"

"No. Not the police. By people like you." She grabbed his arm and wiped the blade of her hand over his skin. "Anglos did this."

"A white person attacked her?"

"Yes. Three of them. They come here and try to make us pay to stay here. If we do not do as they ask, they give our names to immigration."

"These men threaten to out the undocumented? How do they even know what someone's status is?"

"At first, we thought it was a guess, at random. There are many of us here. But it became clear they knew exactly who they were looking for."

"But, why Mrs. Hernandez? She isn't undocumented."

"Who knows why they do what they do?"

Parker pulled his cell phone out, pulled up a photo of Clement, and held it out to her. "Does this man look familiar?"

She leaned in and squinted at the cell phone screen. "I don't think so. The men who come do not have long hair like him."

The ambulance pulled away, spiriting Mrs. Hernandez to the hospital. With her departure, the crowd melted away. The old woman joined arms with her old friend, and they supported one another as they shuffled to a duplex across the street.

If the old woman lived directly opposite the market, she knew the temporary housing arrangements the business provided for those coming over the border. The question was, who else knew? The Immigrant Coalition.

Parker reentered the market and returned to the backroom. Any evidence of twenty migrants once camped in the space was gone. Mrs. Hernandez was efficient and careful to move her charges without leaving a trace behind for someone to find them.

On the kitchen counter, he found a small notepad with an uneven, shaky message scrawled on the page. "Tomaso, $50,000, 48 hours, Rocky Wash."

Parker's hand shook. Rocky Wash was the remote desert road where his partner died four years ago, murdered by Esteban Castaneda. Who else would use the location as a kidnap ransom exchange? Castaneda was here, and Parker knew where he would be in forty-eight hours.

Chapter Twenty-Five

P arker locked up the market as best as he could, hoping the community would band together and keep the place from being looted. He didn't figure the threat came from the people living nearby, but from outside opportunists who would move in and try to exploit the unattended store.

A vibrating cell phone pulled his attention from the darkened storefront. He recognized the incoming number.

"Hey, Billie. What's up?"

"I heard about Mrs. Hernandez. Is she gonna be okay?"

"She took a beating. Someone of her age—it's hard to tell how she'll recover. We got her to the hospital, and we'll wait and see."

"Robbery?"

"Doesn't look like it. She called me a few minutes before they attacked her. Her grandson, Tomaso, she said Los Muertos took him."

"Why would them assholes nab a kid?"

"Ransom. They want fifty grand from her."

"If they wanted cash, then why give her a beat down? Don't make no sense. Unless she told them no."

"I think there's two things going on. Los Muertos took the kid. Someone else hurt the old woman."

"With her in the hospital, she ain't gonna be able to pay off Los Muertos. That ain't gonna be good for her grandson. They don't leave no loose ends."

Parker's mind shifted to the killing of his partner, McMillan. Castaneda didn't need to kill Mac after he discovered the Los Muertos hitman with a van full of undocumented migrants. No loose ends. Mac bled out on a remote desert road, and the migrants were found two days later, dead in a steel storage container.

"It's Castaneda. He set the meetup for the spot where he killed McMillan."

"You believe me now? I told you I saw him."

"I know Billie. Part of me hoped he disappeared."

"People like him don't stay gone for long. There's always a reason for them to crawl out from under their rock."

"What's so important to draw him out, expose him here north of the border? And why would he be interested in grabbing kids like Tomaso?"

"He respects power and money. He can't get enough of either."

"A kidnap for ransom is kind of small-time for Los Muertos, isn't it?"

"I heard they been snatchin' up politicians and judges outside of Mexico City."

"Gangs been kidnapping high-profile folks south of the border for years. Grabbing young, college-aged men here makes no sense. It's not as if they're trust fund kids. Has to be more to it for Castaneda to risk showing up."

"I haven't heard nothin'."

"Neither has Lynne at the FBI."

"How is Lynne? She ever warm up to you?"

Parker sidestepped the question because he really didn't know how to answer. "I need to be at the exchange. Could you give me a heads up if you see anything out there that might tell me where Castaneda's holding the kids? Can't be too far from the drop point. He can't risk driving around Phoenix with hostages."

Billie agreed to keep an eye out while she made her scrapping rounds in the north valley desert before she hung up.

A text message popped up on his phone before he shoved it in his pocket. It was from Barry Johns. Clement made bail, and he was being processed out. Tully was set to follow Clement once he left the Sheriff's building.

Parker started typing in a reply, and Johns sent a follow-up text. The attorney, Ambrose R. Turner, posted bail.

So much for finding out who wanted Clement on the street. The defense attorney would not disclose who funded the bail bond. Who was paying the billable hours for the slick attorney?

Parker got into his SUV and knew it would take someone who swam in the murky depths of legal defense work to find out who held the purse strings on Clement. He retrieved the number on the phone's web browser; The Law Offices of Sutton, Wimmer, and Hoster.

He paused before he called. Sutton was an opportunistic bottom-feeder, and those were his most redeeming qualities. The lawyer defended Cartel hitmen, human traffickers, and was feared in the courthouse. If Ambrose R. Turner was a front for dark money, Sutton would know.

He put the call through and, to his surprise, the secretary didn't transfer him to Larry Sutton's voicemail. Within thirty seconds, the lawyer came on the line.

"Detective. I didn't expect you to come calling. Finally got caught up in the grift and corruption permeating your department?

"And hello to you, too. I'm doing my best to stay on this side of the bars, thank you. I'm wondering if you can tell me about a colleague."

"Why would I give up someone playing for my team?"

"I'm not sure which team this one plays for."

"Who we talking about, Detective? I may or may not tell you anything you don't already know."

"Fair enough. I'm working a case, and this attorney shows up before the guy makes a phone call."

"Everyone has the right to counsel, Detective."

"The guy we had in custody was a person of interest in a series of homicides."

"Was a person of interest. I take it you failed to gather enough to charge the alleged killer?"

Parker ignored the comment on the investigation and changed focus. "The guy has no apparent means of income, a registered sex offender. He wants to be aligned with the Aryan Nation, but even they have standards. Yet, this high-priced attorney shows up out of nowhere, and posts bail for the guy."

"Nothing illegal about what you've told me. He has the right to representation. Attorneys are assigned on a rotation basis when the public defender has a conflict on a case, or if they are all assigned."

"This attorney doesn't strike me as an ambulance chaser trolling for criminal defense clients. No offense."

"All right. Who we talking about?"

"Ambrose R. Turner, ring a bell?"

"Come by the office. I think we need to talk about this in person."

Sutton gestured to a stocked bar on a cart in a corner of the office. "Want a drink, Detective?"

"Thanks, but I'm on the clock. Don't let me stop you."

"Turner, huh? Competent, worked with him on a couple of cases. He hadn't taken on police misconduct complaints before and needed to learn the process. Picked it up quickly and haven't seen him since."

"Who does he work for?"

"He's a private attorney. Isn't associated with any law firm I'm aware of. He's a hired gun."

"What kind of client would he work with?"

Sutton poured himself a generous serving from a crystal decanter. He sniffed the amber liquid. "Parker, we've crossed paths a time or two. You have no reason to believe me. My advice to you is give young Ambrose a wide berth. It's why I thought this conversation should be face-to-face. As much as it pains me to admit, Turner trolls in some dark waters. Some people he represents are not the kind you'd want to cross."

"This coming from a man who represented Sinaloa Cartel gunmen?"

"They're nothing compared to Turner's friends."

Parker watched as Sutton downed the Scotch in once quick motion. He'd never seen Sutton shaken, and the mention of Turner rattled him.

"The cartel played by the rules—their rules, but there was some level of understanding in that. The people Turner involves himself with are without any sense of—I guess honor isn't the word. What I'm trying to say is clients like the Aryan Nation, or domestic terrorists, don't play by the rules. Eventually, young Mr. Turner is going to pay for his hubris, and the price will be steep."

"You think the Aryan Nation is bankrolling him?"

"Everyone is entitled to representation, even the Aryan Nation."

"What's in it for them?"

Sutton poured another drink, and his hand shook as he sat the decanter on the cart. "I had a client who tried to disassociate himself from the Nation. I took him on after an arrest—bogus, I might add—for possession of methamphetamine. Like your person of interest, my client had no job, lived in public housing, and he was going to sit in jail until trial."

"Let me guess, the Aryan Nation posted his bail."

"I was approached by someone who gave me cash to bail him out. Not the ten percent bail bond, but the full twenty-five thousand cash bail. The guy was a big dude dressed in biker leathers and Nazi tattoos on both arms. He said his right-minded friends appreciated my help, and there was money in it for me if I wanted to keep playing along."

"You think this guy was from the nation?"

"I asked around afterward, and turns out he was. Tommy Nash. Supposed to be an enforcer for the Aryan Nation."

"Why would they want to bail out a guy who wanted to walk away from the group?"

"My client was dead within six hours." Sutton slammed the empty glass down on the cart.

"Ambrose doesn't know who he's dealing with. His client is a dead man. He'll be next if he's not careful."

Sutton's receptionist knocked on the doorframe. "Mr. Sutton, your next appointment is here."

He nodded at her, dismissing the receptionist to her post.

"Parker, whoever Turner is in bed with, give them a wide berth. You don't want to be in the way when it blows up—and it will."

Parker begged off and left Sutton's office. He didn't pass anyone waiting for an appointment in the lobby area.

He called Pete from his SUV, and Tully picked up on the first ring.

"Hey, boss. Was about to call you. Clement's been processed, and his attorney, Turner, picked him up. Barry's following them now. Last report was heading west on the 10. Looks like he's homeward bound."

Parker gave him the recap of his conversation with Sutton.

"You think the Nazis would waste their time on a low life like Clement?"

"If Clement targeted his victims with the approval of the Aryan Nation, they may want to tie up loose ends."

"You think they'd make a move on him, knowing we're watching his ass?"

"Who knows what they will do for their cause? Make sure you watch your ass out there."

Chapter Twenty-Six

Parker called Miguel's cell to find out if he wanted him to pick up dinner on his way home. The call clicked over to voicemail. Parker looked at his watch and figured Miguel was about done with his last class of the day. It would be good to spend some time with the kid, just the two of them. Wouldn't be long before Miguel was off on his own.

Their shared experience—trauma if he was honest—resulted in a deep bond between them. In little more than a year, he thought of Miguel as family. He knew Miguel was eager to live independently, and it scared the hell out of Parker. Miguel was innocent and naïve when it came to the world. He was also a strong, resilient survivor. Parker hoped the balance of the two would prepare the young man for life after living with him. Parker would miss him when it came time to move on.

Parker spotted a local coffee shop known for roasting their own beans, and he wanted to grab a bag. He and Miguel enjoyed a brief morning cup together before they set off for the day. It was the one moment they could connect before the demands of school and work pulled them in separate directions.

The aroma of freshly roasted coffee hit the moment he entered. Deep, dark, and rich. He paused for a moment and scanned the chalkboard menu listing the day's roast.

"Detective Parker?"

He spotted Sofia Martinez, Nia Saldana's sister, standing at the register. "Hello, Ms. Martinez."

"I wasn't sure you were going to come. The envelope from the car is in my locker."

Parker nearly forgot her call because it was overshadowed by the labor organizer getting shot and arresting Clement.

"The computer drive?"

"Yes. I'll go grab it for you." She called out to a co-worker, saying she needed a ten-minute break. She disappeared into a back room and returned holding a white envelope. She directed Parker to an empty table in the corner of the busy shop.

"This was in Nia's car," she said and passed the envelope to Parker.

"Have you looked at what's on this?" Parker said, and he slid the red USB drive onto the table.

"My sister didn't have a computer. There is no reason she would use one of those. I haven't looked at it."

Parker pointed to the envelope. "Any thought to who 'RB' might be?"

She shook her head.

"When you called, you said your sister got referrals for her work. Could one have been an 'RB'?"

"I don't know."

Parker stared at the envelope. "You mentioned Nia got referrals from the Immigrant Coalition for work. Is that right?"

"Yes, they helped find her homes to clean where the families were understanding of her situation."

"Being undocumented?"

"Yes. And she needed time off to care for her children."

"Did she ever tell you who gave her the referrals?"

"No. I got one call while I was watching the girls from the Coalition about a new job for her. I took the message and gave it to Nia."

"A message about a new home to clean?"

"Yes. I think it was. The message struck me as a little strange. The man said Nia needed to do a little picking up at the address. Usually, people want a deep cleaning. Picking up wouldn't pay much."

"Remember who called, or the address?"

"No. I don't think I ever got a name. I'm sorry, I wish I had. You think it's important?"

The 'RB' on the envelope was a mystery. The 'R' Parker thought of died alongside Nia. A bolt shot through Parker's mind.

"Ever hear Nia mention a man named Jessup? Roger Jessup?"

She sat up straight at the mention of the dead man's name. "Jessup? That was one of the houses she cleaned. I heard her talk about him. She said he was a nice man."

"Anything specific about him?"

Sofia frowned and bit her bottom lip. "It might not mean much, but Mr. Jessup called her the day before she died. I heard part of what Nia was saying before she hid in her room to finish the call. I remember her saying she didn't want to work at this one place. She was afraid to get caught." She tapped a finger on the envelope. "Maybe she meant this. She took it and wasn't supposed to. It doesn't make sense. My sister didn't steal from the houses she cleaned."

"It sounded like Mr. Jessup wanted Nia to find a specific item. No idea where she was going?"

Sofia shook her head.

Parker sat back, swept the USB drive back inside the envelope, and placed it in his jacket pocket.

"How are the girls doing?"

Sofia tilted her head and brushed her dark hair behind her ear. "The youngest keeps asking when Mama is coming home. The older one knows and has become quiet and withdrawn. I'm worried about her. They both miss my sister so very much."

"I can give you some counseling referrals."

"We found someone. She's having her first appointment the day after tomorrow. The counselor specializes in childhood trauma, especially in the undocumented community."

"Good. I'm glad to hear you found a therapist who can deal with her specific needs."

Sofia pushed back from the table. "I've got to get back to work. I hope whatever is in that thing helps you."

Parker left the coffee shop and dialed Miguel. Again, the call transferred to voicemail. He checked his watch and was certain Miguel was out of class. Was he avoiding his calls now?

He shifted the sand in his mind, trying to figure out why Miguel was avoiding him. He thought they'd come to an understanding about his involvement with the protests and was going to stay away from the fringe activities of the Immigrant Coalition.

Parker arrived at the detective bureau, and his gut twisted when he spotted Billie and Miguel waiting for him.

The pair sat in his office, and Miguel hung his head, and Billie was rubbing his back, trying to comfort him.

"Miguel, what's wrong?"

"Is it true? Marco Cavalrubio is dead?"

Parker glanced at Billie, and her jaw tightened.

"How do you know him, Miguel?"

"He worked to help people find jobs once they came here."

"Right. He was a labor organizer."

Miguel raised his eyes to Parker. There was worry hidden there. For someone who experienced the violence and trauma from his trek from El Salvador, the anxiety the boy showed now was concerning.

"He was more than an organizer."

"I'm sure he was. I didn't mean—"

"Stop treating me like a child."

Parker put his hands up. "Okay, Okay. How did you know Cavalrubio?"

"He was on the board for the Immigrant Coalition."

"He was a contract employee. That's what I was told. What's this about a board?"

Billie cleared her throat. "Remember when we was at their offices? Brunell said he was the board vice chairman."

"And Jessup was the executive director."

"Roger Jessup, Emilio Hernandez, and Marco Cavalrubio were all board members."

Parker leaned against his desk.

"How do you know?"

"Because I'm a member, too," Miguel said.

Parker jolted upright. "You're what?"

"I'm a student representative to the Board."

"Jesus, Miguel. I thought we had an understanding about this."

"Didn't think you needed to know. You're all twisted up in knots over immigration issues."

"Not without reason?"

"I'm not saying you don't. But I need to make sure what happened to me doesn't happen to others."

Parker sighed and rubbed the back of his neck.

"All three were Coalition board members? You're sure?"

Billie piped up. "They were. That ain't what got Miguel worried." She nudged the boy. "Tell him."

"Tell me what?"

"I'm a student representative to the Board—"

"I heard."

"I'm one of three. The other two are missing."

Chapter Twenty-Seven

"Taken?" Parker asked. "Wait, he's one of these student reps, Mrs. Hernandez's grandson, Tomaso?"

"Yes, he is," Miguel said.

Parker plopped down on a sofa in the office. "Mrs. Hernandez was assaulted at the market. Maybe someone looking for Tomaso."

"Is she bad hurt?" Miguel asked.

"She took a beating. She's at the hospital now."

"Had to be Los Muertos," Billie said.

"That was my first thought, too. Until a witness said she saw three white guys rush into the store."

"White? You think them Aryan assholes had a hand in this?"

"I don't know who the muscle was. I found a note—looks like Mrs. Hernandez had forty-eight hours to come up with fifty grand to buy Tomaso back."

"She don't have no fifty grand lying around."

"The part of the note bothering me is where she was supposed to drop off the money. Out on Rocky Wash."

"Rocky Wash, where deputy McMillan got killed?"

He nodded.

"You know what it means, don't ya? That note was left for you."

"I know. It was Castaneda. He's going to be there in forty-eight hours."

"You think Los Muertos is gonna hand over the kid like that?"

Miguel sat up. "We have to get Tomaso back."

"It's not as simple as it sounds. You said you were one of three student

143

representatives on the Coalition's board? Tomaso is one. Is a kid named Juan another?"

Miguel's eyes widened. "Juan Estrada. Tomaso, Juan, and I were supposed to meet up this afternoon and talk about a student demonstration for next week. They never showed up. I need to call Juan," Miguel said and pulled up his phone.

The trill of a cell phone rang in Parker's hand. Juan's cell phone was in a plastic evidence bag.

"I found this left behind in his car. A woman said she saw some gangbangers pull him from his car."

"They took him, too?" Miguel's voice cracked as he spoke.

"Looks like it. Miguel, why would someone nab Tomaso and Juan? Are you in some kind of trouble?"

"The three of us backed Roger Jessup at the last board meeting." Miguel locked eyes with Parker. "So did Mr. Hernandez and Marco."

"What was the issue all of you supported?"

"Mr. Jessup wanted to increase the Coalition's efforts to serve migrants here. It meant paying for coyotes to make the crossing. The weather will change, and the hundreds waiting on the other side of the border will freeze. They're without food, no medical care, and every day many are lost to corruption and crime while they wait."

"Roger asked me if I could start making trips to bring families over," Billie said.

"Jessup had to know it was illegal."

"That's where the opposition came in. They didn't want the Coalition to be caught smuggling migrants. The federal government is cracking down. They want everyone to wait on the other side while paperwork gets passed from desk to desk. Nothing happens. Ever. The number of people waiting keeps going up."

"You know the conditions these people face," Billie said.

Parker nodded. "I understand. I do. Helping people after they get here is one thing, but I think the Coalition didn't want to get trapped in the middle of trafficking people over the border."

"With the board members who supported Mr. Jessup gone, they will abandon hundreds when they need help the most," Miguel said.

"Who opposed Jessup's proposal?"

"Three members. We had the numbers, and a vote was supposed to happen today. That's why I was looking for Tomaso and Juan."

Parker moved to his desk, brought up a web browser, and typed in a series of words. With a mouse click, he brought up a webpage. He turned the monitor toward Billie and Miguel.

"Tim Brunell opposed expanding the Coalition's work to bring migrants over, I bet."

The bright red, white, and blue Brunell for Senate webpage filled the monitor. Snappy quotes and endorsements lined the edge of the page. Photos of Brunell with a diverse lineup of state and nationally recognized powerbrokers dominated the screen. Highlighted policy positions scrolled into the space, and Parker tapped the screen when the first two points appeared. "Compassionate Immigration Reform and Controlled Borders."

"All it means is ain't no one getting in," Billie said.

"There's always a way in. Legal or otherwise. I understand what he's trying to do here, balance on the razor's edge and pander for votes. He'll never win the election if he comes out supporting illegal immigration and is caught paying for coyotes to smuggle people over the border."

"Looks like the anti-immigrant faction wins again," Miguel said.

Parker sat back and pondered for a moment. The targeting of the pro-migrant Coalition members wasn't random. This was the piece he needed to convince the captain, and the brass the Immigrant Coalition was at the center of the killings.

"Who knew Jessup's position—all your positions on the issue? Was it a secret thing, or was it out in the open?" Parker asked.

"It came up––the question of backing away from helping people seek freedom started last month. It wasn't a secret. Mr. Hernandez was pissed-off about what he saw as abandoning people in need of our help. Mr. Jessup was quick to agree. There wasn't any loud disagreement or argument. It was a difference in opinion in the direction the organization was going to take. Sure, Mr. Hernandez was vocal about it, but it was his way."

Billie nodded. "He was a passionate man. Especially when it came to helping undocumented folks. It's why he let us use his store as a bunkhouse."

"Of all of them, Mr. Jessup was the most upset. He started this organization to serve the undocumented population. He took the change in direction as undoing everything he stood for."

Tully rounded the corner to the office and interrupted. "We got a report of shots fired at the Immigrant Coalition offices. One victim down."

"Where's Clement? Does Johns have him covered?"

Tully held his cell phone. "He was my first call. Clement ducked into his house and hasn't so much as poked his head out since."

Parker snapped to his feet. "Pete, tell Barry to contact Clement. Go knock on the door. I want him to see skin. Let me know when he does."

Tully put the phone to his ear. "You got that?" He shot Parker a thumbs up.

Billie and Miguel rose to their feet and followed Parker from his office. He turned. "Where do you think you're going?"

"I'm coming with you," Miguel said.

"The hell you are. You could be a target. You told me everyone who took your side is dead or missing. I don't want you to be next. Billie, you watch over him."

"I'm not a child."

"You're my son, for what it's worth, and I don't want anything to happen to you."

Parker never said the words before. There was always an unsaid agreement between them of respect and support. He felt foolish for blurting it out. But there it was, and he wouldn't take it back.

Miguel's eyes misted over before he looked away.

"I know you want to help. The second I know anything, I'll let you know. In the meantime, stay here where you're safe."

Tully pulled on his jacket and joined Parker. "Update from the scene. Victim is Tim Brunell."

Tully's phone rang. He listened to the caller for a moment. "Wait. I'm putting you on speaker."

"Go ahead," Tully said.

"Clement's gone. Back door was open. He ducked out moments after he got home. He turned on the lights and made it look like he was staying put. He knew we were watching. I lost him." Johns said.

"How long was he out of sight?"

"Thirty minutes. Couldn't see the back door from where I parked. Didn't see anyone drive by who picked him up. The property backs up to open desert. I'm behind the place now, and there is a set of fresh tracks from an off-road vehicle. A quad, maybe. I don't remember seeing one of those out here when we took him down."

"Me either," Parker said.

"Sorry, boss. I lost him."

"Look around. See if you can figure out where he went, or if anyone picked him up behind his property. Meet Pete and me at the Immigrant Coalition offices."

"Look, I'm sorry—"

"He beat us. It happens. Finish up there and hook up with us soon as you can."

Parker handed the phone back to Tully.

"Barry's going to beat himself up for letting Clement slip out on him."

"Billie, promise me you'll look after Miguel."

"I should see if I can reach the board members. They need to know what's happenin.'"

"You can use my office. You know where to find me if you hear from them."

Parker nodded to Miguel, who balled his fists, unhappy he was sidelined.

"What about Tomaso and Juan?" the boy asked.

"We've got time before the drop."

"What happens when they find out we don't have the money? What about Juan? You didn't find a note about him."

"We're doing everything we can. I've gotta run. Find out what the Coalition is working on, planning—if there is a rally, it's the kind of thing

Clement would try to zero in on."

"I need to help. I can't sit on my ass and hope everything turns out okay," Miguel said.

"I know. You might be a target, too. I need to make sure you're safe here with Billie."

Parker left with Tully as Miguel slumped onto the sofa, resigned to his sidelined role.

One by one, the Immigrant Coalition members were taken off the board. Parker felt the backlash coming, and there was no getting out of the way.

Chapter Twenty-Eight

The strip mall offices of the Coalition were swarmed by news media vans with remote live broadcasts of the breaking news. The responding units set up a perimeter, keeping the cameras and the curious crowd away from the parking lot. Thick traffic on the main road bled around the double-parked news vans.

A uniformed deputy lifted the yellow plastic ribbon to let Parker drive under and park amongst the six patrol units, three fire department engines, and an ambulance. The medical examiner's white and blue van hadn't arrived.

Parker spotted the broken front window as he stepped from his vehicle. The deputy standing at the broken window jotting notes on a tablet was Linda Marsh, Miguel's savior after the Friendship Park rally.

"Hey, Linda. You first on scene?"

"I was. Deputy Lincoln and I pulled up at the same time. Reporting party says a shot came through the front window here and hit the victim. No one saw where the shot came from. Best guess is on the curb there where I asked one of our deputies to post up until the crime scene tech roll up."

"Good idea. That makes it a straight shot from there into the office. Less than fifty yards, I'd wager." Parker leaned in and noticed the window blinds were up and retracted fully.

"Last time I was here, these were down. You find them like this?"

"Yes."

"Our victim inside? The medical examiner hasn't transported him yet, have they?"

Linda tilted her head, and her dark brown ponytail flipped over her shoulder.

"He won't need the M.E."

It was Parker's turn to tilt his head.

"He's not dead," she said.

Parker shifted and peered into the office through the shot-out window. Tim Brunell sat in an office chair, being attended to by a pair of paramedics. The interim Coalition director looked more put out than hurt.

"I should go have a word with my victim," Parker said.

"Have fun with that. He's a piece of work, that one."

Parker strode into the offices and stood behind the paramedics attending to Brunell.

Brunell brushed shards of broken glass from his shoulder. "Detective, I was told you had the man responsible for killing Roger in custody."

"I was told you were shot."

"Sorry to disappoint you. It wasn't for a lack of effort. Seriously, Detective, there is a killer out there trying to destroy everyone and everything associated with the Coalition. These bigots can't stand helping disadvantaged persons who end up in our country. They claim they come here to take our jobs and live off the welfare state. We need a safety net where they are protected and given a chance in our society."

Parker thought it sounded like the press copy in his election brochure.

"Where were you when it happened?"

Brunell pointed to Isa's desk. "I answered the phone. Picked it up, and no one was there. Then a loud bang, the window blew out, showered me with broken glass, and I fell backwards."

"You see anyone before the gunshot?"

"I wasn't looking outside. I was picking up the phone."

"On Isa's desk. Where is she?"

"I sent her home. She was upset, as you can imagine. She was making copies when they tried to kill me. She called 911, and here we are..."

"I wish you hadn't told her to leave. I need to speak with her. She's a witness here and may have seen something you didn't."

150

"The copy machine is in the back room." Brunell pointed to a small space in the rear, out of the line of sight from the window. "She didn't see him."

"Still, I'm going to need to reach her."

Brunell waved his hand. "Whatever."

"Last time I was here, the blinds were down and closed. You mentioned keeping protestors away. When were they opened?"

Brunell glanced at the broken window. "Hadn't noticed. They were closed when I opened this morning."

"You didn't raise them?"

"No."

"Who else was here? Who pulled them up?"

"Isa. Oh, a workman came in and looked at the electrical box. We've been getting the breaker popping every time the copy machine and the printer run at the same time."

"You didn't see who opened them?"

"Why are you worried about my damn window blinds? Someone tried to kill me."

"They lured you to the desk to answer a phone in direct view of the window."

Brunell glanced from the window to the desk and back again.

"I am wondering why the shooter missed."

"He didn't miss! Look at me," Brunell said, gesturing to the cuts and lacerations from the broken glass.

"Everyone else he shot at is dead."

A vein on Brunell's forehead pulsed. "If you'd done your job, he wouldn't be out here shooting at me. You're like the rest of them. You don't care what happens to people who don't think like you, don't believe in the same values, and want nothing but a better life for those less privileged than you."

Parker bit back his response. Brunell was in shock from someone taking a shot at him. Lucky though it was, he could talk about it because none of the Sun Valley Sniper's victims could provide their account of the events.

"The shootings—witnesses spotted a vehicle parked on the roadside. You notice a car, truck, or someone stopped out there on the main road?"

Paramedics stopped the bleeding from the lacerations on Brunell's face with butterfly bandages. They were working on one stubborn bleeder above his left eye.

"I focused on the phone. Didn't look outside. You think the call was to lure me to where he could take a shot?"

"It's possible. What'd you hear on the call?"

"Nothing. All I heard was an open line."

"Okay. Can you give me Isa's phone number? I'd like to call and speak with her."

Brunell pushed the paramedic's arm away and stormed to Isa's desk. He grabbed a business card from a small silver stand and handed it to Parker. "Her cell phone is the best way to reach her."

Parker regarded the business card with Isa's new title, "Brunell for Senate—Campaign Manager."

"Campaign Manager?"

"She knows the issues."

Parker pocketed the business card.

One paramedic started buckling straps on the ambulance gurney.

"I'm not going."

"Sir, you should get these wounds checked. There may be one or two that could use a stitch or two to avoid scarring."

"I'm not giving whoever did this the benefit of thinking they won."

"Sir, I—"

"I'm not going. I'm refusing further medical treatment. I appreciate what you did, and I'll follow up with my personal physician."

The paramedic who treated Brunell's wounds tossed packages of gauze and butterfly bandages on the desktop. "You heard the man. We're out."

The two paramedics set their equipment bags on the gurney and rolled out the front door.

"Mr. Brunell, since we're alone now, I want to circle back to something you mentioned the last time I was here. Los Muertos."

Brunell bristled. "What of them?"

"You said Los Muertos were taking over the migrant routes from the independent coyotes."

"Vultures. They extort and victimize the desperate ones who want to make the crossing."

"As I understand it, the Coalition's board was considering a vote to increase the number of undocumented brought over. Would this mean an agreement with Los Muertos?"

Brunell leaned against the desk where he was shot. "Roger didn't understand. Los Muertos will not ignore a move to take their action. These people are nothing but a revenue stream to them. If the Coalition started down the path Roger advocated, using our own people as coyotes, there would be a bloodbath."

"You wanted to back away from the Coalition's involvement with bringing the undocumented over."

Brunell eyed Parker. "Who have you been talking to? But, yes. My position is we can offer financial assistance, housing, social services, and employment training to the undocumented here in the region. We shouldn't be involved with the act of illegal entry into the country."

"A bit of a shift for the Coalition, isn't it? I mean, for years, the organization has been knee-deep in bringing the undocumented over."

"The organization is evolving. In response to the previous Administration's border policies, we took an aggressive approach to sponsor migrants."

"Sponsoring as in arranging transport over the border?"

"I'm not going to comment further on the Coalition's activity under Roger's reign."

"And now, it seems you're changing course."

"A non-governmental organization must be able to pivot and adapt to provide services where most appropriate. Meaning, getting services to the undocumented already living and working in our community."

"If the board votes along those lines, you mean," Parker added.

"Yes, yes, of course. Until we reconstitute our board, we won't make any permanent decisions."

A uniformed deputy entered and motioned for Parker.

Brunell straightened his shoulders and left to address the assembled news media at the crime scene tape.

"Detective, we've got something for you to check out. Oh, the crime scene techs are pulling in. Where do you want them?"

Parker spotted the Maricopa County van park, and a tall man stepped from the driver's side. Sam Turner cast his own shadow at six-foot-eight, with a rough, craggy face that seemed like it was carved out of hard, dark granite. Tall and athletic, Sam was an imposing figure and an intimidating shot-blocker in the N.B.A. until he blew out his knee. Rather than grow bitter from the abrupt end of a promising career, Sam used his intensity and focus on becoming Maricopa County Sheriff's Office's top Crime Scene Technician.

"Sam, all by yourself today?"

"Willy called in lame this morning. That boy is gonna get an earful tomorrow."

"We got us a shooting scene. The trigger-puller was probably out on the road. Sent one shot through the window, missing the intended victim. I'm gonna need that slug. Likely buried itself in a wall."

"I'll find it," Sam said and carried an equipment bag through the office door.

Parker followed the deputy to the edge of the main road.

The deputy pointed to two yellow plastic evidence markers. One was next to three cigarette butts, while the second was near a bright brass shell casing.

"Looks like a .308 casing. I'll ask Sam to document the location."

A bright red laser strobed from within the offices. Sam found the slug and lined up a laser to show the likely shot's trajectory. It hit Parker in mid-chest.

Parker waved to let Sam know he'd spotted the light. He assessed the height was near what he'd expect from a shooter in a vehicle. Except for the brass souvenir he found on his windshield, the Sun Valley Sniper was careful not to leave evidence behind.

Clement wasn't going to wait around.

On cue, Detective Barry Johns edged his patrol unit to the barrier. The enormous man looked angry, pissed off after a half-wit Clement gave him the slip. Parker recognized the look because he'd experienced it himself over the years, more than once.

"No sign of Clement. I followed a set of quad tracks from behind his place. A quad was left by a road parallel to Clement's place. Either he stashed a vehicle there, or someone picked him up. The houses on either side of where the quad stopped didn't notice."

"He arranged the pickup," Parker said.

Tully and Sam came from the office, and Sam handed Parker a plastic evidence bag with a flattened lead bullet.

"We'll compare this slug to the others, but it looks like what's left of a .308 round. There was some chipping and deformation from impact with the cement block wall."

Sam took a step back, pulled a single-lens reflex camera from his bag, and knelt near the discarded brass shell casing. After snapping a series of shots from different angles, he used a pair of tweezers and slid the shell into the bag, pausing to smell the casing.

"How long ago did the shooting go down?"

"No more than an hour," Tully said.

"Here, what do you smell?" Sam extended the shell to Tully.

Tully gave it a sniff. "Nothing."

"A recently discharged round would hold on to a burnt gunpowder odor for a while. Maybe it's nothing. I thought it was a little odd," Sam said. "I'll check it out. Could be any number of reasons…."

The news media crews were breaking down their camera equipment. Brunell shot his hands in his pockets as he finished talking with a reporter. He looked up and caught Parker's attention. Brunell barreled toward the detectives.

"Parker!"

"Someone's got a hornet in their underwear, as my grandma used to say," Sam said.

Parker dealt with victims after assaults. A common thread was anger. Why them? Why didn't law enforcement stop it from happening? Brunell's bluster and red face marked him in the latter category.

"Why do I get it from some reporter?" Brunell said.

"What?" Parker said.

"You let the man who shot me out of jail—that's what."

"We didn't let anyone out of jail. That's not our call. You said you didn't see who shot you."

"It was him. It had to be. You arrested a known Aryan Nation associate after assassinating one of my board members, then you let him go."

"He's a person of interest, and we'll pursue all the evidence—"

"Person of interest. You people and your meaningless words. I was shot. And you're standing here doing nothing." A small trickle of blood leaked from beneath the bandage on Brunell's forehead.

"You should really have that looked at."

Brunell wiped his hand near the bandage and came away with blood smeared on his fingers. He sneered at his hand, turned, and strode back to the offices.

Parker turned to Tully and Johns. "Find Clement."

Johns slumped his shoulders.

Chapter Twenty-Nine

Parker reached Isa, and she agreed to meet him at her midtown condo. The doorman-attended high-rise was richly appointed, and he wasn't allowed access to the elevator without the doorman calling her up and getting her approval. Even then, the elevator wouldn't open without the doorman inserting his card key in a slot near the up button.

The elevator was quiet on the ride to the sixth floor. Parker spent the short ride staring at the ceiling-mounted camera until the doors parted in Isa's living room.

Isa greeted him wearing a green silk kimono, revealing bare legs. She held a glass of white wine in one hand and wrapped the other arm across her waist. Her tired eyes narrowed when the elevator door closed behind Parker.

"Do we really need to do this, Detective?"

"I'm afraid so. It's important to get witness statements as soon as possible. I'd liked to have done this at your office."

She turned on her heel and retreated into her apartment, calling over her shoulder, "Let's get this over with."

She perched on a sofa, tucked her legs under her, and took a sip from her glass. Behind her, the view to the northeast framed Camelback Mountain. The lights on a few of the million-dollar estates dotting the hillside were coming to life.

"You were in the office today when the shooting happened?"

"Yes."

"Anyone else there with you and Tim Brunell?"

"No."

"Where were you when the shooting occurred?"

"The copy room."

"Where was Mr. Brunell?"

"I couldn't say."

Parker recognized the attorney-like responses, answering what was asked and nothing beyond.

"Run it down for me. Walk me through your day from when you arrived to the time you left."

She sighed and drew another sip from her glass.

"I was the first one in this morning. I opened up—you know—turned on the lights, warmed up the copy machine, and turned on my computer."

"You were the first in. When did Mr. Brunell arrive?"

"I came in at seven-forty-five. Tim arrived around noon."

"And what time did the shooting occur?"

She squinted at the question. "It wasn't like I was sitting around with a stopwatch."

"All right. How long was Mr. Brunell in the office before the shooting?"

"Maybe a half hour. It wasn't long after."

"Anyone call and ask about him?"

"No."

"When you heard—"

"Wait. About an hour before Tim came in, a maintenance man from the property owner dropped in and asked if Tim was coming in today. I assumed it was about the lease. Tim handles those issues."

"A maintenance guy? They often show up during the day?"

She took another sip, draining her wine glass. Isa unfolded and padded to a bar on one end of the living room and poured another generous helping of chardonnay. She leaned on the bar, glanced at the red nail polish on her toes, and knitted her brow.

"Maintenance comes in when we need repairs. They are pretty good about taking care of the businesses in the complex. Funny though, it's usually Martin."

Parker perked up. "You ever met the guy today?"

"No. He said he was new. I didn't really pay much attention to him."

"What did he do? What needed fixing?"

"I didn't call him, so I don't know if Tim did. I thought it's why he was asking when he was going to come in."

"What did he do in the office?"

"I was busy. He was messing around in the front of the office. He had a tape measure at one point. I don't know what he was doing. He pulled up the blinds and messed around with the window pulls."

"Were the blinds broken?"

She shrugged. "I don't know. I've never opened them—ever. It was for our client's privacy, as you can imagine."

He nodded.

"Brunell mentioned some problem with the electrical breaker. Did the guy seem interested in the junction box?"

"I didn't notice."

"This maintenance guy—he give you a name?"

She sipped again. Parker was going to need to wrap this up based on Isa's blinks getting longer.

"I don't remember. I was preoccupied."

"What did he look like?"

"Tallish, maybe. Brown hair, kind of scruffy looking. Martin always said his boss enforced a grooming standard. This guy didn't get the memo. He was Hispanic, with that Latin swagger going on."

The wine hit. Parker stood from the sofa. "Anything else you can recall?"

"Not really. He wore brown coveralls, like Martin, but the sleeves were rolled up. He had this little tattoo on his arm."

Parker froze.

"A star on his left forearm?"

She pivoted to face Parker. "How did you know?"

Parker joined Isa near the bar and noticed her wobble a bit. The wine bottle was empty. He fished out his cell phone and pulled up a photograph.

"This guy? Was he the maintenance man?"

Parker tensed while Isa bent to the phone, holding her dark hair back as she regarded the photo.

"Him? Yes, I think it was. Why would he pretend to be a maintenance man?" Isa uncorked another bottle of Cakebread chardonnay.

"Thank you."

Parker left Isa and thumbed the elevator button with a sour note in his stomach. Parker glanced at the photo Isa identified. Esteban Castaneda. His hand tightened around the phone. He was close.

Chapter Thirty

Parker made it back to his SUV, his mind spinning after Isa identified Esteban Castaneda in the Immigration Coalition offices. From her accounting, Castaneda asked about Brunell and opened the blinds to clear the field of fire for the attempt on Brunell's life.

His knuckles grew white as he gripped the steering wheel, trying to make sense of the connection. Brunell admitted Castaneda's Los Muertos connections were established to smuggle the undocumented over the border. They also brought the violence and extortion the gang relied upon for years. Snatching Juan and Tomaso and holding twenty migrants in a locked storage room were all markings of Los Muertos activity.

Brunell's position on supporting the smuggling of migrants over the border put him at odds with the board members—the dead and missing board members. The board votes would increase the flow of the undocumented, putting the group at odds with Los Muertos' claim on the smuggling routes. Los Muertos wasn't someone you wanted coming after you.

The puzzle piece not fitting into the whole was a connection between Castaneda's Los Muertos with Clement and the Aryan Nation. Avowed white supremacists in bed with a Mexican gang? Nothing about the pairing made any sense.

By the time Parker arrived back at the detective bureau, the television screens were on, covering local news reports. Captain Morris stood in the center of the room with a television remote in hand. "You're gonna want to hear this," Morris said when he spotted Parker.

The captain thumbed up the volume.

"Today's events serve as a reminder for all of us. It's not enough to pretend racism is behind us. It lurks in every dark crevasse, in small minds, and out of ignorance. When people are targeted because of the color of their skin, or because of where they were born, it diminishes all of us. We cannot allow hate to win. We cannot allow bigotry to win while our institutions enable and support those who perpetrate violence against the most vulnerable in our community. Our own Sheriff's Office let the man responsible for today's attack out of jail because his victims weren't important enough or weren't white enough. This ends today. It's why I've committed to run for State Senate—"

Morris muted the feed. "It's on all the networks. I don't need to tell you how this is going over in the corner office."

Parker sighed and stared at the smug image on the television screen. Brunell posturing for the media made him angry.

Barry Johns came into the squad room and stopped in his tracks when he caught the captain watching the press conference.

"Captain, I—"

"Got the cigarette butts down to the lab," Parker finished for him. He cut a glare at the junior detective.

"Yes, sir. I asked them to rush the analysis. They also said they would expedite lifting any prints from the spent shell casing they collected at the scene. Nina said she'd send it and the shell you snagged off your window off to NIBIN and let them know we're in a rush."

NIBIN was the National Integrated Ballistic Information Network, and Parker knew any case information from the feds would take weeks.

"Is Nina going to run DNA on the cigarette butts?"

"That's the plan. We have Clement's DNA on file as a sex offender. Still, take a day or two, at best."

"We need to find the weapon," Parker said.

"I have a thought."

Johns trotted to his desk and grabbed a folder. Opening the red cardboard cover, Johns unfolded a map of the western valley from Buckeye to the 303.

He stabbed a finger on the map surface near the 303 and Glendale Avenue, where Marco Cavalrubio was shot.

"We know Clement and the van were at this spot when Cavalrubio was murdered. We found GSR inside the van and traffic camera footage of the van leaving the scene."

Morris nodded.

"The last image of the van is off of Bell Road, here."

"And we didn't regain sight of the van until we spotted him pulling up to his place. Here," Parker said.

"Exactly. There are three potential routes I've traced here. The most direct would put him home in twenty minutes from 303 and Bell. This one," Johns tapped a blue line, passes the only Nashville Hot Chicken restaurant in the area. "That would put him forty-five minutes out."

"We lost him for over an hour," Parker said.

Johns tapped a finger on a green line. "If Clement headed west on Bell, stopped at his chicken joint, then made a stop, it would put him air closer to an hour."

"Lots of places he could stop. Gas, liquor store—"

"Or a storage unit."

Johns pulled out photos of the van pulling in and leaving a storage facility. "This place is out past Sun City Festival and mostly caters to the snowbirds who live there for a few months a year. The timestamp on the photos shows he was there for fifteen minutes."

"How'd you do all this?" Captain Morris said.

"I drove every probable route from where we lost contact with the van. These were the most likely. Then I found the photos of the van coming in and leaving the storage unit. There's a service station across the street."

"This is good work, Detective," the captain said.

"If I hadn't—" Johns started.

"Very good work, Barry," Parker said.

"Good enough for a warrant for the storage place?"

"If we knew what unit, sure. Without narrowing it down, the judge will call it a fishing expedition," Morris said.

"How about for unit 2118?"

Morris and Parker looked at one another.

"How would you know the unit number, Barry?" Parker said.

"I stopped in and asked. Showed the manager a photo of Clement and he recognized him. Said he goes in and out every couple of days. The unit is paid a year in advance. The manager's the nosy type, but's never been able to see what Clement brings in or takes out."

"You're thinking he stashed the rifle in the unit?" Captain Morris said.

"It explains why we didn't find it when we searched his home."

"We have to overcome the lack of GSR on his hands and clothes."

"The manager of the chicken joint remembered Clement using the bathroom and was in there a while. Didn't recall if he'd changed clothes, though. So, he could've scrubbed down enough to show a negative for residue."

"You spoke with the restaurant manager?"

Johns nodded.

"Damn, Barry. That's good work. When did you have the time to do all this?"

"My off time. This guy is not getting away."

"All right, I'll call in a favor over at the DA's office," Morris said. "We'll ask for a warrant. Head over to the storage unit and make sure no one opens the unit until we secure it. Unit 2118, right?"

"Yes, Captain."

"Fine work, Detective."

"Thank you, sir."

"Barry, I assume you want lead on this one?"

"I want to shake the starch out of his Klan robes."

"Okay, you and Tully head out. I'll catch up after I—hey, where's Miguel and Billy?"

The inner office was empty.

"Barry looked at Tully."

"I didn't see them leave," Tully said.

Parker dialed Miguel's cell, and it fell to voicemail. Billie picked up on the third ring.

"Billie. Where are you? You were supposed to wait in my office?"

"Miguel and me figured out a way to bring Tomaso and Juan back."

"Stay away from it. Los Muertos is up to their neck in it."

"All Los Muertos wants is money. You know how they operate. I found us a way to get the fifty-grand they want and get them boys back."

"Don't do anything. Where are you?"

"Don't worry. I'll keep Miguel out of trouble."

"Who's gonna keep you out of trouble? Where is the money coming from?"

Silence on the end of the line. Parker could hear Billie breathing and voices in the background. One was Miguel. The other was Tim Brunell.

Chapter Thirty-One

Parker paced in his office, ruminating over the call. Billie wouldn't admit Brunell fronted the money for the hostage exchange. Billie had a big heart and would do whatever it took to bring Tomaso and Juan back, and she could talk Brunell into funding their recovery. He'd want to keep the questions around a gang-spawned kidnapping and ransom far from his budding senate campaign. Miguel was at risk out there. Whoever targeted the board members could be looking for him. The ransom payoff didn't mean Miguel was safe.

His mind spun, knowing Miguel survived so much in his seventeen years. He witnessed his family destroyed by MS-13 gang members, fled the country to avoid being drawn into the violence enveloping his home country, and traveled solo across Cartel-controlled Mexican territory for a faint glimmer of a life. If his story ended because of anti-migrant vigilante terrorism, Parker could never forgive himself. He promised the boy he'd provide him a safe place to live and completed all the tedious, formal processes to become Miguel's foster parent.

Yet, here Miguel was, caught in the middle of a violent web again. White power thugs like the Aryan Nation were targeting the Immigrant Coalition because of their widely known open borders philosophy. There were boxes of files next to his desk, attesting to the level of hate directed at the group.

Parker woke his computer with a flick of the mouse. What did he really know about Brunell?

The first six websites listed in the search engine painted Brunell as a firebrand advocate for the undocumented. As the public face for the

Immigrant Coalition, Brunell wasn't shy about his stance on border policy, treatment of separated families, and defunding ICE. Two articles appeared after federal authorities intercepted migrant caravans north of the border. Brunell argued they should release the undocumented travelers on their own recognizance pending a hearing before an immigration court. The federal prosecution team considered the deal until they found three previously deported drug smugglers among the travelers in the caravans.

Through it all, Brunell never wavered from his advocacy—until he announced his run for state senate.

Parker clicked on a link for a bio. The piece referenced Brunell's experience in the financial world and how his fiscal background enabled him to be such an effective fundraiser for the Coalition. It was a puff piece; Parker could see through it, but it didn't mention where his financial experience came from. No references to where Brunell worked, where he went to school, or his life before associating with the Immigrant Coalition.

It was as if Brunell didn't exist until forty-eight months ago. Parker switched applications and brought up the Arizona Motor Vehicle Department database. Tim Brunell's Arizona MVD record showed an initial application two years ago, but nothing before. He tried alternate spellings and derivations of the name—Tim Brunell didn't exist until recently.

It wouldn't be the first time someone changed their name for a new start, or if they were hiding from their past. There was usually some wisp of a trail but, in this case, nothing.

He picked up his desk phone and dialed.

"Detective Littlefield, Missing Persons."

"Hey, Little."

"Parker, what do I owe this honor? I mean, missing persons rarely gets the pleasure."

"I need your expertise."

"I'm regretting this already."

"You have experience tracking people who are hard to find—how about ones who want to disappear?"

"Sometimes. You know, not every reported missing person wants to be found."

"What gives them away? I mean, where should I look to find someone who might be hiding?"

"Depends. If they really want to disappear, all connections to the old life must go. No credit cards, no electronic footprint. If it was me, I'd go old school and off the grid, live in some Unabomber cabin."

"Not very social, are you, Little?"

"When I retire, I'm out. I'm tired of the city, tired of people, and all this."

"You wouldn't be the first cop to go live out in the sticks after they pull the plug. But, the guy I'm looking for—how do I say this? I know where he is—and who he is now. What I'm trying to do is find out who somebody was before he became who he is now?"

"What the hell are you saying? If you know him, go ask?"

"I've got a guy who, on the surface, lives a public life. I can't find a paper trail of him over four years old. Found a recent current motor vehicle registration under his name, but that's it. How can I dig back and find out who he was before?"

"And you can't approach him directly?"

"Nuh-uh."

Littlefield paused. Parker could hear the big man wheeze over the connection.

"If he changed his name, there would be a court record. Problem is, you need to know what court the guy used to file his petition for a change. You know, you haven't mentioned WitSec. I mean, is the guy a federal witness hiding out from the mafia or something?"

"I doubt it. Where would I start?"

"Work back from the oldest contact you have. Sometimes the context of the information will let you know where to look next. It's turning over one rock at a time."

"Thanks, Little. There's a lot of rocks in this pile."

"There's always something there, Parker. You gotta look at it from a different angle. You know how to do it."

Parker finished the call and sat back in his chair, studying the image of Tim Brunell at a fund-raising event representing the Coalition. The Senate candidate would back away from soliciting funds for the group. The non-profit organization would take a financial hit.

His eye caught the USB drive Nia Saldana's sister found in the wreckage. Parker held it, and the inch-long device appeared ordinary and boasted a one-gigabyte storage capacity. Not unusually large. The sister thought it odd because there was no computer in the family home.

Parker plugged the USB drive into a slot on his desk computer. He ran a quick virus scan, and it was clean. Six months ago, another detective inadvertently downloaded a virus to the server. It ended up being a harmless one. Every time a detective logged on to the network, a screen popped up, and a robotic voice screamed, "I watch porn at work!" Captain Morris was in the middle of a slide presentation to a community church group when it first hit. Everyone was careful to virus scan any outside device accessing the system after "The Morris Meltdown."

The drive was clean and held a single file, a small one. The file extension identified it as a spreadsheet.

Parker hovered over the enter button for a moment and hit enter.

A spreadsheet filled the monitor. Column after column of numbers. The heading at the top was letters, not full words. JC, DR, ST, LM, AN, J, and on.

Maybe these were the homes Nia Saldana worked at? Parker discounted the theory because the numbers, if in fact they were dollars, were too large. Ten thousand, twenty-five thousand, with the smallest entry of two thousand.

The spreadsheet entries were in date order from the far-right column's label dating back a year, and the last entry was the day Nia died in the accident on the freeway.

"What is this, Nia?"

Dozens of entries. A ledger? Where were the funds coming from, and where were they going to?

Parker's cell rang, and the caller ID said it was Tully.

"You guys at the storage facility? I haven't heard from the captain on the warrant request yet."

"We won't need one."

"Why?"

"The unit was on fire when we got here. The fire department found a body inside. I think it's Clement."

Chapter Thirty-Two

P arker arrived at the storage yard as all, but one fire engine was released from the scene. In a densely packed commercial yard, there was concern about the blaze spreading to the adjoining units. The responding firefighters cut the locks to the units next to the burning one to ensure combustible or explosive materials didn't pose a larger threat.

Tully and Johns stood near the blackened maw of the burnt unit, watching the firefighters mop up.

"What did you find, guys?"

Tully points to a blackened husk on the floor in the center of the unit. "Looks like Gary Clement. I mean, he's a crispy critter now, but the scrap of a tattoo on his neck looks familiar. We'll need dental."

"Size is about the same," Johns said.

"What was he doing here? Where's his van?"

"No sign of it. We've asked the manager to turn over the video to see if we can pin down how he got here—and with who."

Parker took a step toward the unit, and the fire captain held up a hand to stop him.

"We've got a couple hundred rounds of military surplus ammunition in there, and the heat made them unstable. We've already had a couple rounds pop off. I've asked for your bomb disposal team to come and lend a hand clearing the place."

"Looks like crates of the stuff," Parker said.

The fire captain pointed at a charred wooden box. "That one's labeled S4GCA. I recognize the label from my time in the sandbox."

"Afghanistan?"

"Iraq. If the label's correct, the crate contains twenty-five Mark II fragmentation grenades."

Parker instinctively leaned back.

"Your detectives tell me this guy was a vet. He must work some old connections to get his hands on this kind of stuff. The ammo and firearms alone would go for big bucks on the open market."

"You didn't find a .308 caliber rifle?"

"Wasn't paying too much attention while we were putting the flames down. Could be. A couple long guns were on the workbench in the back. We backed out after one of my guys spotted the Mark IIs. What was he into, anyway? There was enough to equip a small militia."

"I'm trying to nail that down, too."

The captain turned at the sound of a large vehicle creeping down the alley between the storage units. The dark green EOD truck lumbered to a stop, and two deputies in olive drab jumpsuits hopped down from the elevated cab. A barrel-chested sergeant spotted Parker and came over to join the detective and the fire captain.

A quick discussion of the wooden crate and ammunition in the storage unit between the EOD Sergeant and the Fire Captain and a plan came together to address the threat.

When a single small pipe bomb is rendered safe, the bomb technicians often cover it with a heavy lead-lined blanket, or seal it in a heavy, steel-reinforced barrel before they destroy it with a controlled detonation. Parker wondered what a box full of military-grade explosives would do to the thin metal and concrete block storage units.

The EOD sergeant waved up one of his bomb technicians, who piloted a squat green robot with rubber treads. The tech used a handheld controller to manage the robot's movement and the articulating arms mounted on either side of the machine. Parker'd seen these devices used when a suspect barricaded themselves in a home. They could deliver a chemical agent canister and effectively blast a less than lethal round from a 12-gauge shotgun.

As the robot drew near, the EOD Sergeant waved everyone back.

"I need a hundred-foot perimeter. Y'all get back behind the next row of storage units."

No one needed to be told a second time.

The tech with the handheld remote used a camera mounted on the front of the machine to guide the path into the unit. Parker looked over his shoulder. "You mind?" Parker asked.

"Nope. Knock yourself out."

Parker found the bomb technicians he knew to be ex-military explosive ordnance disposal specialists. If they could disarm a roadside IED with the Taliban shooting at them, they could handle the odd pipe bomb in the desert. They were a quiet bunch, unlike their tactical unit counterparts. They did their jobs and pressed on. Parker could imagine the steely nerves these techs had when it came to disarming a device capable of blowing off an arm.

The view on the screen displayed the smoke-blackened interior of the storage unit. The crate of fragmentation grenades was in the far back corner. Between the robot and the explosives lay Clement's burnt body.

The tech inched the robot closer with subtle movements of a joystick.

Parker wondered if they were going to drive over the body with the heavy rubber treads.

"Sergeant, we got us a secondary."

"What's that mean?" Parker asked.

"Bottom on the screen on the right side," the tech said as he inched the machine closer.

"I don't see anything."

"Timmy, whatcha got?" the EOD Sergeant said.

"Body's booby-trapped. Looks like a single Mark II tucked under the body near its waist. Pin's pulled, and the body weight is keeping the spoon depressed."

The Sergeant leaned in on the screen.

"Warren, suit up."

The second tech donned the heavy protective suit consisting of three layers of blast, heat, and overpressure protection. The seventy-pound package looked like a deep-sea diving suit until the additional blast plates were mounted on the front, back, and groin of the operator.

A microphone check after the helmet went on showed Warren was ready.

"Warren, there's a Mark II fragmentation grenade under the body, left side, midline. I'll have Timmy point at it with the robot."

Warren waddled to the mouth of the storage unit and slowly paced to the rear of the robot.

"I see it. Back Junior off a bit, would you?"

Timmy toggled back on the joystick, and Junior, the robot, reversed away from Clement's burnt body.

Warren activated a helmet-mounted flashlight, and the bright white flare against the charred flesh made it seem like a bad horror movie.

"I have it."

Warren didn't approach the device. Instead, he eased to the opposite side of the body.

"What's he doing?"

"Where there's one, there could be others," the sergeant said.

"Got another one," Warren's voice called out over the radio. "Same thing. A Mark II, pin pulled, body holding the spoon down."

"What do you need?" the sergeant asked.

"I've got it. I'm going to neutralize this one first."

Warren opened a pouch on the front of his suit and retrieved a small case. He selected a short length of wire. Settling on his knees, Warren fished his left hand under the burnt corpse.

"I'm rotating the grenade—there—I've got the spoon." Gingerly, he withdrew his hand from under Clement, and a grenade shown on the screen. He kept the body of the explosive under the body, exposing only the head. Warren made sure the body didn't shift, relieving pressure on the other grenade. With his free hand, the tech snaked the length of wire in the holes, securing the spoon in a safe position.

Warren soft-stepped to the first device and repeated the process until the explosive was disarmed.

The tech rose to his feet and aimed his light on the soot-covered floor as he made his way to the rear of the unit. The camera showed his view as he peered into the open wooden crate. Fiberboard tubes contained twenty-three Mark II grenades, and they were intact, with pins in place.

"We're clear. I'm coming out."

"We're good?" Parker asked.

"Give us a minute to get the crate, and the two disarmed Mark II's outta there."

The robot backtracked out of the storage unit, and within five minutes, the EOD crew safely secured the crate of military surplus explosives in a steel compartment on their vehicle.

"What are you gonna do with those?" Parker asked.

"We'll disassemble them and make them inert. The place is yours, Detective."

Parker entered the unit, and the smell of burnt flesh bit into his nostrils.

Johns followed. "I called for the M.E., should be here in fifteen. Crime scene techs are here."

"Let's finish documenting this scene."

Johns waved in the crime scene techs.

"Where do you want us to start, Detective?"

"Let's begin with the body. We're gonna need an inventory of everything in here," Johns said.

"Looks like you called this one, Barry."

"Yeah, I got questions, though. When did he get here? Where's his van? How come he's extra crispy?"

"You never heard of spontaneous combustion?" Tully said.

"Nothing about this seems spontaneous." Johns' brow knitted. He strode to the left wall, where a workbench took up most of the space. On the surface, gun parts and accessories.

"Check this," Johns said.

"Looks like Clement was a gunsmith. We ever see that pop up on his skill sheet?" Parker said.

"We know about his military record. Could've been a holdover from his time in the service. You know the whole, this is my weapon, this is my gun, thing." Tully said.

"You watch too many movies," Johns said.

A wall-mounted rack held eight rifles of different models and calibers. Two empty slots were covered in soot stains, meaning the weapons were taken before the fire started.

Parker pointed at a black-stained length of metal. It was cut in random lengths. Rough ends were flecked with loose metal shavings. A band saw sat on the end of the bench with metal shavings piled under the blade.

"Any bets on if this is our missing sniper rifle?" Parker asked.

"Part of it, anyway," Tully said. "Don't see the receiver lying around."

The lab tech stepped over and snapped a series of photos of the gun barrel fragments, the metal shavings, and the band saw. In the flash of the camera strobe, Parker caught a reflection on the black, soot-slicked wall above the bench.

Parker wiped a glove-covered thumb across the spot on the wall. An image bled through. He brushed a wider spot with the blade of his hand.

"What'd you find?"

Parker leaned over the bench, careful to keep from touching the ash-covered surface. He wiped a two-foot-wide swath, revealing photos stapled to the wall above the workbench. Taken from a distance, images of Roger Jessup, Emilio Hernandez, Tomaso Hernandez, and Juan Estrada were tacked prominently. Each photo bore a sharp red diagonal line, crossing out each of the murdered men.

The two photos shook Parker. An image of Miguel and Billie together and an aerial view of a remote desert road. It looked like any dirt crossing, except for the makeshift, white wooden cross at a swell in the road. The memorial to Sheriff's Deputy McMillan on Rocky Wash—the exact spot Billie and Miguel were heading.

Chapter Thirty-Three

The medical examiner came and left the storage facility, and the cause of death was yet to be determined. No obvious gunshot wound or gaping knife slash. Until a full examination and autopsy, Parker wouldn't know if Clement was dead before the fire.

Clement's death should've eased Parker's anxiety. He was tied to the shootings, if not directly responsible for them. But who killed him? What was the killer's connection to the convicted sex offender, and were they going to finish crossing off the photos on the wall?

On the way to the detective bureau, neither Billie nor Miguel answered their phones. He knew there could be a dozen reasons, but not being able to reach them left him anxious. A glance at his watch confirmed it was twelve hours before the deadline left on the note for Tomaso's blackmail exchange. Billie was a desert dweller and knew the contours of every barren flat and wash within a hundred miles. He knew her pattern. She'd watch the drop for hours ahead of the deadline.

Parker cut north on the 303 and headed past Cave Creek, turning on Rocky Wash. Each time he drove this section of road, guilt washed over him. He'd relived that night countless times, in hours of administrative interviews, in his nightmares, but the most painful was telling Mac's pregnant wife he was never coming home.

Parker wiped a tear with the back of his hand as he spotted the roadside memorial. He pulled the SUV to a stop and waited for the dust to blow by the driver's door before he got out.

Parker straightened the faded white wooden cross in the loose desert soil.

The photo of McMillan on the topmost arm of the cross had faded. Last year, Parker pinned a photo of Esteban Castaneda to the cross and promised Mac he would make the man pay for what he'd done. Castaneda's image was gone. It was probably for the best, not tarnishing Mac's memorial with a photo of the killer. Parker knew Mac's wife never came to this location; she couldn't bear the pain. Few knew of the marker's existence.

Looking to the southeast, Parker gazed through the heat waves rising off the roadway. A glint in the distance signaled another vehicle on the track. It wasn't moving. The single glare off a windshield meant someone else was watching this drop point. Billie wouldn't be out in the open. Los Muertos.

Parker's cell vibrated in his pocket. Billie's number blinked on the screen.

"Billie? Where the hell are you? Is Miguel with you?"

"Nathan, you shouldn't be here."

"Why did you leave the Sheriff's office? It's not safe for either of you."

"The pickup truck is movin'. Comin' your way. Kinda slow."

"Where are you?"

"On the ridge to your left—to the west."

Parker scanned the hilltop until a flash from a reflective surface flickered at the base of a large red bolder. "I see you."

The reflection disappeared.

"Los Muertos reached out and sped up the timeline. They're here now to collect. You're messing things up."

Parker could make out the outline of the pickup through the wavy lines radiating from the hot road surface. It was at least a mile away.

"How did Los Muertos contact you?"

"Well, not me directly. They said we was supposeta drop the money and back away."

"In exchange for Tomaso?"

"Then they'd tell us where to find him."

"Billie, they won't have any reason to turn him over after they get their hands on the money."

"Said, weren't no other way they'd do it."

"And you talked to them? Was it Castaneda?"

"Not me, personally. But it had to be him."

Parker clocked the slow-moving apparition a half mile out.

"Who gave you the information?"

"Tim Brunell got the call. He made them put Tomaso on the line—you know—as proof of life."

"Was this before or after Brunell got shot at?"

"After. Glad the shooter missed. But I hear you found him."

"I don't know what we found. Los Muertos was involved somehow—I know it."

"Truck's pullin' to a stop. Two people inside. It's him behind the wheel. It's Castaneda." Billie's voice carried an urgent tone.

Parker reached to his hip and drew his Glock. He held the weapon down at his side. He glanced at the wooden cross. Mac's death would not go unanswered.

"What's he doing, Billie?"

"Don't know. They was supposeta come pick up the money. But now he seen you."

"Where's the money, Billie?"

"That rock ten yards behind deputy McMillan's cross. There's a bag stashed there."

Parker strode to the rock and, as Billie said, a black nylon bag was tucked behind the rock. Parker holstered his weapon, unzipped the bag, and fifty thousand in cash lay inside. He zipped it up and hefted the bag, and walked to the center of the road. He raised the bag over his head.

"Parker, I gotta call coming in from Brunell."

"Take it. I have a feeling we're in a bit of a standoff here."

Parker dropped the bag at his feet and tapped his holster. Parker couldn't make out the faces in the pickup truck.

Billie rang his cell once again.

"Brunell says Castaneda wants you to leave the money and go."

"Ain't happening."

"I told him you'd say that. He said Castaneda is ready to make an example if you don't back down."

Parker caught movement on the road ahead. The driver's door opened, and Castaneda strode around to the passenger door and flung it open. A pop sounded and echoed against the hillside. Castaneda pulled the passenger from the seat and tossed him to the pavement.

"Billie? What happened?"

"Castaneda shot him. He shot Tomaso!"

Parker began running toward the truck.

Castaneda stomped to the driver's side, stepping over the downed man, got behind the wheel, and spun the wheels in reverse. The truck pulled a quick turn and sped off in the opposite direction.

Parker was out of breath when he arrived at the crumpled body. A black hood covered the boy's head.

He knelt and felt for a pulse on his neck while pulling back the hood.

A bullet hole in the boy's temple. There would not be a pulse.

It wasn't Tomaso.

A cell phone rang in the dead boy's shirt pocket.

Parker snagged the phone and hit the connect button.

"Hello, Detective Parker. It's about time we became acquainted."

Chapter Thirty-Four

Castaneda's voice in Parker's ear burned. The dead boy at Parker's feet was Juan Estrada; the boy pulled from his Nissan Sentra by a pair of gangbangers.

"Parker, I want my money, and you want your kid."

"I want you."

"If you want to see him again, you'll follow my instructions to the letter."

Parker closed his eyes and tightened his jaw.

"Are you listening to me, Parker?

"I'm here."

"Keep this phone on you. I'll call you in an hour and tell you where to bring my money."

"I'm coming for you. You hear me?" Parker spoke to dead air. Castaneda disconnected the call.

Billie ran to Parker's side and fell to her knees at the dead boy.

"It's Juan. Why would he do that? The kid was an innocent boy. He meant nothing to him."

Parker leaned in and looked at the boy's smooth face, unlined from age or sun, marred by an ugly black hole in the side of his head. There wasn't a lot of blood from a head wound.

Picking up the black hood, Parker thought there was some mercy in that Juan never saw it coming. He crushed the hood in his hands. And glanced at the fabric, speckled with dry blood.

Parker held the hood, pulling it out to expand it, and made a discovery. There was no bullet hole in the hood.

"Juan was already dead when Castaneda got here."

"What's that?"

"He would never release the kid. He was already dead."

"But we, I heard the gunshot."

"It was all theatre. It was to make us believe he'd kill Tomaso if we didn't hand over the money."

"If he hasn't already," Billie said.

"Where's Miguel?"

"I didn't want to risk him comin' out here. I dropped him off at home. He promised me he'd lock down and stay in."

Parker fished out his cell phone and placed a call to Miguel. After five rings, it landed in voice mail. Parker hung up and dialed his home number.

"He's not picking up."

"He's prolly got those darned headphones on again," Billie said.

Parker gazed into the distance, where Castaneda's truck disappeared.

"Something's not right. I got a bad feeling. Castaneda said, 'I want my money, and you want your kid.' Your kid. My kid. He meant Miguel. I—I gotta go."

Parker called dispatch and asked for a deputy to make a welfare check at his home. Hopefully, Billie was right, and he was ignoring the calls, or deep in some video game and didn't hear them. A second call went to Johns and Tully. They were to call out the M.E., evidence techs, and respond to Rocky Wash. Billie would wait for them.

"I got this, Detective. You go make sure Miguel is okay. He's a smart kid. He knows better than to go poking around on his own."

Parker hoped she was right. But ever since he became involved in the Immigrant Coalition, he'd become secretive and unpredictable. The behavior change was especially noticeable since Emilio Hernandez died in his market over a stupid Coalition poster.

The drive from the north valley to home was the longest forty-five minutes in Parker's life. Luckily it was against the commute traffic going away from the city, or it would've been double the time. He skidded into his driveway, and his heart skipped a beat at the sight of a Sheriff's patrol unit position curbside.

Deputy Linda Marsh stepped from the patrol unit.

"I took the dispatch call when I heard the address."

"He okay?"

"No one's home, Nathan."

"You positive?"

"Back door was unlocked. I entered and checked. Miguel's not home."

Parker trotted to the front porch, fumbled with his keys, and unlocked the door. Linda followed behind. "Any idea where he would hang out? Friends, A girl, maybe?" she asked.

"He was supposed to stay put."

"I asked the neighbor next door if she noticed him leave."

"Mrs. Imperieli? She'd know. She's our own unofficial neighborhood watch."

"She noticed a car leave about fifteen minutes ago. Couldn't say who was in it and didn't see Miguel. Got a description of the vehicle."

Parker held an uneasy tension in his gut. He wasn't used to walking his own home like a crime scene, looking for evidence pointing to where Miguel was, who he was with, or if the boy was okay.

A vibration rattled, and the cell phone left on Juan Estrada's body rang. Parker glanced at his watch, and true to his promise, an hour had passed since Castaneda called.

"Are you ready to listen, Parker?"

"Say what you gotta say."

"I'm going to let you know exactly what's at risk if you don't do exactly as I tell you."

"You want your money, I get it."

"That's not all. I sent you a photo. Let me know when you have it."

Parker felt the phone vibrate with a text message. He clicked over to an app and opened the new text message. A photo, a proof of life photo, filled the screen. It wasn't Tomaso—it was Miguel.

Chapter Thirty-Five

The animal had Miguel. His worst fears come true.

"What have you done?"

"I want to make absolutely sure you know what's at risk if you don't carry out my instructions to the letter."

"I'm coming for you, Castaneda."

A dry laugh sounded over the phone. "You aren't in any position to threaten me, Parker. You know what I'm capable of. Do you want Miguel to end up like the Estrada boy, with a bullet to the head?"

"What do you want? The money? Tell me where, and we'll make a trade. The cash for Miguel and Tomaso."

Deputy Marsh overheard enough of the call to know what was going on. She got on her cell and called Tully and Johns.

"The money is a start. But I need more from you now."

"More? What the hell do you mean?"

"Do exactly as I tell you. Don't deviate from my instructions. You do, the boy dies. If you're late, the boy dies, if you bring in the FBI, or I see another cop, he dies. Tell me you understand."

Deputy Marsh returned to the room and nodded to Parker. He hit the speaker function on the phone. "I understand."

"We'll see if you do. Be at the Westfield Mall, near the arena's east entrance. You have twenty minutes."

Castaneda disconnected the call.

"He has Miguel."

"I heard. Johns and Tully are standing by. Whatever you need. We're there."

"He can't know you're following. I'd be a fool if I wandered around blind with this guy."

"Why take Miguel? He's just a kid," she said.

"Leverage. He wants me."

"I've got to move. I don't have much time to get north to the mall."

"What do you need me to do?"

"Stay close. I'll keep you up to speed on the drop. I can't risk Castaneda hurting Miguel because I didn't follow through."

"And Johns and Tully? What do I tell them?"

"Have them head to Goodyear and stand by. I don't know where this is going. The Mall is an open, public setting. I don't know what he'll do. Anything going on there tonight?"

Linda pulled up a browser on her phone. Her brow knitted. "A Phoenix Coyotes home game. Gates don't open for another hour. Chicago. There will be tons of Blackhawks fans in the mall. He couldn't have planned it better."

"I'll let you know what's up."

Parker trotted to his SUV, opened the back hatch, and removed the black nylon cash bag. He jumped in his personal vehicle, a four-wheel-drive Jeep, and backed out, tires barking when he shot down the street.

Game night traffic near the Westfield Mall snarled the access roads, and acres of the parking lot were roped off for the twenty-thousand hockey fans descending on the arena. Blackhawk jerseys were everywhere, attesting to the Midwest snowbird population's origins.

Parker tucked his Jeep in the closest parking slot he could find and hoofed it to the plaza in front of the arena, lugging the black nylon bag.

The gates hadn't opened, and the fans crowded the front of the arena complex. A few hockey fans started partying early and were well into a beer buzz. Parker scanned the crowd for Miguel and Castaneda. They'd be hard to find within the teeming mass.

At a spot between the east gate and the main entrance, Parker leaned against a barrier and studied each face as it passed. He glanced at his watch every few minutes, and the deadline passed. Nothing from Castaneda. The crowds pushed into the arena until a handful remained outside.

A text message alert sounded on his phone. Tully and Johns parked a block away in a casino parking lot. Parker gave a quick response and pocketed the phone. The phone Castaneda left for him was silent. Soon the only people near the arena gates were the ticket scalpers, who were careful to remain two-hundred feet from the stadium entrance as required by the local ordinance.

Parker strolled to the east entrance, now empty of ticketed hockey fans when he spotted one scalper holding a cardboard sign. "Parker," written in thick black Sharpie.

He jogged to the scalper, a tall, thin, balding man who twitched like he was on a three-day meth binge.

"You want tickets?" The scalper said with sour breath.

"What's with the sign?"

"Dude paid me to hold this until some guy named Parker shows up. How many tickets you need? I'll give you a good deal."

"What you supposed to do when Parker comes?"

The man squinted. "You him? Parker, I mean."

"Yeah." Parker tensed and glanced into the adjoining parking lot for Miguel.

"I'm supposed to give you this." The scalper dropped the cardboard on the ground and fished a folded envelope out of his back pocket.

"Who gave this to you?"

"Some guy. You should know. He said you and your kid were gonna go on a little drive."

"Hand it over."

"What do I get in exchange?"

Parker pulled his badge. "How about an all-expense paid weekend in tent city? You said you already got paid." Parker snatched the envelope from the scalper's hand.

The folded, wrinkled envelope was wet with sweat.

"Damn, don't gotta be all shitty about it." He threw up his hands and skulked away.

Parker tore the flap open and pulled out a single folded sheet of paper. The typewritten note inside with a Phoenix address. Nothing further.

The East Buckeye Road address was familiar, but Parker couldn't place it. He entered the address into the search engine on his phone, and it traced to the Phoenix Greyhound bus terminal near the airport.

He called Tully and Johns while he jogged back to his Jeep.

"He's sending me on a snipe hunt. I'm heading to the bus terminal on East Buckeye Road."

"Don't get on a bus. We can't cover what happens inside," Tully said.

"I might not have a choice. I think he's doing this to make sure I'm not bringing a Sheriff's posse with me. He'll be watching."

"We'll hang way back from the terminal if you need us to swoop in and save your ass."

"Put your superhero cape away, Pete. I got a feeling Castaneda's going to be running me all over the valley before we make the drop."

The bus terminal was tucked into an industrial district near the airport. The grey concrete brick and red trim was a busy metropolitan terminal with ten gates leading out to waiting buses. As Parker entered, a boarding announcement sounded over the public address system for a last call for the bus to Las Vegas.

Castaneda's note didn't carry additional information, only the bus terminal address. Parker scanned the seats, ticket lines, and vending machine lines for Miguel. Once he was certain neither Miguel nor Castaneda was in the terminal, Parker approached the gate doors, peering outside.

"Nathan Parker to the information desk. Nathan Parker—to the information desk." A woman's voice called out over the address system.

Parker searched for the information desk and spotted a long counter at the back of the terminal. Before he made his approach, he glanced in the terminal's restroom and the smoking area, to make sure Castaneda wasn't waiting for him. Any of these unfamiliar faces could work for the Los Muertos hitman.

He stepped up to the information desk where a small, older woman perched on a tall stool. Her legs dangled from the stool, and her cloudy eyes locked on Parker.

"Can I helps you?"

"You called over the intercom. Nathan Parker."

"Oh, yes. I have something for you here. Let me see where I put it." She patted the desk surface, and her gnarled fingers found a ticket. She held it up, inches from her eyes. "Here it is." She held it out for him.

"What's this?"

"Baggage claim. Outside, around the corner." She pointed to the exit.

"Where'd this come from?" Parker asked.

"Someone said they found it. You should be careful. I was about to give up on you. I paged you three times."

Parker hadn't heard the two earlier calls. "You know who it was who found it. I'd like to thank them."

"No. I don't. My eyesight isn't what it used to be."

"Thank you."

She nodded and pointed at the exit. "Out and to the right."

Parker spotted the Package Express sign and was a bit relieved he wasn't boarding a bus to Barstow. He handed the clerk the claim check. A minute later, the clerk hefted a three-foot-long cardboard box and plopped it on the counter.

"Sign here," the clerk asked, holding a clipboard for Parker.

Parker scrawled his name and carried the box to the hood of his jeep. It wasn't heavy, but felt bulky. Parker used a pocket knife to slice the tape on the top of the box. Inside, a black zippered case. Tugging on a heavy zipper, Parker parted the heavily padded canvas sides, and the sunlight gleamed off a disassembled Remington 700 sniper rifle. Another folded letter lay on top of the blue steel barrel.

Parker unfolded it, and a photo fell out. Tim Brunell's face stared back at him. The text of the note sent a chill up Parker's spine. "Six hours. Brunell or the boy. One must die. You choose."

Chapter Thirty-Six

Parker hit redial on the burner cell, and there was no answer. Castaneda dumped his phone. There wouldn't be an easy way to trace the man. Glancing at the note, Parker couldn't imagine turning into Castaneda's hitman, but it's exactly what the Los Muertos assassin wanted. A life for a life.

A series of rationalizations shot through his brain. The value of one life over another, the worth of a man's character. Miguel's unrealized potential hit him the hardest. One life to be snuffed out at Castaneda's command. Parker would sacrifice himself before he harmed Miguel. Murdering Tim Brunell was the emotional choice, but Parker couldn't become an extension of Los Muertos, killing on command. Castaneda wouldn't stop with Brunell. And, Parker knew, even if he did as Castaneda ordered, Miguel's safety was far from guaranteed.

Saving Miguel meant he needed to find the Los Muertos kingpin first. Castaneda's hair-trigger meant Parker needed to act fast. He'd failed McMillan and was too late to save Juan Estrada. He couldn't make the mistake again. Not with Miguel's life held in the balance.

Parker zipped up the rifle bag and tossed it in the front seat of his Jeep. He cast his eyes from car to car passing in the street and those parked along the street in front of the bus terminal. Castaneda would be watching. Parker could feel the man's presence.

Pulling out of the Greyhound terminal, Parker kept checking his mirrors. The paranoia ticked up a few levels when he spotted a black sedan run a red light and pull behind him. Careful to stay two or three cars back, the dark car switched lanes as Parker maneuvered through traffic. The outline of two people in the plain-looking sedan shown in Parker's rearview. No front plate visible, although Arizona didn't require one.

After three miles, the black car held steady, veering out occasionally to make sure Parker's SUV was in sight. Parker waited for the next check, and as the black car veered left, he cut right into the far lane. Seconds later, the black car merged into the traffic behind him.

Parker spun the wheel and fishtailed down the next street. He floored the accelerator and shot down the two-lane road. He bounced over a speed bump and into a parking lot, tucking his SUV behind a delivery truck.

He slunk down behind the wheel and waited. Thirty seconds later, the black sedan crept past. The tinted window made it impossible to identify his pursuers. When the car pulled past, Parker shot out into the parking lot toward the street, to find it blocked by a second black sedan. Trapped.

The sedan ahead sat diagonally in the entrance, and the man stepping from the passenger seat wasn't one of Castaneda's thugs. FBI Special Agent Collins ambled to the front of the car and leaned against the hood.

The second black car turned around in the lot and now sat idling behind Parker's vehicle.

Parker shut off his engine and opened the door. Collins wasn't acting like this was a felony stop. He wasn't holding Parker at gunpoint, ordering him down on the hot asphalt. The look on the FBI agent's face was annoyance.

"What's up, Agent Collins?" Parker said, climbing out of his Jeep.

"Mind telling me where you were going?"

"Out for a drive."

"Really, Parker? You want to play it like this?"

"Like what?"

"Agent Finch said you'd spot us. What gave it away?"

"The tail? It wasn't hard to spot. I mean, Jeez, drive a Prius once in a while. How come you're following me?"

Collins spread his arms wide. "Don't you know the cavalry when you see it? You can't leave a dead body out in the desert and walk away."

Juan's body—the kid Castaneda murdered at Rocky Wash.

Parker didn't know how to begin. Castaneda warned him to keep law enforcement out if he wanted to keep Miguel alive.

"Deputy Marsh and the Carson woman told us what's going on. What are you thinking, going after Castaneda by yourself?"

"Listen, if he thinks you're involved, Miguel's dead. I can't risk it."

Collins put his hands up. "I get it, I do. But you're playing into his hands."

"If Castaneda so much as sees me talking to you, it's over for the kid."

"I know, I know. I'm not saying you need to step aside and let us take over. I'm suggesting a little help if you need it."

Parker heard a clunk from behind him. An FBI agent shimmied out from under his Jeep.

"It's a GPS tracker and transmitter." Collins caught a small plastic object from the agent and handed it to Parker.

"A key fob?" Parker asked, looking at the Jeep logo on the front of the black plastic case.

"Agent Finch and I would feel better if you used this one if you're determined to do your lone wolf routine."

"My Jeep doesn't even come with electric locks."

"You can pretend to live the high life. You've probably guessed this isn't a panic button. Hit that red button on the back the minute you have Castaneda in sight. Don't get drawn into his game. There's a tactical team on standby, and the minute you have eyes on him, press that button, and we'll swoop in."

"I'm more concerned about freeing Miguel and another kid Castaneda has."

"You have a photo of Miguel? I want to show it to the tactical guys so they can spot him."

Parker found one on his phone and sent it to Collins.

"Nice looking kid," Collins said. "How old?"

"Seventeen."

"My sympathies. Tough age. Wanna be all grown, but not ready to leave the nest. I got three of them."

"That's a handful."

"Tell me about it. The oldest is applying for colleges, and there is no way he's ready to live halfway across the country."

"Miguel's the same. Wants his independence and gets frustrated because he thinks I treat him like a kid. After what he's been through, leaving El Salvador and making a new home in a strange land, I understand why he wants to make his own path—his own place in the world."

"Agent Finch told me about how you met him and how the Sinaloa Cartel nabbed him coming over the border. Something like that could mess a kid up."

Parker nodded. "His resilience amazes me."

"All right, where you meeting Castaneda? I need to get the team staged."

"I don't know where he is. He's had me running all over the valley. He'll contact me when he contacts me."

Collins eyed Parker and crossed his arms across his chest. He pushed off the car. "You know how to reach us when he does. Don't be stupid. The kid's life might depend on it."

Collins stepped back to his vehicle, and the driver backed the sedan from the lot, followed by the second black vehicle.

Parker was alone, except for the GPS tracker on his Jeep and Castaneda's sniper rifle. A glance at his watch told him he had five and a half hours to find Miguel, or Castaneda would expect him to kill Brunell.

Chapter Thirty-Seven

Parker dropped the black nylon bag with the disassembled Remington 700 rifle on Tully's desk, startling the detective.

"I know it ain't Christmas, boss. What did ya bring me?"

"Get this down to the lab geeks and have them run ballistics. Did we ever pull the results on the barrel pieces we found in Clement's storage locker?"

Tully rolled back in his chair. "Nothing yet. They got a lot going on down there. Said might take a day or two. I thought it was fine since Clement is dead and all."

"I got this from our friend, Castaneda."

"You what? Word on Miguel?"

"Get the ballistics on both rifle barrels. I want to know which one was used in the Sun Valley Sniper cases."

Tully picked up the phone. Parker slammed his finger on the receiver.

"Get up and walk this down to the lab. Light a fire under them and make sure they know there is no higher priority."

Tully blinked. "Yeah, okay. What's going on, boss? Miguel?"

"Nothing yet. Castaneda wouldn't give me this rifle for no reason. I need you to check this out for me, Pete."

Parker didn't include the demand he murder Tim Brunell.

Pete grabbed the bag and strode to the door.

"Thanks, Pete. Tell them the clock's ticking on this. I need to know the second they have a read on it."

"I won't leave them until they finish."

"Barry?"

"Should be back any minute. Finishing up with the Estrada kid's family."

Parker nodded. "Thanks, Pete. Let me know what they come up with."

Pete left with the sniper rifle Castaneda delivered to Parker. Why would he provide him with the means to kill Brunell? Why not simply point out the target? The drama of it was Castaneda's style.

Parker stepped into his office and called Lynette Finch. Once past her guardian, Parker heard Lynne, "Is this the Lone Ranger calling for help?"

Parker let the comment pass. "Lynne, I know you're watching Tim Brunell."

"Why would we watch?"

"Save it, Lynne. Castaneda is coming for him."

"What would he have against Brunell?"

"I'm working on a thread Brunell mentioned. The Immigrant Coalition's been hiring Castaneda's people to coyote migrants over the border."

"Los Muertos?"

"Brunell cut them out of their operation, and Castaneda took exception."

"How is it you know this?"

"Brunell told me about the relationship. And Castaneda wants me to kill Brunell."

"What?"

"If Brunell isn't served up on a platter in," Parker checked the office wall clock, "five hours, he'll kill Miguel."

"Jesus, Nathan. He can't—you can't."

"He will, Lynne. You know what this guy is."

"We can help find him—"

"Do you have a fix on Brunell or not?"

"Nathan, what are you going to do?"

"Whatever it takes."

Nathan hung up.

He shuffled through the notes on the surface of his desk and found the number for the Immigrant Coalition offices. He called, and no one answered.

"Dammit!" Parker slammed the phone down on the receiver.

The shaking movement of the desktop woke up the computer on Parker's desk. The screen blossomed to life, and Nia Saldana's mysterious spreadsheet filled the screen. Line upon line of numbers. Code? From all accounts, Nia wasn't an undercover agent ferreting secrets from the undocumented community.

Parker's hand closed around the USB drive as he prepared to pull it from his computer. He spotted a pattern among the numbers; the same series of letters and numbers preceded many of the lines. The label on the first column was CLABE.

Parker opened another window and punched in CLABE into a search engine. The hit identified CLABE as Clave Bancaria Estandarizada, the standard for identifying bank accounts in Mexico.

"What were you up to, Nia?"

Parker ran a finger down the spreadsheet on the screen. The lines with the Mexican Bank account were revealing deposits regularly—significant deposits. On the page Parker opened, there were at least a quarter-million dollars in transfers.

Was Nia money laundering for the Cartel? From everything her sister described, she didn't seem the type. She came off as a woman who put her children first, and laundering cash for organized crime didn't scream "Mom of the Year."

A rapping at the door got Parker's attention. Barry Johns stepped in, looking a bit worn. His tie was loosened, and his eyes were puffy.

"Any word on Miguel?"

"No, Castaneda's gone dark. I'm expecting him to pop up and tell me where to go next."

Johns dropped a clear plastic evidence bag on Parker's desk. "Juan Estrada's belongings."

"How did the next of kin notification go?"

"One of the tougher ones. Large family. He was the oldest of seven kids. Mom collapsed at the news. Everything seemed to be going for the kid. He had a job, going to college, ran with a good crowd. Then this happens. Juan's father said they left home in Guatemala to escape the violence. It followed them here."

"They know of any connection with Juan and Los Muertos?"

"They're aware of them, like anyone hopping the border, but I didn't feel a sense they knew of any interaction between their son and the gang."

Johns poked a finger at the plastic surface of the evidence bag. "I found this inside the kid's wallet." He withdrew a three-by-five creased photograph from his jacket pocket. "Thought you should have it."

The photo featured Miguel, Juan, and Tomaso mugging for the camera. They posed in front of a graffiti-stained concrete wall with broad smiles. The back of the photo bore a single word "Hermanos," brothers.

"Thanks." Parker tucked the photo next to his computer screen.

"Say, Barry, you worked on that European crime ring using local business to launder drug money, didn't you?"

"Ivan the Car Wash King. Yeah, cash flowing in from all over the western states."

"How'd they unravel the money trail?"

"Ivan got greedy, started siphoning off cash from the payoffs, and someone dropped a dime on him."

"I got something here. I don't know how it's related. Remember Nia Saldana—the woman killed in the accident when Roger Jessup was shot?"

"Uh, huh."

"She ended up with a USB drive full of what looks like financial transactions when she died. The family swears she didn't even own a computer."

"She ran a cleaning service, didn't she? What would she be doing with that?"

"Coupled with what her sister told me—she got most of her work from referrals from the Immigrant Coalition. Something's going on there, and I can't quite put my finger on it."

"I know some people in financial crimes. Want me to run it by them?"

Parker disconnected the USB drive from his computer and handed it to Johns.

"I've gotten as far as identifying some of these transactions hit accounts in Mexico. Don't know why, or who was involved in either end of the deal. Could be something, could be nothing, but I can't help asking myself why Nia Saldana would end up with it?"

"On it. I'll run this down and see if we can find out. If she was money laundering for the Cartel, it could blow back on what's left of her family here. Hope it doesn't come to that."

"Me either. Thanks, Barry."

Parker's desk phone rang, and the caller ID made him sigh. "I gotta get this. Thanks again, Barry."

Parker closed his eyes and picked up the phone. "Hi, Lynne. Didn't think I hear from you—well—like ever again."

"Listen, Nathan, deep down, I know you're a good man. You've always done the right thing. I didn't always agree with how you got it done, but I don't think you're one of the bad guys."

"Okay—thanks—I think."

"Tim Brunell is at City Hall and will give a press conference in twenty minutes. It is supposed to be an announcement about his Senate run. That's all we could find out. It was a last-minute kind of thing. I hear the news media are scrambling to set up for it."

Parker felt his heart rate increase. He stood from his desk with the phone held tight to his ear. "Thank you, Lynne."

"Don't make me regret this, Nathan."

"When have I ever caused you regret—never mind. Castaneda wants the man dead. I don't. I need him alive. He can give up the goods on Castaneda and Los Muertos."

"Agent Collins is heading to City Hall."

"Is the event inside or on the street?"

"Outside."

"Of course it is. Grandstanding is pure Brunell."

"If Castaneda has a torpedo in the crowd, we might not know until it's too late. You be careful, Nathan."

"Thanks, Lynne," Parker said to a dead connection.

Parker patted his service weapon on his hip. He stole a glance at the photo of Miguel and his friends. He snagged it and shoved it in his jacket pocket. He wanted Miguel with him for what he had to do next.

Chapter Thirty-Eight

For a hastily announced press event, the sidewalks in front of city hall were teeming with onlookers. There were none of the sign-toting street protesters this time, but fifty to sixty people were pressing toward the city hall steps. And unlike the last gathering, the crowd was predominately white. A few backward baseball caps with "Build the Wall" and "Go Back Home" gave a forecast of where this crowd was heading.

Parker watched the assembly from across the street. Isa weaved through the crowd, passing out Brunell for State Senate banners. He spotted Agent Collins sitting on a concrete wall sipping on a white paper cup. He wasn't hard to find during what was looking like an Aryan Nation meeting.

He waited until Collins nodded to him before joining him on the short concrete wall.

"This doesn't feel like a pro-migrant rally, does it?"

Collins raised his coffee cup and, instead of taking a sip, spoke into a microphone hidden in the plastic cover.

"Alpha-1, status?"

Parker couldn't hear the response as the transmission went to a small earwig receiver in Collins' left ear.

"Affirmative. Press conference is scheduled to start in ten minutes."

Collins tipped his cup at Parker. "Nice of you to set this up for us, Detective."

"Wasn't me. This is all Brunell. He knows Castaneda is gunning for him. He missed once and isn't likely to make the same mistake again. This is a ballsy move."

"Does he want to draw him out?"

"If he did, he would've reached out to the Sheriff or the police, and he did neither, from what I hear. I don't know what this is about. Based on his reaction after Castaneda shot up the Coalition office, I'd put my money on another bash at law enforcement for not keeping the public safe."

"Or, how about don't get in bed with criminals? Yeah, Agent Finch told me about Brunell and Castaneda's deal to smuggle immigrants over the border."

"How many people you have here?" Parker asked.

"One on the building to the left, one on top of city hall, and three in the crowd."

"You believe Castaneda will make a move here?"

"He's angry enough. If not him, he'd send a soldier to make a move on Brunell."

Collins tapped his ear. "We're about to find out. Come on."

Collins hopped off the wall and trotted across the street into the back of the crowd. Parker followed on his heel and waded into the gathering.

Two news crews positioned cameras on tripods pointed at a wooden podium. A red and white "Brunell for a Safer Community" banner was plastered to the front.

The city hall doors opened, and Brunell strode to the podium. His posture, stiff and determined. He gripped the podium with both hands, and from where Parker stood, he felt the man's presence.

He wasn't the only one. A chorus of cheers greeted him from the people closest to the podium. From among the back of the gathering, where Parker and Collins stood, the mood was darker.

Brunell waved to quiet his supporters and began reading from a folded paper he withdrew from his breast pocket.

"Hours ago, I became another statistic. Another needless crime victim.

"There will be those who are quick to blame the immigrant community for this violence. Make no mistake, the criminals who targeted me are from another country, but they are not from our immigrant community."

"What's the difference?" a potbellied man wearing a border patrol hat shouted.

"I'll tell you the difference," Brunell said. "The people who come to our country to make a better life for themselves and their families, the same people who work to make sure you're fed, your homes are cared for, and—"

A pair of men began shoving one another at the base of the stairs.

"Alpha-1, you see this?" Collins said into his microphone.

Collins cupped his ear to shield out the growing crowd noise around him.

"Castaneda?" Parker asked. His heart rate raced at the thought of getting the Los Muertos killer and putting Miguel out of harm's way.

"Gun!" someone yelled in front of Parker.

Collins and Parker pushed through the crowd, shoving bystanders as they waded in.

Parker spotted two men tussling. A large, red-bearded man with a black leather vest grappled with another smaller man in a long-sleeved blue t-shirt. The man in the t-shirt had his back to Parker, but the man's build, and his black, slicked hair, looked like Castaneda. The long sleeves covered any identifying tattoo on the man's arm.

The men struggled with one another, and their hands locked around a handgun. The blue steel barrel glinted as the two men fought for control.

Two men from the crowd rushed the podium and shoved Brunell back. Both wore FBI badges hanging from chains around their necks.

Parker and Collins closed on the combatants. Collins locked his hands around the barrel of the gun, controlling the direction of the weapon. He wrenched the barrel downward, and the man screamed when a bone cracked.

Parker dove on Castaneda's back, pinning him to the concrete, face down.

"Where is he, you son-of-a-bitch? Where's Miguel?"

Parker handcuffed the man and rolled him over.

"Who's Miguel?" the strange man asked.

He wasn't Castaneda. The logo on the front of his t-shirt read, "Defend our Borders."

"What the hell were you doing?"

"People like him make our country weak."

"So, you decided you were going to shoot him?"

"Hell, no. It wasn't my gun. That biker asshole thought it'd be fun to pop off a couple rounds."

"Why?"

"Ask him."

Collins handcuffed the large pot-bellied biker and needed to cuff him with his hands in front because the man was too fat to cuff from behind. Red beard cradled his hand, with an index finger pointing in the wrong direction.

Brunell shrugged off his protectors and returned to the microphone. The event was captured on live television, and the candidate would not let the opportunity slip away.

"Is this what we've come to? We resort to violence whenever we disagree with one another? We are better than this. We have to be better than this. For as long as this country has existed, we welcomed those who wish to come here to escape violence and persecution. People are dying here from the very thing they fled their homes from. We must be a better example."

A few murmurs of support rose from the crowd.

"Criminals are cowards. They prey upon the most vulnerable in our society. As we witnessed with the recent shooting spree by the Sun Valley Sniper, a known white supremacist targeted members of the immigrant community and their allies. As law enforcement closed in on him, the coward took his own life."

Uniformed Phoenix Police officers took the two handcuffed combatants away.

Collins brushed the dust from his pant leg and joined Parker.

"I want it noted that I took the big guy," Collins said.

"This was your party, after all."

Collins tipped his head at Brunell. "The Sniper—that's not how I heard it went down."

"Don't have the M.E.'s report, but it's safe to say it wasn't suicide."

"Then what's he peddling?"

"Smoke. It's all a smoke screen."

A young man tapped Parker on the shoulder.

He was brown-skinned, five and a half feet tall and thin. His clothes were grimy and well-worn.

"Are you Nathan Parker?"

"What is it?" The hair on the back of his neck tingled.

"I'm supposed to give you this."

The young man held a sealed envelope and extended it to Parker.

"Who gave this to you?" Parker knew the answer. He glanced around, looking for Castaneda.

"A terrible man. He told me to give this to you, or he'd kill my family. I know he'll do it. Please take it."

Parker took the envelope. "How did you know to find me here?"

"He dropped me off here and said he knew you'd be here because of him," he said, pointing at Brunell.

"How did you know to find me in this crowd?"

"He gave me this." He pulled a photo from his pants pocket. And the image buckled his knees. A photo of Parker and Miguel at a Diamondbacks game. The crease in the paper meant it came from Miguel's wallet.

"Have you seen him? Miguel?" Parker pointed at the photo image.

The kid nodded.

"Where, where is he? Is he okay?" Parker grabbed the man by his arms.

The young man pulled away. "I don't know, I swear. They kept us in small cages. I know it's north of here because there are Palo Verde trees and cactus on the hillside I could see. They put a hood on my head, and they drove me here. I thought I was going to die."

"He let you go?"

"As long as I did everything he asked."

Parker tore open the envelope and withdrew another photo. This new image bore a date and timestamp today less than two hours ago. They tied Miguel to a metal pole in a wire cage. His lip was bloodied, and his left eye swollen shut.

"Did you see this?"

The kid nodded.

"This was taken before they drove you here."

Another nod.

Proof of life.

Parker removed another folded slip of paper. He unfolded the page, and a handwritten statement burned onto the page. *The deal's off.*

"What?"

"I'm sorry, but I don't have a choice." The young man pulled a stubby, black semi-automatic handgun from his waistband and pointed it at Parker. He held a cell phone in his other hand, filming what he was about to do.

Parker backed off a half step before the man trained the weapon on Brunell. Tears filled the young man's eyes.

The crack of the gunshot rang out in the city hall plaza.

Chapter Thirty-Nine

The young man lay motionless on the pavement where he fell. The crowd panicked and fled in all directions, escaping while a few shouted out "active shooter," fearing a gunman roamed the city hall plaza.

Parker knelt over the dead man. The look in the man's eyes before the shot ending his life was sorrow, regret, and desperation. The expression would etch deep into Parker's soul. He wasn't angry at the man, even though he intended to kill him. Castaneda gave the poor kid no choice. Kill him, or Castaneda would massacre his entire family.

Collins stooped close and gathered the black semi-automatic handgun. He removed the magazine, racked back the slide, and ejected a round from the chamber.

"Alpha-1, confirmed. Target down, weapon secure." Then to Parker, "You all right?"

Parker pocketed the dead man's cell phone and struggled to his feet. "One of your guys take him down?"

Collins nodded.

"Damn Castaneda. A coward, making a poor kid like him do his dirty work."

"This isn't one of his soldiers?"

"Hardly. Castaneda threatened he'd kill his family if he didn't take me out. Wanted me to know it, too. Gave me a note saying the deal was off."

"Deal? The deal Agent Finch told me about? The one where Castaneda wanted you to take out Brunell?"

It didn't surprise Parker Finch passed on his conversation with her.

He locked eyes with Collins. "Your sharpshooter up there. He was looking at me, wasn't he?"

Collins shrugged it off. "Aren't you glad he was?"

"This kid was my ticket to finding where Castaneda's holding Miguel. I needed him to help me figure it out. They threw a hood on him, but he knew where they were holding him, the sounds, smells even. Now, I—I don't know where to start."

Ahead of him, a news camera lay toppled over. The second one was still running with a camera operator shooting footage of the aftermath. Brunell for Senate signs trampled on the steps, an overturned podium, and a law enforcement presence sweeping through the area.

"Where's Brunell?"

"Inside city hall."

"I need to see him."

Collins grabbed Parker by the elbow.

"That's not happening."

Parker jerked his arm out of Collin's grasp. "What do you mean? He needs to tell me what he knows about Castaneda. He's in bed with Los Muertos and paying them to traffic migrants over the border. He knows more than he's giving up."

"We'll take it from here. If there's any evidence of his involvement in human trafficking or migrant smuggling, hand it over and stay out of my way."

Parker clenched his fists. He knew a bureaucratic stonewall was inevitable, but Parker didn't think the Feds would step in so quickly. A public attempted murder is hard to ignore. Collins was right. Brunell was a shrewd politician. The scant evidence was hidden in Brunell's own words.

Throwing up his hands, Parker backed away, taking a last glance at the dead man who carried Castaneda's secrets to the grave. He shoved the photo of Miguel in his back pocket and uttered a brief prayer for Miguel and the dead man. Hopefully, they wouldn't share the same fate.

Parker drifted away from city hall and leaned against a building a block away. His chest tightened; it was hard to breathe. A panic attack. He hadn't felt one since his partner, McMillan, was killed. For a month after the murder, Parker suffered daily panic attacks where he felt like he was going to die.

He attended counseling off the books because he didn't want the stigma following him. The sessions were provided by the department, but he knew the reactions he'd face from deputies, who wondered if he'd crack again when they depended on him. Best to keep that stuffed down where it could fester in its own juices. It didn't help to hear his physical and emotional reactions were normal after a traumatic event. He knew what normal was, and this didn't feel normal. He wasn't the one shot after all.

The self-imposed isolation was partially responsible for ending his relationship with Lynnette Finch.

The panic attack today surprised him. A man pointed a gun at him and prepared to kill him—and would have if an FBI sniper didn't take him out first. That he was also considered a target by the same gunman didn't calm his breathing, either. But it was losing Miguel that hurt the most and made him feel absolutely helpless, exactly like the night he lost McMillan.

The Sheriff's Office pushed to lessen the negative stigma mental health issues carried. Still, the Old Guard, and Parker considered himself one, felt if you couldn't deal with your own demons, you weren't fit to carry a badge. That old line of thought was responsible for the skyrocketing alcohol abuse, domestic violence, and suicide rate plaguing the profession.

Lynne tried to convince him to find help, take a leave of absence, and take time to heal from his partner's death. The administrative time off he was forced to take after the incident forced him to ruminate over finding his partner bleeding out on the road. Over and over.

Instead, he threw himself back into the job. Extra hours, extra shifts, anything to avoid the downtime where McMillan's murder would creep out from the darkness.

Here he was again, paralyzed by fear.

"Shit. Get it together, Nathan."

"Detective Parker? Are—are you all right?"

Isa, Brunell's Immigrant Coalition assistant and recently appointed campaign manager, stood a few feet away. She looked lost and as fragile as Parker felt.

"Fine—fine, I'm fine." The mantra of the unwell everywhere.

"Detective, Tim has to be stopped."

She reached and grabbed his arm, steadying both of them.

"I'm sorry, Isa. I don't understand."

She pointed two storefronts down to a coffee shop. "I think we could both do with a sit-down."

Parker felt the cool air-conditioning the second the door cracked open. After ordering a couple of iced coffees, they found a quiet table in the back.

The first swig of caffeine hit Parker's system, and his mind began to unfreeze. He'd felt this before and joked the stimulant was a brain lubricant.

"This was a good idea, Isa. Thanks for suggesting it. I'm a bit off after that poor kid died in front of me. There was nothing I could do to help him."

She clamped her manicured hands around her cup. "This is the second time someone's been shot at in less than twenty-four hours. Tim doesn't care as long as the fundraising keeps going."

"I'm sorry. Your boss seems to bring out the worst in people."

"He's always done it. Antagonizing the far right was fun for him. This is far different. People around us are dying, and he's concerned about his precious poll ratings. He should be happy now. This is going to make him a martyr."

"How's that? A kid got himself killed. Because of a Los Muertos thug."

Isa's forehead wrinkled up. "That's not the way Tim's spinning it. Two reporters hustled inside with Tim and the two officers who pulled him away from the podium. He does this every single time—people get hurt, and he comes out pretending to be the hero."

"FBI Agents—"

"FBI? The FBI is onto him?" Isa stiffened.

"Why don't you tell me what's going on, Isa."

She drew a deep breath. Her coffee cup remained in front of her, untouched.

"Tim is—ugh, Tim isn't even his real name."

Parker nodded and took a sip of his coffee, encouraging her to fill in the gaps in what he knew about the man.

"I connected with him in my last year of law school. I wanted to be an attorney to start over—start a new life for myself, and it led to an intern gig at the Coalition. The organization was brand new, him and Roger. They wanted to set up the Coalition as a legitimate not-for-profit entity, and my job was to pull the filing documents together to make it happen. Roger was the idea man behind the operation—always was. It was his idea to secure not-for-profit status for fundraising. Tim was the public face—the used car salesman who would court big money donations to the cause."

"What was the cause? Back then?"

"At first, it started as sponsoring a migrant family. You know, the people who come here and have absolutely zero when it comes to resources, and their families end up hungry and homeless. There was no shortage of them—still isn't, really. But one family grew to five, to a dozen, and before we knew it, hundreds of undocumented were supported, housed, and given a foot up by the Immigrant Coalition.

"Go back to your non-profit work. That's when you realized Tim Brunell isn't his real name." Not a question, a statement.

"I knew before Roger. I was ready to file the Coalition's paperwork, and Tim told me to hold off."

"Because you couldn't file with his name."

"Exactly. Roger didn't even know."

"He ever say why he changed his name?"

"He was running from his past. I mean, we run up against skeletons in our closets, Detective. But this one, he wanted it kept a secret."

"A secret he kept from Roger?"

"What Ruben Burns did, he didn't want his business partner to know about it. They had a big blow-up over it."

"Ruben Burns? How did Roger take the news?"

"It was tense for a long time. I needed to file the not-for-profit with Roger's name only."

"I thought I saw Brunell's name on the documents, too."

"Eventually. I refiled last year. I helped Tim, or Ruben, or whoever, petition to have his name legally changed. He insisted I file it out-of-state. I told him it wouldn't matter, but he insisted I file in San Bernardino."

"Why there? What was the reason he gave to file in California?"

"Something about a prior residence there—something along those lines. He wasn't exactly forthcoming. He let it slip—"

"He lived in San Bernardino. Not where I'd choose to live, but no mystery there."

"No, the prior address he told me to use—Central Avenue, in Chino."

Parker shook his head, unsure where she was going.

"I checked. It's the California Institution for Men. He was in prison."

Chapter Forty

"Prison? Are you kidding me? Brunell is a felon?"

"Ex-felon, apparently."

"We'll see if that holds true," Parker said.

"He left to go to live in San Bernardino for a few months while this was going on to prove he was a state resident."

"I didn't think a court would grant an ex-con a name change."

"It's discretionary. Courts in California are open to granting these petitions—if it isn't for fraudulent purposes or to avoid debt."

"Huh. Good to know."

"Any idea what he went to prison for?"

"I don't think he knew I put the pieces together."

"That history didn't come up when he filed as a candidate for State Senate?"

"Technically, he is eligible because his voting rights were deemed restored when he completed his prison sentence."

"Definitely not a history his campaign contributors would look kindly on."

"That's the weird thing. The campaign money. I've taken in donations from people Tim met with. The deposits go into his campaign account, separate and fire-walled off from the Coalition's books. Roger demanded it."

"Good idea."

"Except the money in the campaign account and a good chunk of the Coalition's funds—gone—all of it. I thought it had to be a mistake and asked our account manager at the bank about it. She told me there was no mistake, and Tim wired the money from the account."

"To Mexico?"

Her eyes widened. "Yes—how did you know? Not all at once, but the largest share ended up in accounts down south."

"What was Brunell's explanation?"

"He told me to mind my own business. This is my business. It's my business when someone takes a shot at Coalition members."

Parker's mind began sorting out the bits and pieces Isa revealed. What were the odds of the missing campaign funds wired to Mexico, coinciding with the spreadsheet found on Nia's USB?

"He never mentioned transferring any of the money?"

Isa's face lost color as she glanced over Parker's shoulder.

"Isa? What are you doing here?" It wasn't a friendly voice from behind Parker.

Parker swung around. Sofia Martinez stopped cleaning a table across the room. She dropped the paper cups, wiped her hands on her apron, and strode to where Parker and Isa sat.

"Isa, you have nerve showing up—Detective Parker? What are you doing here?"

"Miss Martinez. I take it you two are acquainted?"

"Why are you here, both of you?"

"Sofia, I'm sorry I haven't had the chance to say how sorry I was about Nia's passing. The girls? How are they handling this?"

"How are they handling this? Handling this? Like it's some minor inconvenience? To you, that's all Nia was."

"That's not fair—"

"Fair? You talk about fair? Why is my sister dead? What's fair about that? You people put her in harm's way. Told her where to go work, where to pick up cleaning supplies, and where to pick up things for their employers. Fair?"

"I'm sorry it happened. She was a beautiful spirit. I'm sure her terrible accident was simply an accident."

Parker cleared his throat. "Miss Martinez mentioned before many of the jobs Nia worked were referrals from the Immigrant Coalition."

Isa drew a shallow sip from her iced coffee. It was to bide time rather than to slake her thirst.

"She did," Sofia said. "My sister was controlled by you people. Her entire world was consumed with the Coalition. She couldn't work for anyone outside of the referrals you gave her. You even threatened her when you found out she was taking on cleaning jobs for people."

Sofia's outburst drew the attention of coffee drinkers. Heads turned, and another green-aproned employee peered over the counter.

"We did no such thing. Nia was always free to work when and where she chose. We help everyone find jobs, and we offer referrals where we can. It's what we did *for* Nia, not *to* her," Isa said.

"I know what my sister told me. The worst of them was Mr. Brunell. She'd see his face on the television, and she'd leave the room. Said he made her do things."

"What kind of things?" Parker asked.

"She said he wanted her to listen at first. She was to tell him what people were saying."

"A spy?" Parker asked.

She nodded.

"Why would he ask Nia to spy while she was cleaning houses?" Isa said.

"He told her where she had to work—they were people he said he couldn't trust."

"Your sister cleaned Roger Jessup's home right before her accident. She ever mention him?"

"The night before she died, she couldn't sleep. I found her in the kitchen, sitting in the dark. When I asked her what was wrong, she told me she needed to do something—something Brunell told her to do. She was upset because it might hurt someone else."

"Jessup?" Parker asked.

"I don't know. I think she was supposed to look for something in his house."

"What makes you say that?"

"She was worried about getting caught. She didn't want the girls thinking she was a bad person for what she had to do."

"What was she supposed to do?" Isa asked, leaning forward, listening to Sofia.

"I don't know for sure. She was to go to see Brunell after she was done."

"To tell him what she found out? To give him something?"

"My sister was not a thief."

"Was Brunell threatening her?"

"I couldn't tell. She wasn't comfortable around him. I saw them once when I drove her to the Coalition offices. She looked—I don't know—scared, maybe."

"Why didn't she speak up?" Isa asked.

"Who was she supposed to go to? He's a leader of the Coalition. Who'd believe what she had to say? She's an undocumented cleaning woman. Faceless and worthless in their eyes."

"Someone would have listened—"

"How can you say such a thing? You're one generation removed from the very place where my sister existed. One wrong move, a traffic stop, or God forbid she needs to take one of her girls to the emergency room, one mistake and they'd rip her away from her family and deport her."

Isa started to speak, and Sofia took a step backwards. "What are the two of you doing working together? You're selling out our people to the police."

Parker scooted his chair around so he could face Sofia. "Remember when we met? I told you, you could talk to me. I'm not concerned with your sister's immigration status, and I'm not after you or the girls. What I want is to find out why Nia died."

"You told me it was a car crash."

"It was—it was. I mean, why was she on the road then? A neighbor saw her run from Roger Jessup's home and leave. Roger followed her less than a minute later. Their vehicles were together in the crash. Why did Roger follow her? Now you're telling me she took something from him?"

"I never said she stole anything." Sofia was quieter now, and her tone became less confident.

"The computer drive you found in your sister's property—did she find it at Roger's?"

"She wouldn't—"

Isa perked up. "A drive? A USB drive?"

Parker nodded.

"Was it red and silver? Wait." Isa lugged her purse from the floor and plopped it on the chair next to her. After a few seconds of rummaging, she withdrew a pair of USB drives, exactly like the one Parker received from Sofia.

"That's what I found in my sister's belongings."

Parker pointed at the drives. "Immigrant Coalition drives?"

Isa shook her head. "No, I gave one of these to Roger with everything I found out about Brunell—about his felony conviction—all of it."

"I didn't see documents. Could be there. I stopped with the first thing I found, a spreadsheet."

"Roger was a spreadsheet fanatic. He was comfortable with numbers, less so with people. Kinda why he and Tim split the duties to run the Coalition that way. Tim handled the public, and Roger managed the business side. Roger would write the checks, and Tim would rack up the bills."

"If I showed you a spreadsheet, could you tell if it was one of Roger's and what it means?"

She shrugged. "Maybe. He had his own style. Roger used account codes, never labels. It would drive me nuts."

"Account codes, like bank accounts and wire transfers?"

"Yeah, I guess."

Parker pulled his cell phone and opened a file containing a photograph of the spreadsheet. He set the phone on the table and slid it to Isa. "Look familiar?"

She pulled the phone closer and bent to the small screen. Isa's forehead creased, and her jaw tightened. "This is one of Roger's sheets. I don't know what these labels across the top represent. How did you find…"

"I've got someone working on it. Question is, what was Roger tracking?

And why did Nia have it with her when she died?"

Isa leaned back. Her eyes darted as she looked away. "You said you knew Tim transferred the campaign funds to Mexico. Was this what you meant?"

"I don't know what accounts these are yet. But if it's what you're thinking it is, Tim Brunell wouldn't want this to see the light of day."

"He made Nia take it from Roger. It's why she died. It's why they both died," Isa said.

Parker took his phone back. "Wonder if it was worth killing for?"

Chapter Forty-One

"Wait, Roger Jessup was chasing my sister?"

"Not sure if it was a chase. He left his home after Nia ran out, presumably with the USB drive. They were both on the freeway together, heading in the same direction."

Isa shook her head. "I knew Roger was up to something. He kept asking me about the campaign accounts, who had access, and how we were tracking the donations coming in. He knew there was a problem. Damn, I wish he'd told me." Isa's palms pressed on the tabletop.

"What direction was my sister heading before she crashed?"

"Eastbound on the 101."

Sofia's forehead wrinkled. "It doesn't make sense. Mr. Jessup was her last house of the day. East on the 101 wouldn't take her home. She always took the 17 south."

"It makes perfect sense." Isa straightened in her chair. "East on 101 would take her to Tim's place. She was bringing him the USB drive."

"Hey Sofia, I could use your help at the register," a barista called out while drawing shots of espresso from an elaborate chrome-plated machine.

"I need to get back to work. The Coalition is responsible for my sister's death. I will make it my mission to make sure everyone in my community knows what they did and who Brunell really is—another white savior getting rich off the backs of the undocumented. It ends now."

Sofia turned on her heel and strode to the counter, where six new patrons waited to order their caffeine fix.

"I can't believe Tim used Nia to spy on Roger. What are you going to do about him? I'm heading to the office and cleaning out my desk. I will not be associated with that—that bastard anymore."

"The Immigrant Coalition did some good work for people with nothing when they land in a strange land. Tim used it for his own twisted purposes. But the mission of the organization is something not to give up on. Miguel taught me to never give up when so many need so much. I mean, look at him, he's new to this country, and he's risking everything so others like him will have a chance. Now—I've lost him."

"Lost? I'm not following?"

"He's been taken. The man you saw in the office—the maintenance man—he's a Los Muertos killer by the name of Esteban Castaneda. He's got him, and he's killed Juan Estrada."

She put a hand to her chest. "Juan and Miguel? Why would someone go after college kids? I'm so sorry, Detective."

"The kid killed back there at the city hall plaza. He was my hope of finding Miguel."

"What would someone like Castaneda want with them? I can imagine what they're going through. Is there anything I can do to help?"

"I don't know. If you hear from Brunell, or the Coalition, it might help. All I know is they held Miguel and the dead kid somewhere north. Higher elevation than the valley floor, and Miguel was in a cage."

She stiffened. "A cage. Like some kind of jail?"

"I don't know. The kid said it was a small cage."

She shook her head. "I can ask around."

"Don't. If the wrong person gets wind of us asking about the place, we might put Miguel and the others at risk."

"I'd only ask the people I trust."

"I know you wouldn't put Miguel in harm's way on purpose. I don't know how deeply Los Muertos has their claws into the Coalition. Too many people affiliated with the organization end up in a bad way. I can't risk it. Please don't. I have another idea to find the place."

Parker stood up. "Please be careful of Brunell. I don't know what he'll do next. He's acting like a desperate man."

"I've seen what desperate men can do."

Parker left Isa at the coffee shop, wondering if Sofia would tear into her again now that he wasn't there as a mediator.

On the walk back to his Jeep, he passed by the city hall plaza. The Phoenix Police Department secured the scene and collected evidence trying to recreate the scene. Under normal circumstances, he would assist.

He spotted a lean woman in a tailored blue jacket. He'd recognize her red hair anywhere. He flashed his badge at the officer at the perimeter and ducked under.

"Detective Murphy."

She turned and waved him over. "Nathan Parker, as I live and breathe. What brings you out to *my* crime scene?" she said, emphasizing her case, her jurisdiction.

"I'm not here to poach. The kid, he looks familiar. Have an ID on him yet?"

Murphy motioned for a city evidence tech. The detective asked for an evidence bag.

"According to the matrícula consular card in his wallet, the deceased is Enrique Vaszquez Ramos-Costa. Ring a bell?"

"No. Mind if I snap a photo of the card?"

"Help yourself." She held the bag out but didn't release it. She would not risk breaking the chain of custody.

Parker snapped a photo of the card with his cell.

"Twenty years old. Man. What got him to turn killer?" Murphy asked.

She didn't know Ramos-Costa was trying to kill him. If she did, it would tie him up for hours—hours Miguel may not have left.

"Thanks, Murph. I'll get out of your hair and let you get back at it."

"Nathan, you owe me a run. You promised me you were going to start running after you bottomed out with Lynne." She cast an eye at his belt line. "I see you haven't started yet."

Parker instinctively sucked in his gut. "That hurts Murph. I'll be in touch."

Detective Murphy was a long-distance runner, Boston Marathon Qualifier, and threw down ten-mile training runs at a dizzying pace. She would crush Parker and leave him gasping after a mile.

"Sure you will. Good to see you, Nathan."

"You too."

Parker retreated outside the yellow tape barrier, and Murphy went back to work directing her team.

A last glance at Ramos-Costa, a twenty-year-old who pulled a gun on him. The kid's body was now tarp-covered for some small measure of dignity. Parker dug out the kid's cell phone from his own back pocket and snapped a photo of the covered body.

Parker sat in his Jeep and called the one person he knew who would know the exact location of an abandoned dog track. Billie picked up on the first ring.

"Miguel? You have him?"

"Not yet, Billie. Castaneda backed out of the deal. Sent a damn kid to kill me."

"Good God, Nathan. You okay?"

"Not even close to okay. Billie, the kid said Miguel and others were being held in small cages. Seemed to think it's up in the hills, maybe north of here. You know of anywhere that might fit the bill? Something isolated, where Castaneda can hide?"

Billie chewed her lip for a moment. "I heard about an abandoned dog track up north. Kids usedta head there to make out and stuff. That might be where they stashed him."

"You know where?"

"It was called Black Diamond Racing. Yeah, I know where it is. Heard rumors about some drug operation runnin' the kids away from a long-time make-out spot."

"Los Muertos. Makes perfect sense. Castaneda, drug trafficking, it all comes together."

"Where you at now?"

"I'm leaving downtown."

"Take the 60 north. I'll meet you in Morristown. Look for North Castle Hot Springs Road. I'll meet you there."

"Billie, you can't run up on these guys. Los Muertos will have it guarded and locked down tight."

"Ain't my first run-in with them assholes. We're gonna come in the back way, and they'll never see us comin'."

"You sure? I don't want to make them do something stupid and hurt Miguel or the others if we get found out."

"I know the place. Been there dozens of times. Hell, I used ta park my rig there before they tore down the stands and stuff. We'll be invisible."

Parker sighed. He knew Billie memorized every rock outcropping in the north valley. Her livelihood depended on knowing where she could camp, scavenge, and hide when needed. "All right. I'll meet you at the 60 and North Castle Hot Springs. I'll look for your rig."

"I'm heading that way now. About fifty miles, Nathan."

Parker disconnected the call and pulled the Jeep into the westbound traffic. Fifty minutes was a long time. Enough time for Brunell to figure out the kid he coerced into shooting him failed in his task. Miguel would pay for the miss with his life.

Parker slipped his Jeep into the Maricopa County Sheriff's Office garage. He needed a few things before he confronted Castaneda. Parker grabbed his tactical vest and wrote out a note to Johns. "Run the name Ruben Burns and let me know the minute you get a hit. Should find a California prison record."

It was time to confront Esteban Castaneda.

Chapter Forty-Two

It was the longest fifty miles in Parker's life. His anxiety levels whipsawed every time he found himself stuck behind a big rig, making the northbound trip to Prescott and Sedona. He swore every eighteen-wheeler in the state was on the 60, and Parker would hug the center line until the gap in the southbound traffic was enough to allow him to shoot past the slow trucks. Every second's delay put Miguel closer to suffering Castaneda's vengeance. Parker pinned the gas pedal to the floor as the image of the beaten boy flashed through his mind.

Billie's battered red Toyota truck stood out at the intersection ahead. Parker pulled off the highway on the shoulder near Billie's truck. He didn't wait for the red dust cloud to settle before he shoved the door open.

Parker hopped from his Jeep and trotted to Billie's window.

"How far from here?" Parker asked.

"Five miles."

"You sure? How long has it been since you've been there? Can we make it to the dog track this way? You said it was a back road?" Parker spat out nervously.

Billie pointed to the road ahead. A faded sign on the shoulder read Black Diamond Dog Racing. A greyhound profile in the center of a diamond. It read "5 mi."

She started the truck, and the exhaust was earsplitting. Billie motioned Parker to the passenger door. He grabbed two black plastic bags of beer cans she'd collected for recycling and tossed them in the truck bed. Parker jogged back to his jeep and snagged a handful of zip-tie restraints and a spotting scope from his glove box.

Billie leaned in as Parker sat. "Sorry 'bout the noise. Some jerk stole my catalytic converter. Gonna live with it 'till I can afford to get it fixed."

"Wanna take my Jeep? Won't they hear us coming?"

Billie answered by shifting into gear and pulling onto the road. The landscape was sparse. Low-hung creosote brush popped up from the red clay desert floor.

"This can't be the place. The kid mentioned more vegetation, not less."

"Up ahead," Billie yelled over the exhaust noise.

At the crest of a small rise, clusters of Palo Verde and Scrub Oak dotted the landscape. They weren't dense, but seemed to sprout up in small groves in random spots along the road.

"There are natural springs along here. They bubble up, and you get them trees takin' advantage of the water."

Parker thought the kid who tried to kill him was held near these groves. Easy to believe they were in the higher elevation if all you saw was a green patch.

The Toyota slowed down, and Billie aimed the truck at a set of off-road tracks pitching north from the main road. It was a rough slog, and Parker's head bounced off the roof after they hit a deep rut. He grabbed the handle near the window to keep him on the seat.

A minute of bumping through the low desert brush and Billie pulled off. She shut the engine off and motioned Parker to a high spot on the road above them. They scrambled up a fifty-foot dirt trail and found themselves on a hilltop, looking across a wash to the abandoned Black Diamond Dog Track.

As the kid described, there were clusters of trees and vegetation around the site. Patches of creosote brush and Palo Verde crept through the alleyways and roads in between the remaining buildings. Parker peered across the hundred-yard wash and couldn't see where Miguel, or the others, were held. A pile of rubble dominated the foreground and butted against a flat round oval of dirt—all that remained of the track and the stands. No movement, no vehicles for an occupying Los Muertos army. It looked every bit the abandoned dog racing track.

Parker stood and took a step toward the track, but Billie pulled him back. "Get down."

"What?"

"Two o'clock at the base of the trees."

Parker squinted and couldn't spot what drove Billie's warning. He ran back to Billie's truck and snagged his spotting scope, and rejoined her on the rise. Kneeling alongside her, he raised the scope.

Billie pointed to a dark green blotch near a weathered concrete block building.

Parker held the scope to his eye and focused in on the spot. What Billie could see in the open was a green plastic tarp tied to the nearby trees for a makeshift shade cover. Movement from the shadow under the tarp drew his attention.

"Good eye Billie. Looks like we have a sentry watching this side of the wash."

"There'll be more of 'em."

"How many do you figure?"

"If it were me, two on this side, one opposite, and I'd find me a high spot for over-watch."

"At least four? Why only one on the far side of the complex?"

"There's one road into the complex, and it's gated and fenced, funnelin' into the track. All you'd need is one guy."

Parker swung his scope to the left. A flicker of sunlight glinted in the rubble of the grandstands. Parker fell flat as a shot rang over his head.

"You were right about the second man on this side. He's hidden in the broken concrete at the left edge of what used to be the stands."

"Now they know we're here," she said.

Parker crawled to the edge of the drop-off, staying in the shadow of a tree and a small rock outcropping. He pointed the scope at the first sentry and the man appeared from under the tarp and peered up at the rise, using his hand to block the sun. No binoculars, or a scope mounted on a rifle. The man grabbed an object from his belt and held it to his head. Through

Parker's scope, he recognized it as a walkie-talkie. Whatever was said, the gunman didn't rush toward them. The opposite, in fact. The sentry waved off the call, tossed the radio on a blanket, and retreated under the tarp. Pulling the scope to the left and Parker spotted a man scanning the hill with a rifle. The glint he'd seen before was from a rifle scope.

The man wore grey and black camouflaged shirt and pants, blending in with the concrete debris. Lean and compact, the shooter pulled his rifle down and held it across his chest. A moment later, he backed into the rubble and nearly disappeared beneath the broken concrete. The man leaned back and tipped his hat down over his eyes.

"They aren't coming after us."

"Probably thought you were a kid comin' up to hang out at the track. I heard they was chasin' people off. That's one way to do it."

"How do we sneak in?" Parker asked.

"Wanna wait till dark?"

"Not really."

"Then we need us a diversion."

Parker patted his pockets. "I didn't pack any."

"I got me an idea. How quick can you cross that wash?"

"Depends. Is anyone gonna be shooting at me?"

"Only if I don't draw their attention. Don't worry, I don't plan on them shootin' at me neither. We gotta draw 'em out."

"Can't imagine these guys will leave their posts to scare off a trespasser."

"They will iffen they think they're threatened."

Billie scrambled from the rise and plodded back to her truck. Parker followed and watched as she tore through the bags stacked in the bed of her truck.

"What do you need me to do, Billie?"

"You'll know when they do. Get ready to run across the wash. Be careful. I don't know how long I can keep them occupied."

"Billie, don't do anything foolish."

She cracked a smile. "When did I ever—never mind. Just be ready, and if this works like I hope it will, we'll get us some reinforcements."

225

Parker watched as she leaned over the side of the truck bed, reaching for a hidden item. She slid down to her feet and held four oil-stained road flares and a wrinkled paper bag.

"Billie?"

"There's one thing everyone out here fears. There's little chance of a fire burning out of control here in the wash, but I bet our Los Muertos thugs don't know that. They'll rush to put it out before the forest service spots the smoke."

"The reinforcements? We can't put the fire crews in danger, luring them into an armed camp."

"As soon as Los Muertos realizes they can't put it out, they'll run. They won't risk getting caught, 'specially when they hear a fire truck siren comin' at 'em."

"What's gonna keep them from putting the fire out?"

"Leave it to me. Now, you go up there and be ready to make a break across the wash when these guys come a runnin'."

Billie trotted down the road and disappeared into the tall creosote brush. She waded into the thick dry brush and kept the fragile limbs from snapping and popping, giving away her movement. Parker smiled at another example of her ability to survive in the harsh desert.

He scrambled to the rise and waited for Billie's diversion. He spotted both sentries with his scope and ran the lens across the roofline of the tallest structure within the complex. Billie swore there would be an overlook established. Parker was about to move to another structure when he caught movement on the rooftop. A man emerged from a rooftop hideaway, clad in a black t-shirt and ball cap. He shoved a rifle back on a shoulder sling and raised a pair of binoculars, and gazed into the distance.

Parker glanced to his left and found the source of the lookout's attention. A wisp of grey smoke lofted into the air. This wasn't what Billie hoped for. The sentries remained at their posts, paying no attention to the tendrils of light smoke.

Parker prepared to make a break across the wide-open expanse. This was the chance he had to rescue Miguel.

A pop sounded in the distance, near where Billie started the fire. Both sentries popped up from their posts at the sound. The smoke grew darker from the fire, and a second lighter blaze started throwing up smoke.

Parker grabbed the scope from his front pants pocket and strained to find Billie. Another pop caused the sentries to flinch and seek cover. He finally found Billie huddled behind a tree, where she took firecrackers from the wrinkled paper bag and tossed them at the flame.

The second fire began spitting out dark black smoke from the creosote brush, and Parker heard the hiss and pop of the dry brush as it burnt.

The watcher on the roof of the building spoke into a radio and waved his arms in manic gestures as he described the fires to whoever was on the receiving end of the connection. Seconds later, he disappeared from the roof. The sentries rushed toward the fire and were met with a rapid pop-pop-pop of fireworks. They fell to the ground, thinking they were gunshots.

Parker watched as their indecision unfolded. They tried to edge forward, but the smoke wafted in their direction, and the "gunfire" increased. Both men ran to the center of the complex, and Parker spotted them with his scope, talking with the man who was on the roof. A cell phone came out, and the man from the roof held a quick conversation, then motioned to the two men.

Parker sprinted across the dusty wash, his legs pumping in the thick sandy soil. His foot caught on a snag, and he tripped, landing face-first in the dirt. He didn't bother to brush himself off. He pushed up and continued his run to the edge of the central building.

As he rounded the corner, a blue truck shot away to the main exit. Four bodies were framed together in the truck's rear window. In the distance, the wail of fire engine sirens carried in on the breeze. Billie's diversion worked.

Parker came on a worn path from the building to a line of wire-framed dog kennels, presumably where the racing greyhounds were staged before their races. Something much darker happened in these cages recently. Handcuffs hung suspended from five of the kennels. Scraps of clothing lay strewn in the cages.

Castaneda used these dog cages to hold his captives. Parker patted his pocket and pulled out the photo the kid offered as proof of life. Miguel in a cage, beaten and bruised. The animal pen was the second one to the right, and Parker's gut tightened when he noticed Miguel's maroon hoodie on the dirt floor of the cage.

A banging noise from the central building caught his attention. Parker ran from the pens to an open door on the side of the structure. The Los Muertos soldiers were in a hurry and abandoned the encampment. Parker peeked inside and found three rows of larger cells, each filled with men, women, and children. Parker's arm flew over his nose. The smell was overpowering. Those who remained alive were forced to sit in their own waste. The cages weren't tall enough for a grown adult to stand.

"My God."

Parker guessed there must be fifty people penned up in the metal enclosures. At least four were dead. Most of the survivors looked frail and weak. God knows how long they were held in these conditions.

Fire department responders burst through the door and stopped in their tracks when they realized what they'd found. One doubled over and threw up.

Parker started prying locks off the cells. The captives were so weak they couldn't crawl from the cages to freedom. Firefighters began gently helping them from the pens.

When the last cell was opened, Parker circled around the survivors, looking, hoping.

Miguel was gone. Parker was too late.

Chapter Forty-Three

Parker felt his world crumble. He'd failed Miguel. The one person he'd sworn to keep safe, and he'd broken his promise. All the struggle for passage to a free country, getting an immigration visa, completing his GED, and going to college—all of it for nothing. Miguel was better off in El Salvador with the drugs, violence, and gangs.

He withdrew the creased photo of the two of them, the one Miguel tucked away in his wallet, and rubbed his thumb over the boy's image. His jaw quivered, and he was going to lose control.

"Hey, could you give me a hand over here?" an EMT called to Parker. The slight blonde EMT was struggling to pull a straggler from a cage. The frail man was older, with gray hair, thin arms, and a waxy pallor.

Parker knelt at the cage door, and despite the oppressive heat in the enclosed building, the man's clothing was soaked through with sweat, and he shivered. His eyes fluttered open and locked onto Parker's. He tried to speak, but the words were lost in his dry throat.

"Can you hear me?" the EMT said.

The man's head lolled to the side and rested against the cage's metal wire.

"He dehydrated?" Parker asked.

"Don't know. He's got an empty bottle of water in his lap. Not sure how long he's gone thirsty." She held a fresh bottle under his lips, and the old man pushed it away and mumbled.

Parker leaned close to the man and listened. "I don't understand what he's saying. Diablo, diab—I can't make it out."

The EMT felt the man's pulse. "Rapid." She leaned close to the man.

"Diabético?"

A slight nod followed by a muffled "Sí."

"Okay—okay. I'll take care of you." She began rummaging through her red plastic case.

"What can I do?" Parker asked.

"Help me pull him out of this damn cage. Who treats another human being like this?"

Parker knew exactly who—Esteban Castaneda.

He lifted the man under his thin arms and dragged him from the wire cell. The EMT rolled up a soiled blanket she pulled from a dusty corner of the building. "This will have to do." She rolled up his sleeve and inserted an IV on the first try in the man's collapsing veins. She pricked his rough fingertip and collected a blood drop on a test strip.

"Insulin?" Parker asked.

"No. This is simple saline and potassium to pump his fluids up and prevent cerebral swelling from diabetic ketoacidosis." She prepared a second IV bag and motioned her partner over with a gurney. Triaging the walking wounded in this building was a tough choice.

"Get this one started on insulin and monitor his blood glucose levels. He's above five hundred now."

Parker helped the two EMTs load the frail man to the gurney. They rolled him out, and two pairs of EMTs entered the building.

Parker felt helpless. He spotted a case of bottled water dropped off by the firefighters, and he began passing them out to the survivors waiting for their turn at treatment.

He'd ask if anyone saw the boy in the photo he held. Most simply shook their head or looked away. Until a woman squinted at stared at Parker.

"I know you," she said in halting English.

"I'm Nathan, Nathan Parker."

"Celia Cruz." She held a thin hand out to Parker. She shook his with a firm grip.

"Where did we meet?"

"Los Aztecas Mercado. You took us there after they brought us to the machine shop."

"I thought you moved on to someplace safe."

"We were until Los Muertos took us again. They threatened to kill the people who were guiding us unless they turned us over and started working for them."

"I'm sorry—I—I didn't know."

"You did what you knew to do. It gave us a chance. It's not your fault these animals came to us. But here you are."

"I know you haven't been here long, but did you see this boy?" He handed her the photo of him and Miguel.

She held the photo in both hands and waited for a moment before she spoke. "Yes, I remember him."

"He was here? Miguel?"

"Yes. They had him here. I know they took him outside to the cages where they hurt people. I'm sorry."

"I can't find him. Is he here somewhere?"

"I don't know. There has been talk of—no—I should not say." Celia quickly formed the sign of the cross over her chest.

"Talk of what?"

Her lips tightened.

"Please, where can I find Miguel?"

"On the track. We heard Los Muertos would bury people on the track, where the dirt was soft."

Parker felt sick to his stomach. He felt a hand on his shoulder. Billie made it back from her adventure.

"I never suspected they'd have this many people holed up," she said.

"Los Muertos brought us over the border. If our families didn't pay what they demanded, they would keep them until they complied." The woman's gaze at the line of dead brought tears to her eyes. "Los Muertos would change the price after we arrived. There was no possibility of meeting their demands. They would argue between them. Some men wanted to kill us and walk away."

Parker fished out his phone and brought up the photo of Esteban

Castaneda. "Ever see this man?"

She took a quick glance, and it was all she needed. "Yes. He was here. He was the big man. He would yell at his men and tell them they were going to get paid for us. I didn't understand most of what they were saying. He was going to make 'him' pay. I don't know who he meant."

The EMTs came to Celia, and Parker backed away.

Responding medical personnel and law enforcement arrived at the makeshift detention center. Parker needed air, and Billie noticed him wobble.

"Let's go outside and let these folks do their work," Billie said, tugging on Parker's arm.

She snagged a bottle of water on the way out and handed it to him. "Drink. You don't look good."

It wasn't the first time Billie made him hydrate, but at least this time, he wasn't the one buried in the desert.

"Buried."

"We don't know for sure. It could be all talk to keep them people scared."

Parker downed a long chug from the bottle, and the warm water sat heavily in his gut.

"You heard Celia, the woman in there, say Los Muertos would keep people here until the families paid for their release—ransom, basically."

"Uh-huh. They'd pull off kidnappings down south all the time. Snatch a family member of a prominent businessman and make their demands."

"If they didn't get paid?"

"Most of the time, they did. It's part of the underground economy in Hermosillo these days."

"If they didn't get paid," Parker said again.

"Detective, you don't know they done anythin' to Miguel."

"Castaneda thinks I'm dead. Why would he keep Miguel alive? He was willing to let these people rot...."

"Somethin' that woman Celia said is sticking in my head. She overheard Castaneda sayin' the big man's gonna pay. What if the big man is Brunell? What if he wants Brunell to pay for Miguel—him being a Coalition board

232

member and all?"

Parker straightened and looked at Billie. "Castaneda was pissed at Brunell for cutting off payment for bringing in groups of undocumented people. Brunell claimed he was being forced to pay Los Muertos. If the money flow suddenly stopped—"

"Los Muertos wouldn't take kindly to it and find another way to take what they think they're owed."

"The ledgers on the USB drive—if they verify payments from Brunell's campaign account to Castaneda—"

"Then they're both toast."

A uniformed Sheriff's deputy led a small pack of new arrivals into the compound. Even at a distance, Parker could read the body language—anxious, disturbed, uncertain. What made it worse were the three people wearing dark blue FBI windbreakers. Agent Collins and Lynette Finch spotted him and left the flustered Sheriff's deputy in mid-sentence.

"I thought we had an understanding, Detective?" Collins said.

"And that was?"

"Don't play ignorant, Nathan. You know full well you were to alert Agent Collins and his team when you spotted Los Muertos."

"After Collins and his sniper team targeted me at city hall, let's say my confidence is a bit shaken."

Lynne shot Collins a glare.

"We needed to cover all threats against a political candidate."

"Who happens to be laundering campaign money to a known criminal organization," Parker said.

"We've not seen any evidence of improper transactions."

"Have you looked?"

"It's not been my focus."

"Your focus is to gun down a kid who was pressured to act on behalf of Los Muertos."

"You forget he was going to kill you?" Collins said.

"Enough!" Lynne said.

She stepped between the two men. "Collins, call the bus in here for these people."

"Immigration? Lynne, they don't deserve to get locked up again and deported if they're lucky. Just look at them. They can barely walk. They need medical attention, more than the EMTs here can give. They are victims, Lynne. They could help us build a case against Castaneda and Los Muertos. We need to press ICE to grant them T Visas."

"Trafficking victims?" Collins said.

"They were taken and held by force. Starved, beaten, and a few of them died. If that doesn't define a trafficking victim, I don't know what does."

Lynne scanned the surrounding faces. A mother with a child no older than six sat in the shade while a firefighter tended to a bruise under the woman's eye.

"All right. I'll make a call. Collins, see if the medical staff want to use the bus to transport the less severe cases to the closest hospital."

"But, legally, they—"

"Get it done, Agent."

Collins turned away and strode off, unhappy about the change in plans.

"Thank you, Lynne."

"It's not their fault—"

"Detective! I'm glad you're here. You need to see this." A young deputy broke into a trot, and he was out of breath.

"There's—it's—so many."

"Take a breath. What's going on?" Parker glanced at the deputy's name tag, Minton. "Minton, what?"

"Down on the old track. A grave. A mass grave.

Parker, Lynne, and Billie followed the deputy to the pile of rubble that once served as a grandstand. A well-trod path wound around the edge of the rough, crumbled concrete to the old track.

A pile of freshly dug soil lay next to an open pit. A small tractor parked by the open hole, ready to backfill the soil. Parker's gut tightened. He spotted four similar mounds, dug, and filled around the track.

The deputy didn't want to approach any closer. He couldn't speak. He pointed to the pit, turned, and threw up.

Parker trod closer to the edge of the opening until three pairs of legs were visible. Another step meant more of the bodies were exposed. Parker inched closer, expecting and fearing one of the dead would be Miguel.

Billie sensed his anxiety and joined alongside, placing a hand on his shoulder.

All the dead were face down in the mass grave. Each suffered a gunshot wound to the back of the head. Two were older and bigger than Miguel. The third—the third body on the far left was Miguel's size and age.

Parker jumped into the pit and approached the body. He knelt and gently rolled the corpse. Guilty relief swept over him. It wasn't Miguel.

"Oh, no," Billie uttered.

"Who is it?" Lynne asked.

Parker released the body and stepped away. "It's Tomaso Hernandez, the grandson of the couple who run the Los Azteca Market."

Chapter Forty-Four

"This is going to kill Mrs. Hernandez," Billie said.

Parker knew what she meant. The aging storekeeper lost her husband to the sniper, took a severe beating, and now she'd lost her grandson. Of course, she'd ask what families ask, "Why did this happen?"

What could he tell her to ease the pain? The woman had seen enough violence in her life to know what her grandson suffered in his ending moments.

Castaneda was responsible for this—all of it. The mass graves, the kidnapping, the inhuman treatment of his captives, he was behind it. The things that mattered to him were money and power. Leverage.

A thought flashed through Parker's mind.

"Give me a minute."

Parker pulled out the phone he took from Ramos-Costa's body, and the cheap burner didn't need a password.

In the messaging application, there was one phone number. Three messages coming in. Nothing sent from Ramos-Costa. They must be from Castaneda. Curiously, though, the messages were in English rather than Spanish.

Parker scrolled to the home screen. All the labels on the applications were in English. Perhaps Castaneda bought the cheap burner here. But the messages bothered him. Still, they offered a point of leverage Parker could use.

Back in the messaging application, the first message read, "Tell me when it's done." Scrolling down to the next message, Castaneda was getting tense.

The message was, "Get it done, or your family pays the price."

"You bastard."

"What's that?" Billie said.

"Castaneda. He forced a twenty-year-old kid to—never mind."

The message sent minutes ago was a photo of a man and woman huddled together. The woman was trying to shield her young daughter behind her. Parker knew the background in the photo was from the makeshift prison at the dog track.

"Billie, did you see this family at the track?"

Parker held the phone out to her.

"Can't say for sure."

Parker used his cell phone and snapped a photo of the screen on the phone. It was blurry and wouldn't work.

"Dammit, I was going to ask Lynne if she recognized them."

"You could ask her if they wrote down their names?"

Parker stared at Billie.

"Yeah, I could ask. Thanks, Billie."

Parker tapped a text to Lynne on his phone asking for a family with the name Ramos-Costa.

While he waited, he traded phones and held the burner, and tapped in a reply to the previous message. Too much, and he backspaced until he had an empty screen again. How much English did Ramos-Costa use? Castaneda was using English with the kid, so Parker began typing again. Short phrases, no Americanized slang.

"It is done. Let my family go."

Parker's finger hovered over the send button for a moment before stabbing the little envelope icon.

A reply popped back in seconds. "My proof?"

Parker remembered the kid holding the phone as he readied to shoot him. He was filming proof for Castaneda.

Parker opened the photos application, and there were two files. A ten-second video and the still frame image Parker shot of the tarped body.

He pulled up the video and hit play. The image was shaky, and the sound was difficult to hear. His image was looking back at him. Ramos-Costa couldn't keep the camera centered, and Parker drifted from the frame. A boom sounded from the small phone speaker. The image flickered and faded to black.

It might work. Parker sent the ten-second video to Castaneda.

No response from the Los Muertos thug.

Parker sent the still photo of the tarp-covered body.

Still nothing.

Parker pressed the keyboard keys and composed another text message. "I did as you asked. Let my family go. Are you a man of your word?"

The callous thug couldn't resist questioning his honor.

"You are in no position to make demands. I'll do as I please with your family. You'll never see them again."

Parker's cell buzzed in his lap, and it took him a moment to focus on the second phone. Lynne replied to his question about The Ramos-Costa family. "Mother, father, and daughter all accounted for. In good condition. Anything I should know?"

Castaneda didn't know the facility was overrun. Parker felt the leverage shift.

He typed another message to Castaneda.

"Don't you want the money the Coalition took from you?"

"What money?"

That was too easy.

"Didn't they promise you money? It's what the man said before he died. Miguel told me he knew how to do it."

A pause. Was Castaneda asking Miguel? Parker hoped it was true. It meant he was alive. Castaneda hadn't eliminated him yet. Parker had to make sure he believed the kid held some value.

Parker didn't wait for a reply and pressed on. "Miguel is the only one who knew how to access the accounts." Parker winced and hit send. There was no way the Ramos-Costa kid would know Miguel, or his status within the Coalition. Parker counted on Castaneda's blinding greed.

Parker's screen brightened with a new message.

"Miguel says he doesn't know what you're talking about."

Parker shut his eyes and raised his head. Miguel was alive.

"The man you had me kill mentioned a Tuition Fund. Miguel managed it."

"Parker said that?"

"He tried to buy me. I told him I couldn't because of my family."

Another long lull in the messages.

"Miguel says he knows the account you mentioned. Says he can only find it from the Immigrant Coalition offices."

Smart kid. Get Castaneda to lower his guard and catch him in the open.

"Miguel is staying where he's at. You need to go to the office and do it for him."

"I don't know how. They won't let me walk in and steal their money."

Parker needed to draw Castaneda out.

"You need to figure it out. I'll put Miguel on the phone, and he will walk you through it."

"If I do this—you'll let my family go?"

"Yes."

A simple one-word reply. Lies, greed, and deception blended in a single word. Castaneda's greed would bring him down.

Parker knew this was a delaying tactic, but it meant Miguel was alive, and if Castaneda believed he was useful, or held the keys to the Coalition's money, he had a chance at living another day. Miguel's fate rested in the hands of a savage, deceitful killer.

The burner cell fell silent in Parker's hand. The electronic lifeline to Miguel was all he had.

"Nathan," Billie said in a low whisper. "I couldn't help overhearing. I don't know everything Roger was up to as far the Coalition bookkeeping, but I know there ain't no Tuition Fund."

"I know."

Parker headed for the edge of the compound and the sandy wash where he'd raced across, avoiding the Los Muertos sentries.

Halfway across the wash, Parker turned at a mournful howl behind him.

A half-dozen survivors broke through the barricade strung up near the mass graves. The cries came from a woman on her knees. Her hands were outstretched to the heavens, and if she was asking for a reason her loved one lay in the bottom of a ditch, she would not hear an answer.

If he couldn't convince Castaneda to show himself, Parker would be the one on his knees asking why.

Chapter Forty-Five

Billie wasted no time on the drive from the abandoned dog track to the Immigrant Coalition offices. She skidded the Jeep to a stop in front of the boarded-up window. The assassination attempts on Brunell felt like ancient history.

A blue BMW sat in the lot, and Isa opened the car door when she recognized Parker in the Jeep passenger window. She said she was going to clear out her desk after the shooting downtown, but she hadn't been to the office yet. Parker pleaded, telling her it was important.

"I don't want to be here," Isa said, clutching the office keys in a tight fist.

"Thanks for coming. We're running out of time."

"So, you said. If Castaneda has Miguel, he's probably left the country. I don't know if there's anything we can do about it now...."

"I have to try. I owe him that much."

She huffed and unlocked the door, holding it open for Parker and Billie.

After they entered, she poked her head out and looked into the parking lot before closing and locking the door.

She strode to her workstation and booted up her computer.

"You wanted me to log into the Coalition files, you said?"

She tapped a few keys, and the monitor displayed a list of files and folders.

"What were you looking for specifically?"

"I need to send Castaneda the money he thinks he's owed."

Isa pushed back from the desk. "You want to do what?"

"Pay him. It's the only chance to save Miguel."

"You want to pay Los Muertos with Coalition money? What makes you think he'll give the kid back?"

"It's how these people work. A kid named Enrique Ramos-Costa can transfer the money with Miguel's help."

"Who's that? I don't know him."

"They killed him today at city hall plaza."

Isa knitted her brow. "What? I don't understand."

Parker sat at the desk and scooted his chair forward. "You have the campaign transaction account numbers?"

"The campaign funds we talked about Brunell moving to a Mexican bank?"

"That's the one."

"What are you thinking?"

"I need to keep Castaneda believing Miguel and Enrique are working on his money."

"Because you believe he has Miguel?"

"He does. Miguel would know what I meant when I mentioned a tuition fund. It's something I've been nagging him about."

Billie clapped her hands together. "That's what you were talking about!"

"Castaneda wouldn't know any different. From what you and Billie say, no one other than Roger Jessup really knew how the accounts were structured."

"Much to my frustration. Any time I needed a financial report or a tax document, he was our source. I chalk it up to his lack of trust in Tim after he discovered his past."

Parker placed the burner cell on the desk and took a deep breath.

"Ready?"

"Ready? For what?"

"We need to make it look as if we are getting funds together, and he has to believe we're going to give it to him."

Isa centered herself at the computer. She wiggled the mouse and brought it to life. Parker and Billie huddled over her shoulder.

"All right. I think I know what we can do. This will serve Tim for what he's done... what he's always done." Isa's brow knit, and she began typing in a series of keystrokes.

Parker hit the dial button on the cell phone and waited for the line to connect to the man who killed McMillan, Juan Estrada, and Tomaso Hernandez. And Miguel could be next.

The cell phone rang twice and disconnected.

A text message popped up on the screen.

"Are you at the Coalition office?"

"Can I call you? It would be easier to talk this through. Can I speak to Miguel? He'll know what I need to do."

"No. Are you at the office?"

"Yes. I'm there."

"Who else is there?"

Isa tapped on the desk to draw his attention.

"Tell him I'm here. As far as he knows, I'm going on with business."

"You sure?"

She nodded.

Parker typed in his text. "A woman named Isa is here."

"Don't let that two-faced bitch know what you're doing."

"Huh. Judgey asshole."

"Ok, but I need her to let me use a computer?"

"All right. Don't let her stand over you and watch."

"What do I do?" Parker typed.

"Once you're on the computer, find a shared file."

Isa grabbed the mouse from Parker and ran it to a file directory. She clicked on an icon marked shared file.

"Found it. Now what do I do?"

The screen blossomed to life. "Find the file named TB."

"Tim's work files. We each keep a file directory of our own."

Parker watched as Isa clicked on the TB file. Dozens of files scrolled down from the top of the screen.

"What am I looking at?" Parker asked.

"All of Tim's work product. Doc files, press releases, photos, and PowerPoint presentations."

The burner cell alerted again with a new message.

"Did you find it?"

"Yes. Now what?"

"Look for a file named 'bordergaurd' next."

"What's he looking for?" Parker asked.

"How does he know what's in Tim's file server?" Isa asked.

Billie pulled the window blinds apart. "We got somebody coming."

Parker typed his reply. "I found it."

He clicked on the file, and a screen popped up, requiring a password to open the document.

"What the hell is this?" Isa asked.

"You know the password?"

"Not a clue."

"Let's play along," Parker said as he typed a response.

"I can't open it. Something didn't work."

A message back. "Type this in exactly. 11201982."

Parker entered the string of numbers in carefully, one after another. The document came into view.

"More fricken numbers?"

"I know these—that one—it's Brunell's campaign account."

"This is getting interesting," Parker said.

A knock rattled the office door. Billie jumped at the sudden thump.

"Get rid of them, Billie," Parker said.

Billie peeked through the blinds and threw them closed.

"It's the FBI—that Agent Collins guy."

"How the hell did he know—"

Parker pulled the key fob from his pocket and tossed it on the desk.

"What do I do?" Billie asked.

"I'll handle it," Isa said, striding from the desk to the door.

She unlocked the door and opened it a few inches. "Yes, can I help you?"

Collins tried the door, and Isa's foot blocked it from opening. He wasn't putting any weight behind it, but his intent to enter was clear. He flashed his FBI credentials in her face.

"Agent Collins, FBI."

"Again, how can I help you?"

"Why don't you let me in, and we can talk? You, me, and Mr. Parker?"

"I don't think so."

"Excuse me?"

"I said I don't think so. I'm busy at the moment."

"I'm here on official business."

"So am I."

"I could arrest you for obstruction."

"No. No, you couldn't. You have no probable cause to enter a private business, no exigent circumstances to override the need for a warrant to enter and search. You're blowing smoke Agent Collins."

"How do you know I don't have a warrant?"

"Because if you had one, we wouldn't be having this conversation."

"If you make me get one, it won't be easy for you."

"Are you threatening to violate my fourth amendment rights, Agent Collins?"

"I can call and get a warrant, and I'll drag it out all day."

"I can call Judge Theresa Límon and see what she has to say about it. She's on the federal district court of appeals. She was my law school professor."

Collins's face tightened, and Parker leaned back and caught the Agent's expression. Collins locked eyes with Parker, and as the Agent opened his mouth to speak, Isa closed the door on him after saying, "Thank you for dropping by."

Parker grinned. "You didn't make a new friend there."

"Believe me, I've brushed off overzealous feds before. This one is no different."

"You keep Judge Límon on speed dial?"

Isa locked the door and returned to the desk. "Hope you never need to find out."

Parker glanced at the screen. Castaneda messaged, and he hadn't noticed while Isa held off the FBI.

"Now he wants us to transfer money from the Coalition tuition fund to this account," Parker said.

"You mean the fund that doesn't exist?"

"That's the one."

Parker began typing his response. "I don't know how. Miguel needs to do this part."

"Get it done." Parker could feel the frustration bleeding through the cell phone.

"I can't. Miguel needs to walk me through it. I don't want to mess it up." The burner phone rang.

"I can't answer. Castaneda knows my voice."

"Mine, too," Isa said.

Billie stepped to the desk. "I don't know what to say."

"We'll write it down for you. Try to sound like a scared kid."

"That won't be hard, 'cause I am."

Parker hit the accept call button and the speaker icon on the burner cell.

"Miguel?" Billie asked in an accented English tone.

"Yes, it's me."

Parker melted in his chair. Relief swept through him at Miguel's voice.

"I don't know what to do next," Billie said, waving her arms to make Parker jot down the script she needed to lay out.

Parker slid a note in front of Billie. She nodded and recited the script.

"Can you tell me where to find it?"

"It's kind of hidden. It's in a little shell."

"But where? I don't know where to look?"

A pause before Miguel spoke drove Parker's heart rate higher.

"I drew out a plot map for the files. Look in the lower left corner. Let me know if you see it."

Parker pointed at a map on the wall. "What's this?"

Isa whispered in Parker's ear. "It's a map of known routes over the border."

It marked a map of the southern region of Arizona and California, with red and blue lines snaking over the dotted line of the international border separating the United States and Mexico.

Parker nodded to Billie.

"Okay, I found it. Now which file?"

"You'll have to search for it. I don't know which one has what you're looking for. I think it's a blue file, and you've seen it before."

Parker tapped his finger on four routes in the left corner of the state. Three red lines and one blue one.

"Okay. I can find them." Parker handed Billie another note. "Once I find the file, what kind of password protection is there?"

"Six numbers—you can figure it out."

A terse command in the background followed a rustle on the phone. "Get it done, and we're out."

The connection cut off.

The echo of the second voice filled the office because of who it wasn't.

The man holding Miguel wasn't alone. Esteban Castaneda was there, but the second voice belonged to Tim Brunell.

Chapter Forty-Six

"How did Brunell know where Miguel and Castaneda were? When we met up with Castaneda out at Rocky Wash, he was alone."

"He lied," Billie said.

"When did he—how—?"

"Explains how Castaneda knew where to find the file on the shared server. Tim told him.….." Isa said.

"Why would Brunell do that? Tell Castaneda how to steal from him?"

"Tim doesn't know what's in these files. He only knew where they were. That's why Miguel was important to him," Isa said.

"When he realizes there isn't any tuition fund?" Parker said.

"Brunell's a desperate man. No tellin' what he'll do," Billie said.

Parker strode to the map with the undocumented migrant routes.

"Isa, you know how current this is?"

"I don't. When migrants crossed over, they'd tell someone if there were dangers along the passage—from cartels to Federales, to militia groups. Someone would mark the route in red. Blue ones meant no troubles on the journey."

Parker tapped the once-blue route snaking through the Papago Indian reservation.

"Billie, this one seem familiar to you?"

She leaned in and traced her finger along the route.

"Ain't it the route you, me, and Miguel came over on last year?"

"Miguel told us where he is and how many people were with him—six—the password number."

"Smart kid," Isa said.

Parker glanced at the wall clock. "It takes three-three and a half hours to drive there from here. Isa, I need you to keep Castaneda thinking we are transferring him the tuition funds account."

"There is no such thing."

"Could Brunell know it's a fraud?"

"He wouldn't. Sounded like he told Castaneda he had the money. He's paying Castaneda off."

"The accounts in his shared file—what are they?" Parker said.

Isa shoved her chair in front of the monitor and scanned the list of accounts.

"These aren't Coalition accounts. I'm not sure about some of them."

Parker peered over her shoulder. "I recognize the third one down. It has the Mexican bank code I saw on the USB drive. The numbers with it—I'm not sure. I think I know a way to hold Tim off for a while."

Isa squared her shoulders, tucked her hair up into a ponytail, and started tapping keys. "Tim wants money transferred; I can so do that."

Parker patted her shoulder. "Thanks. Let me know how it goes. If I hear anything from Brunell on the burner phone, I'll relay it to you."

"He'll be watching his account—the one he flagged for us."

Billie snapped a photo of the migrant route map with her phone. "Pretty sure I know where this is, but couldn't hurt to have a reference. Some of these red routes run damned close."

"Good thinking." Parker stared at the FBI key fob a moment before grabbing it and shoving it into his pocket.

Parker unlocked the door, and Billie stepped through. Parker called inside to Isa, "Lock this back up. I'll let you know when we have Miguel."

Billie hopped in the passenger side of the Jeep and waited for Parker to start the engine.

"If Castaneda and Brunell are together and have Miguel, where'd they hide?" Parker said.

"The fact Castaneda is parked on the border means he's plannin' to take the money and run."

"What's he running from?"

"Castaneda don't spend much time in one place. You know that. Why?"

"There's more to this. Brunell is running for office, getting the media coverage to paint him as a stand-up guy, protecting us from people like Castaneda. So why is he paying him off now?"

"I see what you mean."

"He's cut Coalition ties to Los Muertos, right? He's desperate to show himself as this immigration reform candidate. All the while, Castaneda claims he's owed for losing the trafficking routes."

Billie straightened in the seat. She shot a look at Parker. "He's paying off Castaneda."

"That's what I'm thinking. It makes sense with Brunell pushing for the cash from the Coalition. Maybe Castaneda took Miguel hoping for a cash exchange. Must have set the drop near the border, on a route he knows he won't run into any cartel problems."

"Los Muertos and the Sinaloa Cartel don't play well together. The cartel sees Castaneda and his boys poachin' on their territory. If Castaneda gets his money from Brunell, he'll slip over the border."

"We can't let him disappear again."

"Let me ask you somethin'. If Brunell fears Castaneda, you think he'll be at the drop? I mean, he needs Brunell until he don't."

Parker's foot let up on the gas for a moment.

"You have a good point, Billie. Brunell wouldn't take the chance."

"Maybe we should tell 'em?"

"You know how to reach him? I don't have Brunell's cell phone number."

"I could put word out in the migrant community. Someone might be willin' to speak up."

Parker fished his cell from his pocket. "Or they might want nothing to do with Los Muertos after they kidnapped people from their own community. You saw what they did to them at the dog track. I have another idea."

Parker found the number he was looking for in his contact list. He dialed the number and hit the speaker.

"Law offices of Larry Sutton. How can I help you?"

"Detective Nathan Parker here. I need to speak with Mr. Sutton. It's urgent."

"Mr. Sutton is busy at the moment—"

"Tell him this concerns a former client from down south. It's important, and the client may be interested in what I have to say."

"I'm sorry, Detective Parker. Mr. Sutton cannot be disturbed."

"Listen, I appreciate you are keeping him on schedule, but—"

"I will pass on the message, Detective. Thank you for calling."

She disconnected the call. Parker smiled, his hand on the steering wheel.

"Sutton? The scumbag lawyer who represented the Cartel?"

"The same."

"But he don't represent Castaneda."

"He definitely does not."

Billie's eyes widened with recognition.

"You want the Cartel to flush Castaneda out?"

"Something like that," Parker said.

The cell phone rang, and the caller ID was Larry Sutton, Esq.

"Mr. Sutton. I need to run something past you."

"Detective, I cannot discuss any client, present or past. You and whoever is listening to this recording should know this."

"No recording."

"Still—"

"Last year, you represented some influential groups in Mexico and their 'import-export' operations."

"I have many international clients, Detective."

"There's one who will want to know about a competitor moving in on their operation. Esteban Castaneda, the head of this competition, will make a move south in the next few hours."

Silence at the end of the connection.

"Sutton, did you hear me?"

"This have to do with what we spoke about yesterday? I ask because my client isn't the only one with an interest in Mr. Castaneda."

"It is connected."

"I understand. You wouldn't know where my client could arrange a meeting with Mr. Castaneda?"

"I should have a fix on it soon."

"Text me."

Sutton hung up.

"Damn! You wanna send the Cartel chasin' after Castaneda? Neither one of 'em give a shit who gets caught in the crossfire."

"I know, Billie. I can't risk Miguel being trapped in between. I want to make Castaneda know the Cartel is out looking for him. He won't be able to hide. He'll surface and make a run for it."

"He won't go without his money."

"If he knows the Cartel is hot on his tail, he'll need to make a choice—wait for Brunell to make good on his deal or stand and fight."

"All well and good, but how is Castaneda gonna hear about Cartel comin' for him?"

"The thing about Sutton is he'll play both sides—his cartel clients and the Aryan Nation. The Nation will want Castaneda's hide because he killed Clement. The Cartel wants him because of his disruption to their smuggling operations. That kind of heat will be hard to miss. Castaneda will feel it and make a move."

"That might work."

"It has to. Miguel is running out of time. I don't know if Isa can move the money fast enough. Castaneda will only wait so long."

"Don't make me feel warm and fuzzy, dependin' on the likes of them."

"Me either, Billie. But you know the old saying, better the devil you know than the devil you don't. We know these devils…."

Chapter Forty-Seven

Parker felt his anxiety increase the closer he and Billie got to the Papago Reservation. They wouldn't be able to drive up to the warehouse in the center of the reservation without alerting whoever Brunell had guarding the building.

Last year, he and Billie got a quick look at the metal-sided warehouse when they were smuggled back across the border with the help of a group of undocumented migrants. The men who ran this stop weren't Cartel players, they were opportunistic meth-heads. No telling who ran the desert depot now.

Parker's cell rang, and he grabbed it from the dash, hoping for another connection to Miguel. The caller ID said otherwise.

"Hey, Lynne, what's up?"

"I should ask you what's up. Agent Collins is sitting here telling me you were at the Immigrant Coalition offices and refused to let him enter."

"Wasn't me. I mean, I was there, but it's not my call who comes and goes. I don't think threatening a private citizen is the best way to endear the bureau to the public."

"I'll come out and ask. Do you know where Esteban Castaneda is?"

"Wish I did."

"Nathan, if you're lying to me—"

"Lynne, you know better. I've never lied to you, and won't start now. I don't know where Castaneda is hiding. I know he's waiting for a payoff from Tim Brunell. I'm heading south—but Agent Collins already knew it because of the GPS in the key fob he gave me."

Collins's voice sounded over the connection. "Why didn't you leave the key fob behind?"

"Because I told you, I would hit the button if and when I spot Castaneda. And I will."

"Why should I trust you to follow through?" Collins said.

"I'm the one you had your sniper team target. Don't talk to me about trust. I'm heading to a spot near the Papago Reservation. A smuggling route Castaneda uses to run people and drugs across the border. If he wants his payoff, chances are that's where it's going to happen. If you want a shot at nabbing him, I suggest you get moving."

Lynne cut off a biting reply from Agent Collins. "How do you know this is the spot Castaneda will turn up? I mean, the guy is a shadow. We've never been able to find intel on where he goes to ground."

"Castaneda nabbed Miguel, and he's stashed him down here near the reservation. Castaneda will surface for his money."

Collins piped up again, but his tone was cautious. "The Papago Reservation? The task force picked up chatter about a coyote coming up today. The strange part is there is no mention of what the coyote is bringing up. When we gather intel on these movements, it typically comes with a head count of the undocumented coming over, or kilos of the drug of the day. This time—nothing. But he is going back south the same day, and he won't be alone. Don't have a fix on the number going home with him."

"That's Castaneda's ticket back across the border. He won't risk crossing with a large group. If he makes the crossing, we'll lose him."

"I'll alert the tribal authorities and ICE to coordinate the takedown."

"You do what you need to do. I'm going in and getting a look at what's happening. Once I press the button, how long will it take to put your team on site?"

"Once the team's in position, less than three minutes."

"How long until they're in position?"

"I'm on my way now."

"It'll take you three hours—we don't have that kind of time."

"Uncle Sam has helicopters. I'll be there in twenty."

"Nathan, are you sure Miguel is there?"

"He's there. Lynne, I need you to find Brunell."

"Because he's being blackmailed? You think he's in danger?"

"You know exactly where he is. I need you to pay him a visit and plant a seed."

"Nathan?"

"Mention campaign finance concerns and see what happens. We have evidence showing Brunell's campaign cash funneled into accounts in Mexico."

"Evidence? What evidence? I can't accuse a political candidate of misappropriation of funds without concrete proof." Lynne was getting snippy with Parker.

"I'll send it to you, Lynne. Financial Crimes is looking into it now to see if we can lock down who is behind the accounts and transfers. Someone needs to sit on Brunell once you drop this bomb on him."

"He's a political candidate—I can't simply—"

"He's an ex-felon, Lynne. Brunell isn't even his real name. Have someone run down Ruben Burns. You'll see who Brunell really is."

Lynne huffed into the phone. "Nathan, what aren't you telling me?"

"Gotta go, Lynne. We're getting close to the drop."

"Nathan. Please be careful."

"I will, Lynne. Tell Collins to be ready to move in on my signal."

Parker disconnected the call and tossed the phone on the seat.

"You didn't tell her the Cartel might be beatin' the bushes for Castaneda."

"Couldn't take the risk they'd find him. I need him to follow Brunell down here. He so much as smells a fed tail, he'll go to ground."

"Won't he know if the Cartel is after him too, then?"

"I'm counting on it."

Parker pulled the Jeep onto a deserted dirt track. The trail was narrow, and creosote brush snapped off the front bumper as he drove on. A wide spot marked where two trails converged. He pulled the Jeep onto a wide bare patch near the intersection and hopped out before the Jeep came to a full stop.

As he stepped from the Jeep, a scream sounded in the underbrush. It wasn't close, and the tall brush alley muffled the sound.

Parker trotted down the trail, rounded a corner, and startled a small knot of migrants resting in the shade.

Billie and Parker didn't expect to see a man emerge from the bush and swing a machete in their direction.

"Whoa. We're not here for you."

The machete-wielding man rushed a step toward them and whipped the blade between them.

"They are mine. I can't let you take them."

"I told you I'm not here about them, or you."

"Please, help us," a woman called out from the pack sitting on the dirt path.

She was thin, young, and her eyes gave away her fear. She was consoling another pretty young woman, holding her ripped shirt together.

Parker recognized the situation instantly. This crazed blade-wielding man was their coyote, and he was terrorizing the women on their trek over the border.

Parker had seen too many reported rapes and assaults of undocumented migrants during their crossing. They were at the hands of their coyote, and many of them were as sadistic as the cartel soldiers these migrants fled to avoid.

"Who do you work for?" Parker asked.

"People more powerful than you."

The man stepped closer, and Parker drew his service weapon.

"Drop it, or I'll drop you."

"Pendejo cabrón."

His eyes glued to the barrel of Parker's Glock, he didn't notice a woman come from behind him and smack the back of his head with a rock. The hollow thunk of the rock against the man's skull was a sickening sound. The machete fell from his hand, and the man's eyes rolled back in his head as he collapsed on the desert floor.

The woman gripped the rock in her trembling hand. Her fingers bore a slash of blood from the man's head wound, and she couldn't take her eyes away from it—and what she'd done.

Parker holstered his weapon, eased to the woman, taking her hand, and unfolded her grip on the rock.

"Are you all right?" Parker asked.

The trembling woman was afraid to speak to the tall American. Billie sensed her fear and knelt near the downed coyote. She placed a fingertip on his neck and felt for a pulse.

"Is—is—he dead?" the woman asked.

"No. He'll have one hell of a headache, though."

"We need to leave before he wakes up and comes after us. He'll kill me for what I did."

"No, he won't," Parker said, tossing two sets of heavy zip ties to Billie. "You do the honors."

Parker held a canteen he'd pulled from the bag and offered it to the women. "Did he work for Los Muertos?"

The young woman with the torn blouse nodded her head.

"I'm Nathan, and this is Billie. Do you need medical attention? Can I call someone for you?"

A slight shake, her eyes cast down at her torn blouse.

"He can't hurt you anymore."

Billie stood and assessed her work, securing the Los Muertos coyote, sitting up with his back to a thick Palo Verde trunk. His arms wrapped around the green tree and locked with the zip ties.

Billie knelt by the women and whispered to them in a low voice. She unbuttoned her long-sleeve red and black plaid shirt and gave it to the woman with the torn blouse. The woman pulled the fresh shirt around her and stood, giving Billie a hug.

The travelers gathered their few possessions and looked at Billie.

"That way. The highway is maybe a half mile. There's a gas station, and you might get a bus pass from Leon if he's working."

"Thank you. Thank you both."

The woman disappeared down the trail, and Parker hoped the worst was behind them.

For him, though, the most difficult challenge lay ahead—rescuing Miguel from a Los Muertos compound.

Chapter Forty-Eight

After a half-hour slogging along the dirt trail, Billie grabbed Parker's arm. She pulled him into the brush where Palo Verde thorns and brittle creosote branches jabbed his back. She put a finger to her lips and motioned up the trail with a tip of the head.

Parker heard voices—Spanish voices. There were at least two men coming down the trail. Their cadence wasn't urgent, so they weren't searching for them.

Four feet off the trail wasn't far enough to become invisible.

The voices grew louder. One spit out a rough laugh at a comment from his partner. They weren't on alert. If they were looking for their wayward, machete-wielding friend. They would find him a mile up the trail.

Billie squeezed Parker's arm as a blue denim pant leg came into view between the branches. A soiled canvas athletic shoe kicked up dust as it strode past their position. The man stopped and fell silent a few feet from where they hid. The second man's boots came to a stop in front of their position. Parker held his breath while the two men lit up cigarettes.

The polished wooden rifle stock on the closest man swung on a shoulder strap. These weren't migrants on a casual trek north after crossing the border. These were enforcers. They burned through the cigarettes, crushed them out in the dirt, and patrolled on. The pair weren't in a rush, but that would change in less than thirty minutes. Parker wondered if the machete rapist remained unconscious after the skull-cracking blow one of his captives gave him. Parker would call for medical treatment for the guy if they survived the day.

Billie waited almost a minute after the two gunmen left their position before she nudged Parker out from the thicket.

They trotted down the trail, putting distance between them and the two men.

The sound of a metal roll-up door slowed them. They were close now.

Parker was the first to spot the metal building in the clearing ahead. A yellow-tinted steel skin gave off a jaundiced vibe.

"See anyone?" Billie asked.

"Nah. Musta missed 'em. I heard the door. It's closed now. Must be inside cause their truck is parked out front. Check the logo on the truck door."

Parker pulled aside a branch and spotted the Diamond Dog Racing logo on the door.

"The same bastards what done them migrants at the track?"

"Looks that way. Maybe they took Miguel with them when they split. If we're in the right place, Miguel told us there were six guys guarding him. We've seen two armed soldiers, and I don't know if the coyote was one of them. Might be four left inside."

"We need to get closer," Billie said.

"And off this trail in case the others come back this way."

"'Member the old school bus?" Billie pointed at a faded yellow school bus, long out of service. The Pima County Department of Education lettering on the side was mostly a ghostly outline. "Been sittin' for a while. Them tires are low. I figure we can crawl under it and put us closer to what's happenin' inside. Shade under that old heap, too."

Billie's tank top was soaked through and clung to her wiry frame. "Come on." She didn't wait for Parker and ran for the old bus. The fifty yards were open space, and if the metal door rolled up while she sprinted to the bus, she'd be done.

She made it to the side of the bus, away from the metal shed, and waved to Parker to make his break.

He glanced at the door, willing it to remain closed, and rushed to the bus.

Ten feet from the bus, he caught his foot on the dry, rough surface and fell forward, breaking his fall with his hands. He slid to the bus and bumped against the bus's metal skin, releasing a dull gong reverberating into the yard.

Seconds later, the metal door flew up on its rails with a clatter. Two men armed with AK-47s crept out, sweeping the yard with their gun barrels. The pair split up and circled out from the door.

Billie and Parker crawled under the bus as quietly as they could. Any sound from a scuffed boot, or a rock skittering underneath the old hulk would be their end. Parker shoved a thick spider web away from his face, and it clung to his ear and the back of his neck as he inched forward. He swore he felt armies of little spider legs scurrying down the collar of his shirt.

Parker lost sight of the gunman on his left as he passed behind the bus. Parker was almost certain he was out of view, but if his legs were sticking out from under the old bus, it wouldn't be good. He rolled to one side and pulled his legs up into his chest, making himself as small as possible. If they leaned to glance under the edge of the bus, they might miss him. Billie noticed and did the same, pulling her thin frame into a tight, compressed ball.

Voices from behind them. They weren't Spanish, but English. Not good English, but the gutter version spoken by the Aryan Nation.

"Told you there weren't nothing out here."

"Boss said we gotta check, so we gotta do it."

"We done it, so let's get our happy asses back inside where it's cooler."

"In a minute. Wanna check somethin' first."

Parker watched as the pair of boots stepped closer. The gunman stopped at the edge of the bus and paused. The rattle of the sling meant he was taking the weapon down from his shoulder. If the thug dropped to a knee and glanced under, they'd be trapped.

Parker was lying on the side of his holstered Glock. He bridged up as quietly as possible and withdrew the weapon. It was no match for the large bore automatic rifle, but it was all he had.

A shadow dropped on the ground three feet in front of Parker. The man's weapon was pointed down.

The gunman dropped to a knee in front of Parker. The rifle was next to move.

Chapter Forty-Nine

Parker jerked with the loud pop echoing under the bus chassis. He glanced at Billie, curled up next to him in the shadows. She hadn't been hit either.

Parker eased his head around and spotted the gunman on his knee using the rifle as a hammer, slamming the butt against a padlock on the bus door frame. After ten hard impacts, the lock gave way and rolled under the bus, coming to rest in the dirt near Parker's head.

If the gunman looked for the lock, he'd find much more than he bargained for.

The man rose from his knee in the dirt, and the metallic scrape above told he forced open the bus door.

"What the hell you doin', Les?" the second gunman called.

"I been asking myself why they been tellin' us to leave this old shit alone? Way I sees it is they be stashin' the good shit out here."

"Really? Out here in this old heap? You lost what's left of your mind, Les. Come on, you don't want him to find you out here."

"No, man. He don't pay us for shit. Gotta get what you can while you can."

The worn shock absorbers sank under the weight of the first man. Rust and dirt particles rained down on Parker and Billie.

"Well? You see shit worth takin'?"

"Nah, ain't a damn—"

A crash sounded above Parker, and the rusted floor buckled outward from the weight of a body falling.

"Holy shit, Mark! There's—there's a dead guy up in here. Scared the shit outta me."

The second man rushed into the bus, and the suspension sagged under their combined weight.

"Lemme see."

Rust flakes fell on Parker. He hoped the aged metal was thick enough to keep these two from falling through.

"All be damned. This one ain't been dead long. This heat makes it hard to tell."

"Who is it? You know?"

A shuffling sound against the metal floorboard told one man edged closer to the body.

"Hard to tell. Lookit. They handcuffed him to the seat."

"They left him here?"

"Clement told you this fucker was crazy."

"Don't I know it. The guy got stuff we can take?"

"I'm not touching him. You do it if you wanna know."

"You're closer."

"Don't you think if he got his ass locked up in here, they'd a took anything worth takin'?"

"Yeah, prolly. Still, makes me wonder why a boy got left like this. I mean, I can't tell if he was white—or what. Hard to tell now."

"I'm getting back. He's supposed to call soon. It's too hot in here anyways."

"Bet that's what he said."

The two men shuffled off the bus, closed the door, and didn't bother to find the lock before they strode to the metal shed. The door rolled back down with a clang.

Parker let out a breath. He wasn't aware he was keeping it in.

"Billie, you all right?"

"Yeah, we gotta get closer to the building."

Parker belly-crawled out from under the derelict bus and sprinted to the side of the metal building. Billie joined him within seconds.

"Them two ain't Los Muertos," Billie said.

"No, they aren't. Wonder who they were talking about—the man who doesn't pay them enough?"

"When the roll-up door was open, I saw light comin' in from the back side," Billie said.

They edged around the corner of the metal building and made sure there wasn't another gunman watching the back.

"Dammit. I woulda swore there was a window," she said, scanning the solid metal skin.

Parker trotted to a metal ladder mounted to the far corner. He grabbed a rung, and it groaned under his weight. He paused, listening for the telltale roll-up door.

Billie pulled on his pant leg, urging him down. He let go of the ladder and dropped two feet back on the dirt.

Billie shoved him aside. "I'm lighter than you." She grabbed the same ladder rung and tested it with her full weight. No metal noise came from her light first touch. She scrambled up the ladder and gently lowered herself onto the flat metal roof.

Parker grimaced because he knew the metal surface would be hot to the touch, and Billie didn't give any indication of her skin burning. She glanced down and whispered.

"Skylight. I'm gonna look." Then she pointed at him and gestured him to take cover in the thick brush and discarded machine parts behind the building.

He considered waiting at the base of the ladder for her until she gestured again. This time, she was animated, pointing and holding two fingers up. The two gunmen from the trail returned.

Parker scampered into the brush behind the building and crept up an incline, where he spotted the two gunmen. They weren't dragging the unconscious body of the Machete Man, and they didn't look like they were in any hurry as they sauntered down the trail. Either they didn't go far up the trail, or the man had broken free.

The two armed men weren't Aryan Nation members unless the white power group was recruiting brown-skinned members. The odd pairing of likely Los Muertos members and Aryan Nation gave Parker an unsettled feeling in the pit of his stomach.

He'd counted on Castaneda being at odds with Brunell, forcing them to bring their fight out into the open. The presence of opposing forces here in the desert meant he was wrong. They were already working together.

The Los Muertos pair stopped at the metal building and pounded on the roll-up door. The rattle of steel on dry tracks reverberated through the building's metal skin.

Parker slid to his left to find a better vantage point. The two Los Muertos gunmen entered, and the two white boys slung their rifles and donned worn ball caps over their mullets as they moved out into the sun.

A changing of the guard. The white pair, Mark and Les, the same two who found the body on the bus, didn't seem happy about their turn on patrol. No pleasantries were exchanged between them. They strolled past the old bus, following a trail in the brush heading south.

Billie waved a hand to get Parker's attention. She pointed to the roof of the building below her. She waved her arms back and forth in front of her like a baseball umpire. Parker knew what she meant. Miguel wasn't inside.

An ugly thought shot through his mind. If Miguel wasn't being held inside the place like Brunell led him to believe, then where was he?

Oh, God. The body on the bus.

Chapter Fifty

Parker ran to the bus. He didn't care if the two sentries heard his footfall. He needed to know.

He reached the bus, and his heart pounded in his chest. Parker pulled the bus door open, throwing the thin metal accordion door to the side. He shot up the three steps to the bus floor and saw a young dark-haired man slumped forward in a seat in the middle of the bus.

From his distance, he couldn't tell if the matted, blood-stained head was Miguel. Parker's feet felt leaden as he approached the aisle seat occupied by a slumped figure the same size and haircut as Miguel.

"Oh, please, no."

Parker dropped to a knee and lifted the dead boy's chin. A gunshot to the back of the head does things to a human being. The explosive force, hydrostatic shock, expands and distorts a face. Even with the disfiguring damage, Parker could tell this wasn't Miguel.

He dropped to the floor and sat, cradling his head in his hands. He thought he had lost Miguel—again. He was no closer to rescuing the boy. For the first time, dread crept into Parker's mind. Would he ever see Miguel again?

A shuffling sound behind him startled Parker from his dark thoughts.

Billie crept up the bus aisle while monitoring the roll-up door.

She froze at the sight of the dead man slumped in the seat.

She dropped to a knee.

"Is—is it?"

"No," Parker said.

Parker's cell phone vibrated in his pocket, and he wriggled it out so he could read the message.

"It's Isa. She's able to send the money."

"Man, she is one smart cookie. Where did the money come from, 'cause we know there ain't no tuition fund?"

"I don't know how she did it. But it means Brunell can pay off Castaneda." Parker patted his pocket. "Shit, I left Enrique Ramos-Costa's phone."

"Brunell, I mean, all he really cares about is payin' off Los Muertos so he can get Castaneda off his ass."

"You're probably right. It doesn't put me closer to finding what's happened to Miguel, though."

"Call him on it. Put it out there. Castaneda got his money. Now turn the kid loose."

Parker leaned against the seat on the opposite side of the aisle. He bit his cheek and stared at the kid shackled in the bus before they executed him. He couldn't let that fate befall Miguel.

"With the money in his hands, Miguel has no value to him. He becomes disposable in his eyes," Parker said.

"We need to get Brunell to make it about him—how he was buyin' the boy back and such."

"You really think Brunell is going to bust a grape to do anything? Unless he thinks he can pull a rainbow out of his ass and come out of this as some kind of hero," Parker said.

"It's who he is. Lookit—he wanted to be the face of the Coalition; he's runnin' for office on account of the attention it gets him. When eyes are on him, he's blind to everything else."

Parker huffed. "Pretty sharp assessment, Billie."

"I spent hours around this guy watchin' him glad-hand and back-slap anyone who he could use. He never paid no attention to me, 'cause I could do nothin' for him. I get it a lot."

"People underestimate you, Billie. There's no one I'd want on my side more than you."

Billie didn't respond, but her chin lifted a bit with the compliment.

"Without the Ramos-Costa kid's phone, I don't know how we can keep up the ruse and convince Castaneda to let Miguel go."

"Go straight to the source. Call Brunell."

"And what? Tell him we know he's been lying to us all along?"

"No. Play along with his game. Tell him the Ramos-Costa kid transferred a bunch of money to some account. You're tellin' him 'cause he's the head man at the Coalition. You could play to his ego and ask him to help Miguel get sprung from Los Muertos."

Parker fell silent. He rubbed the sweat from the back of his neck. "It might work. He is about his public image. Only one thing. I don't know the number to contact him."

"I do."

"Brunell's number? You have it?"

Billie spit out a phone number from memory. She noticed the puzzled look on Parker's face. "I remember things. Numbers and stuff."

He shook his head. "Billie, you never cease to amaze me."

Parker grabbed his cell phone and tapped in the number while Billie recited it. He drew a breath, pressed connect, and waited.

After four rings, a hesitant voice answered. "Yes?"

Parker put it on speaker and began. "Mr. Brunell, Detective Parker."

"Parker? I thought you were—"

"Dead? 'Fraid not. Hey, listen, I'm calling because we've heard Los Muertos, specifically Esteban Castaneda, is on the move. There's been a sighting down south near a reservation. You should know—he's holding Miguel."

"Castaneda? Why would he snatch a kid like Miguel?"

Like he didn't know.

"Apparently, Miguel worked with Roger and knows how to access the Coalition accounts. Castaneda plans to bleed you dry."

"Roger. He was too trusting of the help."

Parker twitched at the disposable reference to Miguel and the others.

"Listen, you're in a position to give him what he wants and get Miguel back," Parker said, ready to lay out the appeal to Brunell's ego.

"Why would I pay that asshole a dime? If you know where he's at. Go find him."

"Listen, I know one of Miguel's friends, Enrique-something, got into the accounts and moved some of your money out. I can't reach him now. I think he's run off."

Silence on the other end of the connection.

"If Castaneda got his money, you can make an appeal to him to release Miguel. You would be the one to make it happen. Think of the press this will generate. State Senate candidate rescues hostage."

"What can I do? I'm only one man!" Brunell said. He was circling the bait.

"Not just one man—*the* man. You're the one who can convince Castaneda to release Miguel to you. Give him what he wants. The feds can take him down after the exchange and freeze his assets later."

"No. I don't want to risk it going wrong and Miguel getting caught up. No takedown. Castaneda walks away. I have to deal with him in good faith. He knows where I live, remember? I screw him, and his Los Muertos thugs will burn me before I rescue Miguel."

It was Parker's turn to pause. "You need protection. If the feds—"

"No feds, no locals. I meet him heads up, and we make the deal."

"But —"

"That's the conditions. I do this alone."

"You know how to reach Castaneda? Think you can make him agree to the exchange?"

"I know him. He won't be able to say no."

"Where will you meet?"

"He'll want to make the exchange near where he has Miguel. You said a reservation. Must be the Papago. I think I know where to find him."

"Where? I can be there—"

"I need to go alone. If he smells a law enforcement presence, he'll disappear and probably take Miguel with him."

Parker realized the ICE intel about a coyote going south was for Castaneda, Miguel, and Brunell. But now Brunell had reason to stay and become a hero. If he rescued Miguel, Brunell would become a media darling and sit back as his political future brightened.

But Miguel could expose the dirty inner workings of the Coalition. If Miguel died, Brunell could spin it as a tragic loss and another example of violence spilling from across the border unless Parker could convince him he was worth more alive. Or at least worth it to someone else.

Parker knew the window to rescue Miguel was about to slam shut forever.

Chapter Fifty-One

Parker held the phone to his chest, calculating the risk of what he was about to tell Brunell. He caught Billie's eye, and she sensed the weight of what he was about to say.

"Mr. Brunell, I shouldn't be telling you this, but we received information Castaneda is going to take Miguel."

"Why would he bother? The boy is a nobody—another brown-skinned kid with his hand out trying to grab freebies from the government."

Parker's jaw tightened. Billie put her hand on Parker's arm.

"What we hear is Castaneda thinks the kid has some dirt. He wants to use it against you and the Coalition."

"What does he think the kid can tell him?" Brunell sounded wary and unsure. The bluster was evaporating from his voice.

"I have no idea. But it must be good if it's worth coming out of hiding to collect."

"I doubt—"

"If you have any idea where he's keeping Miguel, tell me so we can find him before Castaneda takes him away."

"Like I said, I have an idea where—but I need to go alone. I can reach the kid before Castaneda has a chance to use him."

"I really think you should let me go with you," Parker said.

"No cops. The kid won't stand a chance if there's any hint of a cop within a mile. You don't know him like I do. I'll call you when I know something." Brunell abruptly disconnected the call.

"Think he took the bait?" Billie asked.

"I hope so. I feel like I'm playing a game of chicken, and Miguel's the one who'll be run over."

Billie tapped him on the shoulder. She nodded down the southbound trail where the two sentries were coming back toward the metal shed.

Parker and Billie hunched down in the bus as the pair of scraggly white boys approached. The crunch of the gravel under their boots told they were close—too close. Parker and Billie were trapped in the bus if curiosity struck, and these two wanted to take another look at the dead kid inside the bus.

The footsteps stopped as a cell phone sounded. Parker's eyes widened, thinking it was Billie's phone. She shook her head. The man outside complained as he answered his cell.

"Yeah."

The pair were close enough to overhear a high-pitched prattle on the connection. The words spoken weren't clear, but the tone and pace of the one-sided conversation were enough for Parker to recognize the voice, because he'd just spoken with him—Tim Brunell.

"Got it. They ain't gonna be happy about this. No going back," the voice Parker assumed was Mark said.

An angry buzz sounded over the phone.

"I get it, I get it. We'll handle it. When will he be here?"

After a brief pause, Mark said, "We'll be in place at the secondary."

The call ended because the second sentry, Les, started chattering away. "What did he want? Whatta we gotta do? Who's comin'?"

"Lee, shut up and follow my lead. That's all you gotta know for now. We gotta lock them two beaners in the building first."

"Oh, they gonna be pissed."

"It was bound to happen one way or another. Let's get it done."

The footsteps crept away from the bus, and Parker peeked up far enough to watch the pair close in on the roll-up door. Mark handed his rifle to Les while he opened a small metal footlocker next to the building. Careful to keep the lid from clattering down, Mark lowered it slowly and knelt at the base of the door.

"They locked the two Los Muertos guys in the building," Parker whispered.

"They's planning an ambush. Castaneda is on his way, I bet ya."

"Brunell must've called him the second we hung up.

"Think those two can handle Castaneda? He ain't gonna come alone."

"Castaneda isn't stupid. He'll come prepared."

"Them two went down the trail over there. While I was up on the roof, I could see another small clearing 'bout a hundred yards out. Might be somethin' there where they be keeping Miguel."

"Another building? Could be the 'secondary' the guy was talking about."

Billie shrugged. "Don't 'member one from the last time we was here."

Mark and Les backed away from the roll-up door without alerting the two gunmen inside. With two locked up, Mark and Les headed back on the southern trail. There could be two additional sentries if Miguel communicated the number accurately.

Parker waited until the pair of gunmen disappeared around a bend in the trail.

"Hundred yards out? I don't remember another building out here before."

"I think I mighta saw another way around to that clearing."

Parker followed Billie's lead as they left the bus and cut a path past the metal building along a game trail in the brush. Two feet wide, at most, the sharp branches welted their arms as they pressed forward.

"What made this trail, Billie?"

"Prolly javelina."

"Wild boar?"

"Un-huh. You can tell 'cause of the broken limbs 'bout knee height. Them suckers push right through. And the smell."

There was a musky presence in the thick brush. Parker pictured the tusks, beady eyes, and little else. He didn't want to encounter one of the ill-tempered beasts on this narrow trail.

Billie came to a stop and lowered to a knee.

Parker's first thought was a wild pig blocking the trail ahead, but the glint of yellow paint glistened through the screen of brush.

"A cargo box?"

"Like off one of them semi-trucks? Must come in another way. Gotta be another road then."

Billie started forward, and Parker grabbed her shoulder as the scrawny gunman, Lee rounded the back corner of the cargo container. He lit up a cigarette and tossed it in the dirt when an engine noise sounded in the distance.

A white pickup truck bounded into the dirt lot in front of the cargo box. Judging by Les's reaction, a wave, and the rifle slung on his shoulder, the new arrival wasn't Castaneda and Los Muertos soldiers.

Parker posted to a rise to the southwest. The mound was less than twenty feet above the desert floor but would command a view of the access road in and the cargo container. A slight man dressed in desert camo jogged up the rise and ducked behind a rock ledge. At the distance, Parker couldn't see the new arrival's face. What disturbed Parker most was the distinctive outline of a Remington 700 sniper rifle in the shooter's hands.

An ambush waiting for Castaneda. From where Parker hid, the rifle looked like the same model used by the Sun Valley sniper. A coincidence? It wasn't a rare weapon, but the .308 caliber rifle was becoming too common as far as he was concerned.

"You see that, Billie? The rifleman taking cover behind the rock up there."

"Yeah. I don't like what's gonna happen when they snap this trap on Los Muertos. If Miguel is in that cargo box, he's gonna be in the middle of it."

"I'm thinking these are Brunell's guys. They gotta be, right? I wasn't sure about the white power connection before, but it fits together. The witnesses saw a couple of white guys take Juan Estrada from his car. The anti-immigrant bullshit from the Aryan Nation in Clement's place. Brunell's sudden swing to tighten up the border. I don't understand why, but it must be, right?"

"Makes sense to me. I didn't see who else was in the truck, though."

"Can we move around the side and look at the front end of the cargo box?"

"Not without the sniper picking us off."

"I got an idea." Parker dug in his pocket for his cell and tapped out a text message to Isa. "Transfer the funds."

Moments later, a reply text popped on his screen. "Done."

The timing was cutting it close as a pair of black Escalade SUVs pulled into the dirt lot.

Parker's blood drew cold the moment Esteban Castaneda stepped from the passenger side of the lead vehicle.

Parker drew his weapon and centered the sight on Castaneda. Fifty feet wasn't far. Well within the distance, Parker shot at the range during quarterly qualification. A live, moving target, coupled with the adrenaline coursing through his system, didn't make the shot a sure thing.

McMillan's murderer was fifty feet away. He couldn't let the man responsible for killing his partner escape.

Chapter Fifty-Two

Parker drew a deep breath, let half of it out and felt his finger lightly caress the trigger. This was the moment his nightmare begged for four years. Closure for McMillan, the dead deputy's family, and for himself.

His hand trembled. He re-gripped the weapon with both hands and centered the barrel on Castaneda. He let the rest of his breath out and lowered the gun.

"I can't do it, Billie. All this time, I prayed for this chance, only to let it slip away. I let McMillan die, and the man responsible is there."

"That's 'cause you ain't like him. You're no murderer."

Parker silently watched Castaneda pace in front of the building, agitated and growing angrier with each passing minute.

"Why didn't you try to stop me?" Parker asked.

"On account of I got faith in you."

"It wouldn't help Miguel if I'd put Castaneda down. He'd—"

Castaneda's cell rang, and the Los Muertos shot caller answered with an angry whip of a fingertip, reminding Parker of a scorpion.

"Where are you? I want my money!" Castaneda growled. He spun around as if the call had come from nearby. "Show yourself."

Castaneda motioned to his men. They fanned out with stubby-barreled automatic rifles at the ready—not searching, but watching and waiting to unleash their lethal charge.

"Where's Brunell?" Parker asked.

"Maybe he's too afraid to show his face."

"I thought he'd want to do this face-to-face.

I dunno, Brunell always wants to make a shine in public, but deep down, I think he's afraid. Like he's always hidin' somethin'. You know, bein' what he's not. Which he was, I guess, him bein' an ex-con and all."

"Huh. He is afraid. You're right, Billie. Brunell, or Burns, or whoever, is afraid his secrets are going to get out. He can't let anyone know. Everyone who knew is systematically being taken down. Roger, the board members, Mr. Hernandez, the storekeeper, Juan Estrada, and Tomaso Hernandez—all of them."

"Then he ain't done yet. Miguel knows, we know, and him," Billie said as she pointed at Castaneda.

"Brunell's not going to pay up."

The word's echo hadn't died when a shot cracked in the dry desert air. One of Castaneda's men spun and dropped on the red dirt. The gunshot sent Castaneda and the rest of his Los Muertos soldiers to cover.

Castaneda ducked, pulled a gold-plated Desert Eagle handgun, and sent two quick shots, downing Mark and Les, who seemed as surprised as anyone when the first gunshot sounded. The fifty-caliber round lifted Les's skinny frame four inches off the ground. The white supremacist was dead before his body dropped in the dust. Mark's body, pinned against the cargo container until he slid down the metal, crumpling against the door.

The Los Muertos soldiers didn't know where the shot came from based on the urgent clipped Spanish between them.

"You make out any of what they're saying?"

"One says it came from the west. Nobody saw where exactly. It had to be the guy we saw slip up to the rise with his rifle."

Castaneda wheeled around the corner of the cargo container, and another round from the sniper cracked into the steel frame of the box as the Gang leader ducked behind cover.

The three remaining Los Muertos gunmen started peppering the hill with fire. Puffs of dust and rock flew into the air as their bullets struck the ground. It was cover fire, allowing Castaneda to circle around and attempt to approach the sniper from his flank.

Castaneda paused at the rear corner of the cargo box, timed his movement with the cover fire and sprinted to the Black SUV. Instead of moving to the sniper's position, the gang leader crawled into the SUV and started the engine.

One of his men shifted when the engine roared to life, exposing his head from behind cover. The sniper shifted position to the south and put a round through the gang member's neck.

Two seconds later, a second gunshot slammed into the SUV's hood, and the engine sputtered a few seconds before it coughed and died.

Parker removed the key fob from his pocket and crushed the red button. It wasn't out of concern for Castaneda and his men. With these stray rounds popping off in random directions, it was a matter of time until another one pierced the cargo box where Miguel was trapped.

Three minutes—that's what Agent Collins said. His faith in the FBI would be tested.

The gunman closest to Parker and Billie sprinted to the northbound trail and fell behind a rock a fraction of a second before a gunshot hit the dirt behind him. The gangster leveled the barrel of his weapon over the rock and blindly fired off a dozen rounds, the last three pinging off the disabled SUV.

"Billie, I gotta get Miguel outta there. Stay put."

Parker edged down the incline and crept closer to the gunman as he shoved a fresh magazine into his rifle. Once again, he blindly fired three-round bursts to where he believed the sniper's last location was.

While the gunman was occupied, Parker crept up on the man's position. "Drop it!"

The startled gunman turned toward Parker. When he spotted the business end of Parker's Glock, he let go of his weapon and held his empty hands out.

"On your stomach, now."

The Los Muertos gunman complied and lay face down in the dirt. He looked slightly relieved.

Parker pulled a zip tie from his belt and secured the man's hands.

"You stay put. Don't make me regret this."

"I'm not going anywhere."

Parker got on a knee and risked exposing himself to gunfire. The Los Muertos soldier was nowhere to be seen. And with him, Castaneda vanished.

Parker stepped from behind the rock as an armored personnel carrier pulled into the dirt lot by the cargo container. Yellow stenciled FBI lettering on the side and darkened glass gave off a sinister vibe.

Parker glanced at his watch. Four minutes.

"You're late."

Chapter Fifty-Three

Special Agent Collins stepped from the rear of the personnel carrier behind the six tactical team members in black body armor and heavy weapons. The team fanned out and found no one to take down.

Collins stood over a dead Los Muertos gunman at the base of the cargo box.

"Your handiwork?"

"Nope. Castaneda and his men walked into an ambush here."

"Where's he?"

"Castaneda and one of his men slipped away while their team came under fire. Two down here. Another one in restraints over there on the trail and two in the building in the next clearing."

Parker jogged to the cargo box and hefted the heavy padlock securing the door. Four bullet holes pierced the metal door.

"Miguel! Can you hear me?" Parker pounded a hand on the plate's metal surface. No response sounded from within the metal death trap. If the bullets didn't kill him, the oppressive heat inside the container...

One of the tactical team members shoved Parker aside and pulled a set of bolt cutters from his plate carrier. Once the lock was cut, the team stacked behind the lead, who plucked a flash-bang grenade from his belt.

Parker grabbed his arm. "There's no need for that. There's a boy inside."

The FBI man shoved Parker aside, sending him to the ground. "I'm not getting my team hurt."

"Then let me open it."

"Stand down."

Parker stood and pressed toward the door. The FBI man drew back his rifle and struck Parker in the midsection. Parker doubled over and tried to catch his breath. The FBI operator readied to slam the rifle butt on Parker's head.

"Vincent. Back off," Collins ordered.

The rifle butt lowered, and the tactical team member gave Parker a shoulder as he pushed past him.

Parker pulled the remaining lock shard from the hasp and tossed it aside. He slid the heavy ratchet and threw the bolt. The smell from the interior was a putrid mix of sweat and decay. Parker knew the odor. He'd encountered it when undocumented migrants were abandoned by their coyotes and left to die, baked in the desert sun.

"Miguel!"

The light crept in as the cargo box door opened. Three men came into view. Each bound with thick wire around their neck. Their gray, bloated faces gave away they died days ago.

The door swung wider and exposed two human forms. Two men, hands bound with wire behind their back and electrical tape over their mouths. Heads limp. Bodies listless. Parker locked onto the body on the far left.

"Miguel!"

He ran to Miguel, tipped the boy face up, and watched his eyes roll back.

"I need medical attention in here."

A scuffling sound from behind Parker marked the tactical team entering. A black medical bag plopped on the floor next to Miguel.

Parker peeled the tape from Miguel's mouth. The FBI paramedic slipped an oxygen mask over his face and began ripping a shirtsleeve to insert an IV.

"Dehydrated. Vein's rolling… there, got it." A plastic IV bag fed into the back of Miguel's hand. "Hold this."

The paramedic used both hands to force the IV solution into Miguel's system. The IV push could speed up what could take hours for a drip IV to infuse into his system.

"Is he gonna be okay?" Billie asked from the open door.

"Gotta get him out of here, for starters. Need to evac him to the closest hospital. Have to cool his body temp." The paramedic whispered into his throat-mounted microphone.

Two black-clad FBI operators entered with a collapsible stretcher. Parker and the FBI team members placed Miguel on the canvas and aluminum stretcher and carried him out of the metal-sided abattoir. Miguel was the sole survivor.

The stretcher loaded into the rear of the armored vehicle while Miguel received a thorough exam. Collins stepped to the rear door and tapped Parker's arm. "How's he doing?"

"He's been locked in there for a couple days. He's lucky he's not like the others."

"We got a facial ID on two of the victims inside. The ones with the wire neckties—they were known Sinaloa Cartel hitters. The other one, no hit in the system. My guess is he's someone unlucky enough to run into these guys."

"Cartel? They must want Castaneda bad to send a pair of assassins up north." Parker knew his message to the Cartel from Larry Sutton, the attorney was delivered. When the two hitmen didn't report back, the Cartel would send more until Castaneda was done.

"We need to move this kid to a hospital. We need a Medivac," the paramedic said, referring to a medical helicopter.

"Use ours," Collins said. "It's already here."

A black-clad operator behind Collins and Parker said, "What? You gonna waste resources on a—"

Parker spun and grabbed the man by his plate carrier. "You better not finish that sentence, asshole." The same FBI operator who wanted to toss a flash-bang grenade into the enclosed steel box.

"Or what?"

Parker tightened his grip on the man while he balled the fist of his free hand.

"Knock it off, Vincent. Back off."

The FBI man didn't back down, but Parker felt the tension ease in the man's body.

Vincent shoved Parker's hand away. "Shoulda left him in there with the rest of the trash."

Parker swung and caught Vincent square in the mouth, knocking him back a few steps.

Parker shook his hand from the impact.

"Your mine now, asshole," Vincent said, wiping blood from his mouth. "Assaulting a federal officer."

"Stand down, Vincent. Now!" Collins ordered. "You had that coming, and I've wanted to do it for months. Stow your gear and find a ride back to the field office. You're done."

Vincent grunted and stormed off.

"Sorry about that," the paramedic said. "The guy's been on edge for a while now. Don't know what got him wound up."

"Parker, hop in. The chopper is a half-mile away."

Parker jumped into the rear, Billie pointed at herself and then in the direction they came. She was going to point the FBI team to the metal building and backtrack to Parker's jeep. Parker tossed her his keys.

Billie waved as the armored vehicle swept out of the dirt lot. A line of four Pima County Sheriff's and unmarked vehicles slid into positions near the cargo box.

Parker saw the worry on Billie's face. She'd become almost as attached to Miguel as he was. Worry Castaneda was out there, and their plan to lure Brunell to the scene was a failure, but most of all, worry they'd found Miguel too late.

Chapter Fifty-Four

The transfer to the helicopter and the flight north to the sprawling Veteran's Administration hospital in Phoenix swallowed thirty long minutes. Miguel never stirred during the ordeal, and Parker kept watch over the boy the entire time. He'd rub, pat, or hold a hand or arm to reassure himself as much as Miguel that everything was going to be okay. But could it ever be?

The noise in the helicopter made it impossible to whisper words of comfort. He tuned out the buzz of radio communications and crew chatter, which couldn't distract him away from watching the rise and fall of Miguel's chest.

Agent Collins tapped him on the shoulder.

"I said we'll be landing in two minutes."

Parker nodded in response.

"You see who the shooter was picking off Castaneda's men?"

"I saw a guy take a position on the slight rise to the west. Looked like a Remington 700 rifle over his shoulder. Not tall, desert camo pants, long sleeve tan shirt. Had a wide-brimmed hat, so I couldn't make out any facial features."

"A 'boonie' hat? Like one of those sun hats?"

"I guess so."

"Hey, Morgan, you got your 'boonie' on you? Toss it here," Collins said over the radio to a team member to Parker's left.

The man dug in the pocket of his tactical bag and threw a folded black wad to Collins. The FBI agent shook it out and held it to Parker. "Look like

285

this?"

"Yeah, almost exactly, different color is all. More of a brown to match the desert."

Collins tossed the hat to the man next to Parker.

"What you're describing is a military issue. Could be former service member, or militia nut buying out government surplus stores."

"Clement, the guy we tied to the Sun Valley Sniper shootings, was former Army. We tracked him at the location of at least two of the shootings. It looked racially motivated at first. Some Aryan Nation flavor to it."

"What changed your thinking?"

"All the victims were tied to the Immigrant Coalition and supported an increase in the group's activity to move migrants from down south."

"Still sounds racially motivated to me. Aryan Nation don't like anyone who ain't all lily-white and march to the same Nazi drummer. Bringing undocumented immigrants into the country would get their Eva Braun lovin' panties in a twist."

"There's more going on, and I can't quite put it together yet. Los Muertos, Brunell, and money transfers out of the country. It's all involved."

A clipped radio transmission sounded in Parker's headphones. "One minute out."

Parker leaned to look out the window. The hospital helipad loomed into view. He felt his stomach flip as the pilot swooped down to the landing pad. The angle of descent and swift drop to the surface marked an aviator with experience flying in a combat zone.

Fractions of a second before the skids touched down, the Agent next to Parker flung open the side door. A medical team met the helicopter before the rotors slowed. Miguel was transferred from the helicopter bay to a hospital gurney, and the onboard paramedic briefed the green scrub-wearing hospital staff.

The pilot lifted the visor and looked over her shoulder. "Hope the boy will be all okay."

"Thanks for getting him here so quick." Parker didn't notice the pilot was a woman until she pulled up her visor. Deep set-blue eyes stared back at him.

She grinned. "Give us a five-star rating on your Uber app."

Collins hopped out, and Parker followed, after a wave to the helicopter crew. The rotors spun up, and a high-pitched whine grew louder as the helicopter lurched from the landing pad and lifted skyward.

Parker followed on the heels of the medical team with Miguel as they shoved through a set of glass doors into the hospital. The veteran's hospital showed its age but was spotless in appearance. They rushed past a nursing station and rolled into an emergency room bay surrounded by faded blue curtains.

A doctor in a starched white smock pushed through the curtain and stopped short. "I thought this was an FBI case."

"He is," a young nurse said while changing IV bags.

The doctor frowned, causing the spray tan lines around his chin to dimple. "I don't know what kind of joke this is. You pulled me out of a meeting with the regional administrator for this? Another wayward wetback getting caught out in the sun."

Parker pushed the doctor out of the treatment bay and backed him up to a wall with a forearm to his chest.

"Listen here, you officious prick. That kid in there is more of a man than you'll ever be." Parker plucked the doctor's name tag from his spotless starched smock. "Dr. Myers. Let me tell you how it's gonna be. You're gonna go find an actual doctor to treat this kid. I don't want you to put one racist finger on him. You hear me?"

"You can't tell me what to do."

"I can, and I did. Get out of my sight before I feed this name tag to you."

Parker released his forearm pressure, and the doctor sidestepped away from the wall.

"You act like he's your kid." Dr. Myers straightened his coat and brushed off imaginary lint from the pristine creases.

"He is."

The doctor's eyes narrowed as if he couldn't conceive of any relationship between a middle-aged white man and a brown-skinned kid like Miguel.

"Whatever. It takes all kinds."

"I know exactly what kind you are—doctor."

"My name tag?" Dr. Myers held his hand out, demanding the return of the symbol of his station.

Parker tossed it on the ground at his feet.

"Get out of my sight," Parker said in a tone carrying unveiled contempt.

The doctor looked as if he was considering a comeback, but turned on his heels and strode from the emergency room.

Parker slid back inside the blue curtain. The nurse who replaced the IV bags looked at Parker with a slight grin on her face. A second nurse put away a blood pressure cuff and gently tucked a pillow beneath Miguel's head.

The second nurse, Yolanda, according to her name tag, leaned to Parker. "We've been waiting for someone to put him where he belongs."

"I need a doctor for him," Parker said.

"Don't you fret none. We already called for one while you were having your *discussion* with Dr. Myers."

On cue, a young woman stepped through the curtain. Less than five and a half feet tall with ebony dark skin, her gaze focused on Miguel immediately. The name embroidered on her white smock identified her as Dr. Oymango, Medical Director.

"Thank you for coming to the rescue, Dr. O." the lead nurse said.

The nurse then recited a litany of numbers and medical terms to the doctor, most of which Parker didn't understand. Dr. O moved in, held a stethoscope to Miguel's chest, and listened to his heart and breathing.

"Breathing is labored. Put him on two liters O-two. I want his electrolytes up. How long has he been unconscious?"

All eyes turned to Parker.

"They'd held him in a storage container for over twenty-four hours. He wasn't responsive when we found him."

"I want a full workup, a CBC, cardiac biomarkers, metabolic panel, and C-reactive protein. I want to know how much organ failure we're dealing with here."

The words organ failure made Parker's knees buckle. "Is he—is he going to be —?"

"The next twenty-four hours will tell. He's young, so he's got a fighting chance," the doctor said. "Is he your—?"

"Son. Foster son. What does he need? How can I help?"

Dr. O grasped Parker's hand, tipped her head up to meet his gaze, and spoke. "It's up to him now. We'll hydrate him, pump him full of electrolytes, and keep his core temperature regulated. His body is shutting down. We won't know the extent of the damage until we have his blood work back. We're going to do everything we can."

"He was trapped in a damned metal box. If I'd gotten to him sooner."

"Finding him when you did was critical. Any longer, and he would face irreversible organ failure. The next few hours will tell us a great deal. I have hope. I need you to have hope, too."

Parker's chin quivered. "Thank you, doctor. Can I stay with him?"

"Would you leave if I said no?"

"Probably not."

She smiled. "I thought as much. We'll set him up in a room, and you can be with him as much as you want. I need you to rest. You're going to be needed in the weeks to come."

"Thank you."

"You're most welcome. And I'm sorry about your introduction to Dr. Myers. He can be a bit—"

"Irritating."

"I was going to say he can be a bit of an ass. A holdover from a bygone generation, one unwilling to see others as equals if he sees us at all."

"How do you put up with it?"

"I work for the government. As irritating as Dr. Myers is, unfortunately, he's not the worst I have to deal with."

A nurse guided Parker by the arm and directed him to a waiting area. "Let us change him, clean him up a bit, and get him settled. I'll come and let you know after he's in his room."

Parker plopped into a hard plastic chair in the emergency room waiting area. Most of the people here were grey-haired, frail, and confused. He'd seen this before. In a city boasting of its senior living communities, there seemed to be no safety net to catch those who couldn't care for themselves any longer. Alone, or abandoned, yet Parker knew these were the lucky ones.

Head down, he counted the lines on the floor tiles when a pair of dusty, worn black boots stepped into his vision.

Parker didn't glance upward. "Hey, Billie."

"How's Miguel?"

"It's a wait-and-see. They say he's lucky we got to him when we did. Nothing about this is lucky. How'd you get here so fast?"

"It's been three hours."

Parker glanced at a clock on the wall behind the nurse's station. Three hours slipped away while he sat here. It didn't seem possible.

He popped up from his chair, legs stiff from sitting, and approached the nurse behind the counter.

"Excuse me. Is there any update on the boy I came in with, Miguel?"

"Yes, I didn't want to disturb you. We moved him to ICU."

"ICU? Intensive Care? Why didn't someone tell me?"

"Dr. O wanted him closely monitored, and the ICU team is the best to make sure it happens. I tried to wake you, but you were exhausted."

"He didn't get worse, then?"

"No, do you want me to check with ICU for an update?"

"I want to see him. Where's the ICU?"

Parker followed the directions to the ICU on the floor above. When the elevator doors parted, the sounds of a busy hospital ward hit unexpectedly. He'd always thought an ICU was a quiet place where non-responsive people convalesced, or post-surgical patients recovered. The bleep of heart monitors, IV alarms, low respiration warnings, and the raspy whir of ventilators told an unsettling story.

Most unnerving was Tim Brunell, leaning against the nurse's station, waiting for Parker.

Chapter Fifty-Five

"What the hell are you doing here?" Parker said as he rushed from the elevator with Billie in tow.

Brunell broke into a politician's smile, bleached white teeth gleaming with no warmth behind it.

"I wanted to see how our boy is doing."

"How's he doing? He's here because of you. Because he believed in you and what he thought the Coalition stood for. Then you sell him out. You literally sold him out, refusing to pay off Castaneda."

Parker edged closer to Brunell while he spoke, and the slick politician never broke character.

Brunell straightened slightly after Parker finished. "See, the thing is, kids like Miguel are impressionable. Roger and his followers fed them this altruistic open border nonsense. His goal of bringing in as many migrants as possible was always politically naïve. Roger's dealing with the underworld got him killed, and Miguel found himself pulled under as well."

"Weren't you the one Los Muertos wanted?" Parker said.

"Obviously. I cut them off from the Coalition's money. Roger should've never gone into business with them."

"Still doesn't justify using Miguel as a pawn in your game with Castaneda. You could have paid him off and got 'em to release Miguel and the others. They might have lived if you—"

"Negotiate with terrorists? Once you pay them off, they keep coming back. You cannot make deals with these people."

"As long as it's not you being held in a steel prison. If it's a couple of brown-skinned undocumented migrants, that's okay with you?"

"Violence on the border is nothing new—especially for the people who make the personal choice to illegally cross the border. They may have legitimate reasons for fleeing from wherever it was they came from, but extortion, crime, and predators surround them. We can and should help those who arrive, but we cannot be a part of a human trafficking network."

"You've got this worked out, don't you? Your slick talking points and blaming Roger for the deals with the Coalition. You told me about the payoffs to Los Muertos, remember? You knew about them and went along with it."

"I think you misheard me. Besides, Roger was the man in charge, in control of the Coalition's finances, and his misguided approach threatened to reverse the years of good work we'd accomplished."

"You haven't explained why you're here? It's not out of any concern for Miguel."

"Believe what you will. It's a miracle he's alive. I wanted to see if he could tell us what happened. We might never know what terror he experienced. His story could open the eyes of—"

"Stop. Just stop. He doesn't need you making him some poster child for your campaign."

"Or a martyr, depending on how it turns out."

Parker rushed at Brunell. "You son-of-a-bitch."

A man in a dark suit deftly slipped in between Parker and Brunell. He spun Parker away, using a combination of wrist locks and Parker's own momentum.

Parker felt the pressure on his elbow, pressing it to the breaking point.

"Let him go," Brunell commanded.

The bodyguard complied and released Parker with a shove away from his protectee.

The elevator bell chimed, and the door slid open. Lynnette Finch, Tully, and Johns stepped off the car into the ICU waiting area.

Johns was the first to notice Parker was facing off with a thick-necked man in a dark suit. The suit didn't hide the strap of muscle along the man's chest, or the butt of a handgun tucked into a shoulder holster.

Johns stepped next to Parker. "You all right there, boss?"

"Brunell and his friend were just leaving."

A staccato voice called over the intercom. "Code blue, room 4. Code blue, ICU room 4."

Parker didn't need to ask. He knew it was Miguel's room. The medical staff hurried in an efficient rush to room 4. The alarm bells and electronic chirps raised in a crescendo.

A slight smirk appeared on Brunell's face.

Parker ran to Miguel's room. Billie waited at the door, her eyes full of fear.

"I went in to see him. He weren't breathing. Someone disconnected his monitors."

Parker stepped inside the intensive care room, and four medical personnel hovered over Miguel's bed. Chest compressions were being administered, and they pushed new IV drugs into the boy's veins. The monitor tones were constant and flat.

He needed to see Miguel. A tentative step forward caught the eye of one of the attending nurses.

"You should wait outside," she said.

"What happened?"

"Please, sir, wait in the hall."

Parker caught the glint of an object on the floor and a trail of red dust. He pushed past the nurse who was going to escort him from the room and dropped to a knee.

"What's Adenosine?"

A doctor turned in Parker's direction, a puzzled look on his face.

"There's a half-empty vile on the floor and it's labeled Adenosine. Is this what you're giving him?"

Parker witnessed the chaos of an emergency room before, where compresses and supplies are hurriedly used and discarded. Medications, though, were typically tightly controlled.

"Let me see that."

Parker grabbed the vial and handed it to the doctor.

"This isn't ours."

Dr. O rushed into the room and peered over the ICU doctor's shoulder.

"Start 10 milligrams aminophylline."

"It's too late—"

"Do it now," she ordered.

A nurse prepared the syringe with the medication from the crash cart and handed it to the doctor. He slid the needle into an IV port and jammed the plunger down.

The monitors showed no change.

"Defibrillator—charge to 120," Dr. O said.

The first doctor readied the defibrillator paddles and charged the machine. An increasing whine marked the current building strength.

A nurse bared Miguel's thin chest.

"Clear." The doctor placed the paddles and released the charge. Miguel's body convulsed from the electric current flowing through him.

"There." Dr. O pointed at the heart monitor, and the line flickered from flat to an uneven peak before settling into a regular rhythm.

"Is he okay?" Parker asked.

"I want to know how adenosine got in his system," Dr. O said.

"There's nothing indicating he received it on his chart," one nurse said.

"The vial. It's not ours. The drug company—it's not one I recognize."

"Let me see it," Parker asked.

Dr. O nodded her approval, and the doctor handed the small glass vial to Parker.

He turned the glass container in his palm. The small print bore a label in English and Spanish. The pharmaceutical company was vaguely familiar, but Parker couldn't place it.

"Billie, look at this. You see Mexi-Pharm on your runs to Hermosillo?"

"Mexi-Pharm, yeah, I know them. They been stockin' us supplies for the clinics in the outskirts of the city in them squatter camps of people waitin' to make the crossin'. "'Member, I told you about raids on the camp?"

"The stolen medical supplies? Yeah, I do. How did this end up here?"

"It'd be like Castaneda to pull somethin' like this. But I didn't see no sign of him or his Low Muertos lowlifes."

Lynne cleared her throat at the door. "Nathan, is everything okay with Miguel? I heard you talking—"

"Someone tried to kill him."

Her eyes widened. "What? How did anyone know he was here?"

"Someone obviously found him and wanted to keep him quiet."

"Pretty damn risky to try something so desperate—"

"Desperate. Where's Brunell?"

"He and his goon left. Something about a campaign event. Why?"

"He was here before I was—in the ICU. How would he know?"

"Ain't nothin' secret, if you wanna know."

Dr. O tapped Parker's shoulder.

"He's stable. We're going to keep an eye on his heart rhythm and make sure there are no aftereffects from the Adenosine. That's given to patients who present with supraventricular tachycardia."

"What would that do to him? I mean, why would someone use that?"

"Adenosine is extremely short-acting. Usually allows the heart to convert to a normal rhythm in thirty seconds or so. But, in Miguel's weakened condition, it was sufficient to stop his heart. I'm glad your friend found him."

"Billie, you see anyone coming out of his room?" Parker asked.

"Nuh-uh. He was alone when I showed up."

Parker paced in the small room and stopped at the doorway. He jutted his chin toward the nurse's station.

"What are those monitors for?"

Dr. O joined alongside Parker.

"The monitors. Of course. We installed cameras in the hallways to let the on-duty staff know where their partner is."

"The cameras watch each room?"

"No, patient privacy wouldn't allow that. Here, let me show you." She tugged Parker by the arm and led him a few steps outside the room, and turned so they were facing down the hallway toward the elevator. "See next to the fire alarm? The camera captures the hallway in this direction. There are three others facing down the halls."

"Please tell me the feeds are recorded."

"They are. I don't know how long we keep the recorded images."

"Tully, can you go find out?"

"Sure, boss. Oh, I got the California prison records on Ruben Burns. I don't know what to make of them." Tully handed a file to Parker.

"Like you said, Burns was locked up in Chino and ended up in Palm Hall—their segregated wing because he got put on a hit list by a street gang affiliated with the Mexican Mafia. He and another convict got caught doing some kind of scam on inmates."

"That's the kinda thing gets you a shank in the kidney," Billie said.

"That explains the reason for a name change," Parker said.

"Name change? Who are we talking about?" Lynne asked.

"Ruben Burns legally changed his name a few years back. Meet Tim Brunell."

"What?" Lynne said. "The senate candidate running a tough on border crime campaign is a felon?"

"Ex-felon, technically. And apparently, by law, he is allowed to change his name."

"Huh. That really makes this part fit," Tully said.

"What's that, Pete?"

Tully flipped the pages in the file Parker held and tapped a faded copy of a rules violation report. "Read the first line."

Parker scanned the faded document. "You're kidding me."

"What? Lynne said."

"The convict working the prison scam with Brunell—or Burns, then—was Esteban Castaneda."

Chapter Fifty-Six

"Brunell and Castaneda were running scams back then, and they are doing it again now," Parker said.

"I dunno. Someone was shooting at Castaneda, like for reals out there in the desert," Billie said.

"As much as I hate to say it, maybe Brunell was being honest when he said he wanted to break away from Los Muertos involvement in the Immigrant Coalition. Could be a single kernel of truth in what he was selling. Now with Roger Jessup dead, there's no way to prove it wasn't Roger's deal all along."

"Like we done said, Castaneda and Los Muertos are in it for the money. If Brunell cut them off, then them two is at war."

"Speaking of money, our organized crime task force hasn't found a smoking gun in the ledgers you shared," Lynne said.

"Another dead end."

"We'll keep pushing. I've asked the JTTF to pile on as well."

The Joint Terrorism Task Force would bring the resources of multiple agencies to bear on the money trail.

"Thanks for that, Lynne."

Tully accompanied Dr. O to find the camera feed that would pinpoint who entered Miguel's room in the minutes before Billie found him.

"Nathan, I've arranged for U.S. Marshal's coverage here at the hospital for as long as you and Miguel need it."

"Thanks, Lynne, but I think I'd like to have people Miguel knows." He flashed back to the disgruntled FBI operative back at the storage shed. Was he the leak announcing Miguel's location? "We had a bad experience with the feds out there, and I need people I know and trust. I trust you, Lynne, but I can't take any chances here."

Parker filled her in on the details of the FBI operator who wanted to toss a flash bang into the small storage container and who got pushed out of shape when Miguel was put on the helicopter for urgent transport.

"Remember the guy's name?"

"I don't. Collins will know who I'm talking about."

"I'll speak with him. Please let me know if you need anything, Nathan." She leaned in and hugged him. It was the first personal contact they shared in over three years. He missed that in his life.

"I need to make a call. Billie, can you sit with Miguel for a minute?"

She agreed while Parker followed Lynne to the elevator.

"The last couple of years changed you, Nathan. I mean that in a good way. You've always been a good man—a bit headstrong and set in your ways—"

"Look who's talking."

She grinned. "You're—I don't know—caring now. The boy in there has been a good influence on you. It's not all about the job all the time."

"Thanks, Lynne, I think."

She smiled and shook her head. She hugged him once before she ducked into the elevator and pressed the down button.

Once the elevator door closed, Parker found a seat in the waiting room and dialed the Avondale Substation.

"Deputy Marsh, please."

He glanced at the art print posters meant to comfort the family waiting for news of their loved one. But the smiling families and little pep-talk-like words of positive energy came off flat and phony. No one sitting in an ICU waiting room was smiling when getting an update from a movie-star-looking, spray-tanned doctor.

"Marsh." The voice sounded in his ear, ripping him away from the wall hangings.

"Linda, it's Parker."

"Hey, Nathan, what's up?"

Parker quickly gave her a rundown on Miguel's abduction and condition.

"My God, Nathan. Terrible, just terrible. What can I do?"

"I have a favor to ask. I need someone here to watch Miguel. If whoever tried to kill him realizes he failed, then they might try again. Could you come and help me keep an eye on things? Miguel knows you, and when he wakes up, it would be helpful to have people he knows around him."

"I'm on my way. I'll clear it with the Sergeant. Won't be a problem. Give me fifteen minutes."

"Thanks, Linda. I owe you."

"Yes, you do, and I intend to collect. See you in a bit." She disconnected the call, and as Parker pocketed his phone, the elevator chimed.

What did Lynne forget? He wondered.

The doors parted, and Barry Johns stormed from the elevator and nearly ran him down.

Parker held on to Barry's thick arms to avoid falling.

"What's got you steamrolling?"

"Sorry, Nathan. How's Miguel? Tully called and told me someone tried to get to him."

"Tully's looking at video now to see if we can ID who entered Miguel's room."

"But he's gonna be okay?"

Parker felt his chin quiver. "I hope so, Barry."

"That kid's been through the wringer. Everything he's gone through, and he's never let it change him, you know? I don't know how he does it."

"Miguel's been resilient since the day Billie and I met him on the trek north from Hermosillo. No family left, all killed by MS-13 in El Salvador, and he sets out on his own to find a new home in a strange country to avoid being caught up in gang violence. But it finds him anyway. I should've been able to prevent this. I screwed this up, and he's paying the price."

"This ain't on you. There's nothing you could've done to change any of this. Evil is hidden around us. It's always there, and we don't get to choose when and where it finds us. Miguel saw it and stood up to it in his work with the Coalition. The world is a dangerous place to live, not because people are evil, but because of the people who don't do anything about it. Not everyone is who they seem, and Miguel recognized them for who they are."

"When did you become so philosophical?"

"Here. It's the military records you asked about. Ruben Burns... I got help from Lynnette Finch over at the FBI. She was able to put me in touch with the people who pulled these old records. Over eighteen million files were destroyed in a fire back in 1973. Did you know that? Lucky for us, we didn't need to dig back to the 70s."

Parker took the thin file from Johns and opened the pressboard cover. The topmost form was the discharge document, the DD Form 214. Under the type of character of service box, it read "Other than honorable discharge."

"What did Burns do to get him the boot?"

"It doesn't say anything about covering up an assault on another soldier, but check this out." Barry flipped pages to the end of the file and tapped a finger. "Same date. They issued Clement a dishonorable discharge. And this..."

Parker flipped to the front page. "They were both assigned at Fort Irwin."

"In the same unit. We knew Clement's discharge was tied to a sex offense on base. Was Burns involved?"

"And Burns covered it up. What was Burns doing at Fort Irwin? It's a training center, isn't it?"

"The records say he was an instructor. They ran urban warfare scenarios there. Get this—Burns was sniper trained at Fort Benning."

"Son-of-a-bitch. It's Brunell. It's been Brunell all along. Clement was a decoy."

"What are you saying, boss?"

"Burns is Brunell. He changed his name after he went to prison—after his army discharge. He's the Sun Valley Shooter!"

The elevator chime sounded, and Deputy Linda Marsh stepped from the car. She noticed the excited expression on Parker's face.

"What did I miss?" she said.

Linda wasn't wearing her uniform. She'd changed into a pair of light blue jeans and a black polo shirt. She looked smaller without her ballistic vest, utility belt, sidearm, and taser.

"Barry, can you reach out and get a 'twenty' on Brunell? The feds are watching his movements. Lynne or Agent Collins should know where we can find him."

"You don't need to bother," Linda said. "I was listening to the radio on the way over. Brunell is holding a huge campaign rally over at the Ak-Chin Pavilion. Said there were about fifteen hundred campaign donors set to attend. Supposed to kick off in about an hour."

"Perfect. Barry, never mind then. Find Tully and see what happened to the Remington Sniper rifle Castaneda delivered to me. I've got a feeling I know where it came from."

"Brunell?"

"Get the lab reports on that weapon."

"On it," Barry said as he strode off and checked in with a nurse at the counter.

"Any change in Miguel's condition?" Linda asked.

"Not yet. I'll show you where he is." They began down the hallway together. "Thanks for coming over. You changed?"

"I'm here in an unofficial capacity. The station brass are getting sweated about overtime spending. But the sergeant agreed to let me burn some vacation today, then report here tomorrow as a regular assignment for as long as Miguel needs me."

"I'll make it up to you. I didn't mean to make you burn vacation."

"I've got plenty, don't worry. Someone actually had the balls to come in here and try to hurt him? Don't worry, that's not going to happen now."

They entered the ICU room, where Billie sat at Miguel's bedside. She held his hand and looked like she'd been whispering to him.

"Deputy Marsh. Good to see you."

"You too, Billie."

"Doctor O came in and said his organ function tests won't be in for a while, but she thinks we got him in time."

301

"Thanks to you, Billie. If you hadn't gone on down to his room, it might've been too late."

"It's my fault."

"None of this is on you, Billie."

"Miguel got involved in the Immigrant Coalition because of me. He wants to help people like himself and heard me talking about them."

"Would you two stop it," Linda said.

Parker and Billie shut up and turned to the five-five off-duty deputy. She stood with her hands on her hips, scolding the two of them.

"Are you listening to yourselves trying to out-martyr one another? What happened to Miguel isn't on either of you. Someone did this to him and wanted to kill him here in his own bed to prevent him from telling what he knew."

Parker stiffened. "My God. You're right. Everyone was killed to keep them from telling a secret. Miguel knew it. Jessup, Tomaso, Mr. Hernandez—all of them knew it."

Linda raised an uncertain eyebrow.

Billie kicked the toe of her boot into the worn vinyl flooring. "Like I said, the Immigrant Coalition has been making deals with the wrong people, like Castaneda and Los Muertos, to smuggle migrants over the border. Weren't no secret, though."

"This was never Castaneda."

"He took Miguel—the dog track—you saw what he done."

"The secrets. Linda reminded me someone wanted to prevent Miguel from telling what he knew. Castaneda didn't care. He was trying to expose the Coalition's deals. He'd have wanted Miguel to spill it."

Billie's eyes widened.

"You've got it. Only one person knew the secrets, literally where the bodies were buried."

"Brunell," Billie said.

Chapter Fifty-Seven

"Billie, can you and Linda stay with Miguel?"

"Sure, but I—"

"Call me the second anything changes with him."

Billie protested, and Parker cut her off. "Billie, dammit. They almost killed Miguel for what he knew. Whoever did it thinks you're a threat too. You know what the Coalition has done, who they've made deals with—at least enough to make you a threat to Brunell and whoever he has doing his dirty work. You are safer here with Linda."

"I can take care of myself. I been doing it for years with no one watching over my shoulder like a nursemaid."

"I never said you couldn't. But I need you here to make sure nothing happens to Miguel. They might come back and try again once they realize the first attempt didn't work."

Billie reluctantly agreed, not happy with being held back.

"Linda, thanks so much for being here. You gave me the perspective I needed to make this piece of this puzzle fall into place."

"You're welcome, I guess? You going to tell me what you figured out?"

"You said it was about secrets. We knew that all along, but who had the most to lose if the secrets were revealed?"

"Sounds like you know who they are."

"I need a bit to prove it, and I think I know where to find it. It starts with Brunell."

"There's more to it, though?"

"I think so. I need to prove it. Can I borrow your car?"

303

Parker went in for a hug. "Thanks, Linda. I owe you."

"I know you do, and now you're really going to pay up."

"I'll call you when I know anything."

Parker left them with Miguel and found Linda's Volkswagen Jetta, where she told him she'd parked it. He hit his knees on the steering wheel as he got in and needed to move the seat back to accommodate his six-foot height. The light blue Jetta started with a purr, and Parker backed from the slot and tore out of the Veteran's Administration Medical Center parking lot.

He shot east on Indian School Road toward the Ak-Chin Pavilion, where Lynne reported Brunell's campaign stop. He glanced at the clock on the dash. He would not make it there before Brunell was scheduled to meet with his campaign donors.

Parker pressed the gas pedal, and the little Jetta responded. A feathered dreamcatcher hanging from the rearview swung with the increased speed. He sped through the intersection at 83rd Avenue and shot south. The sprawling concert pavilion loomed in the distance.

Flashing his badge let him slip into the parking area. Thankfully, a political rally didn't carry the same draw in this twenty-thousand-seat outdoor arena. There were perhaps a hundred and fifty cars in the lot. Brunell must think this is a bit of a letdown in his campaign to unseat the incumbent State Senator.

Parker jogged into the pavilion and noticed the crowd collected under the shade structure, and most of them stood between the first row of seats and the front of the stage. There would not be a mosh pit at this event, but the biker leathers and a few "Send 'em back where they came from" signs set the tone.

Parker held back toward the rear of the seating. He spotted a burly middle-aged man with a ruddy complexion in a security uniform and waved to him.

"Johnny Hamilton. I heard you retired. You doing this as a side gig?"

"Hey, they pay on time. What can I say? What brings you out here, Parker? These don't seem much like your people," Hamilton said, pointing at a pair of bikers blowing clouds of vape smoke into the air.

"I thought this was supposed to start fifteen minutes ago," Parker said.

"You know these types. Always need to make an entrance. I heard he showed up."

"I need to find Brunell. Where are you staging him?"

"Hold on a sec." Hamilton held a finger to an earpiece while he listened to an incoming message.

"It's going to be another ten minutes. Ought to get these yahoos all riled up by then. Glad they didn't open the beer concession, or we'd be in the middle of a bar fight by now."

"What's the holdup?"

"Beats me. You can ask him yourself. The backstage area is off to the left down there."

Parker thanked Hamilton and started toward the stage when his cell rang.

The caller ID displayed Tully's name.

Parker stopped and answered the call.

"What did you find, Tully? Did either Brunell or his goon go into Miguel's room?"

"No. Neither of them did. The video showed hospital staff coming and going. No one else."

"You sure?"

"Nathan, I've played this thing frontwards and backwards a dozen times. No one but doctors and nurses entered his room."

Parker lowered the phone for a moment and tried to imagine the room and how Miguel was dosed under the watchful eye of the ICU staff. As much as he believed Brunell had a hand in it, the video evidence said otherwise.

"Pete, the last person who went into his room—before Billie found him—who was it?"

"Hold on a second while I cue it up."

Parker heard the keyboard clicking in the background.

"All right, I've got it here. The last person in before Carson was a nurse."

"What did the nurse look like?"

"Average height, long dark shoulder length hair. Didn't see her face. It was like she knew about the camera in the hall."

"Shoulder-length hair? She had it down? Everyone I met at the hospital had their hair pulled up. Was anyone able to tell you who this nurse was?"

"I'll ask. Hold on, one of the staff said something."

In muffled conversation, Tully asked if anyone knew who the woman in the video was? "Are you sure?" Parker overheard Tully seconds before he came back on the line with Parker.

"The woman in the video isn't on staff here. The person I talked to said the blue scrubs our person wore didn't have the VA logo on the front like theirs do. She was an imposter."

"Good work, Tully. Do me a favor and let Linda Marsh know what you've found and make sure no one matching her description comes near his room."

"On it."

Parker hung up and returned his attention to the backstage area. A heavy black curtain served as the only barrier, and he pushed the black canvas aside.

Clustered around a pair of tables were Brunell, his hulking body man, and Isa. They were in deep conversation with someone on a video connection over a laptop.

"You gave us a commitment to be here today," Brunell said.

Parker drew closer without being noticed, but couldn't hear the response from the well-dressed, affluent-looking man on the video feed.

"There are no distractions, Simon. We're able to bring this home. We were counting on your support," Brunell said.

All Parker could make out was a quick brush-off from the absent campaign donor before the screen darkened.

Isa shut the screen and slipped it into her bag. She was dressed for a day on the go. A dark blue suit and athletic shoes instead of her usual heels.

"Detective, I didn't expect you. How's Miguel? Tim told me what happened. I'm sorry. He was a good kid," she said.

"He still is," Parker said.

"I didn't mean it that way. I'm sorry, is all." Her brow knitted.

"Why are you here?" Brunell asked. "I'm about to go on."

"Less than a packed house, though. Donors dropping out on you?"

"None of any importance?"

"We'll adjust and move through this," Isa said.

"What's causing the sudden change of heart from your backers? Did they find out about your past, Ruben?"

Brunell's jaw tightened, and his eyes narrowed. "There's nothing illegal about changing one's name. I'm all about new beginnings."

"Guess your donors don't see it the same way."

"Did you leak it to them? I'll have your ass for that."

"Wasn't me—it's public record, so anyone could have found it if they knew where to look."

Isa looked away for a moment and gave Parker the confirmation he needed. She'd undermined his fundraising efforts. At the coffee shop, she'd mentioned she was done with him, and this was her way of making sure about being done.

"Tell you what wasn't public record—you and Esteban Castaneda were literally thick as thieves back in Chino. Interesting choice of associates."

Brunell shot from his chair. "How dare you?"

"Dare I what? Insinuate you and the head of Los Muertos have been in business together for years?"

"You have no idea what you're talking about."

"I guess he took it personally when you wanted to cut ties with him to run for office."

"You need to leave."

Brunell nodded at his bodyguard, who looked reluctant to toss the detective out of the backstage area, but strode over to Parker and stood in front of him.

"Look, Detective, I'm only doing my job. You gotta leave. Come on, man."

Parker glanced at Brunell and Isa, both with anxious looks on their faces.

"All right, all right, I'm leaving," Parker said.

He turned and pushed back through the curtains, followed by the big man.

Once outside, Parker asked, "How did you and your boss get to the hospital

307

so fast?"

The man shrugged his massive shoulders. "Beats me. He got a call and said he wanted to go look in on someone—I guess he meant the kid."

"Who called, you know?"

The man paused. "Listen, I shouldn't even be talking to you."

"Who was it?"

"Isa. Isa called him and let him know about the kid getting sent to the VA hospital."

The man slipped back through the curtains, and Parker mulled over how Isa would know to tip off Brunell about Miguel's condition?

He nearly tripped over the answer in a trash can at the base of the steps to the backstage area.

Tossed in the garbage was a set of light blue medical scrubs.

Chapter Fifty-Eight

P arker ran back to the curtain and threw it aside. Isa was nowhere in sight.

The sudden movement drew the bodyguard's attention, and he strode to the curtain and Parker.

"Man, don't make this a problem," the big dude said.

"Where's Isa?"

He glanced over his shoulder, back to where Brunell and two men stood. "Don't know. She was here a minute ago. Listen, Mr. Brunell is about to hit the stage. You gotta go now." He pointed back outside.

Across the backstage area, Parker spotted Brunell straightening his collar, casual without a tie, and checking his appearance in a mirror. He noticed Parker in the reflection and issued a little mock salute as he turned and readied to make his entrance on the stage. One man with him slipped a small stack of notecards in Brunell's hand.

Always out front, always making a fuss, and always letting others do the work.

The stage lighting bloomed a pale blue on the stage, washed out in the daylight. A deep baritone voice called from the speakers above the stage. "Ladies and gentlemen, the Patriots of Arizona are proud to support one of our state's leading advocates for public safety through immigration reform. Please welcome your next state senator, Tim Brunell."

The crowd whistled and cheered as Brunell stepped into the spotlight. Waiting in the heat didn't dampen their enthusiasm. The roar from the hundred in the pit echoed under the canopy. Parker realized the crowd noise was enhanced and piped in through the public address system. The collected bikers and militia members in the audience didn't seem to notice and fed off the artificially enhanced fervor.

Brunell stepped forward and seemed to bask in the moment, eyes wide, chin up, and a broad, toothy smile. After he soaked it in, he urged the crowd to stop cheering so he could begin.

There was no podium. Brunell was alone onstage and tucked the notecards in his shirt pocket.

Parker snuck backstage and found a gap in the backdrop where he could watch the performance. He couldn't spot Isa, but she couldn't miss Brunell's address, if for nothing more than to poke holes in his immigration policy.

"What is he doing?" one of Brunell's minders said.

"He's going off script again," the donor said.

Still no sign of Isa. The description of the woman in the hospital video and the scrubs tossed in the trash left little doubt she tried to kill Miguel. But why? She and Miguel seemed ideologically aligned on immigration issues. Both saw the suffering of those trapped in the web of human trafficking by the Cartels and Los Muertos. It couldn't be possible. Isa wasn't the impulsive type to snuff out a kid in a hospital bed.

Brunell started to speak, and it began the same way as the address in front of city hall. "Our citizens live in fear. Fear of being swept up in the wave of violence rolling over the southern border, unchecked and without consequence. The open borders policy is responsible. Failed immigration policy is responsible. The past few weeks alone should give you the evidence you need to enact commonsense immigration reform. Criminals come to this country and kill members of our community. They even tried to silence me."

Boos and jeers sounded from the crowd.

Parker felt the bodyguard's presence. "Your boss is taking a harder line this time around."

"The local party committee aren't too happy about it," the man gestured to the two suits. One was on the phone, and the second watched with his arms crossed and a grim expression.

"Brunell was about helping the undocumented over the border, then he softened to only helping those who were here. Now, this sounds like a keep 'em all out speech."

"I heard him and Isa arguing about the change in position. She wasn't on board with his close-the-border plan. He tried to tell her they could help those who came here and even offer a path to citizenship, but she wasn't hearing it. Isa told him she was done taking orders from him and stormed off."

"That was a few minutes ago?"

"Uh-huh."

"Was she at the hospital with you earlier?"

"Like I said, she called Mr. Brunell. I didn't see her while Mr. B. checked on the kid."

"He went to look in on Miguel?"

"That's what he said. I kept back at the nurse's station while he visited."

He'd check with Tully, but Pete would have mentioned if they spotted Brunell on camera entering Miguel's room. The last person seen going in was a woman. A woman who looked a lot like Isa. Isa, who wore the same shoes the other nurses wore. She dumped the scrubs the moment she arrived at the pavilion.

Parker turned his attention to the stage where Brunell was pandering to the anti-migrant sentiment of the gathered masses. He didn't care where the campaign cash came from as long as it flowed in.

Parker stiffened. The money flow. Brunell was taking the campaign funds and transferring them to accounts in Mexico. But the information came from Isa. How much of it could he believe? She had to be working with Castaneda to undermine and dismantle Brunell.

A glint drew his attention toward the rear of the pavilion. Parker knew instantly. The sun reflected off a rifle scope.

"Shit. Gun."

Parker rushed the stage and dove at Brunell, knocking the man off his feet at the exact moment a gunshot echoed under the pavilion canopy.

At the sharp report of rifle fire, the crowd panicked. They ran from the pit area in all directions.

The bodyguard ran to Parker, and together they rushed Brunell from the stage and into cover behind the screens. The thin partition couldn't stop a bullet, but you can't hit what you can't see.

"Is he hit?" the big man said.

"I'm fine. Get off me, both of you."

"You're welcome," Parker said.

Brunell brushed Parker aside and pushed him back.

"Looks like you pissed the wrong person off."

"Gotta be Castaneda again," Brunell said.

"Would've been easier to pay him off now, wouldn't it?"

Brunell looked scared. Parker knew he'd been shot at, but this time the man gave off a worried vibe he'd ever shown before.

One of the suited men jogged over. "Get back out there. Control what's left of this message. Use this as another example of why we're here."

"Screw that. I'm not going out there," Brunell said.

"Where's Isa?" Parker asked.

Brunell and the party donor scanned the area. Brunell's expression morphed from fear to anger.

The bodyguard swept his protectee away and headed toward a waiting limo.

Parker found the burly security guard in the yellow shirt and told him to shut the place down. No one leaves—especially that limo.

The crowd dissipated and disappeared within a minute of the gunshot's dying echo. Parker glanced around a construction support toward the location he'd seen the glint off the rifle scope. The glare was gone, but there was a hurried movement in the shadows behind it in the window of a concession booth.

Parker rushed to the spot, using an aisle off to one side of the concession window. As he drew close, he noticed the sliding window was open a few inches. The shooter used the booth as concealment. Castaneda was here.

A cluster of bikers huddled near the concession shack. They'd taken cover next to the building where the shooter fired from.

Parker's cell rang, and he snapped it from his pocket. It was Billie's number.

"Is Miguel all okay?"

"He's awake, Nathan. He wants to talk to you."

A wave of relief swept over Parker. He monitored the concession window while he waited.

A weak voice sounded in Parker's ear. "Hello?"

"Miguel. God, it's good to hear you. How are you feeling? We'll find you the care you need to pull through this. I'll be with you the whole time—"

"I—I saw who got me," he said in a hoarse whisper.

"Don't worry. It was Brunell, wasn't it? I've got him here."

"No. It wasn't him, or Los Muertos."

"What are you saying, Miguel? Of course it was. You rest, and we'll—"

"It was Isa. She did this."

Chapter Fifty-Nine

"Isa? What do you mean?"

The concession door opened, and a man the same size as the shooter at the Papago Reservation slipped out and into the crowd. Wearing a dark hoody, head down, ball cap covering their eyes, the shooter strode away, lugging a duffle bag. The same posture and movement as the one who picked off the gunmen in the desert. It was the same. Parker was certain of it. But if it wasn't Brunell?

The shooter waded through the knot of bikers and headed for the exit. Parker followed behind, moving to the side, making a parallel path with the shooter.

One biker pointed at Parker. "Him. That's the one who grabbed Brunell."

The shooter's face was concealed under the brim of a ball cap, ignoring the commotion.

Four bikers started toward Parker. Puffed up and angry, they blocked the sidewalk. Parker was grateful the beer concession wasn't open to fuel their poor decisions.

Parker stopped to listen to Miguel and the shouts from the small biker convention in his path.

"What was that? Miguel, can you tell me who?" Parker asked. The boy was barely conscious and might be confused over what he remembered from being held in the steel death trap. Isa was involved. Parker was sure of it. No way Isa could manhandle a seventeen-year-old, five-foot-nine man. Abducting someone, beating them, and locking them in a sunbaked metal box was far more extreme than he'd expected from a buttoned-up not-for-profit lawyer. Killing was killing.

The closest biker in a beer-stained t-shirt yelled about building the wall and criminals and rapists infiltrating the country. The man enjoyed a tailgate party before the rally, and he was stumbling and nearly twisted his ankle as he approached Parker.

"I'm sure. Isa isn't what she seems. She turned me over to Los Muertos at some old racetrack."

Parker's mind raced. Isa? Was it possible he misjudged her and bought into her mild-mannered, all about the good of the undocumented people's approach?

He got his answer a second later when the shooter glanced up, revealing cold eyes and a hardened glare. That face. Parker knew in an instant. Isa dropped the duffle and sprinted away toward the parking lot.

"Miguel, gotta go. Stay put."

He shoved the phone in his pocket and ran after Isa. The drunk biker tried to grab him, but the pot-bellied racist's reflexes were dulled, and Parker ducked under his grasp.

Isa was deceptively quick. Parker picked up his pace, reached to snag the dropped duffle, and kept after her.

A pair of Maricopa County Sheriff's black and yellow cruisers cut into the parking lot. The report of shots fired at the public venue got a prompt response.

The first car slid to a stop in Isa's path. The deputy jumped from the car and spotted Parker chasing a woman.

The deputy commanded Parker to stop and drop to his knees. He placed his hand on his sidearm but hadn't drawn it yet.

"Thank you!" Isa said. "He's the shooter. There's a big gun in his bag."

Now the deputy's gun came out.

"I said, on the ground, now."

"I'm Detective Parker—"

"I don't care who you say you are. Get down now and drop the bag."

Parker stopped his approach and held his arms out after gently placing the duffle bag on the ground.

"Listen, I'm a detective, and she's—"

"Thank you, deputy," Isa said as she slid behind the deputy.

The small woman snapped out a hand and wrestled the deputy's Glock from his hand, breaking his finger. Isa pivoted around and struck the deputy in the throat with the web of her hand. The deputy dropped to his knees and grabbed his throat, struggling to draw a breath.

Isa lined the sights on Parker's head. There was no sign of emotion on her face.

Parker saw the knuckles on her hand tighten slightly as she prepared to pull the trigger.

From behind her, the deputy recovered his breath enough to whip his leg out and strike the back of Isa's knees, sending her off balance.

Parker jumped and dove on Isa, wrapping his hand around the gun in her grip. The weapon had no external hammer he could jam to prevent a discharge. And he knew the department policy was to keep a live round in the chamber. All he could do was control the muzzle direction as they struggled.

Isa rolled under him, trying to bring the business end of the weapon to his chest. She was strong, and he felt her muscles coil as she moved. Parker's arm got caught in an awkward position, and she used his weight against him, bending his elbow backward.

The muzzle flicked at eye level, and Parker ducked as she pulled the trigger, sending a .40 round past his ear. He felt the heat, and the sound deafened him. All he could hear was his heartbeat under the ringing in his ear.

Parker kept his hand locked around the weapon and prevented the slide from shooting backwards to load another bullet into the chamber.

Isa pressed hard against his locked elbow, and he felt something give. Sharp pain erupted, and it was the distraction Isa needed. She freed the weapon, racked the slide back, and chambered another round.

She swung the barrel around when a pop and sizzle sounded behind her. Two Taser darts stuck to her back, and her body arched and tensed. The muscle contractions in her gun hand twitched on the trigger, and a second round buried itself in the asphalt a foot from Parker.

Parker shoved away from Isa, and rolled her on her stomach, his injured left arm crying out. He grabbed a set of handcuffs from the deputy's utility belt and snapped them on Isa's thin wrists.

The electric current tingled Parker's hand as he applied the cuffs.

"You can let up now," he told the injured deputy.

"The hell I will."

He did anyway and released the trigger on his Taser. He dropped to the ground and continued to struggle for a full breath.

"You doing okay, deputy?"

He held his throat and gave Parker a thumbs up. "Who was she?"

"An attorney," Parker said.

Additional responding units arrived at the active shooter call. Parker signaled for an ambulance crew to look at the injured deputy. He knew a blow to the throat like that could cause swelling and block off the man's airway.

He grabbed an ice pack for his swollen elbow.

Parker knelt over the duffle bag Isa dropped and zipped it open with his good hand. Pushing the bag open, he spotted a disassembled Remington sniper rifle. It was identical to the rifle Castaneda delivered to him near Westfield Mall. Under the rifle, a set of desert camo—the same color and pattern as he'd witnessed in the desert while Castaneda's men were being picked off.

Isa's eyes remained locked on Parker.

He struggled to pull his cell phone with his injured arm to answer the incoming call. It was probably Miguel wondering why he got cut off.

"Boss, you sitting down?" It was Pete Tully.

"I wish, Pete. Everything okay there?"

"Got the report back on the sniper rifle you wanted. Strange thing—nothing to tie it to Brunell or his California priors."

"I'm beginning to understand." Parker stared at Isa.

"But here's the surprise part—they found a set of prints on the inside of the receiver. And we got a hit."

"Isa Sanchez."

"Damn. Good guess. Her prints were on file because she was a member of the Arizona Bar Association."

"Good work, Pete."

"Thanks, boss. We got our Sun Valley sniper."

"Yeah, we do." Parker watched two deputies grab Isa under her arms and walk her to the back of a patrol car. She didn't struggle against them. She glanced at Parker and gave him a smile. It was the coldest look he'd ever seen from a suspect.

"Hey, Pete? Can you do me a favor? Look in on Miguel and Billie, then come pick me up at Ak-Chin?"

"The pavilion? What's playing?"

"Nothing anymore."

Chapter Sixty

P arker heard Billie from down the hall, four rooms away.

"Dammit, that ain't right. You can't go shootin' people for no damned reason."

Castaneda. He's here. His heart rate skipped up a notch, and he sprinted to the door, his injured left arm throbbing with each footfall.

Parker's hand tapped his holster, ready to take on the next threat.

As he rounded the corner and peeked into the room, there was no gunman, no threat, no Los Muertos thug. Billie and Miguel were propped up on Miguel's bed, playing a video game.

Billie's eyes flicked to the doorway for a moment before her attention returned to the television screen. Her fingers and thumbs struggled to hit the buttons while Miguel pressed and toggled the joysticks with practiced ease.

"Nathan, I got a bone to pick with you. You let an impressionable young man play a damn video game where you're supposta run over prostitutes, rip off drug dealers, and hit people as they cross the street. I ask you, is that any way to parent?" Billie said.

"She's only saying that because she's a big loser," Miguel said.

Parker entered the room and lowered himself into the hard plastic visitor chair. But even that felt like heaven now.

"Where's Linda?"

"She run out to grab some grub. The hospital food tastes like sawdust. Should be back any second."

Billie squinted at Parker. "You doin' okay there, Nathan?"

"I'll be fine, Billie." He grimaced as he readjusted his arm.

"The hell you say." Billie hollered at a nurse passing in the hallway. "Hey, Miss Tompkins, could you take a look at my friend here?"

"You know everyone by name around here now?"

"She does," Miguel said, setting his game controller down.

"It is true? You got Isa?" Miguel said.

Parker nodded. "She can't hurt you or anyone now."

"I—I can't wrap my head around the idea she was taking out members of the Immigrant Coalition board. Why—why would she do such a thing? She helped pick most of them."

"I haven't talked to her yet. I didn't expect to finger her as the Sun Valley Sniper. My money was on Brunell all along. She fooled me. I wish I saw it earlier. Maybe then Tomaso and Juan might have survived, and you wouldn't be here. How did she get to you, anyway?"

"Isa called when I was at home. You told me to stay there, and I should have listened, but she said you wanted me to go with her and check out a camp of undocumented people up north to see if they were safe."

"The dog track?"

He nodded, and his face paled, remembering what he witnessed at the track. "They—the people—what they did to them."

"What did Isa do once you got there?"

A slight nod. Miguel hung his head and mumbled. "She made me watch while they killed Tomaso and dumped him in a hole. She—she said I was going to be next. I—I thought—every time they came for me, I was next.

"All those people. Brunell sold them out to Los Muertos."

"How can you be sure?"

"Oh, I'm sure. I heard the Los Muertos leader—he called Brunell. He was arguing with him. He told Brunell those people belonged to him and reminded him Los Muertos wasn't going to get cut out of their deal."

"The deal being Los Muertos would be the ones running migrants over the border," Parker said.

Miguel nodded. "I heard Mr. Brunell over the phone—on speaker. He said he didn't care what happened to them. He didn't care…"

"I don't think he ever did. It was all a big scam to him. Using the undocumented to make a buck. He was funneling the donations to other accounts," Parker said.

"The Castaneda guy told me he had plans for me. I thought he meant like what he did to Tomaso." Miguel's voice trailed off, remembering the events.

"I think he was going to do it until some fires started up, and his men panicked. They shoved me in a truck and took off."

"That was us," Billie said. "We lit them fires."

"We were coming for you, Miguel. I'll always come for you. I wish I'd been there in time."

Miguel's eyes welled as he glanced at Parker. "You were."

"Castaneda had me in that box when you and Billie called. He had Brunell on another phone–one of his guys held a phone with him on speaker so I could tell you about the accounts. I'm glad you figured out I was talking about the migrant trail map."

"That there was damn smart," Billie said.

"That's why we heard Brunell on the line."

Parker got up from the chair and sat on the edge of the bed next to Miguel. He put his left arm around him and didn't care about how much it hurt. Miguel leaned into Parker and shuddered.

"I'm sorry. So sorry," Parker said.

This trauma was going to take time to overcome, if ever. Parker could imagine Isa and the thugs manning the dog track coming for Miguel and making him suffer through mock executions, each time the boy wondering if this would be the time his life snuffed out.

Escaping the violence and gang pressures in El Salvador only to come to the country and face even more heinous punishment. It made Parker seethe with anger.

"Who were those guys guarding the dog track?"

"Los Muertos."

"Isa was with Los Muertos?"

He shook his head. "No, not really. Well, maybe, kind of. She turned me over to Castaneda like I was some prize, or something. She said Los

Muertos wanted the same thing. I didn't know until later what she meant."

"What?"

"The enemy of my enemy is my friend. That's what she said. She and Los Muertos wanted one thing—to make Mr. Brunell suffer and pay for it."

"Los Muertos, I understand. Isa seemed to be in Brunell's camp from the beginning. She ran the Coalition offices, worked the donors, and agreed to work on his campaign."

"It was all fake. I don't know what it was, but they have history—and it isn't a good one."

Miguel felt heavy in Parker's arms. He let him back gently onto his pillow.

"You need to get some rest. It's all going to be okay." Parker knew it would never really be okay. How could it be after what Miguel went through?

Miguel settled and popped his eyes open, shifting from Parker to Billie.

"We're here, and we're not going anywhere."

Miguel closed his eyes and shuddered as he drew a breath.

Parker jutted his chin to the door, and Billie met him at the threshold.

He leaned close to Billie. "How's he seem?"

"He's pretendin' like nothin' happened. Even I know he's gotta deal with this before he gets better. So, Isa did this to him? Makes it my fault on account of introducing him. Man, I'm sorry, Nathan. I had no idea..."

"No one did. This isn't on you, Billie."

"Castaneda got away again?"

Parker shrugged. "You saw the same thing I did out by the storage container."

The shuffle of rubber soles on the worn hospital flooring drew Parker's attention. Pete Tully rounded the corner and seemed in a red-faced rush.

"Glad I found you." Tully needed to catch his breath. He handed an eight-by-ten black-and-white photo to Parker. "We grabbed this when we took down Clement's place—the storage unit. Had some soot covering the photo. We cleaned it up."

Parker smelled the smoke on the copy and felt a fine grit under his thumb. He held the photo at arm's length and examined it. An Army unit photo of five soldiers in desert camouflage with sniper rifles cradled in their arms.

Clement on the left, two others who looked unfamiliar, and on the far end, a much younger Tim Brunell. A close look at the uniform showed the name R. Burns. Before the name change to Tim Brunell.

Parker held it for Tully. He rubbed a thumb in his throbbing temple. "It confirms what we know, Pete. Brunell and Clement were stationed together at Fort Irwin. Urban warfare training."

"Turn it over," Pete said, pushing the photo back.

Parker flipped the photograph, and handwritten on the rear were the names of the soldiers in the photo, including Clement and Burns. What drew his attention was a line under the roster of names. "Photo taken by Staff Sergeant I. Sanchez." Under her name, an inscription read, "I'm coming for you."

"Now that's a trip. Isa never let on she knew Brunell from their military service. Explains her proficiency with the rifle. That line sounded like a threat. Any idea what it was about?"

"Not a clue. Her service records are on the way."

A soft voice called out from the room. "I can hear you, you know?" Miguel called out.

"Sorry, buddy. We keeping you awake?"

"No. I think I like it when you guys are in here talking. Makes me feel like I'm part of things, you know?"

Parker led everyone back into the room. "You remember Pete Tully?"

"Sure do."

Linda Hunt entered the room with bags of takeout. "Make way."

She plopped the bags on the table next to Miguel.

Pete peeked in one bag, and Linda slapped his hand away.

"That's not for you."

"Jeez, no wonder you're not married," Tully said.

Linda hip-checked Tully out of the way and removed two containers from the bags, arranging them on the table.

"I hope I picked out the things you wanted. I don't know the first thing about Salvadoran food."

Miguel scooted up, and Linda fluffed a pillow under his back.

323

Miguel popped open the first Styrofoam clamshell, and he inhaled the scent wafting up from the dish. A stack of thick corn tortillas stuffed with pork and beans filled the container.

"Pupusas. I haven't had these in a long time."

He dug in and groaned. "This is what I was telling you. Try it." He passed the container and opened the next.

Comfort food. Parker was grateful Miguel responded to the offering. And grateful for Linda's nurturing side.

"Where'd you find this, Linda?"

She swallowed a bite. "My neighbor is from Central America. She knew where to take me. Little place in El Mirage. She introduced me to the owner, a sweet older guy. Turns out he came from a little town outside of San Salvador called Apopa, or something."

"Apopa? That's where I came from," Miguel said.

"Huh, that's a coincidence. Is it a big city?"

"Not really. Maybe a hundred thousand people. Smaller than San Salvador. Did you learn his name?"

"Everyone called him Tio Diego."

"Diego? Tio Diego Rosales?"

"I didn't hear his last name. Could be?"

"Who is he?" Parker said.

"He could be my uncle. He crossed over about a year before I did. I never heard from him again."

Miguel had family. Parker was happy for him. He was also a little jealous and worried Miguel would drift away from him and gravitate to a blood relative.

"Let's get you recovered, and we'll go meet Tio Diego."

"I think I'd like to." He paused. "Could you come with me? I want him to meet my new family."

324

Chapter Sixty-One

Captain Morris demanded a debrief following the shooting at the Ak-Chin Pavilion. It was standard policy, even though Parker never fired a shot in the exchange. Administrative quicksand.

Parker got the order to appear in the form of a personal escort from Lieutenant Gunderson, the head of the Sheriff's Office Division of Professional Standards—the politically correct label for internal affairs. Cops who hunted cops. As far as headhunters go, Lieutenant Gunderson was fair when he zeroed in. But he was unrelenting when he found a dirty cop.

Gunderson didn't say the reason Captain Morris demanded his immediate appearance on the drive over to the Sheriff's Office. He didn't want to leave Miguel, but the Lieutenant was clear about coming with him, or turn in his badge.

Parker had one hand on his badge, pulling it from his belt, when Billie put a hand on his arm.

"We got him, Nathan. Do what you gotta do and come back here when you can."

Linda and Tully nodded.

"Call me if—well, just call me."

After they got underway, Gunderson broke the silence. "Miguel gonna be okay?"

"The doctors say he's young and strong, so he should pull through."

"He can use your Employee Assistance Program for post-trauma counseling. Foster kids are eligible, you know, if you want to."

"Probably not an awful place to start. He's gonna need help after what he's been put through. I didn't know he'd be eligible under my benefits, him being a foster kid, not adopted."

"As far as the Admin. Division is concerned, Miguel is family."

"That's well and good if the captain isn't being pressured to show me the door because I didn't follow the company line—painting Clement as the Sun Valley Sniper."

"You know Morris. He'll do what he can to protect the troops."

"I know Morris is getting close to retirement."

The rest of the drive passed in silence.

Once in the building, Gunderson and Parker wound through the halls until they arrived at the captain's office. The outer office was sparse, and the secretary's desk was empty. Two empty chairs sat against the wall where visitors parked until called.

Parker didn't want to sit, so he paced as Lieutenant Gunderson entered the captain's inner office. He could hear the low rumble of the captain's voice and a lighter voice in response. He recognized Lynne's speech pattern, quick tempo, and to the point. Sharp if you were on the receiving end of it, as he often was recently.

The door popped open, and Morris called out. "Parker, don't keep us waiting."

Inside, Morris was standing in front of his desk. Usually a good sign, as bad things came down when he ruled behind the massive mahogany barrier. He was standing with Lynne, and they were looking over a file together.

"If you don't need my Uber services any further, Captain, I'll get back to my job," Gunderson said with a slight grin.

Morris waved him off. "Parker, what do you make of this?"

Parker strode to the desk, trying to assess Lynne's expression. Confidence? A secret, perhaps?

He recognized the spreadsheet of account transactions from the Coalition and Brunell's campaign accounts to a series of numbered accounts. The transfers to the Mexican bank were circled in red, along with a half a dozen others.

"We've got him, Nathan," Lynne said.

"Campaign finance violations are a big gotcha."

"Your Detective Johns and our FBI JTTF found more than sloppy campaign finance transactions. These accounts, the ones circled in red, are red flagged by Homeland Security."

"Since when does Homeland care about campaign money?"

"Any funds moving in or out of these accounts are tracked because we tied them to known terrorist organizations and arms dealers."

"The bank in Mexico is a terrorist front?"

"Not the bank, but the transactions. They were to an account held by Esteban Castaneda, who I believe you know. He tried to hide it within a shell company, but it's his."

"Brunell was paying Los Muertos to smuggle migrants. He'll spin this as blackmail, buckling under pressure from Los Muertos."

Morris spoke up. "Here's where Barry Johns pitched in. He correlated these transfers to Castaneda with groups of migrants being smuggled over the border. Barry confirmed Brunell wasn't paying blackmail. He was paying a criminal coyote to bring people over the border. And you know full well not all of them made it to where they were supposed to go."

"These others?" Parker tapped a fingertip on a red-circled account.

"That one is an anti-government terror network in Central America. The others include the Juarez Cartel, MS-13, Hezbollah, and the Aryan Nation."

"Brunell was funding these groups?"

"Best we can figure is the Cartel and Central American accounts bought passage through their territories and paid them for kidnapping government officials, maybe an execution or two. The Aryan Nation—you figured that one out already."

"Brunell worked the Aryan Nation up in an anti-migrant frenzy to bolster his state senate campaign. Some of it found its way to Clement and Isa—"

"The white power yokel paying Clement, I get, but Isa? They know she's Mexican American, right?"

"As long as she targeted brown-skinned people or anyone who supported the immigrant cause, like Roger Jessup, they wouldn't care," Lynne said.

Lynne pointed at the page where three blue-lined accounts stood out.

"These—we couldn't break through. No known terrorist connection, or who ended up with the funds, only that they passed through the Coalition to the campaign account before they disappeared."

"What does the FBI plan on doing with Brunell? Watching and waiting?"

"That's the reason I called you in," Morris said.

"Detective Johns and Special Agent Collins are about to take Brunell down on a laundry list of federal crimes."

"Multiple violations of 18 U.S. Code § 2339B - Providing material support or resources to designated foreign terrorist organizations, each count carries a life sentence. Thought you'd want to be there when he's taken down."

"Now you know why I needed you brought here forthwith," Morris said.

"When do we leave?"

Chapter Sixty-Two

"State senate candidate Tim Brunell was taken into custody this afternoon by federal authorities on what officials label as a major disruption to international terrorist organizations. Brunell allegedly embezzled hundreds of thousands of dollars from a not-for-profit organization he ran and directed most of his campaign funds to these foreign criminals—money intended to provide relief for the undocumented migrants he promised to serve. Channel 7 News has learned Tim Brunell has a criminal record himself and served three years in prison for fraud. State charges for fraud and conspiracy are pending. Seems like we need to do a better job vetting our candidates for public office," an on-scene reporter said while footage of Brunell being placed in handcuffs played.

"Well, lookie there," Billie said, pointing at the screen in Miguel's hospital room.

"I can't believe Mr. Brunell used us like he did. He had Mr. Jessup killed because he didn't want his ties to terrorist groups uncovered. Tomaso, Juan, and Mr. Hernandez. And he sent Isa to do it. I can't believe it."

"It's done now. See who's putting Brunell in the back of the police car?"

Miguel smiled when he spotted Parker leading the handcuffed Brunell to the back of the waiting FBI prisoner transport van.

"Way to go, Dad."

"Knock-knock," Parker said at Miguel's door.

"Hey, Nathan, we was just watching your performance on the tee vee. How did Brunell take it?" Billie asked.

Parker entered and plopped into a chair next to Miguel's bed. "He was about to go on camera to finish the speech he started when Isa cut him off at the Ak-Chin Pavilion. The news cameras were already there and got more than they bargained for."

"Is it true, what they said? Mr. Brunell sent donation money given to the Immigrant Coalition off to terrorists?"

"Looks that way. The FBI identified bank accounts tied to cartels, hate groups, even MS-13."

Miguel gritted his teeth at the mention of the Salvadoran gang responsible for killing his brother years ago.

"How much money we talkin' about?" Billie asked.

"Never got a final number, but looks to be in the hundreds of thousands, as much as a million, maybe," Parker said.

Billie's forehead scrunched. "Where's the rest of it? Roger was showing me the accounts about a month ago—why I don't know—said it was important that I know. There was like three times as much saved up."

"I don't know, Billie. Brunell might have taken the money and sent it on to his friends."

"People depended on the money for help and help set up once they arrive here. What are they going to do now? It's not right they suffer because of him," Miguel said.

Parker sat back and regarded the young man. He'd been through so much, kidnapped, beaten, and left for dead. Facing months of rehab and therapy, here he was concerned about the fate of people he didn't even know. Parker was proud of him.

"The need is too great to ignore. Something will fill the hole the Immigrant Coalition left. This time, the organization will actually serve the needs of the community it's supposed to represent."

"I hope so. In the meantime, what happens to those caught in between?"

"I'm afraid I don't have any answers," Parker said.

"I can pick up on my trips down to Hermosillo again. The more help and medical supplies I can bring down there, the less they might need here."

"Didn't the Coalition pay for most of the supplies?"

"Most of them. Until we find someone willing to donate medicine, supplies, food, and clothing, I'll pick up the slack."

"You can't afford to replace what the Coalition was providing."

"I got enough."

Linda Hunt appeared in the doorway. She looked refreshed by a change of clothes and her hair was damp from a shower. Athletically trim and quite attractive in street clothes, Parker sucked in his gut a little. He'd done that enough in the past few days it seemed like exercise.

"My shift, Billie," Linda said.

"I could probably do with a lie down and a shower."

Parker dug in his pockets and tossed Billie his keys. "Use my place. It's closer." Parker also knew Billie's run-down rig North of Cave Creek didn't boast any working plumbing.

"You sure, Nathan? I don't wanna be no problem."

"You're never a problem, Billie—far from it."

"All right then," she said and pocketed the keys, looking like she'd won an all-expense paid resort vacation.

Billie bid goodbye, and Linda settled in a chair opposite Parker. "Caught your little piece on the news. Good to see Brunell go down."

"It's really over then?" Miguel said.

"Looks that way," Parker said. A quick glance at Linda gave away what he really thought. There were months of trials, testimony, and legal wrangling ahead. But for today, yes, it was over.

Miguel noticed the look between them. "When you gonna finally ask Linda out? You know you want to. It's like all you talk about at home."

"I—I do not," Parker said.

"You don't want to ask me out?"

"No—I mean yes, I do, but…,"

"But what?"

"I don't go around talking about you all the time."

"Not even a little?" Linda asked with a smirk.

"Well, maybe once or twice."

"So?"

"So what?"

"You gonna ask or what?"

Parker saw she was enjoying him squirm. Her green eyes twinkled.

"So, you wanna go out sometime?"

"I don't know…I'm kind of busy, you know."

Parker laughed, and the movement made his injured left arm twinge.

"Okay, okay. I'll go out with you. But first, we got to have you looked at."

Linda found Dr. O, who was looking to check up on Miguel and asked her to give Parker a once over. After an hour of scans and X-rays, Parker came back to the room with a sling and instructions for follow-up care with her personal doctor.

"What'd they say?" Linda asked.

"Nothing torn, nothing broken, a sprain and ligament damage."

"Good, then you can take me to a proper dinner, say tomorrow?"

"Tomorrow it is," Parker said.

Miguel pretended to be asleep but couldn't help but grin.

It was good to see him smile again.

Chapter Sixty-Three

The name on the caller ID surprised Parker.

"Hi there, Lynne. What's up?"

"I have someone here who says they want to talk to you."

"Agent Collins wants his GPS key fob back, I suppose? Just as well. I don't want him tracking me around anymore."

Lynne paused. "Isa Sanchez says she wants to talk, but she'll only do it with you."

"Why am I so lucky? Last thing she wanted was to put a bullet in my head. I think I'll pass."

"Nathan, she gave up what she knows about Brunell's involvement in funding the terrorist organizations south of the border."

"Don't forget the Aryan Nation is home-grown."

"True, but she could help us unlock—"

"What's in it for her? I know Isa didn't simply wake up with a conscience this morning."

"The U.S. Attorney is taking the death penalty off the table."

Parker lowered the cell phone. He imagined life behind bars wouldn't be easy for a young woman like Isa. It was suitable punishment for the broken lives and devastation she left in her wake. The death penalty wouldn't bring back Tomaso, Juan, or Roger. Nia's two little girls were without their mother. And putting Isa to death wouldn't lessen the grief of an aging shopkeeper who lost her husband and grandson. Knowing Isa would languish away for decades, never able to flee from the memories of those she harmed, was fitting.

He raised the phone. "Fine. If she's already given you what you need, why me?"

"She said she needed to tell you something," Lynne said.

Lynne arranged for Isa to meet with Parker in the FBI's offices rather than the federal pretrial detention center north of Phoenix. When Parker arrived, he found Isa sitting in a conference room with two Bureau of Prisons officers at the door and a third in the room with her. She was handcuffed and wore a set of baggy tan-colored prison clothes making her look small, but not frail.

"I knew you'd come," she said.

Parker chose a chair opposite her. "Say what you gotta say."

"I told Agent Finch I'd tell what I know about Brunell and Castaneda as long as we had this face-to-face." She paused, and when Parker didn't respond, she continued. "When I was in the Army, I thought I was part of something. Especially as part of a sniper team. It's always the two of you looking out for one another—or so I thought."

"Is this going to get to the point anytime soon?"

"At Fort Irwin, Ruben Burns, Tim Brunell now, was my spotter. He was supposed to have my back. That redneck Clement raped me. Burns wanted me to let it go. Let it go, he said. Claimed it was nothing worth ruining Clement's name over. Well, I didn't drop it, and Burns turned the entire base against me. He and Clement both got tossed out over it, but I lost my career too."

But Burns and his boy got away with what they did to me—and I wasn't about to let them slide."

"Holding a grudge is one thing, but killing innocent people is quite another, Isa. What did they have to do with revenge against Brunell?"

"Castaneda is the one who holds grudges. Seems Tim set him up as the fall guy for their little scam in prison. Castaneda discovered who Tim Brunell really was and threatened to burn the Coalition down if he didn't get a cut of the action. You can imagine how he reacted when Tim decided to cut him out altogether.

"That's when I started bleeding the Coalition's accounts. It was Castaneda's idea. I got Tim to believe he was hiding the money from Los Muertos. I gave him the accounts, and off he went. Self-inflicted. It was beautiful."

"So Brunell didn't know he was funding terrorist groups?"

"Not at first. Then he realized he could use the muscle of groups like The Nation and the cartels to deal with board members who obstructed his plan to cut off Los Muertos support for getting migrants over the border."

"How can you justify what you did to them—and Miguel? What you did to my boy was inhumane."

A smile formed on her lips. "That was Castaneda's idea. He wanted to make you suffer. I took him and handed him over to Castaneda."

Parker shot from his chair. His hands clenched into tight balls. "What did the kid have to do with any of this?"

"Nothing. Nothing other than his connection to you. People close to you don't do well, do they, Detective? Like your partner, McMillan, I think it was?"

Parker felt his face flush.

"What about Melissa Carson? She never had any ties to the Coalition, or Brunell. Why was she killed?"

"Who?" Isa asked, picking at her chipped nail polish.

"The college student shot outside the theatre a couple of days after Mr. Hernandez. Why her?"

"The plan was to make the hits appear random. The girl was in the wrong place at the wrong time. Then things sped up when Castaneda got rid of the board members who wanted to change up the deal he had with Tim. If they were out of the picture, then Tim would have to continue to pay Los Muertos for smuggling migrants. He needed a constant flow of migrants so he could support his fundraising. Roger was going to take the financials to the feds, so he had to go. We couldn't risk him exposing things too soon. He wasn't supposed to be chasing his cleaning lady on the freeway, though. She knew too much and stole the USB drive from Roger. She texted Tim, saying she had it. All I had to do was wait. Then Roger shows up—and well—two birds with one stone. They both had to go down."

"All this. All this killing. To get back at Tim, or Ruben, or whoever the hell he was? It wasn't worth it."

"Who are you to say? It was totally worth it. I got to watch Tim's world fall apart. I found Clement and talked him into being my driver when I took out the cleaning lady, Roger, and the labor leader in the fields. Funny thing was, I made Tim pay for him. I think Tim knew what I had in mind for Clement. He didn't blink an eye. You should have seen Clement's face when he finally realized who I was. Right before I put him down."

"Who took the shot at Brunell at the office? It wasn't you."

She smiled, and it sent a chill up Parker's spine. "That was Castaneda. He wanted to put a little scare into Tim and to keep him from believing it was me taking his world apart from the inside."

Parker shook his head. Isa was smiling at him. He turned for the door.

"Where are you going, Detective?"

"You've told your story. I'm done here."

"I have a message for you. A message from Esteban."

Parker turned, faced her, waiting.

"He says he's coming for you. You won't see it until it's too late. It could be another sniper, a truck running you off the road, or maybe he'll take you apart one piece at a time. The people you know, Miguel, Agent Finch, that troublesome Billie Carson, and even that pretty deputy Marsh you've taken an interest in are fair game. You've cost him too much, and it's time to pay."

Parker was in the hallway and let the door slam as her words echoed in his head. Let Castaneda come—Parker would be ready.

Chapter Sixty-Four

In the four months since Miguel was released from the hospital, he'd mended his physical injuries completely. The doctors were right on that count. His youth and good condition aided his quick recovery.

Hidden injuries lingered—the unseen damage from the trauma he experienced.

Parker found him asleep on the sofa this morning, a pattern which began in the days after he returned home. Miguel said he looked forward to his own familiar bed, but the first night sent him into a panic attack. Claustrophobia set in once in the bedroom. Doors must remain open, blinds and curtains up, or the lingering effects of the steel container in the desert pressed down on him.

Miguel started back at college this week, and Parker hoped a busy school schedule would help him reengage with others. He was quieter, less outgoing than before. All the therapists said it was to be expected and full recovery would take time.

It was hard for Parker to wait. He would sacrifice to help Miguel heal. But there was little to do but wait and be there for support.

The unexpected bright spot came with Billie Carson. When Billie came around, Miguel would perk up, actively take part in the conversation, and looked like his old self. After Billie left, Miguel would revert—almost visibly retreat into a protective shell.

Without the Immigrant Coalition, Miguel found it hard to connect with people sharing his experience. He'd help Billie prepare for her frequent supply trips to Hermosillo, but Parker wouldn't let him accompany her south.

Parker got coffee going and was about to nudge Miguel awake to get ready for school when a slight knock at the door sounded.

The Ring camera showed Billie Carson on the doorstep.

Parker opened the door, and Billie swept in.

"Morning. Didn't know you were dropping by. Maybe you can help me get Miguel up and running."

Billie grabbed the pillow from under his head. "Get your lazy ass up. I got news."

Miguel's sleep-filled eyes turned up at Billie standing over him.

"What?" Miguel mumbled.

"We're back. The Coalition. Well, not exactly. But you and me can start a new organization to help the undocumented."

Miguel sat up. "We've talked about this, but we can't replace the resources we lost when the Coalition folded."

Parker sat next to Miguel and eyed Billie. She was excited, animated, and bouncing on her toes. "Billie, slow down and explain what you mean."

"I found it. I mean, I have it."

"Have what?" Parker said.

"I know why Roger Jessup wanted me to look at them reports so many times. He knew what Brunell was up to with stealing from the Coalition. He transferred the funds to a new account. It's there. I found it."

"Roger set up a new account, so Brunell couldn't steal it? Smart thinking. How much we talking about?"

"Three and a half million."

"What?" Parker and Miguel said in unison.

"Yes. See, Miguel, we can go back to helping these people again."

"I'd like to do that."

"How can you access the money, Billie? I mean, the Coalition doesn't exist anymore?"

"Roger set up the account in my name. I checked with the bank, and I'm an honest-to-God millionaire. We can make this happen, Miguel. You in?"

"Hell yes, I'm in."

It was the most alive he'd seen Miguel in months. This outlet might be the best thing for Miguel.

"Me too, and I know where to start."

Two hours later, Parker, Billie, and Miguel stood on a doorstep in the Guad. Billie knocked, and Sofia Martinez opened the door.

Sofia looked from face to face, settling on Parker. "Detective, what's the meaning of this?"

"Miss Martinez, my friends here have something to say to you."

Parker stepped back.

"Miss Hernandez, I didn't know your sister Nia. But what I've discovered was she was incredibly brave. She found proof people in positions of privilege were stealing money from the Immigrant Coalition, money meant to help families like your sister's," Miguel said.

"And it got her killed."

"It did. I know we can never repay her sacrifice, but we want to give you this. It's twenty thousand dollars to help with her girls. My dad, the detective, is working with immigration authorities to get them visas, so they won't have to worry again."

Sofia looked at the envelope of cash. "Is this real? You'd do this for the girls?"

"They deserve to know their mother was a hero and wanted nothing but a better life for them," Miguel said.

After an exchange of hugs and tears, Parker waited by the car. It was going to take a while, but he could see Miguel's self-esteem and mental scars healing.

Parker glanced at his watch. He had a lunch date with Linda near her substation, not far from where this began, where Nia Saldana gave her life so others could survive and thrive.

Acknowledgements

The spark for *Devil Within* goes back years—while I served as a Juvenile Probation Officer. When officers arrested a youth, or issued a citation, I would conduct a hearing and decide what sanction was appropriate. During one such hearing, a mother and daughter appeared—the daughter cited for shoplifting. A minor offense which we would have resolved informally, however, the first thing the mother did was surrender both hers and her daughter's "green cards." They were Mexican citizens, in this country legally, but the mother was certain her daughter's criminal act was going to result in their deportation. I gave the young lady a few community service hours, and the mother was surprised when I gave back their "green cards."

That event always stuck with me. How vulnerable that mother felt, believing at any moment their legal status could be stripped away, and the family would be shipped off to another country. Vulnerable. Unfortunately, non-governmental agencies have a long history of exploiting the weak and vulnerable. *Devil Within* is drawn from these experiences.

I'm forever grateful to my friend and editor, Shawn Reilly Simmons, at Level Best Books. Shawn is superhuman and I love working with her. She's guided this series and enabled us to share Nathan Parker's story with you. Most of all, I'm happy to call her a friend.

A special thanks to my advance readers, Jessica Windham, Janis Herbert, and Megan Cuff, who aren't shy about telling me what works and what doesn't.

The book community is incredible, and I appreciate the support of independent bookstores like Face in a Book (Tina Ferguson and Janis Herbert) and Book Passage (Kathy Petrocelli and Luisa Smith). They make a bookstore feel like home.

Sometimes it's words of encouragement that came when they were most needed. J.T. Ellison, Wendall Thomas, Karen Dionne, Hank Phillippi Ryan, Baron Birtcher, and Bruce Robert Coffin. I thank you for your support. A special shout out to my fellow Capitol Crimes Chapter of Sisters-in-Crime members for the love and support.

Thanks to my kids, Jessica and Michael—I love you guys.

I wasn't always alone at the keyboard, and I owe Emma and Bryn the Corgis extra treats for all the plot points they helped me work through on countless walks. The book would have been done a month earlier if not for their constant demands.

A special thank you to Ann-Marie L'Etoile for tolerating my nonsense over the years. You let me disappear behind my keyboard and still love me when I come up for air. Love you.

And finally, thanks to you, dear reader. It's only possible because of you.

About the Author

James L'Etoile uses his twenty-nine years behind bars as an influence in his award winning novels, short stories, and screenplays. He is a former associate warden in a maximum-security prison, a hostage negotiator, facility captain, and director of California's state parole system. He is a nationally recognized expert witness on prison and jail operations. He has been twice nominated for the Silver Falchion for Best Procedural Mystery, and Best Thriller. L'Etoile's *Dead Drop* was a Lefty and Anthony Award nominee, and *Black Label* garnered the Silver Falchion Award for Best Book at Killer Nashville in 2022. His published novels include *Black Label, Dead Drop,* and the Detective Penley series. He is an active member of Mystery Writers of America, International Thriller Writers, and Sisters in Crime.

SOCIAL MEDIA HANDLES:
  https://jamesletoile.com
  https://twitter.com/JamesLEtoile
  https://www.facebook.com/AuthorJamesLetoile/?fref=ts
  https://www.instagram.com/authorjamesletoile

AUTHOR WEBSITE:

jamesletoile.com

Also by James L'Etoile

Dead Drop

Black Label

Bury the Past

At What Cost

Little River—the Other Side of Paradise

www.ingramcontent.com/pod-product-compliance
Lightning Source LLC
Chambersburg PA
CBHW030239120726
47903CB00005B/1545